The Guardians of

BOOK 1

Justin Isaacs

Justin Isaacs (signature)

To San

All my love and thank you

v

For all things soon pass away and become a mere tale ...

Meditations, Marcus Aurelius

The Eastern Roman Empire circa 395 AD

Near Constantinople

Part 1

395 AD

Chapter 1

Hebdomon near Constantinople, 27th November 395 AD

Flags and banners snapped and quivered in the chill wind that blew in from the Sea of Marmara. Gainas glanced up at them, closed his eyes, breathed in deeply and breathed out slowly, seeking to quieten the butterflies that stirred in his stomach. After a few attempts, he decided it was not helping, so he blinked a few times, gritted his teeth, and lowered his gaze to the army gathering before him.

Considering where he had come from, he could not quite believe that he was here: a full Roman general. He was quite literally surrounded by the elite of the Imperial court, all dressed in their silk and woollen finery, all adorned with jewellery fashioned from gold, silver, and precious stones. Twenty years ago, he had been a scrawny youth of the Turvingi tribe, in chains; cold, hungry, and desperate. He had been given a choice; fight for Rome or die. He had chosen to fight for Rome. Obviously. He had been desperate, not stupid.

And after many torrid years, many bloody campaigns, many agonizing wounds, and many hard-earned promotions, here he was.

No, he could not quite believe it.

Inside, he was still that desperate, scrawny youth, unworthy to be mingling with the *illustrii*, the rulers of the empire. He was encompassed on all sides by them as they gathered on a raised dais standing on the vast, flat, sand-covered parade ground within the confines of the Campus Tribunalis at Hebdomon. One of the largest training camps for Imperial troops of the Eastern Empire, it lay seven miles from the Milion stone in Constantinople. New Rome.

From their elevated position, with the sun at their backs, the Imperial party could see in the distance, the glints from the spears and helmets of men marching along the Via Egnacia, the thousand-mile-long road from Dyrrachium to Constantinople. Where the road passed the Campus Tribunalis, the men had peeled off from the cobbled stone surface, marched through the huge gates of the camp, past the tents and barracks, along the dusty thoroughfares and onto the immense parade ground in front of the dais.

The empty road to the right wound its way towards the seventh hill of Constantinople, disappearing into the hazy distance. Gainas watched apprehensively as the parade ground filled with men. His men. Men who had been marching for days. The *praepositi* officers organised them neatly into their centuries, with the experienced veteran *optios* yelling and bellowing out orders. The general, with his practised military eye, could see that they were all tired, thirsty, and hungry.

Someone who was not tired, thirsty, or hungry was the young man standing at the front of the dais drinking wine from a large, bejewelled cup. He wore gold-plated armour with a gem encrusted sword scabbard, and a purple silk cloak was draped over his right shoulder. Gainas contemplated Flavius Arcadius, Emperor of the Eastern Roman Empire.

He was the oldest son of the great Theodosius, and the legitimate ruler of the East. However, in the general's opinion, he did not appear to be half the man his father had been. He seemed soft and indecisive; Gainas reckoned his cook was probably a better military strategist.

Either side of the emperor stood a large, straight-backed palace guard, a powerful *Candidati*, dressed immaculately in white robes and gold armour. Their imposing presence made the man they guarded look small and insignificant.

And then there was the tall, thin man with a scowl on his face hovering by the emperor's left elbow. Rufinus, the Gaul. Praetorian Prefect of the East, the second most powerful man in the Empire. It was plain to Gainas that Arcadius was intimidated and controlled by Rufinus. Stilicho, Gainas' old commander in the West had been right. On his arrival two days ago Gainas had met with Rufinus to plan this parade. The snide and belittling comments made by the prefect directed at him and others, including the emperor, had confirmed what he had heard. Stilicho had told Gainas of how Rufinus had humiliated the generals Promotus and Timasius and of how Rufinus was feared and detested by all the Imperial Court.

But Rufinus was untouchable. He controlled the army, the palace guard, the administration, and the emperor. And just to be doubly sure, he was never without his private bodyguard. There they sat on their horses, below the dais, amongst the slaves who held the reins of the mounts that the Imperial party would ride to inspect the troops. Eight large Hunnic warriors. Their fearsome reputation added to their imposing looks. Gainas however, was not intimidated. He had battled Huns before. They were men, just as he was. They might follow the prefect around like a pack of hunting dogs, but run an arrow, a spear, or a sword through them, and they would die, just like anyone else. Without the bodyguards, Rufinus would be an easy target. Many members of the court who bustled around him today would not weep to see him dead.

Certainly, General Timasius would not. The old soldier stood behind the emperor next to his long-time friend and brother in arms, General Abundantius. Gainas knew them both by reputation long before his arrival at the capital and had briefly served with Timasius many years ago. He intended to get to know the two men much better. They had power and authority still, both very rich, and both very influential in the senate despite Rufinus' attempts to dispossess them. Timasius was staring at the back of Rufinus' neck with undisguised loathing.

Another who had positioned himself behind the emperor, was the eunuch Eutropius, the *Praepositus Sacri Cubiculi*. The chamberlain. He had the closest day-to-day contact with the Imperial family. Responsible for the personal security of the emperor and his consort Eudoxia, they in turn had complete trust in him, and that trust bestowed an enormous amount of influence. Gainas had met him only once, two days ago, but at that meeting he discovered that the chamberlain didn't behave like the other eunuchs he had known. There was a cold ruthlessness about him, a surprising arrogance, a confidence, and a hint of ambition that worried him greatly. Stilicho had warned him Eutropius was not to be trusted. Gainas now believed that the eunuch was a very, very dangerous person.

The banners above cracked sharply again in the stiff breeze, drawing Gainas out of his musings. Again, he breathed in deeply and then out slowly, still trying to calm his nerves. He had a job to do. He would get one chance to do it today. To put the empire on a path to unity under one man. He glanced across at the unprepossessing emperor and shook his head. He felt the burden on his shoulders. He heard his heart beating loudly in his chest and felt sure the other people around him must hear it too. Instinctively he touched his breast with his gloved hand, but then chided himself for his stupidity and forced himself to focus on the parade in front.

The last of the cavalry units had arrived and were positioned to the left of the main body of troops. The leading officers had already dismounted, handing the reins to their servants. The Eagle bearers and other standard-bearers took up their positions. Dust, disturbed by the horse's hooves and soldiers' boots, was whipped up by the breeze and swirled around the parade ground; it looked as if the lines of soldiers were steaming in the cold sunlight.

'Quite a sight, isn't it?' said the emperor to no one in particular; he took another cup of wine from one of the slaves serving drinks and tasty morsels to the Imperial party. Rufinus nodded but said nothing. He waved away the slave impatiently.

Finally, after the last of the infantry units had entered the parade ground, a horn sounded, followed by the roaring voices of the *praepositi*, and like a giant creature: the shields its scales, the spears its spines, the army of the East rippled with movement as it was called to attention.

4

All went still.

The muttered conversations of the courtiers died away. The wind still murmured and above them the flags and banners still flapped and quivered, but all Gainas could hear, was his blood pumping in his ears.

A group of eight cavalry officers then remounted, formed up and rode towards the dais: Gainas' personal guard, his *bucellarii*, led by the veteran soldier Euthymius, a Goth like Gainas, who he had known for years and trusted implicitly. The man bore many scars on his face and arms and sported a neat, grey-streaked beard. Euthymius reigned in his horse and called up to Arcadius.

'The Imperial Army of the East, returned by your orders from the West, is ready for your inspection, Imperator!' Euthymius saluted smartly.

The emperor placed his cup down on a small table, stepped to the edge of the platform and returned the salute then spoke as loudly as he could.

'Thank you, my good man! It is wonderful to see my late, great father's army returned safely to our sacred city, praise be to God.' He then descended the stairs from the dais, protected front and back by the *Candidati* guards, Rufinus following.

Gainas gripped his hands tightly to stop them trembling, then trying to ignore the pit in his stomach, he too descended the steps onto the parade ground below. The emperor and his guards were assisted onto their horses, as were Rufinus and Gainas. Rufinus was immediately surrounded by his Hunnic bodyguards. Euthymius and his bucellarii fell in beside Gainas.

The Imperial party cantered towards the cavalry cohorts to begin the inspection; that was the tradition. They formed up, ready for the formal ride past, Arcadius leading with the *Candidati*, Rufinus following with his Hunnic bodyguard and bringing up the rear was Gainas and his men. Gainas glanced at Rufinus, who just scowled. The general took great pleasure in smiling pleasantly back at the prefect; after all, this was his army. He had led them here across Thessaly. He knew these men. They were his men. But despite his smile, he heard his heart thudding in his chest and his stomach was twisting itself in knots. He breathed in deep and breathed out slowly. The moment was approaching.

So began the long laborious review of troops by the emperor, as had happened many times before. Passing the mounted cavalry, the leading *praepositi* and *primicerii* saluted smartly. At one point Arcadius called out to one of the men, 'And how are you today, *praepositus* ?' The man responded as he had been taught, 'You do us a great honour, Imperator, we live to serve you, the Empire and God.'

They continued down the line, past the end of the first cohorts of cavalry. A small group of soldier's servants, the *cacula*, waited there. Next was the infantry, who were brought to attention by their primicerii as the inspection party approached. Before they reached the first standing cohorts however, the emperor raised his hand and called a halt. Gainas stopped his horse. The emperor turned and called to Rufinus behind him, 'We will dismount and walk whilst we inspect the infantry, prefect. We can then see the men face to face.' Without waiting for an answer, he and his *Candidati* dismounted. Gainas and Euthymius quickly followed suit and called out to the cacula to take their horses. The *Candidati* swiftly fell into formation around Arcadius. Gainas licked his dry lips and swallowed. The moment was almost here.

Just ahead of him, Gainas looked and saw a confused Rufinus dismounting, signalling to his bodyguard to do the same. The Hunnic guards looked puzzled at this spur-of-the-moment change of plan.

When they were all ready, Arcadius said, 'Let us continue then.' His drooping eyelids and pale complexion made him a laughable figure. Gainas almost felt sorry for the young man; he looked completely out of his depth. Gainas and his bucellarii formed up, the general at the centre of his men with a line of four either side. Just before the emperor turned to continue the inspection, he looked directly at Gainas and gave a wan smile. Gainas kept his face implacable. He could not afford to get distracted by the youth.

Rufinus' party set off behind the emperor. Gainas kept his face emotionless as he nodded to his men to. He felt calmer now. As he knew he would.

This was it.

As they approached the very centre of the line of troops, Gainas gave a hand signal and his bucellarii slowly and silently drew their swords. He had ordered them to line their scabbards with linen to muffle the sound. At a second signal from the general, they all quickened their pace, closing up behind the Huns.

'Now!' hissed Gainas and with that, the two leading bucellarii leapt up and slashed at the backs and necks of the rear of the Hunnic guard. Two men tumbled forward to the floor, blood gushing. Gainas' other men rushed forward and fell on the remaining Huns before they could react, hacking and slashing in a whirlwind of violence. Gainas found himself faced with a large Hun, struggling to draw his blade, not knowing which way to turn. So Gainas swung his sword, slicing deep into an arm. The man was tough, and tried to strike back, but the thrust was weak and Gainas easily batted the weapon away burying his own sword into the man's belly and heaving upwards. The Hun screamed and fumbled with blood-soaked arms and hands trying to hold his guts in as the general dragged his sword free. The man collapsed to the ground and Gainas arced his weapon viciously across the Hun's throat and shoulder, blood spattering his arms.

Stepping over the body, Gainas looked into the face of Rufinus, who was staring in disbelief as his bodyguard fell around him. Two had reacted quickly enough to fend off the initial attack, but now they were dying too. The end was swift, and soon they lay bloody, contorted, and motionless at the feet of their master.

Rufinus glared at Gainas, hatred burning in his eyes. He raised his own weapon towards the general, but a bucellarii slammed his sword down, severing the prefect's lower arm; weapon and limb clattered to the ground. Rufinus cried out a curse as a second merciless blow took his other arm. Another of Gainas' men kicked the now whimpering prefect behind the knees, driving him down onto the ground. Finally, Euthymius stepped forward and, with a vicious swing of his long cavalry sword, parted head from shoulders in a single blow. The lifeless body slumped to the ground, blood gushing from the gaping neck and soaking into the sand and dust of the parade ground.

The soldiers in the lines were murmuring; a buzz of excitement had spread through the nearest cohorts. Some of the rear ranks had broken formation to try to see what was happening, but Euthymius roared at the men to get back into their lines and to hold their positions and their tongues, or else.

Silence fell.

Gainas, breathing heavily, stared down at the ruined body of the Praetorian Prefect. After what seemed an age, he looked up and saw the emperor staring back at him, the bland face expressionless, yet paler even than normal.

Then the general barked orders at the *Candidati* and the cacula to get the emperor away and within a few seconds Arcadius was mounted and riding back to the dais. One of the Gainas' men hacked at the corpse's wrists and picked up the two grisly trophies, whilst another hoisted the head on a spear showing it to the troops who let out an involuntary cheer, even though most must have had no idea whose head it was.

Gainas waited until the emperor was back on the dais with the Imperial Court, then he turned to his troops and boomed out, in his loudest parade ground voice.

'The traitor Rufinus is dead! Long live Emperor Arcadius! Long live the Empire!'

The troops chorused in reply, 'Long live Emperor Arcadius! Long live the Empire!' They beat their swords and spears on their shields, a rhythm built and grew to a thunderous crescendo, rippling and echoing across the parade ground, joined by cheers and shouts. Gainas let the men have their moment and then eventually called them to order. He handed command to the officers with instructions to get the men billeted and housed. The *praepositi* barked out their orders, and the army began to disperse.

Gainas stared back at the dais. His eyes narrowed and he gritted his teeth as he saw the chamberlain, Eutropius, step up beside Arcadius and begin to talk to him at length. Gainas suddenly realised he was taking deep breaths and gripping his fists.

'Sir?' inquired a voice behind Gainas. Euthymius smiled and held out his hand to the general. 'Good work, sir.'

Gainas grabbed his officer's hand to shake it; but it suddenly came away and he was left holding the dripping, severed hand of Rufinus, whilst his men doubled up laughing around him.

'Bastards!' he cursed. But the laughter relaxed him, and he felt the tension drain from him and soon he was laughing with his men. He was exultant, surprised, and again there was that feeling that somehow, this was not real. It had gone so quickly and so smoothly.

Gathering his thoughts, he growled at the youngest of the bucellarii, the one who had first dismembered the prefect, 'Amalaric!'

'Sir!'

'Catch!' Gainas threw the hand of Rufinus at the young man, who deftly caught it, still smiling as blood spattered across his uniform and face. 'Organise a crew to clear this up. I want *them* dumped in the sea.' He nodded towards the scattered corpses. 'The rest of you get back to

the troops and organise tents, billets, and housing. And all of you …'
he paused and waited for the bucellarii to looked at him '…well done.
That was well done.'

The men smiled, straightened, and saluted then set off back to the main
camp. All except Euthymius.

Gainas turned back and watched the Imperial party as they descended
from the dais and mounted their horses again. He could not help but
notice that Eutropius and the emperor were side by side the whole
time.

'You OK sir?'

When the general didn't reply, Euthymius stepped up beside him and
followed his gaze. 'Can we trust that bastard?'

Gainas snorted and spat in the dirt.

'The eunuch? Not for one second. In fact, I think even now he is
screwing us over. We're in danger of being overtaken by events.' He
sighed and clapped Euthymius on the shoulders. With Rufinus dead,
his own men around him, he should have felt like his time had come at
last. But as Arcadius and his chamberlain rode off, side by side with the
rest of the Imperial party in tow, Gainas was unable to shake off the
feeling that it was not the emperor he was watching depart, but his
ambitions and dreams.

Chapter 2

Two Days Earlier, Constantinople, 25th November 395 AD

Eutropius walked through corridors, down and up flights of stairs until finally, he came to the end of a dimly lit passageway. Outside the doors stood two of his guards, eunuchs such himself him of course, part of the inner circle of protectors who shielded the emperor day and night in his private rooms. This was one of the most secluded and isolated areas of the palace.

Quietly, he pushed open the heavy, intricately carved cedarwood doors. Blinking in the rush of bright light, he stepped into the room. Daylight streamed into the room through a row of carved stone arches in the far wall. Beyond lay a balcony overlooking the Bosphorus, which today was a deep azure blue, flecked with white as the tops of the waves broke in the breeze and the crests caught the bright, late afternoon sunlight. The room was a muddle of luxurious chairs and couches. In the centre was a long low table, laden with bowls of succulent fruit, platters of bread and cakes and golden goblets of wine.

There were only three people in the room. General Abundantius, consul two years ago; General Timasius, another old warrior, friend of Abundantius, who had fought at Adrianople; and the emperor, Flavius Arcadius, who looked like a child alongside the two old warriors. The three were standing close together but already in a deep and heated conversation; Eutropius observed the animated body language. He turned, closed, and locked the doors carefully behind him with the iron bar; the men turned at the sound.

'Ah, there you are at last!' said Abundantius, stepping forward and placing his drink on the table.

Eutropius could see that the emperor was particularly agitated.

'General Abundantius has just told me some very upsetting things, Chamberlain. Did you know about this?'

'About what, Imperator?' asked Eutropius, as pleasantly as he could. He knew exactly what Abundantius had said but for the sake of the emperors' ego, pretended he didn't.

'About Rufinus, of course!'

'What about him, Imperator?'

'Abundantius and Timasius have both accused him of plotting to take my throne!' Arcadius almost shouted the words, a petulant child among adults.

'I would not be in the least bit surprised, Imperator,' Eutropius replied calmly.

'You are not?' Arcadius seemed taken aback, but then he wasn't the brightest of young men, thought the chamberlain.

'No,' said Eutropius. 'No, not at all. He has spent his entire career trying to worm his way into your Imperial family. He tried to marry his daughter to you, did he not? That would have made any grandsons of his heir to the throne.'

The emperor frowned and started to bite his fingernails, a nervous childhood habit he had failed to shed. He sat down on one of the reclining couches and motioned for the others to sit too.

'That's true … that is true, Eutropius, you are right.' He sighed and continued in a quieter voice, 'I'll be frank with you, gentlemen; I've never much cared for the man. But he always seems to know what to do. He always seems so … so … clever. It seems I can never argue with what he says.'

'May I speak freely?' Eutropius looked at the young emperor and smiled as kindly as he could manage.

12

'Of course, always.'

'Rufinus is a talented man, no doubt about it. But he is also ambitious. He's long been using his position for his own benefit more than anyone else's. He has threatened, lied, charmed, and blackmailed his way into power. Your father was very taken with him. Much as I admired him, forgive my bluntness, he was a fool when it came to Rufinus. How he could favour him over the two generals in this room is beyond my understanding.'

The two generals both looked suitably flattered and nodded and smiled in agreement with the chamberlain's words. Eutropius knew the long-standing enmity between the prefect and these two men. Both generals were wealthy, respected, popular, and had wide support in the senate. Eutropius knew that if things went as he hoped and planned, one day soon they would prove to be a problem; but right now, he needed their support. Rufinus must go. He looked at Timasius.

'He has taken lands from most of the *illustrii* in one form or another, is that not so, general?'

Timasius nodded.

'Indeed, it is the case, the prefect has forced me to hand over several large estates, which I originally held in trust for the widow of my friend Promotus, making her homeless until I found her and her household suitable lodgings.'

'He did that to a general's widow?' Arcadius paled.

'And she was only a widow because he had her husband, my good friend, murdered,' snapped Timasius. 'He was a loyal servant of the Empire, Imperator, an honourable man, and a brave fighter.' The general stood up and started pacing, his hands behind his back. 'Rufinus had him killed out of pure envy, and probably because he was secretly scared of him. Promotus never shied away from challenging him. Humph!' He turned and looked at the other three. 'He struck him once, at a dinner hosted by your father, Imperator.' Timasius laughed gently. 'You should have seen the look on his face …'

Eutropius interrupted. 'And then there was Tatianus and his son Proclus, who both, as far as we can ascertain, never took a bribe from anyone. Rufinus had them arrested on false charges. Tatianus was exiled but Proclus was executed.'

Arcadius said, 'What about the courts? They must have investigated the charges, and decided they had cases to answer?'

Eutropius smiled like a teacher to a naive pupil, 'But Imperator, what can the courts do when the judges and prosecutors are in the pay of the prefect? They ruled as he directed.'

Abundantius chimed in with his deep sonorous voice. 'Your father tried to stop the execution, Imperator, but Rufinus held back the messenger until it was too late. I heard that from the messenger himself, who now works on one of my estates. Rufinus went against your father's explicit order.' He tapped his finger on the tabletop. 'That is treason right there! But like the serpent he is, he managed to wriggle out of it and, forgive me too, Imperator, but I agree with the chamberlain, your father was unable to see him for what he is.'

'And this just a hint of what the man is truly like... That is not the worst of it.' Timasius broke in before the emperor could respond.

The room fell silent. Eutropius looked at the generals; Arcadius saw the look and said, 'Well, what? Speak up, what is the worst of it?'

Abundantius held up his hand and stood stiffly. 'Imperator, we believe that Rufinus ordered the return of the Eastern Legions to prevent Stilicho from defeating Alaric. We think he plans to join with Alaric this year to defeat Stilicho and gain control over your younger brother, and thereby the Western Empire, whilst increasing his control over you. He used you, Imperator, for his own political gain.'

For what seemed an age, none of the men spoke. The only sound was the screeching of gulls over the Golden Horn. Arcadius was utterly lost for words. Eutropius could see that. So, he went in for the kill, to seal Rufinus' fate once and for all.

'And I am afraid, Imperator... it does not end there.'

Out of the folds of his gowns, the eunuch flourished a small slip of parchment, rough and split, as if it had been folded too many times. He handed it to the emperor.

Arcadius read the message and looked up sharply at the chamberlain.

'What does this mean? Attempting to obtain hemlock? Is he planning to poison me?'

'Oh no, Imperator, not you,' said Eutropius, smiling kindly. 'From interrogating the messenger, I believe the poison was to be delivered to one of your wife's handmaidens; she used to be a whore that Rufinus frequented. He is apparently blackmailing her. I believe she was to poison the empress, opening up the possibility of you marrying his daughter once again. He is nothing if not persistent.'

Even a man as young and dull-witted as Arcadius could see where this was going. He rose to his feet and said, 'He must be arrested and tried for treason and attempted murder! He cannot continue as he does ...'

Timasius snorted. 'Imperator, with the greatest respect, Rufinus owns the courts, most of the palace guards are loyal to him and the urban cohorts too; even if we could get his own men to arrest him, the courts would acquit him.'

'I will command them to arrest and convict him!' Arcadius shouted.

'You do that, Imperator, and you will force his hand; he could turn around and instigate a coup and likely win,' said Timasius calmly. 'He controls too much of the administration and the army.'

'What then do you advise, general?' the emperor said in frustration. Before Timasius could respond, Eutropius said, 'I believe person who is the solution to our problem is already with us.'

'Who?' prompted Abundantius. The emperor and the two generals both stared at the chamberlain, who smiled a small but triumphant smile and spoke a name.

'Gainas.'

General Gainas was busy in the offices of the *Comes Sacrarum Largitionum*, the finance ministry, with Euthymius and his military administrators. He was in the middle of sorting out details of clothing and bonuses for the returning troops, when a tall, muscled black slave delivered a message that he was summoned to meet the chamberlain Eutropius as a matter of urgency. The note was signed by the emperor himself. Leaving his administrators to finish the victualing work, he and Euthymius followed the slave through the labyrinth of corridors until they came to a plain wooden door. The slave opened the door but did not enter, indicating that the general should do so by himself; he stood in front of Euthymius, calm but menacing. Gainas nodded silently to his commander, indicating he should stay outside. Inside the bare and dusty room, he found the chamberlain. Neither man offered any greeting; they just looked at one another, sizing each other up.

Eutropius was surprised when he saw Gainas. He had expected a barbarian foederatus, unkempt and rough, dressed in skins and leather, but here was a man, yes with a beard, but it was a finely cut beard, trimmed, and styled in the modern fashion. His receding hair he wore long, and tied at the back, in the traditional Gothic style. He wore the standard uniform of a Roman General in camp, but his tunic was of fine silk, his cloak and broach were of excellent quality wool, and his sword scabbard was latticed in gold plate. He looked fit and healthy, though his forearms and face showed the scars of battle. His nose was slightly bent where it had been broken in the past, and his eyes were a deep brown, almost black. Eutropius reassessed. This was no parochial barbarian. A Goth by birth he may be, and a deserter from his native army, but now he was, without doubt, a full Roman citizen and, he reminded himself, a full Roman General in charge of Roman troops.

Gainas was less surprised at Eutropius. The man was big, but not powerful. His mutilation had affected his growth and body shape. He stood slightly slouched, his paunch showing through his robes, his shoulders rounded. Above his double chin was a long face with a wide mouth, curving down in a way that made him appear humourless. A face that held a grudge, thought Gainas. Though in the eunuch's situation he thought he would probably hold a grudge too, especially against the bastard who had chopped his privates off.

Eutropius spoke without preamble. 'I understand, General, that you were personally picked by Stilicho himself to bring the army home?'

'You are correct,' Gainas replied stiffly. He had been warned by Stilicho that this eunuch was as devious as they come.

'Might I enquire if you have any orders from Stilicho other than to return the emperor's army?'

Gainas did not answer the question. Instead, he snapped, 'If you have something to say eunuch, say it.'

Eutropius didn't answer; he seemed quite at ease.

Gainas was unsure if this impotent was trying to determine his secret directives to help him or to thwart him. Stilicho had told him that he had been in communication with the chamberlain over the past few months and that Eutropius had hinted very strongly that, should Rufinus fall to illness or injury, the entire court at Constantinople would be more than willing to entertain a stand-in recommended by

Stilicho until the prefect recovered. If he ever did. But Stilicho did not trust the eunuch one inch.

Gainas changed tack. 'I have simply been ordered to serve the emperor to the best of my ability.'

Eutropius tried a grin. It didn't suit him. 'Don't we all? Don't we all?' A short silence. Gainas couldn't read the chamberlain's expression.

'The emperor's order to return the army was a very clever measure, I might say. Very clever indeed,' Eutropius continued.

Gainas snorted. 'We were about to kick Alaric's arse out of Thessaly when the order came. The only reason General Stilicho obeyed was out of deference to the memory of the emperor's father.'

Eutropius nodded. 'I'm sure that Stilicho was showing full respect to the memory of our late, great Augustus.' The sentence was laced with irony, but Gainas gritted his teeth and stayed silent. 'But really, to refuse the Eastern Emperor would be an open declaration of war between Ravenna and Constantinople, which neither of us wants. It would also undermine his claim to be the protector of the young Arcadius by blatantly going against him. So, he had to return the army, and in doing so, it left him too weak to continue the fight against Alaric, and so the Goth escapes from Stilicho's clutches yet again.' The eunuch signed a heavy, theatrical sigh. 'The good gentlemen of the Western senate must be wondering by now, just what is the relationship between those two? A half-Vandal Roman general and a Goth King who seem to continually dance around one another on the battlefield. And so, in one fell swoop the emperor gains back the Eastern Legions, and in the process undermines Stilicho both in the West and the East. I must say it was a brilliant move.'

Eutropius gave a small snort and then looked directly at Gainas. 'But you and I of course know, General, that Rufinus told our emperor to order Stilicho to return the army to us? The boy on the throne has neither the wit nor focus to think of a move like that for himself.'

'You should mind your tongue, eunuch, when you speak of our Imperator. Everyone knows that Rufinus is an imposter as regent. Theodosius chose Stilicho for that role for both his sons. What's your point?'

'Would I also be correct in my assumption that you have no great love for our esteemed Praetorian prefect?'

'From what I hear, nobody does, what's your point?' Gainas found his patience thinning.

'My point is, General, nothing happens in this palace without Rufinus saying 'yea' or 'nay', as you well know. So whatever Stilicho may or may not have been told by the late emperor doesn't matter. Here, what Rufinus says goes. His judgement on matters is all that counts. You don't cross him unless you have a death wish.'

Eutropius glanced around exaggeratedly, like some lowly actor in a street theatre, then continued, 'His spies are everywhere around the palace, General, and around the city. I could be one of them.' again that sinister grin.

'I doubt that very much.'

'And yet you tell me nothing and answer my questions with banalities.' Eutropius circled Gainas. 'And I understand why. I could be a spy for the prefect, or at the very least his loyal man, and I could be here to try to trick you into revealing the secret orders that I – and Rufinus – are convinced Stilicho has given you.'

Gainas said nothing, though he had balled his right fist to calm himself. Eutropius continued.

'But if I suspected that you intended harm to our illustrious perfect, I wouldn't need proof; I could simply go to him and say that I had a contact in the army or the court who had alerted me to a plot where you plan to kill him so that Stilicho can assume the regency over both

East and West, as he seems to think he should. Rufinus knows you're Stilicho's man, why would he question me?'

Eutropius shrugged nonchalantly. 'I've nothing to lose by betraying you to Rufinus and everything to gain. It would raise my standing in court and gain me more influence with the emperor and the prefect. And that influence, by the way, is of far greater worth than any gold that you might try to bribe me with to stop me informing on you.' The chamberlain paused and drew breath.

When Gainas said nothing, he continued. 'So, you see, it wouldn't bother me in the slightest, exposing your little secret. Things would improve greatly for me and definitely go worse for you. You would be executed, without any torture beforehand if you're lucky, and your body dumped in the Golden Horn. The East would gain an army, Rufinus and I would expose Stilicho's treachery, the threat to the regent would be gone …' He paused to emphasise his words, '… and the emperor would be even more in our debt than he already is.'

Gainas snorted. 'What is stopping you then, eunuch?'

Eutropius ceased his circling and confronted Gainas, their faces mere inches apart, each holding the other's gaze. Then Eutropius blinked and stepped away saying in an almost light-hearted tone, 'On the other hand, like everybody else in the court, I may detest the Gaul with every bone in my body and maybe I am trying to find an ally with the courage, motive and means to cut him down to size. So, I could be trying to determine what orders you have, hoping that they are to depose the hated Gaul, for all our sakes, and perhaps offer you my help in the matter?' He stared at Gainas. 'Only you can decide, General, whether you and I are on the same side.'

Gainas said nothing. So Eutropius gave a small bow and walked to the door. But he turned back to the Goth with a hard expression on his face.

'One more thing, General. You should mind your tongue yourself, and address me as Eutropius, or Chamberlain, not 'eunuch'. You would do well to remember that over the coming days.'

He opened the door and was about to shut it behind him when Gainas called out, 'Tell the emperor to dismount when he inspects the infantry.'

Eutropius paused on the threshold, smiled to himself then pulled the door closed.

It was late in the evening when Eutropius, Abundantius and Timasius met again, in the same remote room as earlier in the day. This time Arcadius was not present. The room was dark now, lit by only a few wall mounted burning torches and some tall tallow candles which dotted the tables. The three men stood on the balcony, under the stars, looking out over the Golden Horn to the hills beyond, the lights of the night-time fishermen flickering across the bay below them.

'What did he say?' asked Timasius.

'Tell the emperor to dismount when he inspects the infantry,' replied Eutropius.

'Is that all?' asked the old general waspishly.

'That's all he needed to or could say.'

'But how does it help us?' insisted Timasius.

Abundantius cut in. 'He is telling us to trust him. He has a plan; we just need to do as he says.'

'But how can we trust him?'

'We cannot, but we have nothing to lose here,' said Eutropius. 'If he is planning to assassinate Rufinus, and he succeeds, we win; if he fails or he is not planning anything, we don't lose, as there is nothing to link us back to Gainas.'

'What if he does nothing?' Timasius was sweating, despite the cool sea breeze.

The chamberlain sighed. 'Then we are no worse or better off than we are now. The emperor is aware of the problem; we will just have to find another way to deal with him.'

'What if the emperor decides to take matters into his own hands?'

'Then General, that will be the first time he has ever done anything on of his own initiative, and we should probably be grateful for that. But it's not a course of action I would recommend we place our faith in. I say we assume our Romanised Goth has something planned, as he, like you, has no love for our prefect, and we make plans for what happens if he is successful. That will be the most dangerous moment.'

'We may trade a Gaul for a Goth as prefect,' said Abundantius.

'The senate and the people would not support that; there are still too many memories of Adrianople, and Alaric has only just been driven out of Thrace and is now a threat in Thessaly.' Timasius was vehement. 'There would be riots, rightly so; I might even join them myself!'

Abundantius' low voice cut in. 'We need a competent administrator, a fair hand and above all a Roman, not a Goth or a German. I would be happy to see our friend Caesarius take on the role; he has proved himself an able diplomat and administrator and is known for his fairness in dealings with people.'

Eutropius went to say something then thought better of it. Abundantius had been his route out of slavery, an incredibly wealthy patron who owned huge estates. That patronage had lasted years. One very small part of the chamberlain admired the old man, but for the most part, he loathed him. Their relationship went back many, many years, too many to count, and filled with too much pain and humiliation for him to want to count. Yes, the general had been key in his elevation from a soldier's sexual plaything to close advisor of the emperor, but throughout that lay their very personal history together.

The ageing general held too much influence for Eutropius to even consider challenging him – yet. He had been consul two years earlier, and the prestige of that even now emanated from the man. People still listened and cared about what he said and what he thought. So, he needed to do as Abundantius said, not because he felt obliged to follow the old man's orders, but because he needed to prepare the emperor for the assassination of Rufinus and make sure that the transition of the prefect's role was smooth. This was no time to cause huge divisions; the Empire needed continuity, not disruption. The army must be brought under the control of the emperor, or at least out of the control of generals like Stilicho, Rufinus and Gainas. With many troops in the legions of Goth origin, or from other barbarian tribes, having senior generals of the same ethnic origin was a very dangerous situation, even if the emperor could not see it.

But the first and most pressing need was to rid themselves of Rufinus. The *illustrii* in turn would advise the impotent Senate, who would then 'approve' the new prefect. Then the emperor, or whoever controlled him, would really approve the position. Eutropius wanted to make sure that it was he who made that decision, but he had not yet got into a position where he was secure from the likes of Abundantius. So Eutropius swallowed his immediate irritation and acquiesced to the general's suggestion.

The old general continued, 'As soon as the deed is done, I will seek out Caesarius and convince him to take up the role. The other *illustrii* will fall in behind him, I am sure.'

'It is key that we are in the senate building when the news arrives of Rufinus' death; there will quickly be a quorum and we will need to steer the conversation,' said Timasius. Abundantius nodded. 'Either you or I must be in the senate chamber, ready the moment the messenger arrives.'

'Chamberlain,' said Abundantius, and Eutropius looked at his patron – he hoped – with due deference. 'You need to go to the emperor and brief him about General Gainas and what he said. In the meantime, Timasius and I will ready our arguments for the senate in support of Caesarius. Are we all agreed?'

All three nodded and departed the room, the decision on the next Praetorian Prefect of the East all but made.

Chapter 3

On the road to Constantinople, 27th November 395 AD

It was a two-hour ride back to Constantinople from Hebdomon. The vanguard was led by general Abundantius, along with Eutropius. Either side of them rode the *Candidati* guards, and behind them came the other members of the court and units of the palace guard. The Empress, who chose not to ride, sat in a litter carried by eight huge slaves, who trudged with practised steps to make her journey smooth, and they too were guarded by yet more mounted palace guards.

As they proceeded, Abundantius spoke in his gruff voice of Rufinus and his treason. Arcadius only appeared to be half-listening. He studiously gazed at the dusty ground as they rode, avoiding eye contact with anyone, his lips pursed in a petulant fashion, his eyelids drooping.

Eutropius studied the young emperor. The boy's father had been a man of many faults and contradictions, he had been overly keen to appear a pious god-fearing man, but in reality, he was an utterly ruthless emperor when he needed to be, unafraid to make the tough decisions. God must have favoured him Eutropius decided , because he had won all his battles. And it had to be said he was a great man. His two sons though, were another matter.

The irony was that in reality he was grateful that neither offspring showed the mettle that the father had. Under no circumstances would Theodosius have let himself become the puppet emperor that Arcadius had been under Rufinus. The boy needed guidance for certain, and now Eutropius had the opportunity to be that guide. He might not be in a position to become praetorian prefect, master of the offices, or consul, but he had something all of those other powerful *illustrii* did not have.

His office was *Praepositus Sacri Cubiculi*, the 'Provost of the Sacred Bedchamber'. His whole life's purpose was to serve and look after the well-being of the emperor. He oversaw the emperors' private residencies, the reception rooms and the running of the imperial palace. Through his network of palace servants, he knew every little thing that went on with everybody. Who liked who, who hated who, who slept with who and who wanted who dead. The other *illustrii*, the senior senators who sat in the consistorium and made up the inner circle of the emperor's advisors, did not have access to this goldmine of information and Eutropius was slowly coming to the realisation that he could possibly hold the key to real power at court.

Because aside from the gossip and the secrets, above all else, both the Emperor Arcadius and his Empress Eudoxia trusted him. After all, it was *he* who had brought them together. They had both seen powerful men scheme and plot and betray to gain influence, attempting to establish their own dynasties, all seeking to get into the palace and perhaps even onto the throne. Eutropius had no such ambition. He was happy to be the puppet master, happy to guide and to steer. His mutilation denied him the ability to found a dynasty, so he was no threat and the emperor did not fear him. Indeed, the emperor had every reason to go to him as a neutral advisor when he was unsure which of the generals or officials were giving him the best advice.

'Are you OK, my master?' asked Eutropius.

'Of course, Chamberlain. I had a better view than if it had been in the Hippodrome,' said Arcadius with a faint smile. 'But I'm glad it's over.'

Eutropius nodded. 'I was somewhat surprised myself. I thought Rufinus would put up more of a fight, but Gainas' men were too fast, he never had time to draw his sword.'

'Never underestimate the element of surprise in a fight, Imperator,' said Abundantius.

'They were fast, weren't they?' Arcadius agreed. 'So … what happens now?' the question was asked with little interest, and more out of a sense of obligation it seemed.

'The senate is already discussing the successor to the traitor, Imperator,' replied Abundantius.

'Do they know what has happened already?'

'I sent a messenger ahead with the news, my master. General Timasius will be leading the senate in their deliberations by the time we arrive back,' said Eutropius. He paused, aware of Abundantius staring at him, and said, 'If I may be so bold, I might recommend that you at least consider the very talented Eutychainus, Imperator.'

Abundantius snorted.

Eutropius paused but decided to press his case. 'He is a highly respected administrator, Imperator, and there is great need to ensure the proper collection of taxes to fund the armies and the auxiliary foederati , plus there is all the administration and re-organisation of the armies now that they are back in the East.'

Again, Abundantius snorted.

Even the dull-witted Arcadius could not fail to feel the old general's disapproval. 'You don't agree, General?'

'No, Imperator, I do not. And neither will the senate.'

'Why?'

'I'd rather not say in public, Imperator,' Abundantius eyed Eutropius with a frown.

'So, who do think the senate will recommend?' asked Arcadius. They all knew that the senate had no real power, but it was politically necessary to gain their tacit approval for any major appointments.

'I believe they will favour Caesarius,' said Abundantius. 'He is known for his diplomacy and fairness, and he is a very competent, if somewhat uninspiring, administrator. He is his own man and not susceptible to bribes or corruption.' He looked pointedly at Eutropius, who ignored his old patron's stare.

'What do you think, Chamberlain?' Arcadius arched an eyebrow.

'He certainly is competent but has a reputation for perhaps a bit too much leniency, especially when it comes to heretics.'

Then, feeling the eyes of his old general on him, he lowered his head deferentially. 'What I think doesn't really matter, does it, my master? I'm your servant, the consistorium are your political advisors. General Abundantius for example, and General Timasius too.'

They rode on for just over an hour until they came to the Golden Gate in the city walls; the guards on the walls and around the gate snapped to attention. They continued up the Mese, which was lined with city militia guards, because the city had come out to greet the emperor.

Crowds cheered and threw flowers at the procession as it wound its way through the main city thoroughfare, through the forums, and up the hill towards the Great Palace. Arcadius waved to the crowds as he passed them, which raised more cheers. Eutropius reflected that most of the population had no idea what Arcadius was like as a person, but everybody knew he was the son of Theodosius, the Warrior Emperor, and that made him the legitimate ruler of the Empire as far as they were concerned. Their protector. God's representative on earth. And so, they cheered

Under the noise of the crowd, Arcadius rode in close to Eutropius and spoke quietly, for his ears only.

'I know, chamberlain, the consistorium are my political advisors but most of them are so ... so ...stuck up and arrogant. They think I'm some kind of idiot. I can see it in their faces. I'd rather ask you. You've got no agenda, because ... well because ...' his voice trailed off and he blushed.

'Because I'm a eunuch, master. You can say it, it doesn't offend. It's what I am. And you are right. I have no agenda. I cannot sire children; I have no desire for women or men. My life is serving you, my Imperator, and if I may be of service from time to time in offering advice, then that would please me greatly.'

Eutropius waved to the still cheering crowd. Arcadius followed his chamberlain's lead and waved too; more cheers went up and more flowers were thrown towards the young emperor.

The procession eventually completed the climb to the palace, leaving the crowds behind them. Arcadius and Eutropius still rode together but had positioned themselves at the back of the Imperial party with two large *Candidati* guards.

'It would please me too, Chamberlain. I feel I can actually trust you. I can't trust the others.' Arcadius had lowered his voice to a whisper, though it was unlikely the guards beside him could hear him. The noise from the crowds behind them still echoed around loudly.

The emperor halted his horse just outside the Chalca Gate, Eutropius did likewise, and they watched as the procession ahead of them entered the great palace complex. Inside the gate they knew a host of slaves and courtiers waited, ready to take the horses to the stables and to provide refreshments and drinks. Members of the Imperial party started dismounting, Abundantius among them.

 The chamberlain shook his head.

'Oh no my master, the officials, the senate and generals of the consistorium are dedicated to serving you, but I can understand, after Rufinus, why you might find it difficult to trust the people who he hired. I will deal with them. I can assure you.'

'Thank you, chamberlain, that's a great relief.'

Ahead, Abundantius waited impatiently. It was the custom for the emperor to lead the Imperial party into the palace.

'Please go-ahead, gentlemen!' called out Eutropius. 'We will follow shortly.'

The courtiers looked puzzled; this was not the normal way of doing things. Abundantius looked annoyed too. But the captain of the *Candidati* stepped in and started directing them to the palace doors.

'As I said on the way here Imperator' said Eutropius, 'most of the palace staff detested the man for his avarice and greed, his attempts to worm his way into your family, his betrayal of Promotus. All of those things undermined him and endeared him to no one in the palace or the administration. I can assure you of that.'

Arcadius nodded slowly and kicked his horse back into motion. They rode to the centre of the now empty courtyard, where the last remaining cacula grabbed the horses' bridles and helped the emperor and chamberlain dismount.

'Still,' said Arcadius a little more brightly. 'It would make me happy, and I would feel more secure if I knew I could count on your advice and counsel when I need it. And I believe I will need it in the coming months.'

Eutropius bowed low. 'Indeed, my master, there is much that we need to do to ensure that the capital and you are protected from all threats. We have Alaric to deal with, and then there are the Huns and Stilicho, and the Avars and the Persians always need watching.'

'So where do we begin?' asked Arcadius. 'It all seems so much to consider and to do. I ... I really don't know where to start.' The emperor looked intently at the chamberlain.

'Well, I can tell you that your decision on the new prefect is the first order of the day. But, Imperator, I could prepare an agenda for you for tomorrow's meeting with the consistorium. If that would be of help? I can talk with some of the *illustrii*, and we can prioritise the other tasks.'

'That would be so valuable. I do get lost in some of the meetings. Thank you, chamberlain.' Arcadius nodded and Eutropius bowed low. As the emperor turned to walk towards the palace gardens he looked back and said, 'And I would like you there as well, please. You don't have to get involved, but I would value your insights and opinion.'

Eutropius bowed low again and waited a minute as the emperor and his two guards walked towards the gardens in the fading evening light.

When he looked up and straightened, he noticed Abundantius watching intently him from the far side of the courtyard. Eutropius gave a small bow in his direction, but the old soldier's irate expression did not change and a few seconds later he turned abruptly and entered the palace.

Eutropius sighed to himself. Things appeared to be going the way he wanted them to. But he was under no illusion: he would have to fight hard, to ensure that things kept on going the way he wanted them to.

Interlude

Hebdomon Camp, near Constantinople, 27th November 395 AD

Gadaric pulled off his helmet and gloves. "Fuck me! I wasn't expecting that! They could have warned us!"

"Great move, though." Gerung whistled appreciatively. "Beautiful action. Wham!" He imitated the sword swing that had beheaded Rufinus an hour earlier. "Do you know how hard it is to do that?" he asked. "Cut through the neck with one swing? I've never managed it meself. That fucker knew how to swing that thing for sure."

Gadaric ignored his friend's enthusiasm. "That was one parade I won't forget for a while," he said as he hung his uniform from the roof of the tent and commenced brushing it down, dust falling on the floor.

"So, who's going to get the prefect's job now?" asked Gerung, noisily relieving himself in the bucket in the tent corner.

Gadaric shrugged. "How should I know?"

"You always seem to know that kind of stuff."

"Not this time. I suppose General Gainas must be hoping he'll get the nod, seeing as he seemed to be the one who organised the whole thing." Gadaric finished brushing the leather tunic and started polishing the silver- and gold-plated buckles.

"How do you figure that one out?"

"Didn't you see him with the officers? He was right in there with them, had to be him who organised it."

"I guess." Gerung sighed, finishing up. "Anyway, we're off duty now for two days, so I'm going into the city, get good and drunk and good and laid. I bet we can get a few free drinks at John's tavern retelling today's little episode, eh?"

Chapter 4

Macedonia (Greece) Border, 10th December 395 AD

A vast line of humanity trudged across the dusty plains of Northern Macedonia. Men and women dressed in tunics and furs walked amongst carts and wagons pulled by oxen, ponies and people. Children played and ran, weaving in and out of the line. They were yelled at by their mothers and fathers and brothers to be careful of the wheels and animals. Groups of men plodded along together laughing and singing bawdy songs, groups of women chatted, babies cried. This was not a band of migrants or an army, it was a nation on the move.

Circling the central mass of people rode the outlying cavalry units, vigilant for bandits and raiders that might try to break into the baggage train. They might try to steal food, or worse, steal the children to sell as slaves, depending on whether they were simply hungry locals, or organised brigands trying to make a profit.

Further afield still rode the scouts, out to find foraging for the horses and people and to check the route for any imperial troops. Progress with such a huge group of people was slow; the leaders wanted to know the minute any potential enemies approached. But now they had made it. At last. They were on the border of Macedonia and Thessalia.

Alaric rode at the head of the line, preoccupied. As his horse plodded its slow energy-conserving plod, the King of the Tervingi brooded. Ten months ago, they had escaped from Stilicho, helped by Rufinus ordering the Eastern Legions back to Constantinople. In hindsight, that decision had saved Alaric's people, who had been trapped by the half-Vandal regent. Alaric had immediately sent messengers to New Rome, requesting lands and food from the Romans to support his wandering people through the coming winter, and in return offering their services to defend the Empire. He had requested an official position for himself: *Magister Militum per Illyricum*, supreme commander of military

33

forces in Illyricum, and offered to defend the East from incursions by the West, and any other barbarian invaders. Rufinus had sent the gold and agreed that Alaric and his Tervingi should proceed to Illyricum. But Rufinus had not granted the title Alaric craved. Concerned about the long-term agreement with the prefect, but with nowhere else to go, he had instructed his commanders to ready the army and followers and move into Macedonia.

The orders from Rufinus were to engage with the cities and people of Greece to purchase supplies, and the prefect of the East had sent orders ahead to the cities of the Greek peninsular to support and supply Alaric's people with food, clothing, and weapons; in Corinth an amount of gold would be ready for them to allow them to get provisions on the second half of their journey.

The great city of Thessalonica was thirty miles behind them to the east. It was a huge city, filled with a large stock of grain, vegetables and livestock. Not just the city; the surrounding cultivated fields were richly provisioned too. They had managed to purchase enough grain and livestock for the next two months with the gold that Rufinus had given him. Winter was coming, after all.

But Alaric's messengers had returned the previous day with the news that Rufinus had been assassinated by Gainas' men; the new prefect, Caesarius, had sent the messengers away with a cursory note ordering Alaric not to enter Greece, but to remain where they were until further orders were sent.

He gathered his commanders together and they spent the night discussing what to do. Some wanted to head back east and threaten the capital, but Alaric had dismissed the idea. They had already been down that road and got nowhere. Constantinople was impossible to breach. Others had suggested crossing the Alps to Italy, to join with Stilicho and then look to invade the East, forcing the emperor's hand. Alaric dismissed that too; Stilicho could not be trusted not to turn on them, either before or after any such campaign.

After many hours of talking, and despite some grumblings from several commanders, Alaric decided he would act as if he had not received the message from Caesarius about staying put. So instead, he wrote another message and despatched his own messenger to the prefect of the East, saying he was proceeding with the prefect's plan of acting as the defensive shield against Stilicho. He would continue to put miles between himself and Constantinople. He was done with taking orders, from Old Rome or New Rome.

A crow above him uttered a hoarse cry and Alaric looked up at it. Was that a sign? A sign he was on the wrong path? What do you want me to do God? What should I be doing?

The crow screeched again flying off into the distance, the king of the Turvingi none the wiser, doubting still the wisdom of his choices.

Beneath him, oblivious to his rider's thoughts, his horse continued its steady, slow plod across the plain.

Chapter 5

The Golden Palace, Constantinople, 12th December 395 AD

Eudoxia lifted herself off Arcadius and rolled away, lifting her legs and pulling a pillow under her naked buttocks.

"What are you doing?" asked Arcadius.

"Just making sure that you have a son, my dear," smiled the Empress. "My head courtier says if you do this, it guarantees getting pregnant. Well at least she swears by it, having had … erm … I think she said four healthy children herself?"

Arcadius rolled to her side, feeling her smooth skin against his. "If you say so, but surely a prayer to God would suffice?"

Eudoxia lifted her head and giggled.

"What?" asked the emperor.

His wife turned her head and whispered, "Them," indicating with her eyes the two eunuchs standing by the bedchamber doors, beyond the large curtain of mesh silk which hung semi-transparent and shimmering, surrounding the imperial bed. They stood motionless, wearing long white robes lined with golden thread. From a wide leather belt hung a short sword and a knife. Their backs were to the imperial couple, who lay entwined on the jumble of soft sheets on the massive bed.

"Do you think they sneak a peek, whilst we're doing it?" She smiled coyly at her husband.

"I would not be surprised!" said Arcadius, chuckling.

"Well," she lay back. "They certainly can hear us, I'm sure."

"They can hear you out in the corridor!" laughed the emperor, getting a punch on the arm in response.

Arcadius looked at his new bride as she lay beside him. She was stunningly beautiful. Long, dark hair framed a tanned, blemish-free face, a smoothly curved neck, perfectly proportioned shoulders and breasts, and a narrow waist, curving into strong hips and thighs. He could not get enough of her. In his mind, he thanked God for sending him such a bride. He had been dreading being married to some horse-faced harridan from a wealthy Isaurian family or from Italy or even, God forbid it, Persia, all in the name of some alliance. Rufinus had even tried to unload his ugly offspring into him.

He looked into those dark eyes again and said, "I don't care if they hear us or see us; let them, it's God's will that we lie here together, so why not let them witness what God wishes?"

"No doubt, my dear, but our faithful Eutropius also had a little something to do with it, I think?"

"He did, you are right."

"And ... now that you're free of Rufinus, don't you think that he might be a good person to listen to for advice?" Eudoxia looked intently at the droopy-eyed emperor.

It wasn't an ugly face, but it certainly did not fill her with confidence that this boy had any kind of spirit in him. He might be besotted with her; she, however, was not besotted with him, but she knew her imperial duty. Sure, he could screw well enough, but if she wanted a night of real passion, she had others who could provide that, such as that *Comes*, John, who she had her eye on.

She certainly wanted the emperor to work with Eutropius. She needed to solidify her own position in the palace, and she could trust none of the other court officials, except perhaps Abundantius, who knew her godfather Promotus well, and who had brought the eunuch into the

Eastern Court. Both the old general and the family of Promotus had worked hard with Eutropius to arrange her marriage.

Arcadius nodded. "I know he is. In fact, we spoke as much about that today."

Eudoxia smiled. "Good. Let's face it. He is very good at his job, and he is loyal to you. General Abundantius, who is no fool, advised your father to bring him into the imperial household, so his advice is probably far better than anything you might get from, say, Caesarius or Aurelian, who I think are only interested in what they can get of out this for themselves."

"If you say so."

"I do say so. Eutropius brought us together, my love, didn't he?" She reached across and gently caressed his thigh, working her hand upwards. "And if you think about it, if you have a good advisor, someone you can trust like Eutropius, then think of all the extra time we can have together, or if you so desire it, time you can go hunting with your friends."

Arcadius' eyes closed in delight as her hand reached between his legs. "You're right. Since you put it that way, why not have him do all the hard work?" He placed his hand on her belly and slid it downwards past her belly button and lower still. He opened his eyes and looked at his Empress, admiring her youthfulness, her curves.

"Precisely", said Eudoxia, rolling towards him, and placing her thigh over his hips. "Now, let's get back to our own work." She leaned into Arcadius again.

Chapter 6

The Senate, Constantinople, December 15th 395 AD

The senate was packed, ready to vote for the following year's consul for the East. There was only one name on the list of any import. That of the emperor. Eutropius sat next to the seat on which the emperor would normally have placed himself, awaiting the meaningless but traditional vote from the senate. Arcadius was not there, though. Eutropius was acting as his proxy. The chamberlain knew this whole affair was a huge sham. They all knew it, but it went ahead anyway. It fed the egos of the senators and kept them from contemplating too deeply on just how utterly powerless they really were. The normal windbags had to have their annual speech, toadying up to the emperor in the hope that a well-chosen phrase or over-eager praise might catch the emperor's ears and elicit some kind of preference or favour.

One of Aurelian's distant relatives was speaking, saying how well he thought the emperor had done in his first year as sole ruler of the East. Particularly with getting Stilicho to return the troops, eliminating the hated Rufinus and beginning the re-organisation of the army. There were murmurs of agreement and a nodding of heads from those who were still awake.

Eutropius despised the whole assembly and vowed that one day he would himself become consul, if only to piss off the old bastards who sat on their fat backsides, revelled in their imaginary power and who still pined for the old days of the Republic, when being a consul actually meant something. Now, it was nothing more than a badge, a status symbol, and an expensive one at that. Nobody minded Arcadius being nominated consul, as it saved everyone else having to spend a fortune on games and parades and processions to celebrate the new consulship. And if truth be known, only a very few now could afford that amount of money. Eutropius swore to himself he would ensure that he had both the money and the political clout to gain a consulship.

That would send a few shockwaves through the stuck-up aristocrats, and really give them something to debate for a change. A eunuch as a consul. Unheard of. Impossible. The chamberlain smiled to himself and silently committed himself to try to do the impossible. There were two problems, though, two men who were held in the same esteem as himself by the emperor: Abundantius and Timasius.

A cheer went up and stirred him from his daydreaming. The final votes had been cast and Arcadius, Emperor of the East, was the new consul of the East too. Eutropius stood and caught the eye of the Urban prefect who oversaw the proceedings. He was given the floor and said simply, "Thank you, honourable gentle of the senate, I will pass on the good news to our most gracious Imperator. I know he will be thrilled and will ensure that the consular games are suitably magnificent."

Eutropius whirled around and left the senate auditorium to a chorus of appreciative murmurs, heading for the emperor's private apartments to give him the news.

Part 2

396 AD

Chapter 7

Forum of Constantine, Constantinople, March 31st 396 AD

The Forum of Constantine was bustling with people in the early morning sun. Flavius Anthemius walked as he always did, speedily and with purpose, but without the appearance of effort. He seemed to flow through the crowd and some characteristic of his natural body language caused people to move out of the way. It was a trick he had learnt from his grandfather whilst he was still a youth. Walk confidently, looking forwards and slightly over the heads of the people around you and they naturally give way. Having two of the mint's guards, big, imposing brutes with helmets and swords, helped of course, but the young, swarthy procurator of the Constantinople mint strode on with confidence. They headed straight to a money changer's stall at the southern rim of the forum.

As he arrived at the counter, the stall owner, a Persian, walked out to meet him. "Ah, Flavius Anthemius, what a bright and glorious morning Ahura Mazda has blessed us with." The man's face was round, and still relatively wrinkle-free, but heavily tanned by the sun; he wore a voluminous doublet, with loose arms made of fine quality silk, with matching trousers. He wore a wide belt with a small ceremonial dagger attached.

"Are you still indulging in that pagan heresy, Quaderi?" asked the procurator with a smile.

"Of course," replied the Persian gleefully, "if only to annoy you and your emperor! Hah!"

The two men shook hands and the shopkeeper called to his assistant to man the stall outside; then he ushered Anthemius inside the main shop. They walked past tables, where three more of his assistants were carefully counting piles of coins and writing in ledgers. By each table stood a large, stern -looking and heavily muscled individual; to dissuade any would be thieves the procurator guessed, or there again, maybe to ensure the employees did not run off with the money. They walked through to another door at the back corner of the shop. Quaderi opened it and invited Anthemius to enter, "but not those two," said the Persian, indicating the guards. The soldiers looked at the procurator, who indicated they should comply with the moneychanger's wishes, so they took up position either side of the door.

The back room was lit by only two small windows high up in the back wall. Shafts of light from the early morning sun illuminated the dust devils in the air. Quaderi sat down at his desk and indicated that Anthemius should take one of two soft seats on the opposite side. They were padded with sheep pelts, and the procurator sank deeply into them. Anthemius leaned back and spoke. "Now what is so important that you had me come here so early?"

"No wonder the Roman Empire is in such a state, you're getting soft! This isn't early, the day is half done. Hah!" Quaderi beamed and grinned. His teeth were very white against his brown face, and when he smiled the creases around his eyes gave him a jovial appearance. Anthemius was not fooled, though. He knew very little about this man, but from snippets of gossip he had gathered over the past months, he had established that he was probably not a moneychanger in Constantinople by choice. But he had proved to be a good source of information about goings on in the city, and an honest, if tough, businessman.

Quaderi reached out across the desk and pushed a coin towards the procurator, who picked it up and said, "A *solidus*? I appreciate the offer, but I'm quite well paid as it is. What is it you want?"

"Look at it," insisted the Persian, nodding towards the coin and smiling curiously.

Anthemius looked at it more closely, felt its weight, checked the edges and the embossed face of Arcadius; it all seemed normal. Then he spotted it. There was a chip on the edge of the coin, and by playing with the coin in the shaft of light from the window, he could see the base metal under the gold coating.

"Clever" he said. "It looks like it has been struck, not cast; unlike most other fakes." He hefted the coin again in his hand. "The base metal feels the same weight as gold …"

"It's nearly exactly the same weight," agreed Quaderi.

"How nearly?"

The Persian reached down and heaved a small bag from the floor; he dropped it onto the desktop with a bang, sending dust flying.

"It took that much for me to notice."

Anthemius did his best not to look shocked. But the Persian was observant.

"Surprised, my friend?" he asked lightly. "It seems you have a bit of a problem to solve, I think. Hah!" He took out a handful of dates from his desk drawer and started popping them into his mouth, spitting out the stones onto the floor next to him. Anthemius opened the bag on the table and poured it contents onto the tabletop. The bag itself contained other small bags, plus some loose coins. He inspected several of the coins, and like the first, they were all base metal covered in a thin layer of gold. All looked like they had been struck, not cast.

"Where did you get them all?"

"I've been gathering them over the past month from customers around the city." said the Persian. "I thought I would see how many I could acquire in that time before I bothered you. There are always fakes around, usually low value, and they are normally easy to see and fairly infrequent. That one, though …" he pointed at the coin he had first shown the procurator. "…that fooled me until I accidentally chipped it. After that, I started assessing every coin." He reached across the desk and picked up a small silk purse dyed blue and shook it. "This little bag has twenty of them. I kept them all together as they came. But this seems a little odd, don't you think? Quite a fine little item?"

The Persian fingered the purse for a few seconds then said, "I know this is important to you and you asked me to keep an eye out for fakes, but what does it really matter? Most people can't tell, they see a solidus and that's good enough for them. They'll spend it like any other coin."

The procurator opened up his own purse and brought out a real solidus and held it up in the beam of light from the low sun. Reflections leapt around the room as he rolled it between his finger and thumb.

"What does this mean to you, Quadi?" Anthemius used the Persian's informal name.

"A week of eating well, a roll of medium-quality silk, food for my horse for a week, any number of things."

"Exactly," agreed the procurator. "Have you ever stopped to think about that?"

"Can't say I have."

"It's an amazing thing when you do. This little round plate of gold with our emperor's face stamped into it. It can be used to buy anything you like. Here, in Antioch, in Ravenna, Alexandria even. Anywhere in the empire. Even outside our borders. You'd take this in Persia, even the Huns will take this and use it. It's a promise. I'll give you this, in return you give me something of equal value, say your roll of medium-quality silk. You take this solidus and trust that you could go yourself and buy another roll of medium silk, or your week of eating good meals. It works for you just like it works for me." Anthemius stared at the coin as if in deep contemplation. "But it's more than that." He glanced at the Persian. "Who produces coins like this?"

Quaderi shrugged. "You Romans have got mints everywhere here …"

"Yes, I know that. I mean who apart from us creates coins?"

"Well, the Persians, and …" The moneychanger paused and scratched his beard, "I'm not entirely sure. I've heard that the peoples of the Far East do, but I've never seen them."

"Nobody around or near our sea makes coins, apart from Rome and Ctesiphon," said Anthemius eagerly. "Not the Scythians, Huns, Numidians, Gepids, Northmen, Arabs; none of them. This sets us apart. It's why the barbarians, sitting in their hovels in the freezing snow, are plotting their next raid on the Empire. It's why the Numidians raid the African provinces. They see the Empire as a source of infinite wealth. And coins like this are the embodiment of the empire, of bringing order out of chaos and anarchy." He looked up at the Persian and asked, " Did you ever think of the work it takes to make a coin?"

The Persian shook his head, smiling as if slightly amused by his friend's passionate rhetoric.

"Think of the slaves, the work, the effort it takes to just get the metals from the earth, the food it takes to feed those men and children; think about the buildings, the tools, the overseers, the transport of the raw metal; and think about the smelting, casting and the striking." Anthemius peered at the coin as if scrutinising its history. "All that effort by hundreds, if not thousands, of people. All that organisation, all that administration. All of that work."

He tossed the coin at the Persian, who caught it deftly. "If that is not a symbol of civilisation and the triumph of the empire over chaos, then I don't know what is."

Quaderi gave a short laugh. "That was a fine speech, my friend, I'm sure the senate are suitably impressed by your mastery of rhetoric, when they finally let you speak! Hah."

Anthemius reddened; he did get carried away every now and again. He remembered his father; "Stay on subject Flavius!" he used to snap.

The procurator got up, pulled the coins back into the bag and said, "These fakes undermine the stability of all that. If the barbarians find out that our gold is fake, that our coins are fake, they will see our weakness. We are God's chosen empire on earth, but who is afraid of an empire when their armies are destroyed by barbarians and their coins are nothing but cheap base metal, which any village blacksmith could go out into his local hills and dig up?" He offered the Persian his hand. "Thank you, my friend, for bringing this to me. It would be useful if you could remember who gave you these coins, or at least some of them."

Quaderi sighed, gripping Anthemius' hand in a tight grasp. "I am just a simple money-changer." He smiled with a glint in his eye. "But luckily for you, I keep detailed records of all my customers; it's good for business, and apparently useful when my friend the procurator comes asking who is using counterfeit money." He held up a tube of rolled papyrus and handed it to Anthemius.

As they opened the door, they chatted about the consular games due the following week and in particular the chariot races. Quaderi was a big fan of the races and offered Anthemius several good betting tips.

The mint guards had not moved from their position and quickly they fell in behind Anthemius as he bid the money-changer farewell and walked out across the forum, past the magnificent column of Constantine, heading for the palace and the city mint.

Chapter 8

Provost of the Sacred Bedchamber, Constantinople, April 2nd 396 AD

Eutropius signed off the document that granted safe passage for Rufinus' widow and daughter to Jerusalem. He saw no reason to have them killed as long as they caused no problems. He had sent his court officers to commandeer all of the prefect's properties in the city and the countryside in the name of the emperor. The property would be returned to the state and come under his control, as the emperor's chamberlain. Just a natural state of affairs, he told himself. He would of course move into the most luxurious apartments within the palace district, with their own private baths and a household full of prime slaves, male and female. It would be a shame to have them unused and unappreciated.

Next, he wrote a letter on parchment and sealed it within a bamboo tube from the Far East. He called for Zafur, his errand boy.

The boy was small and thin, originally from Egypt and about eight years old. He stayed in Eutropius' private quarters and was only permitted to go out of them on errands for his master. One time he had tried to run, but the chamberlain's men had caught him before he could even leave the palace. Eutropius had had the boy beaten on the soles of his feet with willow rods, then had personally tended him back to health. The boy had not tried to run again.

Eutropius told Zahur to take the letter to one of his trusted subordinates, Dius. He was another eunuch, of Berber descent and distantly related to Gildo, the general who ruled Mauritania in North Africa. Zafur scuttled out the door swiftly. When he had gone, Eutropius sat back, and looked up at the person standing in front of him.

The man was dirty, unshaven, with a patchy, unkempt beard. His clothes appeared to be of high quality, but they were tattered, torn and filthy. He reeked of urine and faeces and his hands and ankles were chaffed and raw from the hemp rope that bound them; around his neck hung the rope the city militiamen had used to lead him to this meeting in a dim room in the city jail. Eutropius wrinkled his nose at the smell and waved away the militiaman, who quickly left the room. Eutropius couldn't blame him.

"Bargus, isn't it?" he said.

"*Praepositus* Marcus Aurelius Flavius Bargus," the prisoner replied, his voice slightly slurred due to his swollen lips and bruised jaw. The man straightened slightly and trying to sound dignified he added. "And I object to this outrage. Why was I detained when I arrived?"

"We'll come to that." Eutropius unrolled a small scroll in front of him, then asked, "You were the commander of the personal bodyguard of General Timasius, is that correct?"

"No, it is not. I still am the commander of his bodyguard, and he will be extremely annoyed and angry at this outrageous act." Bargus straightened some more, flexing his neck, although it was obviously painful for him to do so.

Timasius must indeed like this man, thought Eutropius, because when the general found out that the commander of his bodyguards had been arrested, he had gone straight to urban prefect, and leveraging his extensive senatorial influence he had managed to get all charges dropped and his man freed.

However, Eutropius, had heard about Bargus from his own contacts inside the city jail and had decided to interview the man before he was released. He told the urban prefect that he wanted to be sure that the man was no threat to the emperor, as through his close affiliation with the general he would be allowed within the palace grounds. The prefect had agreed of course.

Eutropius nodded as if siding with the prisoner, "The general is more than annoyed, he is furious, and I'm here to ensure that you are released today," he said agreeably. Bargus blinked and relaxed. The chamberlain continued "But for our records, I do need to ask some questions of you, *Praepositus*. Why don't you take a seat, you look uncomfortable?" Eutropius indicated the chair the other side of his desk. Bargus shuffled sideways then with obvious relief sat down.

"I believe you met the general in Saris?" It was more a statement than a question from Eutropius.

Bargus looked puzzled but nodded. "Yes, that's quite right; how did you know?"

"*Praepositus* Bargus, there is very little I don't know. It's my job to look after the emperor's safety; I am obliged to find out things about people, so I can better him."

He opened another scroll of parchment and eyed the *praepositus* carefully. "Tell me, what did you do before you took charge of the general's bodyguard?"

"A bit of this and a bit of that." Bargus fidgeted in his seat.

"I have it here that you come originally from Laodicea, where you worked in the town market…" Eutropius looked up from reading, smiling, "…selling sausages?"

"Nothing wrong with working in the markets." said Bargus,

"Not if you are an honest trader, no." The chamberlain smiled without warmth. "But still …rather a lowly occupation, don't you think, for a man of your talents. Sausages? Really? All that offal and guts, and whatever else goes into them, I hate to think."

"It was a start. I worked my way up through society. I worked hard, and now I'm a *praepositus* in the Roman army."

Eutropius steepled his hands, tapping his fingertips. "Yes, and how did that happen? Sausage seller to *praepositus*." He kept a steady gaze on the man. "And how did you come by that praenomen and nomen? Marcus Aurelius Flavius is quite a name for a sausage-seller."

"As you know, many people took the name Marcus Aurelius after the Emperor Antoninus granted citizenship to all people of the Empire; and Flavius, well, that I took from my benefactor."

"And just how did you manage to come across such a gracious benefactor as the general?" asked Eutropius.

"The general has estates in the region of Sardis where I was working …"

"After you left Laodicea due to a misunderstanding, so I am led to believe," prompted Eutropius.

"A misunderstanding between another trader and myself," Bargus said smoothly. He had recovered a little of his composure.

"You seem to have had a few misunderstandings in your life, *Praepositus*."

"Me personally, no; I cannot speak for others though. I met the general in the market in Sardis; he was shopping for gifts for his mistress at the time. We became good friends and, when he left Sardis to return to Constantinople after a few months, he offered me a place as commander of his personal bodyguard."

"Why?"

"Why what?"

"Why did he make you the commander of his personal bodyguard? He barely knew you."

"He got to know me very well after a couple of months."

Eutropius stared intently at the *praepositus*.

"You were his lover?"

Bargus shook his head, "No, as I say, he had a mistress for that. I needed a patron, so I helped him out with finding gifts initially and I recommended some fine eating establishments to him. He rewarded me with a position on his personal staff as his personal secretary, I knew a lot of people locally."

"I see."

"He and I got along well. It was a good match. My General is a long serving soldier, but many people don't appreciate him as much as he deserves. I try to make sure that he is appreciated for what he has done. You just have to know how to reach that part of him, make him feel important, as if he is the emperor himself, that he deserves it. He loves to hear that about himself all the time."

Eutropius had picked up on Bargus' words.

"He wants to be emperor?"

Bargus looked somewhat taken aback. "No, not at all, well … I think he likes the idea of the prestige and the wealth, but no, not really , it's just his little fantasy."

"A fantasy." Eutropius narrowed his eyes. His heart was thumping with excitement; he could not believe his luck. This was exactly the sort of thing he wanted to hear. He determined to keep the fool talking.

"The general is a loyal servant of the Empire, as am I, but who doesn't fantasize about what they would do if they were emperor?" Bargus looked around the room, at the bare walls and dusty floor. "Surely you do?"

"No, I don't." replied Eutropius casually. "Let us move on. Why did you return to Constantinople?"

"I've told you already, I'm the commander of the general's bodyguard."

"But you're not allowed to come back to the city are you?"

"I don't know what you mean."

"Yes you do."

Eutropius fell silent; he stared at the *praepositus*, who stared back but said nothing.

The chamberlain sighed. He opened up a third parchment scroll and began reading. "On April 15th, three years ago, you were accused of defrauding the sum of 24 solidi from the merchant Iovinus Stauricius …"

"Accused but …" Bargus attempted to interrupt but Eutropius ignored him.

"…who deals in fine pottery and marble statuettes in the Forum of Constantine. You managed to convince him to invest the money in an imaginary marble mine …"

"It wasn't an imaginary mine." insisted Bargus.

"The marble was though, wasn't it?"

"There was marble there."

"Barely enough to cover this floor."

Bargus chose to stay silent.

"You were convicted of fraud. You spent a year in prison, and you were banned from re-entering the city."

Eutropius sat back and smiled unpleasantly. "And yet here you are … in Constantinople."

Silence.

"The urban prefect arrested you and threw you in jail, and it was only due to the intervention of your patron, Timasius, that you are being released. I could quite easily speak to the emperor and get your release revoked, of course."

"You won't," said Bargus quietly.

"I won't?"

"No, you won't. Because you want something from me, otherwise you wouldn't have wasted your time on our conversation today. I have something you want."

Eutropius considered the rogue's reply and studied him some more. After his initial shock at being arrested and brought before one of the most powerful men in the empire, the man had settled quickly. Bargus was quite correct that he wanted him for a reason, but Eutropius was well aware of what type of man he was. He had to keep him in line whilst he did the job he wanted him to do. Bargus was a flatterer and a trickster motivated by personal gain and power. Someone he could make good use of certainly, but also someone to be cautious about.

Eutropius got up and stepped around his desk. Bargus got back up also. The two stood toe to toe whilst the chamberlain stared intently at Bargus'. The *praepositus'* s eyes flicked from side to side, avoiding the piercing gaze, and he tried to step back but the seat prevented him.

"It's true," said Eutropius eventually. "I do want something from you. But I could do without it, and I can always find another way to get what I want. Make no mistake, Bargus, sausage-seller-cum-*praepositus*, I know exactly who and what you are. Right now, you are nothing more than a convenience to me; if you start to become inconvenient …", the chamberlain leaned forward so that their noses almost touched, "… then I will make sure that Bargus the sausage-seller is served up as the main appetizer at the next Imperial banquet. As a sausage of course, which I personally will take great delight in eating, as I'm sure will your general and the emperor himself. Quite a fitting end don't you think? I hope I make myself crystal clear?"

Bargus said nothing for a moment, but he had paled slightly, perspiration oozed from his pores and ran down his grimy face in little rivulets. He nodded, attempting to swallow; his mouth and throat dry from lack of drink, and fear. The chamberlain drew slowly back and returned to his seat saying, "You are free to go … for now. We'll chat again when I have need of you. You will continue in your duties for your general, but you will not breathe a word of this meeting to him, you understand?" Again, the nod of understanding.

Eutropius threw him a small bag of coins. Bargus caught it deftly despite his tied hands. The chamberlain indicated the bag and said, "That's a small payment for your troubles. Get yourself cleaned up and sort yourself out with a new uniform. You cross me or speak to anyone of our meeting…". Leaving the sentence unfinished, he rang a small bell on his desk. The door opened and the city militiaman stepped back inside, took up the rope around Bargus' neck and half dragged him from the room.

Chapter 9

Approaches to Larissa, Macedonia, 2nd April 396 AD

When the Tervingi arrived within sight of the city of Larissa, the gates were closed. The spectacle of thousands of Gothic soldiers outside their city walls had made the elders nervous. They ordered the gates barred and the city garrison to stand to and man the large defensive walls.

Alaric on seeing this and having no wish to get involved in any kind of siege at this point in their journey, sent his representative, a half-Goth, half-Greek named Hilderith, to negotiate. The problem was that an imperial messenger had arrived two days before. Alaric had been intercepting the messengers, but this one must have got through somehow. So, the city now knew that Rufinus was dead, and the new prefect Caesarius had prohibited the city from offering offer help to Alaric's forces. Caesarius had re-iterated that Alaric's army should not enter Greece. Too late for that.

With a little persuasion, Hilderith managed to get the city elders to agree that a hundred men and women could approach the city on foot, to trade at the markets outside the city walls on Monday and Tuesday, but they would not allow anyone else from the army into the city itself.

The Tervingi court sat in their tent, a mile from the city, consuming their evening meal. The meal was meagre; food stores were running low, biscuit turning hard, fruit and vegetables beginning to rot. The last of the livestock was due to be slaughtered the following day, but that would only sustain them for a few days. When the meal was done, Alaric called for the last of the wine to be brought and for his commanders to gather around him.

Alaric sat in his chair on a raised platform and looked at his army's leaders. He had in his mind already made a decision on what they should do next, but he wanted agreement from all of his chieftains, because once they had committed to the course of action, there was no going back.

"So, my friends. What should we do? Do we do as the city asks? Pay for the provisions they offer us, and then head on our way to Illyricum, or do we take another course of action?"

A stocky warrior with long grey hair stepped forwards. "We should just take what we need," he said. "The Romans care naught for us. They never have. Likely the food they so generously plan to sell us will be rotten and mildewed."

Alaric motioned for the man to be seated. "I cannot disagree with your feeling, Theodulf," he replied. "Nevertheless, we were tasked by Rufinus to protect the empire from enemies from the West. If we turn on them, we may never gain our own place within the empire."

There were unhappy looks and mutterings amongst the group, which Alaric had expected.

"What? Speak your doubts if you have any, don't sit there gossiping like old women."

An old warrior, Histogild, stood stiffly and said, "My King, Rufinus is dead at the hand of the deserter Gainas. We know you look to serve our people to find them a home, to protect them. But you place too much trust in the Romans to deliver on what we ask. How many messages have you sent to Constantinople?"

Alaric remained silent.

"Many, sire, we know that. And how many have been answered? None that we know of. This new prefect, Caesarius, has ignored us; the towns have not aided us, even though we are supposed to be protecting them. Why? Because to them we're a sub-people they call Goths. They don't call us Tervingi , they insult us with the name of Goth. We're certainly not Roman! They only remember that the "Goths" killed their emperor."

58

Alaric nodded; the last years had been hard. Very hard. Eighteen years ago, three legions, led by Emperor Valens, had been massacred at Adrianople. Since then, the word "Goth" had seeped into the Roman psyche, bringing with it images of death, destruction and fear. Never mind the fact that the Romans had abused and enslaved the Tervingi after they had agreed to let them into the empire. Since then, it had been nothing but turmoil. A constant to-ing and fro-ing between the Romans and those they called "Goth". Sometimes allies, sometimes enemies. Two years ago, he had fought for Theodosius at the Battle of Frigidus, to rid the empire of the usurper Eugenius. He had done it hoping that they would be rewarded with lands and positions in the empire. Instead, ten thousand of his countrymen had been sacrificed on the altar of Roman imperial vanity. When he closed his eyes, Alaric still saw the desperate and futile charges by his fearless tribesmen against the Roman lines. Time and time again they came up against an impenetrable wall of shields, and his men were carved up like meat on a butcher's slab by the stabbing swords of Eugenius' legions. By the end of the day, the battle had seemed lost.

Alaric swore inwardly. The only major casualty that day had been the Tervingi nation. Theodosius had preserved the native Roman troops and used his expendable foederati in the attacks, effectively removing the threat of the "Goth". The next day, some said with divine help, he removed the threat of Eugenius too. Alaric had never forgiven the old emperor for that treachery.

Since then, he had been singular in his effort to force the Roman leadership to grant his people their own land within the empire, to provide them with gold and supplies and him with a formal title and position in the Roman army, commanding both Romans and foederati.

They needed to establish their own client nation inside the empire. Only that way could he see a stable future, or indeed any kind of future, for his people. They could not return to their home in the northeast; that had been overrun by the Huns. The only place they had to go was inside the Roman Empire.

But now Rufinus was dead. He had made the decision to move his whole army and baggage train into Greece, and head for Illyricum on the other side of the central Greek mountains. He had hoped that by completing Rufinus' original plan and effectively occupying Illyricum, they could force the emperor into granting them the land and title he had sought after long and hard. But things had changed. The plan had changed.

Given the choice, Alaric didn't want to rob the common Romans of their livelihoods. But he had come to the conclusion that in fact he had no choice but to do exactly that. He felt like Moses, leading his people through yet more foreign lands year after year, trying to find a home. But there was no manna from heaven here, what food was available they had to take, or else they would starve. So here they were on the move again.

"Sire! What are your orders?"

Alaric realised he had been daydreaming. His commanders had been debating what to do, and now they all stared at him, waiting for his decision.

Slowly he stood. He looked around the room and each of his men.

"We are done with taking orders from the Romans." He saw all the men around him smile. He went on, "If they grant us the lands which we asked for and the titles they have promised us, then and only then will we settle in peace within the empire." Nods greeted his words.

"Until then, since they treat us like enemies, then enemies we shall be!" There were cries of "yes!" and Alaric raised his voice. "Tomorrow we will take the food and supplies we need, and then we move into Greece. No more will we beg for food; we will take what we need, including the gold in Corinth that we have been promised!" He let his words sink in and finished with a roar. "Are you with me?" There was a tumult of yells and cheers as his commanders hugged and slapped each other, and the chant of "Alaric! Alaric!" built up and up and spread throughout the camp.

A mile away, in the dark, on the battlements of Larissa, the sentries heard the cries of the warriors from across the fields, and looked at each other with worried faces.

Chapter 10

The Hippodrome, Constantinople, 2nd April 396 AD

Anthemius walked confidently into the chariot preparation area of the Hippodrome, followed closely by three imposing *Scholae* guards he had requested from the *Magister Officiorum*. The arches above them soared to a dizzying height, supporting the thousands upon thousands of seats in the main arena. Out there, the sun was bright and the day hot; here in the shadows the air was cool and the light dim.

It had been two weeks since his meeting with the Persian, and he had worked through nearly all the names on the list of people who had given the money-changer fake coins. They were an eclectic group of people.

The wife of a senator whose slave clerk had paid the money for a new toga for her husband's fortieth birthday was unable to remember where the coins had come from, either deliberately or genuinely. A mule driver had helped a wealthy aristocrat fix his horse bridle and had been rewarded with a single coin for his troubles. Three others on the list were all wealthy bishops from Italy who were visiting the patriarch of the city. They had done much trading on their journey, so could not remember with whom they had engaged. They had collected many gifts from churches on their visit through Thrace and had no recollection of how they had come into possession of the fake coins.

The small blue bag that the Persian had shown him, he had identified as belonging to the Blues Guild. He decided that he would need protection for that visit, so whilst the wheels of administration whirled to get him an assigned palace guard, he used his own, less able, mint guards to escort him to the other people on the list.

He had gone through the rest of the list by the time the palace guards had been assigned to him, and other work had precluded more investigation.

Anthemius had spoken to Aurelianus, brother of the new prefect, Caesarius, about the fakes. They knew each other from an embassy several years back, with Stilicho, negotiating a new peace with Persia. Aurelianus was younger than Caesarius, and much more ruthless and ambitious, in Anthemius' opinion. Unlike Anthemius, who, whilst a senator through his father and grandfather, was a second-class senator or *spectabiles*, Aurelianus was a senior member, an *illustres* of the senate, though he held no specific office at present. He had been *praefectus urbi* two years ago and had been responsible for the entire urban administration of Constantinople; in that role he had been leader of the Senate, so Anthemius was interested in his opinion, although he never took it as literal truth.

"Go at it doggedly, Flavius," Aurelianus had said when Anthemius revealed his investigation. "Counterfeit coins are a curse and a crime of treason! If the money cannot be trusted, then the very thing that binds and guards the Empire will be tainted. The currency is what guards us from barbarians and chaos. Currency makes us civilised. It is what sets us and the Persians above all other around us."

"I will need men and resources to track down and shut down the source," Anthemius had said pointedly.

"I will speak to my brother and to the *Magister Officiorum* and ensure you get the men you need. Do well in this, Anthemius, and you will gain much prestige; you may make *Comes Sacrarum Largitionum* in the next few years."

Right now, Anthemius needed his wits about him. This was the territory of the guilds. The Blues were in residence today, it was their day of practice, and they, like all the guilds, were protective of their practices and their skills. So, when he and his three men walked into the preparation area, they were immediately surrounded by a large group of big, muscled guildsmen, all taller than the procurator. They did not look like they were afraid of the three soldiers dressed in white and certainly not the rather shorter, wiry procurator.

Anthemius knew that to show fear would be to invite problems, so he mustered himself and stared coolly at the guildsmen, one at a time. He took a scroll from his bag and unrolled it, pretended to read it, then he looked up and called out, "I'm looking for Maurinus."

Nobody answered. The sound of workman repairing chariots and horses being prepared for practice came from behind the wall of blue jacketed men.

"None of you?" said Anthemius brightly. "I have no use for you then, step aside." He walked forwards, but the guildsmen held their ground and blocked him. A stocky, powerfully built figure stood barring this way.

"Move aside!" said Anthemius sharply. But the figure did not move. Anthemius leaned forward and said quietly to the man, "I'm asking you to move aside, nicely. I'm not here to make trouble, I just want to ask Maurinus some questions and then I will be gone, and you can continue with your practice."

"Maurinus does not want to see you."

"How do you know? You haven't passed my message on yet, and besides, I will be making it worth his while."

"Maurinus still does not want to see you," came the level reply.

"Hunulf!" called Anthemius.

"Sir!" came the sharp reply. The nearest of the *Scholae* took a step forward; the Blues guildsmen tensed.

"Please move this man out of my way." Anthemius was still holding the guildsman's stare.

64

Hunulf took another pace forward, he was big in all ways height and width, his eyes were blue, his moustache was big and bushy and merged with the equally generous beard. Brown hair flowed from under the domed helmet. Still the Blues held their ground. So, Hunulf drew his sword smoothly and slowly, placing the tip of it at the throat of the man blocking Anthemius.

"Move aside, like the procurator has asked, arsehole."

There was a sound of multiple swords being drawn. A second sword suddenly appeared in Hunulf's other hand. He pointed it at another of the guildsmen, this one starting to raise a powerful axe. "Don't!" he said sharply.

The younger guildsmen were sweating, one or two visibly shaking. The older men looked hard and determined, but a few still glanced to the side at the man blocking Anthemius, as if seeking assurance that this was the right thing to do.

Anthemius took a deep breath and said, "Think about what you are doing. I am an officer of the Count of the Sacred Bounties, who reports directly to the emperor. Stand down!"

Now the guildsmen glanced at one another perhaps now unsure of themselves. The sword of the Hunulf however was steady as a rock, and the other two guards also with their swords now drawn, assumed positions to defend the procurator.

Anthemius said, in a calm quiet voice, "I'm going to count to three. Hunulf?"

"Sir?"

"If this man has not stood aside on three, you are to kill him for deliberately interfering in imperial business. Understood?"

"Yes sir."

"One." None of the Blues moved, but three of the nearest men were glancing now at the man facing the procurator. Anthemius continued to stare at his opponent and saw doubt in the man's eyes for the first time.

"Two."

"Petrus!" one of the blues hissed. "For God's sake, let him pass, this is pointless."

"First sensible thing I've heard from any of you lot." said Hunulf, still staring at the man in front of Anthemius. "I've cleaned this sword once today already."

Anthemius steeled himself and took a breath, ready to utter the number three. He opened his mouth to speak, but then another voice, deep and clear, bellowed from behind the wall of men. "Petrus! Stand down now! You've made your point."

The tension drained out of the Blues. The *Scholae* maintained their position but relaxed slightly. The man in front of Anthemius backed away to make room for the newcomer. He was an older man, bald, about the same height as the procurator. He was well muscled and looked fit and strong for his years. He stepped confidently up to Anthemius and put out his hand. Next to the procurator, Hunulf tensed, but Anthemius waved for him to relax.

"Procurator, I must apologise for my men, they are very protective of me and proud to serve and guard the guild's practices and secrets. I was busy and had no idea things were getting so … um … tense."

Anthemius looked at the man, something about him was odd, then he noticed that the left ear was missing. He nodded, shook the hand and said, "Flavius Anthemius, procurator for the City Mint." The old man raised an eyebrow, as if he were curious rather than impressed.

"Priscianus Stauricius, head guildsman of the Blues, what can I do for you?"

"I wish to talk to one of your charioteers, Maurinus," said the procurator.

"What's he done now?"

"Nothing as far as I am aware, but he may be able to help me and do a service to the empire."

"Oh well," said Stauricius, not without some irony. "In that case you had better come and sit down and share a cup of wine with me. I will fetch Maurinus, and we will talk, and we can all do a service to the empire."

With that, he ushered the procurator to walk with him. The Blues men walked ahead and the three *Scholae* guards followed closely behind. As they arrived at a stout wooden table near one of the ground arches, which looked out onto the hippodrome track, Priscianus clapped his hands sharply and three slave girls appeared, seemingly from nowhere, and began setting up food and drink. Anthemius and Priscianus sat down opposite each other on rough wooden benches. The Blues guildsman offered Anthemius a cup of wine, but the procurator shook his head. He needed to keep his thoughts clear. Priscianus, however, took a good draught from the cup, licked his lips and spoke.

"So Procurator of the Mint, what brings you here?"

"I'll wait for Maurinus to arrive before I say," said Anthemius bluntly.

"As you wish. I must say I admired your coolness back there, and your guards too; if you had been Greens, we'd be mopping a whole lot of blood off the floor right now."

"I'm a patient man."

"I can see that. Well, your patience is rewarded, because here is your man now." Priscianus waved for a tall young man to sit beside him. He was no older than twenty, Anthemius judged; he had a rather pathetic attempt at a beard, nothing more than a few wisps of light brown, the colour of his curly hair. His face was round, eyes small, and he had a lazy left eye.

"Doesn't that hold him back?" asked Anthemius.

"What? The eye?" asked Priscianus, smiling. "On the contrary, it helps him. All the others think him half-witted, but he can see out of it right enough, eh?" He slapped the young man on the back, an attempt at joviality. But the procurator could see the tension in the young man. He was terrified of Priscianus. "Now what is it you want with my man here?" asked the Blues patriarch.

Anthemius took out the small blue bag of coins and, looking not at the young charioteer, but at Priscianus, dropped them on the table.

"Recognise this?"

The young man looked at the purse, then at Anthemius, then at Priscianus. For a fleeting second, Anthemius saw Priscianus' eyes narrow, and he draw in a small breath. It was only for a very brief moment; had he not been looking directly at the Blues patriarch, he would have missed it. But he hadn't missed it.

Maurinus was nervous, but he nodded. "I didn't steal it, if that's what you're going to ask."

"It's not what I was going to ask." The procurator paused and said, "You gave this to Quaderi, the Persian *Argentarius* in the Forum of Constantine, didn't you?"

The young man nodded.

"So how are you getting hold of counterfeit currency?"

The young man shrugged his shoulders and said, "I don't know what that means."

Priscianus grinned and said, "Use smaller words procurator, you don't need to be Plato to be a charioteer."

"It's fake money, Maurinus," said Anthemius. "Do you know what that means?"

The young man shook his head.

"It means you've committed treason."

The charioteer looked aghast and blurted out, "I'm no traitor! My father was a soldier, just like these men." He pointed at Anthemius' bodyguards. "And I ... I... I'm a loyal servant of the emperor.". Priscianus put a calloused hand on the agitated young man's shoulders and eased him back into his seat. He turned to Anthemius and said with a wry smile, "Shame on you, procurator, you can see this young man knows nothing about your fakes."

"What were you doing with the money then?"

"He was running an errand for me," Priscianus said.

"Let him speak for himself," said Anthemius sharply, ignoring the old man, who visibly bristled at his tone.

The young man stared at the bag of coins on the table. "It's like the boss-man says," he said quietly "I was doing him an errand, taking the money to the argentarius to settle a debt."

"A debt?" asked Anthemius, now looking at the Blues patriarch.

"Simple business transaction, paying back with interest what I had borrowed from the Persian," replied the old man without batting an eyelid. "I was ill that day, or I would have made the payment myself. So, I told one of my clerks to get the money from the strong box and give it to the boy here; he wasn't racing or training that day, and I knew I could trust him."

Priscianus scratched his head where his ear would have been and took another drink of wine.

"Before you ask, I had no idea the money was fake. It was in that bag in the strong box; my clerk merely took it out and gave it to junior here to pass to the Persian. I've no idea who gave us the money to us, so I'm afraid we can't help you there."

"Is this your purse as well?" asked Anthemius, holding up the small blue bag with the money. "It seems more like a woman's purse to me than something you'd use."

"It is a woman's purse," agreed Priscianus. "It was picked up off the arena floor, probably some rich woman threw it on the track. Happens all the time. Normally we collect them and share the money in it amongst the lads in the yard. On this occasion my clerks must have just re-used it for this errand; it was the right weight. I doubt they even opened the bag, other than a cursory look to check it was money." The patriarch shrugged casually, as if it was of no consequence.

"You had no idea that the money you were paying to the Persian was fake?"

"That is correct, procurator," replied Priscianus, calmly but firmly.

"And you have no idea where the fake coins might have come from?"

"Also correct."

Anthemius stared at Priscianus hard for a few seconds, then smiled and nodded, as if coming to decision. He drew in a deep breath and said, "Well, thank you. It was a bit of a long shot coming here anyhow. Tracking fake coins is very hard to do, as I'm sure you can imagine."

The blues patriarch nodded and smiled back. "I am sure it is. Not particularly exciting, I imagine, unlike a chariot race, for example?"

Anthemius laughed gently and stood up and made to leave. "Oh it has its moments, like when I catch the man who is responsible for treason." He smiled again, pleasantly, and offered his hand to Priscianus, who had also stood.

"And do you often get your man?" asked the patriarch.

"What do you think?" responded Anthemius, holding the old man's gaze and his hand. There was silence for a few seconds, then Priscianus said, "I think those counterfeiters need to keep looking over their shoulders. Good day to you, procurator, I'm sorry we could not be of more help."

"No, you've been a great help, thank you. Good day, and God be with you."

With that Anthemius turned and signalled to his escort to close in and they strode towards the nearest exit, back out onto the concourse in front of the Great Palace. When they were outside in the sun and out of earshot of the charioteers and guildsmen, the procurator called a halt.

"What did you make of that, Hunulf?" he asked the guard.

"Didn't believe a fucking word of it, sorry, my pardon your honour."

"Don't worry, I didn't either. He knows who supplied those fakes; a man like that knows exactly what money goes in and out of his organisation. You'd think he would be upset that the coins are worthless if he were not involved, but he didn't bat an eyelid. I'm certain he knows more than he is saying. So, I have a job for you and your men, if you're willing? It will be worth a Solidus each to your men and two to you."

"Who do we have to kill?" asked Hunulf with a grin. He was not as tall compared to the other two, but his shoulders were wide and powerful, and his blue eyes were piercing and full of intelligence, more than the average palace guard. The Master of Offices had assigned Hunulf to him; Anthemius made a mental note to try to get him assigned to him permanently.

"No one, yet," responded the procurator. "But I want you to arrange to have Maurinus and Priscianus watched. I want to know who they go to see, who they meet with, but make sure you are not seen."

"That won't be easy, they have men and women everywhere looking out for them."

"Then you will just have to be careful, won't you?" said Anthemius. "Make sure you get regular reports to me. Use more men if you have to, up to a limit of ten, but make sure you can trust them."

"Do the extra men get paid too?" asked Hunulf.

"Yes, unless they get seen."

"Consider it done, sir."

Chapter 11

The Golden Palace, Constantinople, 3rd April 396 AD

Timasius opened the door to the Grand Chamberlain's offices and walked in. The clerk at the front desk rose and started to protest that the *Praepositus Sacri Cubiculi* was not to be disturbed, but the general simply waved him away. He was in no mood to play games of precedence or rank.

These rooms were the final barrier between the common man and the emperor. The outer defences were the regular palace guards; the *Scholae* provided protection to the emperor's person whilst he was out and about, but when ceremony was done and the darkness and coolness of the evenings descended, it was the role of the *Praepositus Sacri Cubiculi* and his staff to protect the emperor and empress whilst they ate, slept, had sex, bathed, urinated, and defecated. All those bodily functions that even the rulers of the greatest empire on earth could not escape. The staff were mainly eunuchs and women, though a few of the less important posts were occupied by men. Dull men, boring men, men without ambition and with only enough intelligence and ability to do their jobs. Men who were no threat to anyone.

Timasius strode past servants busy tidying and brushing clothes and polishing silver and golden ornaments; a smell of incense lingered in the air, mixed with smells of cooking. There was a separate kitchen here for the private meals of the imperial couple, prepared by trusted servants; but still every meal was pre-tasted by slaves – you could never be too sure.

Not glancing to either side, he quickly mounted three steps and strode through an arch to enter the inner office of Eutropius. The *praepositus* was there with another man, or rather what used to be a man. Philoponus. Timasius knew of him by reputation. He was a veteran tribune of Adrianople. He had become a eunuch not by choice or by decision of his parents or family. A Goth spear and a military doctor had made him a eunuch in the bloody aftermath of battle. He had almost died from his wounds, but fate, the Christian God, or the pagan Gods – whoever you believed in these days – had intervened. He had returned to the capital and Theodosius, always the admirer of bravery and sacrifice, had employed him in the palace. He had remained there ever since. He was ferociously loyal to the young emperor, out of respect for the father. He seemed to have accepted Eutropius' leadership, though Timasius did wonder what the soldier thought of the devious chamberlain, who had never put himself on the field of battle.

"Can I help you, General?" Eutropius asked as Timasius stood there.

"I would like an explanation!" snapped Timasius.

Eutropius said nothing for several seconds as if pondering his next words carefully, but he held the general's stare. Then he drew breath and said, almost casually, "I assume you are referring to the re-assignment of several of your staff and properties?"

"You are damned right that's what I'm talking about!"

"Those people and properties were yours to use whilst you were *Magister Militum Praesentalis*," said Eutropius.

"What do you mean *were*?"

"You are no longer in post, General. The army is undergoing a large-scale re-organisation, as you know. You approved the re-organisation in the consistorium if I recall."

"This is outrageous! Does the emperor know about this?" Timasius bristled, but inside he already knew the answer.

"Of course, he knows, he made the decision that the post of *Magister Militum Praesentalis* will remain vacant until the re-organisation is complete, at which point the emperor will re-appoint the new commanders."

"And when were you or the emperor going to inform me of my dismissal?" Timasius was nearing purple with fury.

"I am informing you now General, I have been busy." Eutropius picked up a scroll and offered it to Timasius, who slapped it away; the scroll bounced off of the wall and rolled under the lowest shelf of a storage unit.

"Just who do you think you are, eunuch?" snapped the general.

Eutropius got up, walked slowly around his desk and stood directly in front of the general. Timasius was stocky, still muscular and strong for his age, but Eutropius towered over him. "I know who I am General, I am *Praepositus Sacri Cubiculi* of the *illustrii*, and the emperor's personal protector and aide. You, however, are an ex-*Magister*, who has no authority now to question my decisions and certainly not those of the Imperator. I would be very careful with your next words, General; questioning the decisions and wisdom of the emperor is tantamount to treason."

Timasius stared up into the face of Eutropius. He didn't like what he saw there. The eyes were alive, twinkling almost, but not with joy or happiness. There was an anger there, and there was hate too but there was also ambition, and that was perhaps the most frightening of all. Eunuchs were supposed to be without that drive and desire. This remnant of a man was dangerous, perhaps more dangerous than anyone around him realised. He felt the beginnings of fear start to stir in his stomach. He looked away and stepped back from the close scrutiny.

"So, who is overseeing the re-deployments?" he asked, trying to keep his voice calm.

"The emperor has seen fit to put me in charge of that task."

"And what exactly do you know about military matters, pray tell?" Timasius could not help but sneer.

Eutropius smirked nastily and turned away to return to his seat behind his desk. He sat down and steepled his fingers together, tapping them one at a time.

"I am making full use of experts in military matters, such as Philoponus here, when it comes to the day-to-day requirements of our soldiers." He indicated the veteran who stood silently beside him. "He is a very experienced veteran, as you know. And I have General Gainas too, as my chief military advisor when it comes to matters of tactics and strategy."

"Gainas?"

"Yes, a capable man."

"A Goth deserter!"

"You can't hold a man's past against him forever, General; he has served the Empire for twenty years. I thought you regarded him as a soldier?"

"He is brave and clever in battle; I'll give him his due."

"Then he is the perfect man for the job." Eutropius smiled condescendingly.

"He is also a fucking barbarian." The unexpected profanity from Timasius surprised and then amused Eutropius. The general truly must be upset; he had never known the old made to swear before. Timasius continued, "And we've enough of those in the army at the lower ranks, let alone in positions of command." Timasius' voice started to rise again. "You're making him *Magister Militum Praesentalis*?" he asked.

Eutropius sighed. "No, I've said already that post will remain vacant until the military re-deployments have been completed. General Gainas works under my direct orders".

76

Timasius was silent for a moment, then he leaned forward and put both his fists on the hard wood of the ornate desk and spoke quietly and deliberately.

"Don't think for one moment I and the others in the senate don't know what you're doing, eunuch." He pointed a bony finger at Eutropius. "You're building yourself up, setting yourself over the rest of us, just like Rufinus did. But don't forget what happened to him. Be careful the same doesn't happen to you!" With that he turned and stormed out of the room. He bumped into one of the tall guards standing by the entrance to the offices of the chamberlain.

Staring after the departing general, Philoponus said quietly, "The general means well, but he is too proud and too vain to see what needs to be done."

Eutropius nodded. "His time is past, the future belongs to us, my friend. Now about those cavalry units in Thrace…"

Interlude

Golden Palace Barracks, Constantinople, 3rd April 397 AD

Gerung swore. "That dozy old fucker nearly broke my arm as he came out today!"

"Stop whinging, you're twice his size," retorted Gadaric, who was changing out of his formal guard uniform and hanging it back up.

They had both been transferred from Hebdomon in February to serve in the palace guard. Their days were taken up with cleaning their uniforms to look pristine, then standing outside doors and offices guarding, or working as protectors, keeping an eye out for potential assassins.

"He did seem a bit pissed off," remarked Gadaric. Gerung had stripped off his uniform and now stood naked at the urinal in the corner of their shared quarters. He started to pee and called over his shoulder, "He just got dismissed by old ball-less himself."

"How do you know?"

"Don't you fucking listen to what they're saying?" asked Gerung.

"No."

"Well, you're a twat, then, aren't you? How are you going to keep up with what's happening around here?" Gerung finished up, turned, and strode across to his bed space and pulled on his civilian clothes.

"Since when did you give a shit about anything around here but whores and wine?" asked Gadaric, who was getting into his tunic and breeches. It was a relief to get out of the heavy armour and cloaks.

Gerung smiled. "Since I met this really amazing whore called Octavia. If I tell her little bits of gossip, she gives me a bit extra."

Gadaric nodded approvingly. "That's more like it, for a moment there I thought you had actually taken an interest in something beyond base pleasures and killing people." He finished off getting dressed and put his dirty underclothes and uniform tunics into a basket.

"Oh, so no bags of gold this year for old Timmy then," laughed Gadaric.

"Nope," agreed Gerung.

"So, let's go to John's tavern via the laundry; I need this lot cleaned for tomorrow."

"Just a couple of glasses of wine tonight," said Gerung.

"Fuck me, what's wrong with you now?" hissed Gadaric.

"Nothing," grinned Gerung, "It's Thursday night, so it's Octavia night. Got to make sure the old pecker stands to attention when ordered!" Laughing, they headed out the door.

Chapter 12

Outside City walls of Larissa, Greece, 3rd April 396 AD

The half-light of early dawn revealed a hundred men and women hauling carts down the road towards the gates of Larissa. They carried torches to make themselves obvious, so that the men on the walls would see the slow movement and realise they posed no threat. The men on the walls of the city saw them coming, but counted the torches and relaxed a little, as the Goths appeared to be obeying the city prefect's command. Outside the gates the market stalls were setting out and the populous was stirring, ready for another day, the traders hoping to profit from the visiting Goths.

Off the road, away from the light, Alaric and a few hundred of his warriors hid under dark cloaks amongst the fields and ditches that surrounded the city walls. They moved individually and slowly, watching the guards on the wall, who as expected were more focussed on the lights of the procession of carts being hauled up the road. By the time the carts reached the market stalls, Alaric and his men were just a hundred yards from the wall and still hidden by the darkness of the dawn.

Alaric watched and waited, not moving. He heard a shout, then another, and then a horn sounded: the signal to move. They leapt up and rushed towards the city walls. As planned, the men hauling the carts had dropped their torches and jammed the city gates open with several of the vehicles. Two dozen men had rushed inside the city, scaled the steps to the walls and could now be seen threatening the militia. There was confusion; the men at the gate had drawn swords there was shouting and cursing, but by the time Alaric reached the gate, nobody was fighting. The guards on the walls above had backed off. Alaric could see that his men had formed a shield wall inside the city gates.

"Gesimund," he called to a tall warrior next to him. "Get a hundred men, take the food and provisions from these stalls and load them on the carts, and send a runner back to tell Athaulf to form the army up outside the walls now."

The remainder of the army was only a few hundred yards away, ready for the order. Alaric walked through the gates between the carts and up to where his men had formed the shield wall. He found a wooden box and stood on it. Looking over his men's shoulders he could see a number of city officials behind another rather poorly formed shield wall of city militia. They were jammed across the main street of the city, which started the other side of a small, paved square that lay just inside the city gates, either side of which rose two-storey buildings of white stone. Several civilians looked out of windows at the scene below.

"Who is in charge here?" boomed out Alaric.

A tall man in long robes, accompanied by a priest, walked forward of the militia's shield wall. "That would be me, Athanakis, city prefect. What is this, Alaric? Did we not make you a fair offer?"

"I've come to make you a better offer," said the Goth King.

"Better for whom?"

"Us of course. You will agree to my terms. If you do no-one will be harmed, no-one will be taken as slaves." Alaric stared around at the people in the doorways and windows, then back at the city prefect. "You have my word of honour, and unlike those politicians in Constantinople, I am a man of my word."

"How can we believe you, when you threaten us so?" asked the prefect unsmilingly.

The Goth king turned and looked at his own men around him and behind him and on the walls. "Any of you who threaten or harm any of the people of this city without provocation will have to answer to me personally!" He swung back and turned his piercing blue eyes on the city leader and said simply, "Good enough?"

"If we refuse your offer?" asked Athanakis.

"Do you really need to ask that?" Alaric raised his hand. Behind him, a commander yelled out an order and the steady beat of thousands of spears on shields boomed from the Goth army outside the gates of the city. The light of dawn had grown, and he could see around him his men grinning, whilst the city people stared in horror towards the city walls. The first rays of the morning sun touched the roof of the city houses, and slowly the Goth King lowered his arm, the sound dying away.

Athanakis turned and spoke with his entourage of officials, then called back to Alaric. "What are your terms?". He looked calm enough, thought the king, but his voice quivered. He knew he was beaten. The Goths had the gates open, a huge army outside ready. There was another army garrison five miles away, which would be at least two hours on foot, even if they started out now, and they would not have the numbers necessary to do battle with Alaric.

To the sound of laughter from his own men behind their shields, Alaric called back, "You will bring out all of your food, all of your wine, all your clothing and bring it to me here. If I think you're hiding anything, I'll set my men on you. I will then tell you what I am going to pay you for your goods. You refuse my offer, I'll set my men on you." He pointed at the eastern wall of the city, "You have until the sun comes up over that wall to bring me your goods. No longer. We're in a hurry!"

Chapter 13

Palace Barracks Training Ground, Constantinople, 4th April 396 AD

Gainas and Euthymius watched from the balustrade of a raised garden as six squads of men were drilled in shield wall discipline by their squad commanders. Dust and gravel flew as the squads shoved and slid, each trying to outmuscle each other. Gainas didn't smile as the men swore and bantered at each other. His mind was racing, his temper short. He was considering his position at the court, or lack of it.

It had been months now since the removal of Rufinus and he had had just one audience with the emperor. The Imperator had been gracious enough. Had thanked him for removing the traitor and gifted him some gold, but he had not endorsed Stilicho's direction that he take command of the men he had brought back from the West, although he would temporarily look after them until they were fully re-deployed. The eunuch Eutropius had been there by the side of the emperor and Gainas had not failed to notice how he subtly controlled the whole meeting, passing messages surreptitiously to Arcadius or in some instances blatantly whispering in the Imperator's ear during their conversation.

He had left the meeting barely containing his rage. He had expected to be at least *Magister Militum* by now, in command of over twenty thousand Roman and foederati troops and with an honoured place at the Eastern court, the man charged with the last line of defence of Constantinople; or maybe *Magister Militum per Illyricum*, heading up the fight against Alaric. Instead, he was simply another Roman commander drilling his tired men at Hebdomon, trying to keep them from causing trouble, waiting on orders from the palace on what to do next. After that one meeting, he found his messages to the emperor were not being responded to, and he was being blocked on all fronts by palace officials when he attempted to insist on an audience.

Like he didn't already know what needed to be done. He needed to chase down Alaric, that was obvious. But he needed to know who he was to work with for planning, who his commanders were, what numbers Alaric had, and most importantly how many men in total he had to work with and what types of troops he had. But he had been told nothing, had heard nothing.

He tried to think if anyone else could be considered for the task. Abundantius was too old and now sat as ex-consul of the East, a fitting title for the old soldier. Timasius was pretty old too and also a respected senator. Caesarius was now praetorian prefect of the East and a decent man by all accounts, but no warrior and no military leader. All seemed happy in their city life, with occasional visits when absolutely necessary to their estates in Pannonia and Dacia. Oh, what he wouldn't do to be in the same fine position. He'd fought under Timasius and Abundantius, he'd fought alongside Theodosius, he had shed much of his own blood in the name of the empire and yet here he was, being snubbed by the very people who expected him to go out and defend their lands should the need arise. He felt frustration rise in the pit of his stomach; he wanted to punch something or someone.

Euthymius said suddenly, "Look who's coming to visit!". Gainas started out of his reverie, and turned to look at the grand chamberlain, who had stepped up beside them.

"Good afternoon, General Gainas!"

The eunuch had sent a message to him asking him to meet with him, but he had been daydreaming. He was glad Euthymius was with him. He cursed inwardly; this eunuch could easily have slid a knife between his ribs had he been alone. He had to stay more alert.

Gainas noticed the small boy; he accompanied the chamberlain everywhere lately. Nobody knew where the child had come from or what relationship he had to Eutropius. Most people were too afraid to ask.

"Who's the boy?" asked Gainas.

"He runs errands for me."

"Whose child is he?"

Ignoring the question, Eutropius pointed at the troops, "How are they doing?".

Gainas turned back to watching them. "They can always improve," he said, non-committal.

"Walk with me General. Your man can follow at a distance.". Euthymius looked in askance at Gainas.

"It's OK," said Gainas. "I'm sure if the chamberlain wanted to harm me, there would be a whole troop of his palace eunuchs surrounding us about now, correct?"

Eutropius nodded, then he looked down at the boy and said, "Go wait with the soldier man."

The small boy obediently went and stood beside Euthymius.

Together Eutropius and Gainas descended the steps and walked at a gentle pace past the practicing soldiers and into some of the most beautifully tended gardens of the palace.

"I imagine you're wondering why you've not been appointed *Magister Militum* of a province or even Prefect of the East?" Eutropius said, his voice full of irony.

Gainas said nothing.

"I'll take that as a yes. What you have to realise is that you are, how shall we say? A bit of an enigma for us here in the court." The eunuch tapped his fingers together, a habit he had when he was thinking. "Up until a few months ago, your name was barely spoken in these corridors and gardens; Gainas was just one of the barbarian generals who fought at Frigidus…"

"And damn well nearly died there," interjected Gainas.

"… and other places," continued Eutropius smoothly. "Now, in the proverbial blink of an eye, you're a name who's gossiped about in every tavern and church throughout the city and beyond. The man who killed the hated Rufinus." The two men stared at each other for a moment.

"I thought that's what you wanted?" snapped Gainas.

"Indeed, it was, and not just me. You would be amazed how many men and women, and others like me, said a little prayer of thanks to God when his head was paraded through the city streets. Not very Christian, I have to agree, but it made the people happy, and when the people are happy, they are not rioting, and that makes the emperor happy."

"So, where is my reward for doing your dirty work for you?" Gainas asked bluntly.

"My dear general, it wasn't my dirty work, it was your General Stilicho, I believe, who gave you the order. I may have been aware of his plan, but I have no wish to take any of the credit, as I told the emperor the day before."

"Presumably so you would take none of the blame if it had all gone wrong, eunuch," Gainas snarled.

"Eutropius or Chamberlain would be appropriate," said Eutropius, staring at the general with an unblinking gaze. Gainas blinked first, inwardly cursing at his lack of knowledge of court politics. He felt like a child amongst adults. The eunuch smiled nastily.

"I did warn you that you should offer me a little more respect, and now you see why." Again, the tapping of the fingers. "Unlike you, I now have the trust of the emperor and of the empress; they are very indebted to me for arranging their little love-nest in the palace. She's a beauty with brains, yes, but she knows who she owes her position to, and how willing the emperor is to listen to me. He for his part wants nothing more than to fuck his beautiful Empress and when he's too sore to do that anymore he wants to go hunting. He's only too happy for someone else to hold the reigns of the empire and place his trust in one who has no desire to usurp his throne. Which I don't, of course. I mean who ever heard of a eunuch being emperor?" The chamberlain gave a short laugh that sounded more like a snort, then straightened up and looked squarely at the gothic general. "So where does that leave you, my dear Gainas?"

"Nowhere, it would seem," he said bitterly.

"Oh not at all, general." Eutropius smiled, though it didn't reach his eyes. "You are a competent, well more than competent, general by all accounts. Your talents will not be wasted. Over the coming months the Eastern Legions will be re-organised, so that we make best use of our military assets and are able to engage with multiple enemies if need be. As you know, the Huns are making threatening noises, as are the Alans and the Gepids. The Persians make noises from time to time, and who knows when a new king of kings may decide to break the peace?"

"I thought General Timasius was *Magister Militum Praesentalis*?" Gainas probed for information.

"No longer, the emperor requested I remove him from post yesterday."

"At your suggestion, no doubt?"

Eutropius ignored the comment. "The General and I do not see eye to eye on many things, and right now we all need to work together. So unfortunately, we had to relieve him of his command." He sighed as if upset by what he had done, but Gainas wasn't fooled for a second.

"But I am not to be appointed Praesentalis." It was a statement not a question.

"No. But nobody else will be either; the troops will be under direct command of the emperor until the necessary reorganisation of the units has been completed."

"What about Alaric? I have it on good authority he is already in Greece."

"That is as maybe; you will not need to concern yourself with Alaric just yet. The cities of Greece are well fortified, he will find little plunder there. We need time to prepare these men, to create a number of armies which can take on Alaric. Do you think you could beat him now with the men you have? Honestly?"

Gainas shook his head. It irked him to admit it, but the eunuch was right. Alaric was a talented and ruthless tactician. Gainas was confident that he was every bit as cunning and determined, but Alaric had the experienced veterans of Frigidus and a dozen other battles with him. The men he himself had brought back from the West had barely fought a few skirmishes with some bands of brigands, who had run at the first sight of any opposition. They would not last five minutes if they came up against Alaric's battle-hardened troops. There was much to do.

"I thought you would agree. So, your role will be to be part of the consistorium, but you will report to me and will assist me in the re-organisation of the legions in the East, to make best use of the men and resources we have and to allow us to defend the empire from multiple enemies quickly and easily."

"I will be working for you?"

"Yes."

"I'm a soldier, not a bureaucrat."

"Sometimes you have to be both; as a general, I thought you knew that," said Eutropius sternly.

"I won't play your political games… Eutropius." Gainas just managed to stop himself from spitting out the word 'eunuch'.

The chamberlain grinned that nasty grin of his. "See, that wasn't so hard. I don't expect you to play any political games, general. I expect you to do the tasks I assign you to do. The safety of the empire, the capital and the emperor depend upon it."

"And if I do this work for you? What reward do I get?"

"You do well and your reputation and status within the consistorium will grow, I'll make sure of that. Once you've established yourself within that inner circle, the rewards will come. *Magister Militum Praesentalis*, perhaps. The emperor is generous, of that you need have no doubt. You saw it yourself a few months ago with that very generous stipend you received."

"But no command appointment."

"It will come, General. It will come."

With that the chamberlain turned and waved for the boy to join him and he walked away holding the small boy's hand, leaving Gainas still fuming and frustrated.

Euthymius walked up to him and asked, "What was that all about sir?"

"Politics Euthymius, just politics."

They watched Eutropius stride away, the child struggling to keep up with him. The boy turned and waved at them and instinctively both men waved back

However, Gainas promised himself that the last thing on God's earth he would do would be to trust the eunuch.

Late that evening, Eutropius sat in his private quarters within the palace. He called for Zahur. Eutropius told the boy to go and fetch a scribe called Domninus Gregoras. Zahur could barely speak any Greek, but he seemed to understand it well enough, and within a few minutes

Gregoras sat in front of Eutropius, with papyrus, pen, and ink ready to write but looking slightly bemused.

Gregoras was also a eunuch and had been in the service of the emperors for the past ten years. He and Eutropius had known of each other for many years, and shared many experiences together, some happy, but not many, and when Eutropius had been originally appointed, he had immediately contacted Gregoras to come and work in the palace alongside him. He was now chief secretary to Caesarius. He had accepted the role gladly. He had been working as a personal attendant to a fussy and demanding rich woman on the south side of the city. Gregoras hated the work, considering it demeaning. But it was better than starving to death or returning to the streets to sell himself night after night to soldiers, bishops, or senators.

The chamberlain ensured that nobody else was around, closed his door and locked it. He sat down and dictated a letter to Gregoras. He looked up at Eutropius at one point during the dictation, but the chamberlain snapped, "Write what I say!" Gregoras shrugged and continued.

When the letter was finished, Eutropius read it through, nodding with satisfaction. He called for Zafur again and asked him to find Bardanes and send him to him, then to go to the house of the *Magister Officiorum* and to extend an invitation to dine with Eutropius tomorrow evening, at his new house off of the Mese. It had previously been owned by Rufinus, but he now used it as a private residence, away from prying eyes and ears in the palace.

Whilst they waited, Eutropius offered Gregoras a drink of wine. Gregoras was pleased and surprised; nobody had ever offered him a goblet of wine before, certainly not in the work he did. He drank it down greedily; it tasted like nectar. He looked up at Eutropius and smiled. The Chamberlain smiled back. "A wine from one of the emperor's own vineyards," he said.

A few seconds later, the goblet hit the marble floor with a clang. Gregoras clutched his stomach and then this throat; he tried to call out, but only a gurgling sound came from his foaming mouth. He collapsed from the chair and hit the ground hard. Eutropius calmly watched as the man writhed in agony for a full minute, his hands clawing at his stomach and then at his throat, grasping thin air, reaching towards him, his blue lips soundlessly moving. Then with a last rattling breath, he fell still. Eutropius took out a small cloth and wiped the man's mouth, removing the foam. He picked up the goblet and amphora of wine and carried them to his toilet. He poured the remaining wine down the hole and then dipped them both in the clean water for hand washing the servants had laid out earlier in the day. He washed both containers out thoroughly and then hung them up in the open courtyard adjacent to his office. He returned to his desk.

A few seconds later there was a knock at the door. A big ugly brute of a man, with a hare lip and a slight stoop and limp, stepped inside. Bardanes. He looked down at the still figure of Gregoras but said nothing.

"He just fell dead," said Eutropius without emotion. "Poor man. He must have had a weak heart."

"Weak heart. Poor man," repeated Bardanes in a rasping voice.

"Indeed," said Eutropius, "Please get rid of that. Make sure nobody sees you. We don't want to upset anyone now, do we?"

"I come back," rumbled Bardanes, and he was gone for several minutes, during which Eutropius examined reports of troop numbers and roles.

Bardanes returned with a stout rope and jute sack. After much grunting and cursing, Gregoras was in the sack. Bardanes picked it up like it weighed nothing.

"That will be all, Bardanes," said Eutropius. The brute nodded and hobbled away with his burden.

The chamberlain returned to his desk and picked up the letter Gregoras had written. He wrapped it in some rough linen and tied it securely with jute. He rose and made his way through the labyrinthine corridors of the palace to the eastern end of the complex, where he descended several large flights of steps and trudged down sloping tunnels until the sound of waves could be heard. He walked out onto the palace's private dock, where a small boat waited, the wooden gunwales creaking as the craft wrestled against its moorings in the evening tide.

There was a tall man waiting on the dock. He wore his hair like a Goth, but Eutropius knew him to be the son of a wealthy merchant of Constantinople, who desired a position in the palace to further his status. Father and son would do anything to gain the approval of one of the *Illustrii* in the slim hope that their family's name might be elevated to one recognised at court.

Eutropius handed him the wrapped papyrus letter. "Deliver this successfully and your father will never know of your little secret, and I may even be able to get you a position within the *Magister Officiorum*."

In the gloom, the man looked at the letter. Eutropius said quietly, "I would recommend you do not open it; it would go badly for you if you did."

"Who do I deliver this to?" asked the man.

Eutropius said a name. The man's eyes opened wide; in the dim, flickering light of the torches on the dockside, he saw the whites of his eyes, and the fear in the face. Eutropius opened his hand; in his palm lay what looked to the man like a coin, but it was much larger than a standard solidus. Eutropius continued, "You are to give him this token from me. Ensure you hand it only to him!" The man took the token; it was heavy, and he stared at it in awe.

"Do you have a question?" said Eutropius with a hint of menace. The man shook his head and said nothing.

"Then go."

Eutropius watched as the man turned and climbed into the boat. The chamberlain stood there as the vessel departed the dock and headed out into the Golden Horn, where it turned left and headed south disappearing behind the headland, headed for Greece.

Chapter 14

Thermopylae, Greece, 11th April 396 AD

The messenger yelled out for the gates to the camp to be opened, and the guards, recognising the scout, complied. He galloped through the camp to the central area, leapt off his sweating horse and ran towards the garrison's commander shelter. "Sir, Gerontius sir!" called a guard.

Gerontius walked out of his tent and stood blinking in the sun. "What's the panic, soldier?" he asked calmly.

The scout was panting and spoke in staccato bursts. "Alaric ... sir ... his army ... sir ... they'll be here ... day after tomorrow."

"How many of them?"

"All of them ... I think."

"You think?"

"Sir, the line stretched to the horizon. There were squads of infantry, cavalry outriders, wagons and carts, some huge wagons carrying the women and children, tents and provisions. I'd say at least seventy thousand strong, if not more."

"Thank you soldier, that will be all, now go and sort your horse out, it looks like it's about to fall down dead!" With that Gerontius turned around and headed back into his tent.

In the dim light sat two people. The first was a Goth Officer called Huneric. He was dressed in the typical style of a barbarian cavalryman. The second was the Proconsul of Achaea, a bulbous, double-chinned man called Antiochus, the second most powerful man in Greece. Gerontius sat back down at the wooden table and said, "You heard that?"

Antiochus nodded, took a sip of wine from his cup, and said, "But how come your man arrived so long after Huneric here; this barbarian's been here all night drinking our wine!"

"Because we're better at riding than you Romans, of course!" replied the Goth. His Latin was fluent, having been educated in Thessalonica as a boy, a rare experience for a barbarian, but one that prepared him for this role of diplomat for Alaric.

"So, what are your orders, proconsul?" asked Gerontius.

"As I was about to say, legate, it's very simple. You are to do nothing. Rufinus' orders were clear; Alaric should be allowed to pass into Greece unhindered." Antiochus took another drink, spilling some down his tunic. He carelessly wiped it away and said, "Did you not say you had some food coming? You've plainly forgotten how to entertain your betters, legate!"

"It's on its way, proconsul. Rufinus is dead, and the last orders we had from Caesarius said that Alaric was in Thessaly, so would not trouble us. Yet here he is, on our doorstep."

"Not for us to reason why, legate. More wine?" Antiochus offered the commander the small amphora. Three slaves walked in carrying a selection of meats, sweetbreads, bread, fruits, shellfish and a variety of sauces. The trays were set on the table and immediately the proconsul grabbed two large chicken thighs and bit into them as if he had not eaten for a week. After he had chewed and swallowed – and not quietly – several mouthfuls, he said, "We've received no orders from Caesarius to stop Alaric, or to engage with him. As far as we are aware, he has been ordered to make his way to Illyricum, where he is to defend the western approaches of the Empire from threats from the West."

"Like Stilicho."

"Like Stilicho," echoed the proconsul.

"I think our guest here should be leaving now," said Gerontius. He wasn't happy entertaining a member of Alaric's army. He wasn't sure if the Goth was friend, neutral or enemy. The lines were very blurred on that matter.

Still eating, Antiochus shook his head, and with his mouth half full said, "No, he is to wait in here until nightfall, and he is to leave as quietly as possible."

"Why?" asked the camp commandant.

"Because, that way, nobody who doesn't need to know will see him leave, just as nobody who doesn't need to know saw him arrive last night. Tongues will wag, the men will get nervous, when there is nothing to be nervous about. You don't want a mutiny on your hands, do you?"

"I might have one when they find out we're just letting the whole of Alaric's army into Greece without so much as a 'by your leave'," muttered Gerontius, but Antiochus gave no sign of hearing him.

"Is it wise to just let this army into Greece?" he asked more loudly.

"What else can you do, legate?" Huneric asked. "Do you really want to fight us?"

Gerontius said nothing.

"Stilicho couldn't beat Alaric with two armies; you've barely got a legion here, and it's full of new recruits and very few veterans."

"How do you know that?" snapped Gerontius.

"I told him, legate," said the proconsul, taking a drink of wine. "Alaric might be a barbarian, but he's not stupid and he's not an animal. A battle against a properly trained army, preferably one led by Stilicho, would be his idea of a fight. Pummelling us into the ground would bring no honour and no booty, and he might lose some of his men unnecessarily. He'll swat us aside like a fly if we attack, but otherwise

96

he'll just ignore us. I'm trying to save you and your men here, legate. I hope you can see that? Excellent oysters, by the way."

"Three hundred Spartans held this pass against a hundred thousand Persians, proconsul."

"But all three hundred died, didn't they, commander?" interjected Huneric. "And Xerces marched through to Athens anyway."

"Just like you're planning to do, perhaps?"

Now it was Huneric who said nothing.

"They only died because they were betrayed, I recall," said Antiochus.

The Goth continued, "You Romans do love your Greek stories, don't you? Ah! The Hellenic heroes from Sparta, battling insurmountable odds … never mind that they were a bunch of mercenaries who had turned up too late for several battles prior to that."

The proconsul wiped his mouth, leaving an oily smear on his chin. "The matter is settled. Commander, I am ordering you to stand your men down, and arrange an escort for our guest to take him discreetly outside the camp gates under cover of darkness and ensure that as few people as possible see him leave. When Alaric arrives the day after tomorrow, he will find this camp empty, because you will have taken all your men, including camp followers, into the hills for exercises for the next four days." He looked at Huneric. "Enough time to get through?" The Goth nodded, smiling.

"Good. Commander you'd best get your men started on their packing, then come back and tuck in, or else I'll finish off the whole lot!"

Chapter 15

Southern Quarter, Constantinople, 11th April 396 AD

Hunulf strolled casually through the market stalls along the side street. Here in this part of the city, the houses were less salubrious than the palace quarter, but the streets were still bustling with people. The smells from the street vendors selling cooked fowl and fish wafted through the air, masking the more unpleasant smells of animal excrement, which lay everywhere on the street, the gift of horses, pigs, sheep, and goats. He wore the rough and uncomfortable clothing of a goat herder and had his hood pulled over his head, but he kept an eye on his target up ahead, who walked purposefully through the bustling traders and merchants.

Priscianus and four of his bodyguards.

They were heading for the docks on the south side of the city, and Hunulf had followed them since they came out of the tavern just off the Mese. The tavern was well known to be one of the headquarters for the Blues guild. They had several around the city which they liked to call "family houses". They which served as taverns, brothels, as well as offices for the guild. Keeping a good distance, Hunulf shuffled along, dodging in amongst the pens of animals along the sides of the street, stopping here to examine a herd of goats, stopping there to examine bags of grain feed, but always keeping an eye on his target. He wasn't alone.

Ahead of Priscianus was Sigeric, a calm but cheerful *optio* who he trusted implicitly. He was posing as a beggar and waited until the Blues patriarch passed him to reach out beseech the man for alms; one of the bodyguards pulled Sigeric away from the guildsman and shoved him hard against the wall. He played his part perfectly and cowered. During this incident, Hunulf saw Sigeric's twin brother, Videric, dressed as a tailor's assistant, carrying a large bolt of cloth, walk unnoticed past Priscianus to position himself ahead of his quarry.

Over the past week the three had perfected this technique whilst trailing Priscianus. Each day they would change their disguises and wander the city, with the Blues head guildsman always in their sights, but always at a distance. Maurinus was not out of bed yet. Hunulf had another two of his men watching his house. But Priscianus was their target now and Hunulf felt a rising excitement, as the Blues' patriarch walked. He had changed his behaviour.

Normally he kept to the city centre and made various trips between the "family houses", always accompanied by two or three of his bodyguards, but today he had four of his men with him and there had been no wandering around the streets; they had set off in a deliberate fashion and very quickly Hunulf had figured out where they were heading.

Having got rid of Sigeric the beggar, the Blues patriarch and his men continued along the street, then turned sharp right, and descended steps down to the South Harbour. Keeping his distance, Hunulf got to the top of the steps then walked past them; there was a second set further on and he hurried along behind the houses to them. Videric was already on the docks, so Hunulf was not worried about losing his quarry. Coming down the second steps, Hunulf entered the packed and noisy harbour area. There were a host of jetties with trade cogs tied up. Each of the jetties were serviced by one or more warehouses. He could see Videric, with his cloth, walking through the throng of people to his right. Priscianus and his men walked in front of him with their eyes firmly ahead. When they had passed, Hunulf plunged into the busy walkway, traders yelling and calling out across the throng, enticing and promoting their goods to the passers-by, who in turn pushed and shoved each other in the crowd, trying to get to wherever it was they were trying to get to. He eventually got across the tumult and found a street vendor selling hot cooked fish. He purchased one and stood there eating, watching his quarry enter a warehouse two jetties further along.

Videric strode past his position with his bolt of cloth on his shoulders, ignoring Hunulf, and took the same route Priscianus and his party had. He walked into the same warehouse and disappeared from sight. A short time later he reappeared, waving his thanks to someone, and headed back into the connecting walkway. Hunulf saw him drop his load off of his shoulders, hand it to a vagabond and point to a jetty further down the harbour. Videric then worked his way through the crowd to where Hunulf stood. He also bought some food and came and stood next to Hunulf.

"It's a warehouse for money changers," said Videric, without preamble.

"What did our man do?"

"He was talking to a Jew with one eye. Gave him a bag of money. Had to leave after that." Videric took a mouthful of hot cooked fish.

"Who was the guy you gave the cloth to?"

"Never seen him before. He looked like he could use the money. I told him where to deliver it for three silver coins."

Hunulf nodded. Videric was a formidable warrior, he knew of no-one else as quick and as lethal with a sword, but behind a quiet, stern exterior was a kind and generous man. "Fair enough. You find your brother and get back to Anthemius and bring him here. I'll wait here to keep an eye on the Jew."

Videric gave a grunt "Was that a joke?"

"Was it funny?"

"No"

"Then I guess it wasn't a joke."

Videric gave another small grunt, then turned and disappeared into the crowd to find this brother.

Chapter 16

Eutropius leaned forward, tapping his fingertips together. "Tell me, Bargus" he said. "Tell me about Timasius' little fantasies of being emperor?"

They were back in the eunuch's private office in the golden palace. Eutropius sat at his desk, with a mess of papyrus scrolls on his desk before him. Mostly it was for show. In the corner, the boy, Zafur, played with some old scrolls that Eutropius had let him have. He was trying to build a tower.

"They are just daydreams. He hired me in Sardis when his previous man died of fever," said Bargus.

"Yes, I know," said Eutropius, shaking his head. "I don't really understand; he had other bodyguards to promote into the role; he could have just written to the *Magister Officiorum* and requested another person to be assigned. Why pick on you?"

"As I said last time, he enjoyed our conversations, what can I say?"

"You told me you flattered his ego and appealed to his vanity."

Bargus nodded. "The general gets no such compliments from his wife, I understand. Men like to be complimented. I fulfilled that need in him. I also introduced him to several local merchants who dealt in silver, horses and slaves; the general is partial to all three." There was a squeak of annoyance from the corner, as the tower of scrolls came crashing down and the boy rushed to gather them together to try again.

"Where did he come from?" asked Bargus.

"So how did you come to know these local merchants?" Eutropius asked, ignoring the question.

"I know things about people. I get to know them. I help them find the people they want to know."

"So, you're a sort of middleman? And you take your cut?"

"Not always. In the general's case I offered him my services full time."

"Because you saw in him someone you can manipulate pretty much as you wish?"

Bargus did not rise to the bait. "The general is powerful. I am but a humble man, but through the general's generosity I've been able to do things many others are denied. Why would I not wish to be associated with him?"

"You might not wish to hang around him if he were guilty of treason."

"That was just fanciful talk. Tavern-talk. As far as I am concerned the general is loyal to the Empire. He certainly has done his share of fighting on its behalf."

"He nearly got Theodosius killed; did you know that?" The *praepositus* was taken aback.

"Plainly not, then. Some people at the time whispered that it was a deliberate ploy to do away with the emperor, so he could take the throne." Eutropius smiled blandly. "But probably, as you say, that was just tavern-talk."

"He never told me that story." Bargus frowned.

"He's probably not given to reciting it. I mean, if it was accidental, then he shows himself to be an incompetent general, needlessly endangering the emperor; if it was a deliberate plot which obviously failed, then he shows himself to be an incompetent traitor."

"You're lying."

"Then there was the time when Theodosius made Rufinus prefect of the East. Apparently, the general was furious with the emperor. After all, he and his friend Promotus had been soldiering on behalf of the empire for years, risking their lives battle after battle, and in comes this Gaul, who can barely speak Greek, and he's given everything that Timasius thinks is due to him and his friend. Now, I can't believe he has not mentioned *that* little episode to you; his anger at the Theodosian dynasty for that insult? That would be classic tavern-talk, I should think."

Bargus looked away. He stared at Zafur, who was just about to place the last scroll on his tower; he placed it too heavily and the whole affair fell to the floor again. Again, a small squeak of frustration, but no other emotion from the child. He just gathered up the scrolls and started again.

"I see he has mentioned it." Eutropius smiled nastily.

"You're imagining treason where none exists," insisted Bargus.

"Am I?" Eutropius raised his eyebrows and gave a short laugh. "Well, *praeposit*us, you say you know people, go speak to them, see if I am not telling the truth about the general."

"Why do you have that child in your office?" asked Bargus.

"He runs errands for me." Eutropius pulled out a small bag of gold *solidi* and pushed it across the desk to Bargus, who opened it and inspected the contents. "It's a small something for your troubles, and to ensure that you keep our conversations strictly between us. We shall meet again in a week and talk some more. Good day."

Chapter 17

Southern Docks, Constantinople, 11th April 396 AD

The sun was setting as Anthemius met with Hunulf on the jetty. Videric and Sigeric positioned themselves either side of the pair, ready for any trouble. The crowd on the docks was thinning. People were quickly making their way home; night-time was not especially safe for the ordinary man of Constantinople. The four men on the jetty were not scared by street thugs; the size and appearance of the three Goths made them the threatening ones, and Anthemius always made the effort to ooze confidence to the casual observer. That usually kept people at distance, but if push came to shove, he was competent with his short narrow blade.

"Is he still in there?" asked Anthemius.

"Unless he is secretly a fish and has swum away, yes he's still there."

"Alone?"

"Not sure. Priscianus and his minions left about forty minutes ago. I've seen six people leave since then, none for the last twenty minutes."

"There could be slaves or servants in there still working," suggested Sigeric.

"Most likely bodyguards. It's getting dark. The Jew won't want to go home alone after dark," said Hunulf.

The final rays of the sun lit up the spires and domes of the great palace nestling on the first hill above them; here on the shores of the Sea of Marmara, amongst the warehouses, the chill of evening was settling in.

"Let us go, then," said Anthemius. "Best we set the agenda, not him."

The four men strode out into the twilight down the harbour walkway, then onto the jetty, the wooden boards creaking beneath their feet as they headed towards the warehouse. As they approached, yellow light spilled out of the doorway and the men's shadows flickered behind them. Oil lamps had been lit and hung from the wall to hold back the night. The Jew with the eye-patch sat at a solitary raised lectern on his own, but as the men entered, three figures emerged from the shadows, and formed a barrier between the visitors and the moneychanger.

The Jew didn't look up but asked aloud, "What do you want?"

"To talk; just to talk," replied Anthemius steadily.

"Your companions don't look much like the talking kind, especially that one." The Jew looked up and pointed at **Videric**, then he returned to writing in his ledger.

"For a one-eyed man, you see a lot."

"What do you want to talk about?" asked the moneychanger.

"I prefer to have our discussion in private."

"What if I don't?"

"Then I'll have to insist."

The Jew looked up, sighed, put down his quill and closed his ledger with a thud. He stepped down from his lectern, grabbing a walking stick, and though he limped, he moved quickly with purpose until he stood before Anthemius.

"You're Egyptian?" asked the Jew.

"My family originated in Egypt."

"Hmm." The moneychanger stroked his short beard. "Who are you anyway? I've never seen you before around here."

"I am Flavius Anthemius, procurator of the Mint here in Constantinople."

"Hmm. Well, come on then. I have an office at the back where we can talk in private, as you seem so set on that." The Jew looked to usher Anthemius ahead of him, but the procurator said, "After you," and waited for the Jew to comply, which he did with a small chuckle and an understanding nod.

"Don't let those men leave," said Anthemius over his shoulder as he followed the Jew.

"They are not going anywhere, sir," said Hunulf.

Two minutes later Anthemius and the Jew were settled on two chairs in a dark office with two newly lit candles. The office was of comparable size to Anthemius' own in the mint. A square desk stood at the centre of the room. It was tidy and organised, also like Anthemius'. He stared at the narrow-faced man opposite and asked. "And what's your name?"

"My name is for my friends," came the sharp reply. "And you're not one of them."

"What should I call you, then?"

"Just call me 'The Jew', everyone around here does."

"Must get confusing. There are a lot of Jews in the city."

"I'm the only Jewish moneychanger with one eye."

"Fair enough. Why did Priscianus visit you today?"

"Private business."

"Not any longer," said Anthemius. "Why did Priscianus visit you today?"

"It's still private business."

Anthemius held the gaze of the Jew, who stared back at his. Shadows from the gently flickering candle danced across his face. "What do I get out of this, considering you are asking me to break a confidence with my customer?"

"You get to not be hanged for treason, so I suggest you start talking quickly."

"If word gets back to Priscianus that I broke his confidence, I think I'd end up dead anyhow, and in a lot nastier way than a nice clean hanging. I'm afraid you're going to have to do better than that."

"He won't find out."

"Tell me you aren't that naïve!" sneered the Jew. "Priscianus knows everything that goes on in this city. He probably already knows that you're here talking to me."

"Unlikely, he left over an hour ago, he didn't know he was being followed."

"So sure, are you?"

"My men are very good at what they do."

"Well, forgive me for not being as confident in your men's abilities as you; the answer is still no. I won't break trust."

The two men stared at each other for a full minute, neither speaking, each weighing up the other.

Anthemius saw a cunning man, experienced in the ways of commerce, but no felon. A man who would drive a hard bargain for certain, with his intimidating looks enhanced by the eye-patch. The procurator knew that moneychangers had to be sharp and ruthless. The opportunity for profit was great but so was the opportunity for ruin. Lend too much money to the wrong person and the earnings of a lifetime could be obliterated overnight. He knew he was asking much to have the Jew break trust, but this was a negotiation, and he had to start high.

For his part the Jew saw a neat, tidy young man, with tanned skin and dark brown eyes, which in the dim flickering light were black as obsidian. The moneychanger had dealt with many palace officials: most of them were either inept and easily fooled, or corrupt and easily bribed. The Jew looked into those dark eyes and realised that this man was neither. He had the look of one driven by duty; likely enough he did not suffer fools gladly and, if God spared this man, it was conceivable that he would end up in one of the high offices, possibly even become one of the *illustrii* **of the senate.** The Jew broke the silence.

"You're the procurator of the city mint?"

"Yes."

The Jew tapped his forefinger on the table in front of him, deep in thought.

"I want guaranteed coin when I order it, any amount, no delays."

Anthemius smiled. "I can't guarantee any amount, you know that.". He leaned forward. Now they were getting somewhere.

"Up to one hundred *solidi* guaranteed anytime, above that one weeks' notice." proposed the Jew.

Anthemius considered for a moment then countered, "Fifty *solidi* anytime, over that, two weeks' notice.".

"Seventy *solidi*, ten days' notice above. You supply the guards. When I need protection, you will provide it."

"I could still hang you."

"Priscianus won't be so nice. You need to know what I know, and I know a lot of things."

"Such as what?"

"That the information I have is worth a guarantee of seventy *solidi* anytime, ten days' notice above."

Anthemius paused then nodded and held out his hand.

The Jew didn't move. "You supply the guards. When I need protection, you will provide it."

Anthemius nodded keeping his hand out.

Still the Jew didn't move. "I have your word of honour; all conversations remain strictly between you and me?"

Anthemius nodded, raised both his hands as if in supplication. "I swear before my God," he said, without a hint of irony.

The Jew paused then reached across and shook hands with the procurator. Then he picked up a quill and for a minute scribbled on a piece of parchment. Once finished he pushed both quill and parchment both towards Anthemius.

"What's this?"

"Our contract."

"We just shook hands."

"You'll have no objection to signing it then."

"You don't trust my word?"

"Do you trust mine?"

Anthemius picked up the quill and signed the parchment. The Jew took the document and rolled it up. With a candle he melted some red wax across the join, sealing it tight. Then he took his signet ring and pressed it into the wax. He held it out to Anthemius who pressed his own signet ring into the wax alongside. The Jew took the scroll back and blew on the wax to cool it. He then pushed himself up and shuffled across to the pigeonholes and placed the scroll in one of the vacant slots.

He sat back down, both elbows on the table, chin resting in his hands. He remained silent. He glanced to the scroll in the pigeonhole. He seemed to be stealing himself. Whether or not to cross the Rubicon guessed Anthemius.

The Jew crossed. He leant back in his chair.

"Priscianus and I had a business transaction today."

Anthemius mimicked the Jew and leant back. "I know."

"He is trying to expand his property holdings in the north of the city. He's been coming to me for about three months now to get coin."

"Why you?"

"I get my coin from the mint at Cyzicus. You don't produce enough in the city for the likes of me to get a decent share, after the court and the senate have had their stipends from the emperor. Cyzicus does good quality, and Priscianus has been taking a regular order of coin recently. Every third Monday for the past three months, he has taken delivery of one hundred *solidi*. It is a loan secured against his existing properties. I make a special request, and the mint at Cyzicus delivers in personalised bags, just for the Blues patrician. It's an extra service he seems to like."

Anthemius reached into his tunic and pulled out one of the *solidi* the Persian had given him. "Do you know Quaderi, the Persian in the Forum of Constantine?"

"Of course, who doesn't? He's the only Persian in our guild; he used to service Priscianus before me."

Anthemius tossed him the coin, which the Jew clumsily caught; no depth of vision, thought the procurator. The moneychanger looked at the coin. "A solidus, so what?"

"Look closer."

The Jew stared with his one eye at the procurator for a few seconds, then he stood up and hobbled around to the other side of the desk. He took one of the candles and placed it on the surface in front of him. Then he took a shallow glass bowl, filled it with a small amount of water from a small earthen jug and placed it in a small three-legged stand in front of him. Moving the candle closer, he held the coin under the bowl and manoeuvred it until he found the view he wanted. He peered closely at the coin through the water, the liquid magnifying the image of the coin, so he could see the tell-tale signs he guessed were there. He looked up at the procurator, and Anthemius could see he was genuinely concerned.

"Fake." He sounded as if he did not believe his own words.

Anthemius nodded.

The Jew looked again through the water-lens. "I would not have noticed, how did you …?"

"Our mutual friend the Persian found it. He chipped a coin accidentally and that alerted him. He checked every other coin he had and found several others. A number of them had come from Priscianus, or rather from one of his young charioteers who was running an errand for him, which is how they ended up in Quaderi's hands."

"Must have been paying off his debts since he was coming to me. What did Priscianus say?"

"He denied all knowledge of the fakes, said the bag must have come from some admirer. He spun a story about a purse being thrown at his charioteer from a wealthy woman in the crowd."

"Humph!" snorted the Jew.

"Yes, I didn't believe him either, which is why I had him followed."

The Jew looked up and smiled for the first time, wrinkles appearing around both the good and the missing eye. "You like to live dangerously. If he had spotted your men ..." he mimed his throat being cut.

Anthemius didn't bat an eyelid "He didn't, but if he did, I would have been annoyed with my men. That's all."

The Jew shook his head. "Priscianus is not above doing away with troublesome officials, there are plenty of stories you must have heard. You are either brave or stupid, I haven't decided which yet."

"I'm not really interested in your opinion on my mental state, but I am interested in your opinion on where that fake may have come from." He indicated the coin, still in the Jew's hand under the water-lens.

"I won't give you an opinion" said the Jew, then held up his hand as Anthemius went to speak. "Because I know exactly where this came from."

"Where?"

"The mint at Cyzicus," said the Jew.

For the first time the moneychanger saw Anthemius look uncertain and confused. Then his black eyes hardened into a stare, and he said coldly, "Stop playing games with me Jew! I can make your life extremely unpleasant if I so wish."

"I play no games with you, procurator. But I assure you that this fake came from the mint. Come, let me show you." He waved for Anthemius to join him at the lens.

"Look at the edging. The coin has plainly been struck, not moulded, like most fakes."

"I know that. It was the first thing I noticed," said Anthemius impatiently.

"You run the mint here in the city. How do you control your dies?"

"We have our people strip searched as they come into work and when they leave. The dies are the most valuable things in the mint. They are personally controlled by my immediate subordinates, who I trust. The dies never leave the building."

"Exactly. Every die is unique. Each one bears the characteristics of the person who made it. The mint in Cyzicus will make its own dies and, whilst they base it on the image they are sent and the image should be identical to the other mints, they never are exactly the same; each carver of the die has his own little trademark, and you get to know them. Look at the emperor's diadem," the Jew pointed under the glass with the point of his quill. Anthemius peered closer; he could see the braided diadem with two small loops to the front to depict jewels. Anthemius stood up. "There are two jewels at the front of the diadem."

"Yes," agreed the Jew.

The procurator reached into a pocket in his tunic and pulled out a real solidus from the Constantinople mint and held it under the water-lens.

"One jewel,"

"Yes," said the Jew. "And that's how I know these coins come from Cyzicus, because that's the only mint in the East where the dies contain two jewels on the diadem. I also recognise the cut of the edges and the proportions of the face. It is with certainty from Cyzicus. One of the die cutters there is quite young but very good at his work; the others are good, one bit mad I hear. Mind you, working a lifetime in one of those places would make you somewhat crazy."

The two men stared in silence for a moment at the coins.

"Why did you not spot these when they arrived? That's part of your job," said Anthemius, even though he knew it to be an unfair assertion.

The Jew snorted and replied sharply, "Do you inspect the coins coming out of your mint to see if they are fakes?"

Anthemius bristled. "We do spot checks on weight and cut before they are bagged. We don't produce fakes."

"And as far as I am concerned neither does Cyzicus. Why should I check if coins coming *out* of an Imperial Mint are fake? I check all coins, especially gold ones coming to me, but coins straight from the mint, if I cannot trust them, then what can I trust?"

And that was what bothered Anthemius the most. Trust in the monetary system. If that was undermined by fakes so good, even the moneychangers could not recognise them, that was dangerous; to have completely debased coins coming out of the mint itself, without Imperial sanction, that was a recipe for disaster. Whatever was going on at Cyzicus had to be stopped and soon.

He shook himself out of his thoughts, turned to the Jew and said, "Thank you for your time. I will keep my side of the bargain and say nothing of which we have spoken. That I promise. I expect the same from you. I was never here; my men were never here. Will your men out there to honour that?"

"They had better, all three of them are my sons!" the Jew laughed gently. Anthemius nodded to the moneychanger and left the room.

He strode back out onto the warehouse floor and waved for Hunulf, Videric and Sigeric to follow him out of the building. They walked down the now dark harbour walkway, lit only dimly by the oil-lights coming through the windows of the city houses and by the faint light of the stars in the velvet blue sky above.

As they walked, Anthemius said, "I will be writing to the *Magister Officiorum* to have you all assigned to me for a trip we are taking."

"Where to?" asked Hunulf.

"Cyzicus, on the other side of the Sea of Marmara." Anthemius heard the Goth groan.

"Can't you get someone else to go with you sir?"

"Why?"

"I fucking hate boats!" Hunulf spat.

Chapter 18

Central Greece, 15th April 396 AD

The raiders came at dawn, when workers were just heading out into the misty fields. Caius and his younger brother, Tiberius, heard them before they saw them. A sound like distant thunder rolled towards them; only when he heard the first scream did Caius realise that they were under attack. He dropped his hoe and tools and grabbed his brother's arm. "Run!" he screamed. Tiberius, who was weak in the head, but strong in the body, looked confused and shook off his brother's arm. "Who are they?" he asked.

"No time to explain, Tibby!" implored Caius, trying to pull his simpleton sibling back towards the village. "We have to go …now!" Now he could clearly see the silhouette of a helmeted warrior on horseback, wielding a huge lance or spear, heading directly for them. Caius grabbed his brother's arm again and heaved, but Tiberius just stared and said aloud, "Why are they riding over the fields, father won't like that … hey! hey!" He shook off his brother again and started walking towards the oncoming shadow. "Hey you! Stop riding over the fields!" Caius again tried to pull him back, but Tiberius was angry now at the men on horses ruining the crops he had so diligently planted. He shrugged off his brother and pushed him away; Caius stumbled and fell backwards.

Caius scrambled to get to his feet; all he could do was stare as the rider charged out of the mist. In slow motion, Caius saw the thick leather tunic, the helmet of the rider, the long hair tailing behind him; he heard the ringing of chainmail and riding tackle clear in the morning air, above the thudding of the hooves in the soil of the field. Powerless to prevent it, he saw the long spear tear into his brother's chest, exiting through his spine, in an explosion of blood. He saw the lifeless body hurled to the floor as the leading shoulder of the horse cannoned into it. Then the rider was gone.

Caius stumbled to his feet and threw himself at his brother, but in the dim light he knew immediately it was too late. His simple-minded, sweet brother lay dead beside him; he kneeled and cradled his head. He heard the sound of another approaching horse and threw himself on the ground next to Tiberius. The rider passed, heard but unseen. Caius lay there, listening to fading thunder of the horse's hooves into the distance, and as the riders found the village, he heard the screams and cries of the villagers and soldiers. He thought he heard the occasional clash of swords, as some of the men, the veterans probably, tried to fend off the enemy. Eventually the screams were silenced, the sound of resistance faded. Just the thunder of the hooves remained; even that died away, and was replaced by the sound of shouting, cheering and laughing as the raiders looted the village. Not knowing what to do, Caius lay by his dead brother, head down, trembling, not daring to move for fear of discovery. He prayed to all the gods to keep him safe, to keep the mist around him, to not let the raiders find him.

Time seemed to become irrelevant, and Caius lay there terrified; he urinated where he lay, unwilling to even stir a muscle. After what seemed like an age, he heard the rumble of the horse's hooves again; the sound built and gathered and grew in volume. The snorting and the panting of the horses above the rumble grew in volume, as the raiders careered across the fields, passing within a few feet of him, covering him and Tiberius with clods of earth kicked up in the wake of the raiding party. Silence settled around him, it seemed to cover him like a blanket; not even the birds were singing their early morning songs.

Slowly, very slowly he raised his head and peered across the fields, keeping an ear open for the slightest sound of riders. Nothing. He saw that the mist had lifted; the early morning sun lay clear above the horizon, and Caius reckoned he must have lain in the field for well over an hour, more likely two, for the sun to be so high. Tentatively he pushed himself to his feet. A bird started to sing in the trees to his left; one by one others joined in, but it sounded muted and hesitant, as if the birds themselves were wary of the raiders' return.

Caius looked towards his village.

His home.

Smoke billowed above the stockade; his friends and acquaintances lay dead in the field. Or were they? A sudden urgency took him, and he raced to-and-fro across the fields, shaking the bodies, but alas, they were all dead. He persisted, working his way back towards the village until he came across a man he vaguely knew. He was on his back, a spear like the one that had killed Tibby lodged in his chest; blood trickled from the side of his mouth, but he was breathing. The sound was erratic and noisy and filled with awful gurgling sounds. Caius knelt beside him and said quietly, "Marcus?"

The man's eyes opened wide, and he grabbed at Caius with a bloody hand. He uttered some words which Caius couldn't understand at first, but then he understood; he was asking if the raiders had gone. "They're gone Marcus, they're gone." The injured man nodded, coughed and spayed Caius with blood. "I'll get help Marcus, I will come back, I promise!"

With that he jumped up and ran towards the village, yelling out for help. He ran past more bodies, none of them moving, several without heads, contorted in the moment of death. He ran in through the village gates. Smoke whirled around him; then the wind cleared it away and he was left staring at what remained of his home. It seemed to him that all of the buildings were on fire. Bodies lay in the street, but there were people alive, some tending to the wounded, some wailing over loved ones; young men, old men, women, and children wandering around aimlessly, looking dazed and confused. He called out for help, then called out for anyone to answer. He wandered into the main street between the houses. He saw Flavius, a veteran legionary who had returned home last Autumn. He half sat up against a wall, his intestines spilled out over his legs, blood staining his chest and legs and the dust around him. He had tried to fight; Caius saw the sword lying next to him, bloodied, so at least he had managed to inflict some harm before they cut him down. Someone bumped into him; it was one of the village councillors, Gallus.

"Gallus!" cried Caius. "Come quick, Marcus is badly hurt, he needs help." But the councillor just pushed himself away and fled down the street.

More people were gradually coming out of the houses: the Superior Magistrate, Lucius, a priest, and a small band of armed men had gathered in front of the Village Forum, grandly named, but nothing more than an open place for the market, with a couple of cheap statues a long-forgotten general had left there. People were starting to gather, and voices were starting to grow in volume and anger.

Caius rushed into the crowd and yelled out, "Help, Marcus is out in the fields, he needs help; can someone please help him?"

"There are many who need help ... Caius isn't it?" said Lucius, "but we will do what we can." He turned to one of the men and said something to him. The man grabbed Caius and said, "Show me where your friend is."

"He's not my friend, but I know him." They ran out to where Marcus lay, but it was too late; the lifeless eyes stared at the sky, and all Caius could do was look down at the dead man. He stood there for a while, not knowing what to do. Then he walked out back to the fields and found Tiberius again.

Tiberius has been a well-known figure in the village. The brothers had lived together for the last five years after the death of their father. Mother had died giving birth to Tiberius. The three of them had been as close a family as possible. Father owned some land outside the village which they tilled and worked to sustain themselves and they had extra most years to sell at market. Father always went to the market, but he never took his boys, didn't want to risk them being stolen by bandits. But then he had got sick. Nothing seemed to work. The village healers tried their best, the priests came and prayed , even some visiting aesthetic monks tried their best, but nothing seemed to help. The lump and the pain grew, and, in the end, he had pleaded with his eldest son to end it. Caius had sent Tiberius out to the fields that day. He had not wanted Tiberius to be there. At the end of the day, he told his brother that Father had had to go away to get better and had left them in charge of his land. Tiberius had asked every day since then, "When will Father be back?".

"Soon Tibby, soon.".

After that day, Caius had been very protective of Tiberius. If he caught anyone sniggering about his simpleton brother, it normally ended in scuffles and broken noses. Caius worked the fields like many, but he was young and enjoyed good health and he was strong from the physical labour he did every day. Soon everyone agreed that Tibby was not the village idiot, because Caius said so. Eventually, everyone came to love the big simple man, who was always polite, always asking questions and above all always wanted to know when he would see his father again.

He knelt down beside his brother, tears welling up in his eyes. "Can you see Father now Tibby?" he asked quietly.

After a while he turned and headed back into the village. As he walked, he wiped his face, ashamed of the tears. You're no wailing woman he snapped at himself. As he walked, his grief turned slowly to a low simmering anger. Somebody would pay for this. Somehow , someway he would get his revenge on the barbarians who did this.

As he entered the village again, he could see that the people had gathered by the forum. The crowd was growing and as he approached Caius heard grumblings and muttering aplenty.

As he approached the forum, Lucius was talking. "From what we can tell, they were Goths, probably from Alaric's army; Sextus here said he recognised their dress and weapons from when he served." He pointed to a stocky, muscled, weather-beaten man of about forty years old. Caius knew of him but had never spoken to him.

"Where are the legions to defend us?" asked someone.

"I do not know," said Lucius honestly.

"How can they be here?" asked another.

"They've taken the entire grain store, and most of the livestock," yelled an old man.

"They took my son!" cried a distraught woman.

"Do not the Goths live hundreds of miles away?"

"Why are they here?"

"Has the empire fallen? Is the emperor dead?" The voices rose in concern and pitch, fear driving people's imaginations.

"Please try to calm down, please calm down," pleaded Lucius. "No, the Empire has not fallen; we met with the councillors from the town only last week. Taxes are being paid, roads are being repaired."

"But no soldiers!" Voices rose in protest. "We pay our taxes! Where are the legions to defend us?"

Lucius looked around helplessly, as confused as the crowd. Someone called out, "Someone needs to go to Larissa and speak to the authorities! Raise the Alarm! Get help, stop this happening to other villages and towns!"

"You should go, Lucius, as leader of the village!" said Agricola, the baker.

"Don't be stupid," said another. "The roads will be full of Goths, he'll be killed; then who will rule the village council?"

"I can think of a few people who'd a better job than Lucius," said a tall thin man, but he was shouted down by several woman, and the

122

situation seemed to be on the verge of descending into chaos, when Caius heard himself say "I'll go." The voices around him continued unabated, so he said it louder. "I'll go!"

Those nearest him paused and the silence spread.

A third time Caius said, "I'll go." He looked around at the faces. "I don't know how to get to Larissa, but if someone can guide me, I'll go and raise the alarm, and get help. There is nothing for me here now. They killed Tiberius."

A woman called Junia, a neighbour and friend of Caius who was nearby, burst into tears when she heard Caius' words. "Oh, my poor Tibby!" she cried. Caius put his arm around her.

"I'll guide you," said a voice. It was Sextus, a veteran soldier. "They killed my old *optio*, Flavius." He pointed back to where Flavius lay dead against the house. "I will make them pay for that!" He looked at the Magistrate.

Lucius nodded and said, "Agreed, the two of you will have a better chance of making it through than a large group. Stay away from the roads, and may the gods speed you."

Without further ado, Sextus grabbed Caius' arm and led him away from the crowd and towards the stables, where the village horses were communally housed. "Go and pack your things. You'll need a blanket and warm clothes for the nights, something to carry water in and food for a day couple of days. I'll meet you back here in half an hour; be quick." With that Sextus spun away into the swirling smoke and Caius was left wondering what in heaven's name he had got himself into.

Chapter 19

The Consistory, Constantinople, 17th April 396 AD

The consistory was in session, the emperor present. They were meeting in the throne room, and the topic of the hour was Alaric. Arcadius sat on the throne, eyes half closed. Two large palace guards stood just behind the throne, Eutropius stood on a step below the emperor, to his right. Aurelianus, who was one of the *illustrii* present, wondered if he was dozing or awake; he could never tell.

Abundantius was finishing off his request for a military expedition to confront Alaric in Greece. "And so, Imperator, due to the ferocity of the enemy and the lack of sufficient military in place, I propose that we raise an expeditionary force to confront, battle and expel Alaric. This should be done with the utmost urgency; we should depart the *praesentalis* within thirty days."

General Timasius raised his hand to speak, the second Abundantius finished. The Urban Prefect, the senior senator in the consistory and acting as the de facto leader of the meeting, representing the emperor, acknowledged him. "I fully support this venture. With the greatest respect to you, Imperator, your father would have already been leading his army to meet the Goths." He held up his hand, as the sleepy emperor shifted uncomfortably in his seat. "Merely that perhaps the advice you have been given has not been the best." The old general looked pointedly at Eutropius with cold eyes. "I've sounded out the senate and there is an overwhelming majority of support for action as soon as possible!"

Hosius, the *Magister Officiorum*, raised his hand to speak, and the Urban Prefect acknowledged him. "Gentlemen, whilst the noble generals have been very eloquent on the matter, the simple fact is, we do not have the resources or the trained men to meet and take on Alaric; my spies and scouts have identified the barbarians to number in excess of sixty thousand, we cannot raise an army big enough to defeat that size of army! I thought that was obvious to all in this room?"

There were nods of the head around the room. Timasius and Abundantius both made noises to counter the statement, but instantly some raised hands, waving papers to attract attention of the Urban Prefect, and they were ignored.

"Senator Eutychainus."

"I have to agree with my friend the *Magister Officiorum,*" said Eutychainus. He was a podgy, balding senator, with a tanned complexion, given to pacing backwards and forwards. "The troops who have returned with General Gainas are in no sense ready to embark on a campaign against a large and experienced enemy who have probably entrenched themselves in Greece by now. We should all recall that it was our Imperator's father who negotiated the arrangement with Alaric's people, in order that peace may be found in the empire, and to allow time for the legions to regroup and retrain. Diplomacy, gentlemen, is often better than war, and I recommend that we send emissaries to Alaric to request terms. We have money, gentlemen; we do not have trained armies."

Aurelian smiled inwardly. Eutychainus was a pragmatist for sure. The senator was known for his belief that words were preferable to weapons. Abundantius was not impressed and snapped impatiently, "Are you suggesting that we offer to pay off these barbarians?"

Eutychainus shook his head and said, "Not at this moment, I am simply saying that we need to find out what Alaric really wants."

"He wants legitimacy within the Empire," said Eutropius from his position by the emperor, a position he seldom left now when the young Imperator was in public. "He wants supplies, he wants gold, and he wants a legitimate place in the Roman Army. He wants to be *Magister Militum*, I believe."

"Humph!" Timasius snorted. "The last thing we need is another barbarian *Magister*."

"General Frivitta is an honourable and loyal servant of the empire, as is our General Gainas," replied Eutropius.

Timasius bristled at the words. "I'm fully aware of both the generals' competence, they are at least true roman soldiers, even if they were born barbarian. At least they don a toga once in a while for senate appearances. Alaric is nothing more than a rampaging animal, who must be stopped!"

"What does the Praetorian Prefect think?" asked Eutropius.

Caesarius stepped forward. His curly hair was dark, his brown eyes alert. He had stayed quiet during the discussions. Now he cleared his throat and said, "I have deliberated with my staff and sought the advice of some of my governors over the past weeks, as I presumed this option would be looked at. All I can say is, personally, I would relish the chance to be able to mount an army fit to challenge Alaric, if only to bring him to the negotiating table. But looking at available tax revenues and discussing it with the *Comes Sacrarum Largitionum*," he nodded to the finance minister, Count John, who dutifully nodded back. "I cannot see how we can raise any size of force that would succeed. The army General Gainas brought back is still not properly provisioned and is in the process of being fully trained; to send it too early would be to send it to its slaughter. However," he continued holding up his hand to stop interruption, "we could put together an expeditionary force, made up of mobile cavalry only. These could get between the cities, providing warning and act as a deterrent to smaller bands of Goths attacking smaller targets."

"The people of Greece are being slaughtered while we do nothing!" said Abundantius.

Before Caesarius could reply, Hosius interrupted. "They are indeed, General, but from the reports I hear, only those that fight back. Alaric is not stupid; he's raiding and taking the easy targets. The latest messages say he has bypassed several cities with significant defences. He cannot afford losses either. He is causing massive disruption, yes, but it is not catastrophic, yet. I urge patience and agree with my colleague, a possible diplomatic overture is preferable." He indicated Eutychainus.

The emperor coughed. All the eyes in the room turned to him, expecting him to speak, but he merely beckoned to Eutropius, who engaged in a whispered conversation with the young ruler. A general buzz arose in the room as consistory members discussed the policy proposed by Abundantius. Then Eutropius stepped forward and said, "Our Imperator has decreed that Alaric is not to be engaged by any Roman forces until the consistory is unanimous in its belief that they will defeat Alaric's hoard. That is the decision for now. Let us now move on to the subject of renovation of the Constantine Walls, a matter raised by senator Aurelianus." Eutropius nodded at the Urban Prefect who said, "Senator Aurelianus!"

Aurelian stepped forward and began his proposed renovation of the city walls, which had been put forward by the procurator Anthemius. He had challenged the younger man to put a proposal before the consistory members as a test of his ability to argue a point. It probably would not get past. The amounts involved were too large, with the threat of Alaric receding, and no discernible threat from the East, but it had given Anthemius a challenge, which the procurator had excelled at. He glanced at the emperor again, and again he had sloped back into the throne, eyes drooping.

Interlude

Gerung was tidying his bunk area. "Well, we know one thing for sure after today," he said. He was stacking his uniforms and belongings neatly on the floor so he could clean the storage shelves.

"What?" replied Gadaric, peeing into the pot in the corner of their room.

"The boy is a fucking waste of space."

"By 'the boy', I presume you mean our illustrious emperor?" Gadaric buttoned himself up then walked back to his bunk and lay down. His space was immaculate, and he kept it that way, unlike Gerung's, which was normally a chaotic mess until he got tired of it. Today he had got tired of it.

"You have the most powerful men there talking about all kinds of important stuff and he falls asleep." Gerung snorted.

"How do you know he fell asleep" asked Gadaric, closing his own eyes.

"I heard him snoring."

"Bullshit."

"I fucking did, it was a little wimpy snore. Like a little girl, but it was definitely a snore." Gerung had cleaned his shelves and was putting his collection of knives and belts back onto them.

"How do you know what his snoring sounds like? Have you slept with him? He could have been clearing this throat."

"Definitely a snore." Putting the last items on shelves, Gerung sat on the edge of his bed. "Only the Empress sleeps with him," he said absently. "I wonder what it's like?"

"What, sleeping with the emperor? Didn't know you were that way inclined?" laughed Gadaric.

"No, dickhead, I wonder what it's like sleeping with the Empress. She's pretty stunning. That would be something." The Goth lay back on his bed and gazed up at the ceiling.

"What about Octavia?"

"What about her?"

"Isn't she stunning?"

"Oh sure … sure. But I have to pay her."

"Why wouldn't you have to pay the Empress? That's about the only way I can ever see her sleeping with you. Not that you could afford her."

Gerung chuckled too. "Well, all I can say is the emperor is a lucky, lucky bastard being married to her, but I pity her in bed; he probably falls asleep on that job too!"

Chapter 20

Praetorian Prefect of the East, Constantinople, 17th April 396 AD

Gainas, with Euthymius shadowing him closely, stormed into the chambers where Caesarius held office and growled "Where is he?" at the first person he saw. A terrified serf pointed with a shaking finger and wide eyes to the imposing, elegant, carved wooden double doors either side of which stood a palace guard. The doors were open and Gainas could see the three small steps that led to the raised floor inside. He strode up to the doors, but guards blocked his passage with crossed spears.

"Move aside now!" bellowed Gainas, the room behind him fell into a hush. The guards held their position, Gainas and Euthymius both tensed and reached for their sword pommels, but before anything else could happen, Caesarius' called from inside the inner chamber.

"Let them through."

Without waiting the barbarian general barged aside the two guards, passed through the doors, and climbed the steps.

The inner sanctum was long but there were only two people in it. Both sat at a long, heavily built and intricately carved wooden table. Caesarius himself sat at the far end furthest from the doors. A clerk sat to his left on the long side of the table. There was an empty chair to his right.

Gainas paused and gazed around at the room. He had not been in here before. The light came from three large candelabras above which held a multitude of candles, the light bright and steady. The walls were stone and painted with scenes depicting Christ at various stages of his life. Behind Caesarius the wall was one large array of pigeonholes each filled with one or more rolled-up scrolls, and in front of Caesarius on the dark wood tabletop, lay a host of wax tablets and papyrus and parchment documents. Close to the two men were a number of gold-plated ink wells with feather quills resting in them and scattered amongst the documents Gainas could see etching markers for the wax, binding ribbons for the scrolls and the wooden umbilicus which scrolls would be attached to. Beside the clerk was an open bronze box containing seals used to stamp and authenticate imperial orders.

Having taken in the scene, Gainas walked around the table to where Caesarius sat and smacked a parchment onto the polished desk surface, the clerk. "What is the meaning of this?" he snapped.

The prefect didn't flinch; he gently put down the quill pen he was holding, reached across and took the document and made a show of reading it, squinting, and holding it at arm's length. "Is it not clear, General?"

"Don't play games with me! You know what I mean. What is going on?"

"I should say nothing is going on, General, which is exactly what the emperor wants, at least today. We are to do nothing; we are not to engage with Alaric in Greece."

"He's ransacked Larissa's food supplies, we've had messages that his men are stealing grain and livestock from other villages and taking the people as slaves, and you're going to let him continue to do this?"

"General, we don't have a lot of choice, do we?" Caesarius looked up at the Goth general sternly, but Gainas thought he saw some understanding in the prefect's stare. "Despite what you and I both would like to see happen, we do not have the numbers of men necessary to engage Alaric. You know that, as well as I. Those men we do have are either untrained or involved in the re-deployments of the armies in and around the capital, to ensure that Thrace, Thessaly, and Anatolia are impregnable to any threat, East or West. You are working on that yourself, I believe?"

"So, we're supposed to sit here and do nothing?"

"No, General, you're supposed to be getting on and doing your job," said a familiar voice from the doorway. He turned and saw Eutropius glaring at him at the top of the three stairs. By his side stood the small, dark-skinned boy. No one said anything as Eutropius slowly walked the length of the huge table, the boy in tow.

Eutropius sat in the empty chair. The boy just stood next to him. The chamberlain reached forward and took a blank wax tablet and etching tool and gave it to the child who immediately sat down cross-legged and began to draw on the tablet.

Then Eutropius looked up at Gainas and said "We have already discussed this. The emperor, the prefect, and the *Magister Militum* are all in agreement that we ignore Alaric for now."

"And when was this decided?"

"This morning, whilst you were reviewing the re-deployment arrangements for Thrace." Eutropius absentmindedly patted the boy on the head.

Caesarius spoke in his clear and practiced voice. "The General has a point, Chamberlain, some kind of show of force would deter Alaric and we could steer him clear of the major cities, make it not worth his while to attack them. He has a formidable force but cannot afford to take heavy casualties."

"If the emperor were to make me *Magister Militum*, I would put an end to the troublemaker Alaric before the end of the year …" said Gainas humping the table.

"We've already debated this point too General. We're covering old ground," said Eutropius and turning to Caesarius he said. "You made a similar point in the consistorium this morning did you not? As did Generals Timasius and Abundantius, and you were overruled by the emperor, who wisely pointed out that we must secure the defences of

New Rome as a top priority. We cannot launch attacks without a secure base of operations and without properly trained and organised troops. You yourself admitted as much to me just a few weeks back, General. The emperor has made it clear, no troops to be sent from the *praesentalis* to Greece until they are ready, and we are certain that no other threats are imminent."

"Meanwhile Greece burns," snapped Gainas.

"The General has a point," agreed Caesarius looking pointedly at Eutropius.

"There are detachments of soldiers in Greece; they are not powerless," retorted Eutropius, clearly displeased at the general's comment and with the prefect taking his side. "They will defend the cities and the arms depots and do what they can to limit the damage Alaric is doing. Our job, gentlemen, is to get the Eastern Roman Army back to strength and to make it a fighting force once again feared by all. Now I suggest you get to it."

With that he stood, took the small boy's hand, almost lifting him from the floor and walked swiftly from the chamber, at such a pace that the child had to run beside him to keep up. As they went down the steps and through the doors , the boy glanced back and gave his small wave.

Gainas turned to Caesarius. "So, what are we going to do?"

Caesarius sighed. "General, we can do nothing. As long as that creature has the emperor's ear and controls what he sees and hears, we are helpless to do anything else. I suggest you focus on getting the army re-deployments organised and completed as soon as possible. Then we can get the armies up to speed and get them into Greece."

"How can you just sit there and do nothing?"

"I'm not doing nothing, General! I'm running the entire administration of the Eastern Empire here, which means collecting taxes to pay your men! Without me, you would have no army to train, or even mercenaries to hire." Caesarius signed and looked at the Goth and smiled. "We are all doing our bit, and I would remind you that I happen to agree with your point of view, and I have ordered Alaric to not enter Greece. An order he has plainly ignored. I'm on your side on this one. But at this moment in time, there is nothing else we can do."

Gainas took a deep breath and nodded. "You're right, my apologies for my words, I meant no disrespect, I am … frustrated. That's all."

Caesarius nodded "You are not the only one, General. Now, if will excuse me, I have an Empire to run, and to add to it all, my personal secretary has gone missing." He indicated the empty seat. "He was very good, and I can't seem to find him anywhere, so if you want to make yourself useful you could help me by sending out search parties into the city to find him! Good day." And with that, the prefect picked up his quill and returned to his writing.

Gainas, seeing that their discussion had been terminated, spun around, and walked back down the steps out through the outer chambers with the crowd of clerks and officials, Euthymius clearing the way ahead of him. The meeting has been as productive as he had guessed it would be. Namely, not at all. But now Gainas knew what he had to do. He had to contact Stilicho.

Back in his chamber, Caesarius continued to write the latest clarification of orders for the Urban Prefect of the city reminding the official of the ban on weapons being carried within the city walls. He glanced across and saw the boy's tablet. He reached across for it and saw the scribblings. It looked like he had been trying to draw a person, a woman perhaps. His mother perhaps? For a few seconds, the prefect mused on the boy and wondered on his relationship with the eunuch. Something to investigate, but not right now.

Chapter 21

Central Greece, 20th April 396 AD

Night had fallen. The man was escorted to Alaric's tent in the heart of the baggage train, the core of his army and the centre of the Gothic world. The man trembled; he was held firmly by the arms by two huge Goth warriors. He was searched, none too gently, for weapons; but he carried nothing but a small knife for self-defence, which he barely knew how to use. The guards took it from him anyhow.

He had approached the camp slowly, under a flag of truce; he had not known how else to do it. So far, the barbarians had honoured the flag, but now he was in the proverbial lion's den, about to meet the most feared man in all of Greece. He had heard rumours of the man in Constantinople. His warriors had briefly laid siege to the city, but had not persisted, they had turned and plunged into the heart of the empire, causing havoc wherever they went.

It was said that Alaric was blessed and cursed. Blessed because he never fell under the power of anyone. Not the emperor, not Stilicho, and yet he was cursed to wander the Empire, homeless and friendless. Some said he and Stilicho were in league with each other, to try to force the emperors to grant him lands and positions; others said he was just a vile monster, rabid and mad for blood, incensed and vengeful for the wrongs he claimed had been done to him and his people by the Romans.

He stepped into the tent and saw a crowd of barbarian's generals around a stout wooden table; they had their heads down, examining maps. One of the guards coughed to attract attention, and one of the generals turned and looked at the visitor. He had a round, handsome face with a short, neat beard, moustache, and the typical long hair of his race, tied back and braided. Barking an order which the visitor couldn't understand immediately, the tent cleared, and the man found himself alone with the round-faced warrior, and one guard who still grasped his left arm firmly.

The warrior said something in the language of the Goths. The man shook his head and indicated he didn't understand. Then the barbarian spoke in perfect Greek. "You're not Goth, are you?"

The man shook his head. He was surprised that this heretic could speak his language. When he didn't reply, the man gave a small smile and then asked, "Why are you here?"

The messenger stammered over his words, feeling foolish as he did so, "I've come … to … to … deliver a letter to K-K-King …King Alaric."

"You can give the letter to me." said the round-faced Goth.

"I can… can only give it to your King," insisted the man, trembling.

"As I said, you can give it to me."

The man's eyes opened wide, and he looked into the kindly face of the scourge of the Romans.

"You look surprised?" said Alaric, smiling with genuine humour.

"I was expecting … I'm sorry … your greatness …" stammered the man.

"Greatness?" laughed the King. "I'm hardly great, am I? King of a baggage train, at most. Perhaps you were expecting a huge fire-breathing monster; or a brute feasting on Roman babies, perhaps?" He stared hard at the visitor and held out his hand. The man stared at it foolishly.

"The letter?" prompted Alaric.

Cursing himself for his witlessness, the man reached inside his tunic and brought out the bundle he had been given by the chamberlain in Constantinople. Alaric took the package, unwrapped it and turned away, holding the letter close to the candles illuminating the table. The barbarian king grimaced as he read the words.

Greetings to you, King Alaric, this communication is for the honoured and legitimate ruler of the Gothic peoples who travel through Roman lands in Greece. I write this with the full authority granted to me by the Emperor Arcadius, Imperator of all the Eastern Empire.

You may avail yourself of supplies and weapons as you see fit in the lands of Thessaly and Southern Greece. Local reluctance may be countered with sufficient force to ensure your people do not suffer, but neither must the local populace be left to starve or endure needlessly.

You should not overtly exert your presence in Greece in any fashion that may enrage the populace to the degree that a deployment of Roman legions from the West, under the leadership of our mutual foe, will be seen as preferable to your continued presence in the area.

If you abide by these terms, your bid for lands and for position will be looked upon favourably when a change of administration occurs in New Rome, and no punitive expeditionary forces will be launched against you by the Emperor of the East.

You should not respond directly to this message; your actions alone will be sufficient notification of your acceptance. I have spies observing you.

This message must be destroyed; confirm with the courier who I am and then kill him. Failure to do so will negate the terms of our understanding.

Alaric sighed and looked at the man. It was a shame. He was young and seemed scared but eager. He was probably some adolescent ambitious senator's son, or someone trying to make his name. He forced a smile and said kindly, "Who gave this to you?"

The man took out the token that the chamberlain had given him and handed it to Alaric.

137

Alaric nodded; he could read the inscription. There was no name, but the inscription stated the office holder was the *Praepositus Sacri Cubiculi*. And everyone knew who that was. He had heard the name and knew of him by reputation. He smiled again at the visitor. "Thank you for bringing this to me, you may go. You will not reveal my people's location to anyone. Is that understood?"

The man nodded and turned; Alaric spoke in Goth tongue to the guard, who nodded his understanding. The king turned back to the letter and held it over the flame until the fire had consumed the message. He accepted Eutropius' terms; he would be a fool not to. He had been given free rein in Greece, as long as he didn't scorch the earth, until Eutropius was in a position to grant him his long-standing demands of land and title. It was glimmer of hope at last, or at least a start.

But it was a shame about the messenger.

Chapter 22

Larissa, Greece 25th April 396 AD

It had been an exhausting ten-day trip, but evening saw Caius and Sextus in sight of Larissa. The first three days of their trip had been the most dangerous as Sextus guided them through the countryside, avoiding Alaric's Army, his raiding parties, and his scouting parties. They had to lead their horses through woods and thickets and along dried-up riverbeds, away from the skylines. At night-time they could light no fire for fear of detection, and they shivered throughout the cold, clear darkness. After that, things had become a little easier, as they had travelled out of the range of the Goth army. But to do so, Sextus had to head further south and west than he wanted, which had added more time to their journey. Caius became restless, worried they were taking too long to raise the alarm, and suggested they could go faster on the roads, but the veteran refused to change his cautious approach, and Caius was now grateful the ex-soldier had ignored his entreaties.

They had passed by Cynus, Opus, through the narrows at Thermopylae; the barracks there was deserted. They had ridden past and through the smaller settlements of Lamia and Narthakion, where they had encountered scenes of desolation. Fields of blackened grass, abandoned buildings, dead livestock being pecked at by buzzards and the occasional dead body. The villages and towns were quiet. They stopped at a few taverns and stables at night and spoken to the locals. They heard the same story over and over again. The Goth had raided the lands, stripped the food from the fields, looted the grain stores, rode off with their livestock and in several cases with women and children too. When they told their hosts they were heading to Larissa to raise the alarm, the people shook their heads and said they had done the same, but no troops had come. They both grew more despondent as they progressed, their mood darkened, though Caius tried to remain positive and hopeful.

Tomorrow they would be at Larissa and Caius would implore the city elders to send troops to drive the Goths out of Greece. Sextus was much more pessimistic; he growled that if troops had been available, they would already have been sent. Something was wrong, he said. Caius hoped Sextus was wrong himself.

All he had known was the empire. Life had been good; the village was not wealthy, but they paid their taxes and every so often, for as many years as the elders could remember, soldiers would visit the village on the way to somewhere. It was interesting to hear about Constantinople and other faraway places. To Caius the emperor was an almost mythical figure. He imagined him riding on a golden chariot, pulled by white horses through streets of white marble and gold as the crowds cheered. How he would love to see the emperor and those wide, white, and golden streets someday. He had never been outside the village in his whole life. He had seen the walls of Larissa late that afternoon and they looked huge to him, even at a distance, but Sextus said Constantinople dwarfed Larissa. Caius had trouble imagining any place that large.

So tomorrow they would find the city decurions and tell them of the raids, and maybe they could go back home to the village to help repair the houses, replant the crops, and hope to make it through to the autumn with some kind of harvest. And maybe some troops would come to protect them.

They arose early the next morning, dew twinkling on the grass and trees around them in the low sunlight. Through the tree branches above them, the sky was a deep clear azure blue, streaked with wispy clouds. The air was cool and refreshing and the horses breathe steamed in it.

140

As they joined the road towards Larissa, they merged into a steady stream of people. There were old men pulling carts loaded with what looked like household possessions. Some carts were pulled by mules led by men, these carts had women and children sat in them, surrounded by blankets, cloths and kitchen household items which rattled as they passed by. There were groups of families, those who plainly could not afford a cart or a mule, walking close together, they carried bundles of clothing and carried jugs and amphoras with them.

"Who are all these people?" asked Caius.

"They're like us," replied Sextus, ", they're headed for Larissa, for help or refuge I guess" They urged their mounts onto the road and picked up a good pace overtaking the walkers and the mule-hauled carts.

Caius had just about got the hang of riding a horse. His family was too poor to own one ,so he had never been properly taught, but Sextus, for all his gruffness, was a good teacher and, after they had cleared the danger of Alaric's army, they had spent a couple of days with Sextus taking him through the rudiments of how to ride. He was still not confident, but he could stop, start, and turn his mount and get it to run full speed if need be.

Sextus looked worried; he kept glancing around, to either side and behind them.

"What's up?" asked Caius.

"Look at them," said Sextus indicating the men and women working the fields.

"So?"

"They look like they're trying to plant more crops. It's very late for that!" Then he pointed ahead. "And that looks like trouble ahead!"

Ahead lay the city.

Caius marvelled at the walls of Larissa. He had heard stories from the veterans of towns like Larissa, with walls and churches and forums. Sextus had been to Constantinople once and said that it was impossible to imagine how huge the city was, how magnificent the palace was. "Imagine in your mind what luxury and paradise would be like," Caius remembered Sextus telling a group of villagers at the tavern one night after harvesting last year. "I can tell you; the sights of New Rome are a thousand times more magnificent than anything you can imagine."

Last night he had asked how Larissa compared to the capital, and the old soldier had laughed and said, "When you see the town tomorrow, you will think it is huge. But I can tell you that Constantinople is as to Larissa as Larissa is to our village."

If that were true and Sextus was not exaggerating, as solders were wont to do, then the city must be truly vast, because Larissa looked enormous as they approached; all he could see were the walls, and the roofs of a few taller buildings. There were what looked like guards atop of them. To Caius the stone walls looked imposing and impenetrable, unlike the feeble wooden stockade of his own home; the people must feel safe inside, he thought.

Then he saw that the gates were shut. And outside the gates was a large crowd. It looked a huge mass of people to Caius; larger than any crowd he had ever seen. He had no idea that many people could gather into one place.

"What's happening?" he asked.

"Not sure." replied Sextus. He pulled up his horse. And Caius did likewise and watched his companion studying the scene intently.

"They've barred the gates, which probably means they can't take any more people inside. We'll never get in that way. We need to get in another way."

"Do you know another way?"

142

"Luckily for you I do. Follow me. Stay close."

Sextus pulled on his horse's reins and guided the beast off of the road, heading out over the fields, riding over bare and patchy ground stripped of its produce. Any fields that were being tended, they skirted around the edges. The workers in the fields looked up as they passed by, some cursing in their direction, some just staring blankly wondering who these new intruders were. They headed toward the Eastern side of the city where stood a large and dense grove of orange trees. They entered the orchard slowing down the horses to a slow walk as they weaved their way between the trunks. The trees were ancient and gnarled but the air was cool and still in the shade of the canopy of leaves. They plodded slowly and soon came on a narrow dusty path which they followed through the trunks, the early morning sunlight behind them slivered through the branches, speckling the ground with shadows and light. Eventually through the trees they saw the pale brown of the walls of the city, and there in front of them was a small but sturdy looking door. It too was shut, but unlike to the south, there were no crowds here surging and pressing to get in.

"How did you know about this?" asked Caius.

"This is not the first time I've been here. This is used by city workers to get out to the orchard when it's picking time. The door is normally locked the rest of the year. Hey up there!" Sextus yelled up to the ramparts.

There was no answer, so Sextus yelled again. Then he dismounted, took a stone, banged it against the door and then yelled again.

"Hey up there!"

There was still no answer, so Sextus picked up some small stones and started throwing them up and over the ramparts which were at least ten to fifteen feet above their heads. The veteran was strong and had an impressive throw. Caius dismounted and joined in. He felt like a

143

naughty boy throwing stones at neighbour's house. Eventually their efforts were rewarded.

"Stop that ! Who are you?" came an annoyed shout from above. Sextus and Caius squinted up and saw guards on the battlements looking down at them; two had arrows aimed at them.

Sextus dismounted and called back up, "My name is Sextus Cassius Velus, this is my friend Caius Plautius Paulinus; we come from near Cynus, to the south. We must see the city decurions! Our village was attacked by Goths, we are here to plead for help to defend our lands."

"Good luck with that!" came the reply, accompanied by laughter.

"Why do you say that?" called up Caius.

"Take a look around, oh visitors from Cynus," said the guard in a mocking tone. "Do you see blossoming trees, fields of wheat and barley starting to push through? Healthy, plump young livestock, just ready for the slaughter?" He indicated the nearly deserted fields, where only a few people worked, the unattended trees.

"The barbarians stripped the city of food, they took the horses, the oxen, so we can't work the fields. The people are hungry and ill; many are too weak to work. There will be a harvest, as we planted in time, but who knows how many of us will live to work it!"

"We still need to see the decurions," insisted Caius. "Someone needs to raise the alarm, tell the emperor what is happening."

The guard sighed and said, "Wait there."

They waited outside the gates for several minutes. Eventually they heard rattling of locks and bolts, the door opened and a *praepositus*, accompanied by two legionaries, stepped out. They stopped a few feet away.

"I'm the commander of the watch. I've been told you wish to see the city Decurions?"

144

"We do," said Caius.

The *praepositus* looked at him. Caius was stocky, of average height, with a broad pair of shoulder and muscular arms from working in the fields year after year from youth. He stood slightly stooped. The *praepositus* looked at Sextus too. He had the same stocky build, was slightly taller than Caius, but stood with a straight back and head held high; he looked back at the *praepositus* directly.

"You a veteran?" he asked Sextus.

"13th Legion."

"Adrianople?"

Sextus nodded.

"Bastard Goths! I hate them. They came through a few weeks back, stripped the town of all its food. We had no choice but to give into Alaric's demands, he tricked his way in; the citizens would have been slaughtered."

"No food at all?" asked Sextus morosely.

The *praepositus* nodded "Oh they left us some, but barely enough to feed the town for the next two months, so some people are out there planting more grain to try to bolster the supply in the Autumn. It's a desperate hope, some people will starve for sure."

"Where are the legions?" asked Caius.

The *praepositus* looked at the field hand, then back at Sextus, who remained stony-faced. He spoke impatiently, like he was speaking to a fool. "There are no legions, son; there are a few cohorts scattered around the area, we've one here in the city. We can keep Alaric out of the main cities, but we've not enough men to defend every single town and village."

"They killed my brother!" burst out Caius. "Why won't anybody do anything?"

The *praepositus'* face softened at the outburst, and he regretted his harsh tone. In a softer voice he said, "Son, I'm sorry, God rest your brother's soul, but there are many people in the same situation. We've got a stream of people coming from villages into the town for protection as the Goths pass through, many telling stories just as you have. Villages raided, woman and children taken, food and drink ransacked. I'm sorry, but if we go up against Alaric we will be slaughtered, and all we'd have done is weakened the already weak defences."

Caius shook his head; this wasn't making any sense. "We pay our taxes to the emperor; he is sworn to defend us!" He looked at Sextus in desperation. "We can't have come all this way for nothing! There must be something we can do."

"I'm sorry, Caius, the *praepositus* is right, we cannot fight such a huge army with the people we have. Perhaps we'd best go home." Sextus sighed, but he suspected that the field hand would not want to do that yet.

Caius was silent for a moment. Then he shook his head. "No, we must tell the emperor what is happening; he must not know that his people are being attacked, we need to tell him. He will help us, I am sure."

The *praepositus* spoke up again, seeing the field hand's distress. "Son, we've already sent messengers to Constantinople, two weeks ago, the day Alaric attacked us. They've not yet returned, but the emperor will know what is happening, and maybe he will send the legions to deal with the Goths soon. "

"I don't care, the more messages he gets and not just from the army, the better, maybe a direct appeal from one of his subjects will help him understand the situation," said Caius.

"You want to petition the emperor?" said Sextus, amazed that this shy farmhand could come up with such an idea.

"Why not, anyone can can't they?" asked Caius.

The *praepositus* frowned "Well, I suppose, yes, they can."

"Well then, that's what I'm going to do. They killed my brother." Caius looked at Sextus. "You don't have to come, Sextus, I'm very grateful to you for helping me so far, but you should go home."

"Caius, you couldn't find your way to the latrine without me to help you; do you honestly think that I would let you go to Constantinople all by yourself?" Sextus laughed. Then he looked at the *praepositus*. "We could do with any supplies you can provide, and we'll carry any messages to the city that you might want to send."

The *praepositus* stared at them both for a period, considering what to do, then he came to a decision.

"You can come in" said the *praepositus* pointing at Sextus, then to Caius he said. "You'll have to wait here with your horses. We can't open the main gates; we cannot risk taking any more people into the city".

Sextus nodded.

"Are you sure, Sextus?" asked Caius.

"Shut up, Caius. I'm coming with you," growled Sextus, then he paused and smiled gently and shrugged. "You've shown guts coming this far, but you would never survive the trip alone. There are brigands and thieves and fraudsters, even slavers along the way." Caius paled as the old veteran talked, but then nodded and said, "I am grateful, Sextus," but the old soldier held up his hand. "You've nothing to be grateful about." He sighed. "Life was getting a little too quiet for me in the old village, if I'm honest; you wanting to head off and save the village gave me the excuse I was looking for. Besides, I'll get to see the palaces and shrines and forums of Constantinople again, something I didn't think

I'd ever do before I died. So, it's me who should be thanking you for shaking me out of my laziness."

He slapped Caius on the back. "You sort out the horses, there is a stream a few hundred paces north and some grazing there too; I'll go try to find some provisions. I'll be back in two hours. We'll stop here tonight and set off at first light." The veteran made to set off, but Caius called out. "Sextus."

"Yes?"

"Thank you."

"I'm sorry about Tiberius … Tibby. He was a nice lad."

Caius nodded, not trusting himself to speak. Sextus spun around and headed into the city with the *praepositus* shutting and locking the door behind them, leaving Caius alone with the horses and his thoughts.

Chapter 23

Sea of Marmara, 2nd May 396 AD

Sigeric was laughing hard as he watched Hunulf rush again to the side of the ship and vomit. The stocky Goth had been ill almost from the moment they had set foot on the ship two days ago. They were now just a day away from Cyzicus, which lay on the southern coast of the Sea of Marmara. Videric wasn't laughing, he rarely did, but there was just a hint of a smile on the otherwise laconic man's face.

"At least that helping went to the fishes that time!" chuckled Sigeric.

"Fuck off, one more smart remark from you and you'll be joining them." snarled Hunulf. Sigeric just laughed louder.

Anthemius could see that the brothers respected Hunulf immensely, and of course that was why they could laugh at his misery without fear. He no doubt would exact some kind of penance from them for their merriment at his expense, even now he glowered at Sigeric and swore again, wiping the flecks of spittle and vomit from his mouth. The big man looked ashen, but he steadied himself and walked, as dignified as he could, back to the ladder that would take him to the lower deck.

"You'd be better off staying up here," said Anthemius. He had never suffered from sea sickness, even in the most violent storm. Hunulf glanced at the procurator, wary that he too was mocking him, but he turned around anyway, and leant on the gunwale next to Anthemius, staring out across the water to the horizon.

In silence they watched the ever-changing surface of the sea; the waves dancing and swirling in a myriad of blues, greens, greys, and whites. The sun was sinking in the West, peering through banks of low clouds, sending shafts of light streaming across the sky and sea.

"Do you think God knew how beautiful sunsets would be when he made the world?" asked Anthemius.

"No idea." said Hunulf.

"You are a Christian right?"

"I guess I am, sir. I've been baptised, but my people believed in many gods until recently. Honestly, I'm not sure what I believe in right now."

"Why do you fight for the empire, then, if you don't believe in the Christian God?"

"Because you pay me to."

"I don't believe you. You're a true believer in the empire, I can tell."

"If you say so, sir."

"I do say so. If you weren't, you'd be out in Greece with Alaric, getting rich on plunder."

"I wouldn't serve under that wanker if he paid me ten times what you do." Hunulf spat into the waves.

"Why not?" asked Anthemius somewhat surprised, "You could get rich very quickly, I'd imagine. You're a good soldier, fast, powerful, I can't imagine Alaric would turn you down."

"He's an arse," said Hunulf tersely.

"Would you care to elaborate?" pressed Anthemius.

Hunulf was silent for a moment, then said quietly. "It's a family feud that goes back many years."

"Go on."

The Goth hesitated at first, appearing reluctant to open up, but then he continued.

"My family come from the Greuthungi. We lived on the steppes but far to the south, so far south that we bordered on the forest around the sea, where the Tervingi lived. When the Huns first came, my people

150

were enslaved by them and forced to fight for them. The Tervingi never lifted a finger to help. Instead, they took over the land our families had farmed for generations and paid tribute to the Huns. Fucking cowards."

"Alaric is a Tervingi?"

"Yes, he's the grandson of the bastard who took my grandfather's land."

"Oh, I see." Anthemius nodded, "What happened to your grandfather?"

"My father told me he escaped from the Huns with his family and made his way to the Danube. I was only a babe at the time. By the time he got to the river, he was old and sick. While we waited for you lot to give us passage across the Danube, he died."

"You have been in the empire all your life?"

"Pretty much." Hunulf nodded.

"That was all a long time ago. Why still the feud?" asked Anthemius.

"Because in those camps by the Danube, the Romans starved us and forced our families to sell their children into slavery for food. It was Alaric's father who acted a slaver, a parasite on his own people! My father challenged him to combat, but instead he betrayed my father to the Romans, who executed him. I was sold into slavery after that." Hunulf paused, he was momentarily back as a boy recalling the fear and loneliness of his childhood. Then he gave a short laugh. "I was lucky though, my owner was a decent enough man in his own way, set me free when I came of age. My brothers weren't so lucky."

"Tough life" Anthemius nodded.

Hunulf continued, "I guess you are right sir, I guess I am a true believer in the empire. It's all I've known, even though you lot screwed my family over, I've worked my way through the ranks of the army, and

151

you've paid me well, and this job as a palace guard is … well can't ask for more."

He spat overboard. "But Alaric's forgotten why our people come into the empire. We wanted your protection from the Huns. Why bite the hand that feeds you? Makes no sense to me. You screwed us over at the Danube. We gave you a spanking at Adrianople, I'd say the score is even. Let bygones be bygones."

"I hear he just wants to have land for his people, and a post in the Imperial Army" said Anthemius.

Hunulf snorted with derision.

"All he is interested in is himself. He wants to be a *proper* Roman general like Gainas that's all. He doesn't care about our people, it's all about him. If I ever met him again, I'd gut him where he stood. Traitorous bastard."

"I don't see many of your fellow countrymen being happy with you if you did that!"

Hunulf didn't reply. He was content now, it seemed, to watch the ruddy sun drop below the low bands of clouds, onto the horizon. The wind was easing as the night approached. Boards creaked as the boat swayed with the rhythm of the sea, and all around them the crew prepared for the night, stowing ropes and equipment. Two sailors had clambered up the mast and were loosening off the linen sail to bring it to bear on the slackening wind.

"I hope the wind doesn't die down altogether," said Anthemius, looking up.

"It won't," said a voice behind them.

They turned and saw the short, fat captain.

"How are you so sure?" asked Hunulf.

"Do I question your competence in your line of work?" asked the captain curtly.

"Sorry I asked," said the Goth, and went back to gazing at the sunset. The captain turned to Anthemius, "We'll be at Cyzicus mid-morning tomorrow; that is for certain."

The procurator studied the captain for a moment. The man had a long, pointed beard and wore a dark red turban wrapped tightly around his head. The harbour master at Constantinople had been fulsome in his recommendation. The man was short tempered, brash, and most definitely Persian, but he was also one of the most accomplished sailors on the sea. At least the harbour master claimed he was. Anthemius suspected the harbour master earned extra coin by promoting the captain and his vessel to would-be passengers.

"Thank you, captain," said Anthemius with a slight bow. Without further comment, but with an annoyed glance at Hunulf's back, the captain walked away. Anthemius saw him take up his favoured place at the high stern of the ship. There he had stood like a statue for the majority of the voyage and now he stood again, surveying the ship, his crew, and the ever-darkening sea around them.

Chapter 24

City of Cyzicus, 2nd May 396 AD

Just as the captain promised, the boat docked at Cyzicus mid-morning. Anthemius was first off of the boat and was met by a *praepositus* and a small squad of around a dozen soldiers.

"Procurator Flavius Anthemius?" asked the soldier.

"That is me."

"I am *Praepositus* Marcus Octavius Probus, reporting as ordered by the *Magister Officiorum*. My men and I are at your command."

Anthemius looked the *praepositus* up and down and liked what he saw. This man plainly took pride in himself, and his men seemed equally well turned out. He hoped the soldiers were as good with their swords as they were with their polishing rags. "Good, then please lead on and escort my men and me to the Mint."

"Sir!" responded Probus, and with that he turned and ordered his men to form a protective guard around the procurator and his Goth bodyguards, and they set off through the throng of people on the dockside into the town.

Cyzicus was a not as big a town compared to the capital, but it was still an impressive metropolis. Two-storey buildings abounded, and the forum with its triumphal column occupied the city centre. The docks were smaller than Constantinople, but they were sturdy and well-built. The street that led from the docks was paved neatly and the shops that lined the docks were every bit as smart and well-stocked as those of the capital. However, there were a few empty shops. The mint's operation had been cut back in the previous year. It was only to be expected that this would affect some other traders. Only two offices now worked issuing coins, most of which were bronze and silver, but it still produced minor amounts of gold solidi every year. It was only a short walk. They passed along the stone-paved main street and then out of the main populated area into a more open space with a single large building, which had its own defensive wall around it.

The Cyzicus Mint.

Anthemius saw the armed guards standing still and stern either side of the gates, which were closed. A small aqueduct fed water to the building from the hills, and the mint had its own outlet and docks. This way, the precious cargo could be much more easily guarded and handled, away from the throng of the city harbour. Only registered cargo boats were allowed to dock there, and they all had specially picked crews, mainly eunuchs, all under the control of the *Comes Sacrarum Largitionum*, Count John, Anthemius' immediate superior.

The group marched smartly up to the gates, which opened as they approached and closed directly they were inside. There in the courtyard waited the procurator of the Cyzicus mint. The man was fat and red-faced, and at least three inches taller than Anthemius. He greeted Anthemius with a curling smile from his thick lips, an attempt at intimidating the visitor. Strictly speaking, the two men were of equal rank, but the size and importance of the Constantinople mint and its location within the great palace, and hence the procurator's proximity to the emperor, gave Anthemius an unspoken seniority, which he planned to make full use of. Anthemius returned the smile but made an effort to appear a little stand-offish. He knew he could trust no one on this mission other than his own bodyguards, certainly until he had found out what under heaven was going on.

"Proculus Veranius Pertacus at your service," said the procurator to Anthemius; his voice was high and slightly rasping. "We had word of your pending arrival two days ago but not why you visit.". The hand he held out in greeting was podgy, the fingers bedecked with gold and silver rings, the wrist draped in gold bracelets. The man smelled of a combination of stale sweat mixed with salts and incense. The resulting odour was slightly nauseating. Anthemius did everything he could to not wrinkle his nose. Reluctantly he took the hand and shook it. It was clammy and greasy. "We need to talk in private, where no one will overhear us.", he said as politely as he could.

The procurator looked mildly surprised at this blunt introduction, but he nodded, looking first at Anthemius' bodyguards then at Anthemius himself. Then he bowed slightly and turned, signalling them to follow him. He waddled more than walked, leading them into the coolness of the mint's extravagantly carved entrance hall, then through plain but brightly lit corridors to a room lined with long wooden shelves. The selves were covered with stacks of documents interspersed with marble and bronze statuettes, all of people engaged in carnal pleasures, Anthemius could not help but notice.

Light came into the room through some tall narrow windows and the sound of waves washing the shore could clearly be heard through them. Anthemius turned to his bodyguard and noticed Hunulf was grinning at the statuettes.

"Guard the door, we're not to be disturbed." said Anthemius.

Hunulf nodded, still grinning, ushered out the mint guards, Sigeric and Videric and closed the door behind him. Anthemius and turned to look at the procurator of the Cyzicus mint.

The obese man sat down at his desk, puffing to catch his breath. The short walk from the entrance to the office, whilst trivial for the visitors, had plainly taxed the mint's commander's body.

"Are you not well?" asked Anthemius. He hoped he sounded concerned, not disdainful.

"It's nothing," puffed Pertacus. "Now, what can I help you with, procurator?"

Anthemius had already decided he was not going to prevaricate, so he said simply, "It's a very serious matter, procurator. I have evidence that illegally debased coins are being minted here at Cyzicus."

156

Pertacus snorted indignantly, "Impossible!" Flecks of spit landed on Anthemius' hand. "Our security procedures are flawless. I oversee the minting process personally, who makes this accusation?"

"Nobody has accused anyone at this time, I merely have evidence of coins minted here which are worthless." Anthemis calmly wiped the back of his hand on his tunic to remove the spittle.

"Show me the evidence then!" snapped Pertacus irritably.

"Certainly." Anthemius took out his purse, opened it and emptied out onto the desk, a handful of the fake *solidi* that Quaderi had given him. The fat man stared at them.

"All of these coins were handed to a Persian money-changer by a member of the Blues guild," said Anthemius. "When I questioned him, he swore blind that he had had no idea where they came from. He said they had probably been thrown onto the arena floor by a wealthy woman as a token of her appreciation of a young charioteer." The procurator paused to see if Pertacus reacted, but the latter just sat there, stern-faced, looking intently at his guest.

"I didn't believe what I was told," Anthemius continued, "and so I had members of the guild followed, which led me to a dockside warehouse where I spoke to a Jewish moneychanger." Again, he paused, assessing the reaction from Pertacus. Still the latter sat stoically, arms folded, staring at the man from Constantinople. He ploughed on with his story.

"Now this moneychanger swears that the Blues regularly collect bags of gold coins against loans arranged by him. Those bags of solidi are delivered to him from this mint."

Pertacus picked up one of the coins and pursed his thick lips. "Well, I know nothing of this, and I'm shocked, to be honest, quite shocked that this appears to be going on. Thank you for bringing this to my attention. I will ensure there is an investigation."

"That is why I am here, to conduct an investigation," said Anthemius.

"But …"

"You don't imagine that I have sailed across the sea just to bring you the news?"

"No …"

"You understand that I'm not just a messenger?"

"Of course, but I …"

"Good, well then, let us begin now." Anthemius stood up.

"Now? You don't wish to freshen up?"

"I'm ready now."

Pertacus continued to sit at his desk looking up at his visitor, bemusement on his face.

Anthemius held his gaze and said quietly, "Do I need to stress to you how serious this matter is?"

"No, I …"

"This is treason of the highest order. You understand that?"

Pertacus paled slightly, beads of perspiration were gathering on his forehead. Anthemius could see the procurator knew all too well the precarious position he was in.

"Of course …" started Pertacus, but Anthemius interrupted him again.

"I don't really have to spell out your position?"

"No, I …"

"So as one trapped between the unpleasant possibilities of being seen as incompetent or corrupt or complicit, I recommend immediate action."

The Cyzicus procurator paled still further, then wiping his brow with a silk handkerchief, he heaved his mass out of the chair, adjusted his robes, and asked, "Where do you wish to start?"

"Show me everything. Die casting, smelting, cutting, striking, packaging. Everything."

"Very well, you have my full support."

Anthemius believed him. "Good, then lead on."

Pertacus walked to the door. "We'll start with the die casting, then. If you would like to follow me." Flanked by four mint guards, he wobbled off down the corridor. Sigeric and Videric followed, with Hunulf and Anthemius bringing up the rear.

"Progress?" asked Hunulf.

"On what?" replied Anthemius.

"On whatever it is you're working on."

"Maybe. Maybe not."

"Not, then."

"Too early to say."

They spent the next three hours being given the tour of the mint. They started with the die casting room, where three men were bent over high benches in the process of carving out the casts, ready to create the dies that would imprint the coins. Pertacus knew them all by name, as he should, as these were skilled men and critical to the whole process.

"These are Vasilis, Suhlamu and Khaemet," he said, "my die makers, and the best of all is Khaemet." He patted a dark-haired and dark-skinned youth on the head. "Egyptian, of course" he said, "Both brother and sister work in the mint. Wonderful artists, the Egyptians, but I guess you know that being one yourself?"

Anthemius didn't rise to the bait, but he made a note that Pertacus might be fat and unpleasant, but he had done his homework on his visitor, so he was not stupid. His own family was indeed originally from Egypt, but that had been four generations ago. Pertacus was continuing to chat pleasantly.

"Khaemet here was found by Balbus, my second. Found him in the markets making adorable mini vases with such delicate engravings, and we were on the lookout for a new die maker at the time." He smiled at Khaemet, who gave what Anthemius felt was a very forced smile back. "Imagine my delight when we heard that his sister was every bit as talented as he was." Pertacus lowered his voice but made sure everyone could hear him. "Maybe even a bit better heh, heh." The die maker smiled that forced smile, nodded, and gave a short laugh, as if he understood the joke. Anthemius guessed he had no idea what was being said.

Pertacus led Anthemius to small room off of the die workshop. "A very useful young man that. He is also quite an accomplished placer of coins in the striking room, very quick and accurate." The room they entered was small, narrow, and lined with shelves taller than a man, all stacked full of rolls of parchments. In the centre of the room was a desk, behind which sat a woman. Anthemius was momentarily taken aback, not because of seeing a female working there – he had several women working at the mint in the capital in administrative capacities – but because the young woman behind the desk was stunningly beautiful.

"Don't stare, procurator, it's rude, don't you know?" Pertacus was grinning. Anthemius flushed, annoyed to be caught off-guard by this bloated prig. "This is Nephtys, Khaemet's sister, and the wife of Balbus, my second in command here. Lucky fellow." Anthemius watched as the procurator sidled around the desk, his bulk making it

160

difficult, and placed his chubby hands on the young woman's shoulders. "Khaemet may be the best die maker, but this little jewel is the best scribe in the mint. Imagine that? A woman! You really are a treasure, aren't you my dear? Balbus really does not appreciate how lucky he is." Nephtys twisted to look up at Pertacus and gave her best attempt at a smile and a laugh, but any fool could see she loathed the fat man's touch. Pertacus glanced at Anthemius and smirked, stroking Nephtys' head. "Come, let us move on. There is much to see." He squeezed back past the desk and indicated the next door, allowing Anthemius to walk ahead. As they exited the room, Anthemius glanced back at Nephtys, whose eyes had followed him.

Pertacus noticed. "Yes, she is quite a beauty is she not? I can't understand what she sees in Balbus, to be frank. But don't be fooled, Procurator Anthemius, she used to forge letters of introduction and accounts for the Blues Guild in the town. Her brother used to make trinkets to sell but she earnt the money, so I am led to believe."

Pertacus was right of course, there was a lot to see. Anthemius saw the aqueduct which brought in water used in the cooling of the coins; he saw the process for the stoking and fuelling of the furnaces, where the gold, silver and copper was melted down. The room was how Anthemius imagined hell must be like, unbearably hot and dirty, a metallic odour hanging in the air. The men who worked here were slaves; most looked ill and many bore scars where their overseers had beaten them. He saw the room where the coins were packed ready for shipping, the room where the orders for coins were checked and administered, where progress of manufacture was tracked. Everywhere he was shown, he spoke to the supervisors and overseers, asking them about their work, their families, their previous employers. Pertacus patiently led him through the various areas. They stopped after a couple of hours to take some food and drink. They were served by a number of very beautiful young men. Pertacus smiled and gazed at them just long enough for Anthemius to understand why such young men would be employed in the mint. He doubted the local bishops would approve.

After they finished their meal, they continued their tour of other workshops and offices and, finally, after descending a large flight of steps, they got to the striking room. A room with a long row of benches where pairs of workers toiled. The air was stale and hot, and the noise was a continuous cacophony, as hammer struck die time and time again. It was the sound of Roman wealth and power being created, one blow at a time.

"Where are the dies kept?" asked Anthemius. Pertacus shuffled across the room and told Probus, who had accompanied them through the tour, to open a heavy wooden door set in the stone wall. Pertacus indicated that Anthemius should go ahead. Taking a large candle, he walked into the die room.

The room was small, no more than six feet by six feet. But it was high, so that looking up he could not clearly see the ceiling in the dark. He was surrounded by shelves loaded with numerous racks, all with different identifying numbers.

On the racks lay the coin dies.

Anthemius looked around. He felt a shiver go down his spine. He always had the same feeling in his own die room in Constantinople. In this room were stored the legacy of decades of the Roman Empire. Emperor Gallienus had first created the mint here a hundred and fifty years ago. He searched up and down the shelves, knowing the storage system; finally, he reached up and picked up a die. He held it to the candle and peered at it. Unlike many, he could easily read the mirror writing of the die; he believed it was because of his left-handedness, his "special gift" as his mother always said. His ability to see patterns where others could not.

The die he held in his hand was an old one, over a century old. It was for a coin of Emperor Lucius Domitius Aurelianus. The emperor

Aurelian. The man who, led by his force of will and personality, guided the empire back from the brink, in a mere five years. This powerful man had always held a fascination for Anthemius, though he knew little detail of his life, but it was well known that he had brought stability back to the empire when times had been darkest for Rome. He stared at the die for a minute and then carefully placed it back in its rack.

Was it his admiration of Aurelian he wondered, that had initially led him to associate with his namesake, the senator Aurelianus, back in Constantinople? He was a powerful and influential man. But though his advice had always been sound so far, lately Anthemius had begun to feel that it might not be in his best interest to get too cosy with him. Personal experience had taught him to trust his own instincts.

"Control procedures?" asked Anthemius.

"The overseer of the striking room books out the dies for the day and personally issues them to the teams. At authorised break times he double checks that all the dies are in place along with checking the number of coins produced. End of the day the overseer checks back in the dies and locks this room. I designed the system of checks myself." Pertacus was brisk and efficient in his description, with a hint of pride. "There have been no thefts of dies, we have lost only a few slaves to accidents, and our strikers are top class. I make sure of that. I also make sure I hire good people. My sub-Procurator has responsibility for this area" he continued. "And he is also very good at his job."

"Where is he now?" asked Anthemius, looking around.

"He is unfortunately rather ill," replied Pertacus, sounding genuinely concerned, "and has been for some time. He has seen a number of physicians and healers, I've even recommended some to him myself, but nothing has helped. He has spent hours in the church too, praying I believe to the Virgin Mary. He still comes into work regularly, but he sent a message that he could not make it in today. I have to admit it is a little unusual for him, especially in view of your visit."

Anthemius was curious. "Do you trust him?"

"Oh yes," replied Pertacus, though Anthemius noticed a moment's hesitation in his answer. Significant or not? He didn't know.

They continued through the striking room, stopping every now and again to watch the strikers at their work.

"Fascinating to watch, is it not?" said Pertacus.

"I certainly don't get tired of it," agreed Anthemius.

They were watching a particularly adept pair performing a sequence of moves that to the observer's eyes appeared almost dance-like. The "placer" was thin and old and shrivelled, his tendons showing taut under his skin. With his left hand he picked up a blank disk of copper and placed it in the die holder even as the hammer of the striker, a bald but powerfully built man who looked of Hunnic origin, was descending. The placer, with his right hand, positioned the obverse die exactly as the hammer found its mark a split second later. Immediately the placer scooped the stamped coin down a small chute, whilst the striker lifted his hammer back up, and with his left hand again, circled it around to pick up the next blank, place it in the die holder as the hammer descended once more.

Hunulf, who had been close to Anthemius all day, leaned forward and whispered over his shoulder, "What if I gave the old bastard a nudge sir? How many fingers do you think he'd lose?"

"Don't even think about it," hissed Anthemius.

They walked on and came to the far end of the room. There was a large and again sturdily built door, which Pertacus's guard opened. Anthemius pointed at a second door to their right, which was barred, "Where does that lead to?" he asked.

"Nowhere" replied Pertacus easily. "It was the old tunnel to the docks where we're headed now, but it collapsed in an earthquake several years back. We tried to repair it, but the rock has shifted. In the end, we decided to dig a new one; the ground is firmer around this one, makes it safer. The procurator reached and took a torch off of a wall rack and lit it from one of the wall lights. It spluttered into flame. Anthemius and his bodyguard grabbed other torches and they entered a narrow corridor, which sloped downward. As they descended Pertacus said, "The tunnel to the docks. We had this built to ensure total security for the finished coin. The next time they see the light of day it is on the dockside, which is separate from the main docks."

After a short walk down, they saw the light ahead of them grow in brightness and they found themselves on a small walkway, blinking in the bright light of day. The sun was to the south, behind them, and the sea of Marmara stretched out in front of them beyond the headland that protected the harbour of Cyzicus. Two ships were in the harbour, one being loaded with new coin and the other unloading what looked like food.

"Food for the slaves," said Pertacus at Anthemius' enquiring glance. "We don't let them leave the mint. They are chained up at night, but we make sure they have plenty of food, as they need their strength."

Anthemius nodded; it made sense to keep the workers contained, less chance of them stealing. A small part of him felt sympathy for the poor creatures, but without their labour the citizens of the empire would have no coin, and coin *was* civilisation as far as he was concerned.

"So, are you satisfied, procurator Anthemius?" asked Pertacus with what appeared to be a genuine smile.

"I'm satisfied that you run an efficient operation, procurator, but that does not explain the debased coins being produced here."

Pertacus took him by the elbow and led him away to the far end of the dock walkway, out of earshot of all the others in their entourage. Pertacus leaned close; the sweat from his exertions had soaked into his robe and his curly hair now clung to his face in damp clumps.

Anthemius resisted the urge to pull away from this repugnant man. But Pertacus whispered sternly, "May I suggest a more subtle approach, procurator?"

Anthemius nodded for him to continue.

"You have one or two of your bodyguard act as mint guards and take duty over the next few days, along with two or three of my most trusted men, especially in the quiet hours. Maybe they can uncover what is going on. It must be out of the normal working day, because, as you can see, there is no opportunity for any such treasonous activity during the working day."

Anthemius studied Pertacus for a moment. There was little about this man he didn't find distasteful. He was he suspected, a pervert, likely a sodomite, definitely a glutton and undoubtedly vain to the point of a narcissist. However, he reminded himself that none of those made him a traitor or a criminal. There seemed little else to do. He reluctantly nodded in agreement. Pertacus smiled and gave a small bow of the head. "In the meantime, I have arranged quarters for you in the city, very luxurious apartments, many beautiful slaves and the food is exquisite!" He led Anthemius by the arm back to where the bodyguards stood waiting patiently for their employers.

Chapter 25

Inside the Cyzicus Mint, 3rd May 396 AD

Hunulf sat cross-legged in the shadows of the striking room, out of sight, and watched and waited. He didn't expect anything to happen, but he watched and waited anyhow. He recalled his reaction to Anthemius' request.

"You want us to pretend to be mint guards?" he had snorted. Sigeric and Videric had both looked equally bemused.

"Call it a temporary assignment," Anthemius had suggested.

Temporary assignment. This was the second night he had hidden in the corner of the room. He had hidden here at the suggestion of Pertacus, who rightly said that if anything "nefarious" was happening, it would be at night, and whoever was making the illegal coins had to have access to the die store. So, he had waited until the building was emptying for the night and the guards were changing and locking up the slaves in their cells adjacent to the striking room, then he slipped in and hid behind some large packing crates at the far end of the room. One of the brothers was hidden down on the docks to prevent anyone escaping that way, whilst the other had joined the mint guard by the main gate. A roaming pair of guards patrolled the building and came through the room once every hour; they had been briefed that the Goths were there but to ignore them.

He had no idea what he was waiting for, but he guessed he would know when it happened, so he sat there and watched.

In the early hours of the morning Hunulf heard footsteps that were not those of the roaming guard. He had been chewing some leaves he'd gotten from a local merchant in the town, which kept him alert and awake. He watched as a slight figure padded quietly through the room, followed by a second person. They headed for what Hunulf knew was the die store. The dark and the shadows made it difficult for him to see exactly what was going on, but he heard the click of the lock mechanism on the door and the high-pitched squeak of the hinges as the door was gently opened. Suddenly there was a flash of a spark, then another. Silhouettes of figures appeared against a yellowy light which was soft but flickering. Shadows danced on the walls and ceiling. Whoever it was, they had lit a candle to see what they were doing.

Hunulf watched as the figures quickly entered and exited the die store and re-locked the door. As they turned to walk away there was a shout. "Stop right there!" He heard the drawing of a sword, that unmistakable rasping sound of metal on metal. The figures froze, and then darted forward, only to run into several other larger dark figures, who had appeared and blocked the exits. The Goth saw and heard their initial struggles die away as they realised that escape was impossible. More torches were lit, and the room was filled with bright, glimmering light. Hunulf stood quietly, uncrossing his legs, but stayed where he was, hidden in the shadows.

"Who have we here, then?" Hunulf recognised the voice of Probus, the captain of the mint's guard. Probus stepped forward and threw back the hoods of the thieves. "Balbus and Khaemet, what are you doing here so late?" The captain sounded surprised.

The slight figure said, in a thin and rasping voice that sounded like he was in pain, "All is well, captain, tell your men to release us. I was simply doing an errand for the Procurator; you can go now."

There was silence for a few seconds and then another voice, also familiar to Hunulf, said, "I thought you were ill Balbus! So, what errand might that be then?" Pertacus stepped forward into the torchlight.

Hunulf saw Balbus' shrink back in fear when the procurator spoke. Pertacus moved close to Balbus, took some items from him, and handed them to Probus; then he saw the fat man strike the shorter man around the face with the back of his hand. A vicious slap which knocked Balbus to the floor. "I cannot believe this! You betray me like this?" yelled the procurator at the man at his feet.

"Pertacus, sir, I ... " started Balbus. Just then Khaemet ducked down and tried to dodge between the guards, but powerful hands grabbed him, and a blow stunned him. "Take them to the atrium!" snapped the procurator to the mint guards, who grabbed the two men roughly and bundled them out of the room. "Who found them?" asked Pertacus. "That was me, Procurator," said the Probus.

"Excellent work, captain. Now search Balbus' office top to bottom and send men to his home, and to the Egyptians' home too. Do it now!"

"What am I looking for, sir?" asked the captain.

"Any more of these." Pertacus gave the captain the items he had taken from Balbus. The captain stared at them as if he was struggling to understand. "Coin blanks, captain; that traitor was going to strike fake coins! He probably has more at his house."

The captain nodded and set about organising his men, whilst Pertacus looked towards where Hunulf stood waiting and said, "Oh, please do come out of your hiding place now ... Hunulf, isn't it?" The procurator's voice was suddenly full of good humour. Hunulf stepped out into the torchlight, facing Pertacus in the flickering light of the torches. Hunulf heard Balbus being escorted away, feebly protesting it was all a huge mistake.

"Who was he?" asked Hunulf.

"That was my deputy here at the mint, along with Khaemet, who you met earlier. Can you believe it? My own deputy!" Pertacus nearly spat the words out. "Let us go outside now and deal with these traitors!"

"I should fetch Procurator Anthemius, sir, he should be here to question the prisoners, don't you think?"

Pertacus waved a podgy hand at him. "Fetch him if you must, but I'll not wait for him to deal out this punishment, so you had better hurry!"

Hunulf nodded and set off at a brisk pace. On his way out through the mint entrance he saw the guards surrounding the two prisoners, they already had their hands tied behind their backs and were kneeling on the ground. One of the guards had drawn a long sword, which glinted in the light from the torches. Hunulf broke into a run.

Anthemius and Hunulf were both out of breath as they reached the gates of the mint. Hunulf was sweating profusely; his leather tunic and heavy weapons made running hard. The guards initially barred them, but a torrent of abuse from Hunulf and various threats of deportation from Anthemius persuaded them to stand aside. As they entered the atrium, lit by torchlight from the walls and by the torches held by the guards, they saw Pertacus, patiently waiting for them to approach, a satisfied smirk on his face.

"Ah, Procurator Anthemius, I'm afraid you have arrived a little late. We have dealt with your traitors already." He indicated, with a wave of his arm, two headless corpses lying on the floor of the atrium, blood pooling around them.

Anthemius surveyed the gruesome scene in the stuttering torchlight, shadows flickering over the dead men. Try as he might he could not stop thinking about Khaemet's sister. Where was Nephtys? He nearly asked Pertacus the question. But he decided against it; he did not want to see the mocking look on the fat procurator's face, as if he had some adolescent crush on another man's wife.

"Why did you not wait for me to arrive before you executed them?" he asked instead.

"Why, Procurator, I am in command here. I have the legal power to summarily carry out justice on the people who work at the mint here, as much as you do in the city. Surely you do not question that?" Anthemius gritted his teeth. Pertacus was right, of course; he had every right to act as he saw fit to punish any treasonous behaviour.

"I am the senior Procurator. Out of courtesy alone, you should have waited." It was not a strong argument, and Anthemius knew it. But he was angry that he had not had a chance to question the prisoners, to try to get to the root of the matter, to see if these truly were the people behind the counterfeit coins.

"We did, Procurator. We waited a good twenty minutes after I sentenced these men to death, but you did not show, and Balbus and Khaemet were making such a fuss, I felt it necessary to just get on with it to stop everyone suffering more than they needed to." The fat man smiled his disagreeable smile.

Inside Anthemius' head warning bells were sounding. Something was not right. But he had nothing else to go on. He faced Pertacus. "Show me the evidence of their treachery; it had better be sufficient."

"Certainly, but let us retire to my office, where we can better discuss this." Pertacus turned to the guards. "You men, clear this mess up; I want their bodies thrown in the sea and I don't want to see a spot of blood in this atrium when morning comes. We don't want to scare the workers." Then he indicated that Anthemius and Hunulf should follow him.

"Go find the brothers and bring them to the procurator's office," said Anthemius. The big Goth nodded and then strode off to find his kinsmen.

Sitting in Pertacus' office, Anthemius was now wide awake. He had insisted that they wait until his bodyguard arrive. Pertacus, sitting at his desk flanked by the captain of the mint guard and a sub-commander of the guard, was looking extremely pleased with himself. Within a few minutes, Hunulf, Sigeric and Videric stood behind Anthemius.

"So, who were the traitors?" he asked.

"Your traitors were my deputy, Balbus …" said Pertacus curtly. "… and the other you met earlier today; Khaemet. I expect very shortly we'll also have any more of their friends who have been helping them in their treason."

"And your evidence?"

"They were caught in the act of stealing a die of our emperor from the die store." Pertacus pointed behind Anthemius. "Your own man saw him, Procurator." Anthemius glanced back at Hunulf who nodded.

"He was caught removing something from the store sir."

"You see?" Pertacus smiled smugly.

"But," interjected Hunulf, "I never saw what it was he took, sir."

Pertacus leaned forward and opened a small bag that lay in front of him; he poured out what appeared at first to be coins, but when Anthemius leaned over to examine them, he could see they were just blanks of gold coin, unstruck. He took out his knife and dug at the coin with the pointed tip. Dull grey showed underneath the gilded exterior.

Pertacus nearly spat out his words. "Base metal! Balbus, you fool; why did you do it?"

Anthemius guessed he was worried about how this would all look in terms of his career. Having a traitor work for him without him knowing about it, for months or even longer, would not look good for the fat man. Pertacus picked up a coin die.

"Taken tonight by Balbus and Khaemet from the die store. Again, your man saw them do it." Pertacus handed Anthemius the die. It was for a *solidus*, with the emperor's half face on it.

Then Pertacus opened up another other bag and pulled out another coin die. The fat man stared at it for a moment and handed it to Anthemius. He was shocked when he read the inverse writing.

"Found in Balbus' office in his safe keeping box," said Pertacus quietly.

"Who has the keys to that box?"

"Balbus holds … held … the only key."

Anthemius stared at the coin die. Staring back at him was a face, but it was not the face of the emperor Arcadius. The face embossed on the die, and the wording encircling the face, were of another man. A man who Anthemius knew of but was not well acquainted with. A powerful man, a powerful senator, and a previous *Magister Militum*: General Abundantius.

"And we also found this in Balbus' office, in the safe along with the die." Fat fingers proffered a letter written on papyrus, in a flowing script. Anthemius speed read the words, which were instructions to Balbus and Khaemet to make a test die as a passing fancy, a fun thing to impress friends with, but to tell no one, and as previously agreed, if the coins were to become legal tender someday, they would be greatly rewarded.

It was signed by Abundantius.

"Why would Abundantius write such an incriminating letter? He is not stupid. Is the letter genuine?" mused Anthemius.

"Well, I cannot say for certain that it is his signature, but you are welcome to take it with you and compare it to any other signature of his you can obtain. He is not stupid, no, but from what I hear he is vain and has no love for the emperor." Anthemius nodded, that much at least was true.

"Abundantius planning a coup?" he said to nobody in particular.

"It would appear so, or it is a joke in very poor taste," said Pertacus flippantly.

"Who made the die; Balbus or Khaemet?"

"From that letter, Khaemet, it is obvious."

"You're sure?"

"Khaemet has the skills to make the die, Balbus too, but it looks more like Khaemet's work."

"Who made the base-metal coins?" asked Anthemius.

"We're not sure yet. My men are questioning the workers now."

"I want to speak to them when you find them."

"Of course you do, but I would suggest ..."

"Why would Balbus do it?" interrupted Anthemius.

Pertacus seemed taken aback by the question. "Why else but wealth and power? He believed he was backing the next emperor."

"But why the counterfeit coins?"

"Taking over an Empire needs support from all kinds of people, you know that, and that is expensive. Better to make fake coins, much cheaper."

"Until they find out they've been cheated."

"That's why the fakes needed so be good, so no one would notice until it was too late. When you're emperor, you have access to the real money and can make good on any promises then, if you have to."

Pertacus steepled his fingers together and leaned forward. His fat jowls wobbled. "Procurator Anthemius, this is critical. We have caught the men red-handed, about to strike fake coins to help fund the traitor Abundantius. We have a die of the usurper, who is plainly so vain and arrogant he designs his own coin before the coup has even started, then is arrogant enough to write a letter to his supporters here. Procurator, you need to get back to the city with this evidence and warn the emperor immediately that he has a traitor in his court!"

Anthemius looked at Pertacus for several seconds, looked at the die in his hand. Re-read the letter. His mind was whirling. Something was not right, but he could not put his finger on it. He felt the die in his hand.

General Abundantius? A traitor?

The old man was vain, yes. Arrogant, yes. But a traitor? He could not see that. The letter was sufficiently vague, dismissing it as a trifle, to avoid outright treason, but when coupled with the actions of tonight, it did not look good. He was certainly wealthy and very influential, especially amongst the military. Theodosius had rewarded him with many commands, he had fought many battles and won them. Perhaps he felt that the young man who wore the purple now was not worthy of the role? Certainly, many in the palace felt that way, but Arcadius was the legitimate heir, the son of Theodosius, the soldier emperor, the man who had saved the empire from the Goth threat.

Though some said at too high a price.

Abundantius being one of them.

Here was the evidence in his hand of treason. A die with Abundantius' face on it. A letter requesting it be made. It was sedition. No doubt. If he failed to act now, he would be culpable too, and he would end up as dead as the headless corpses of Balbus and Khaemet being thrown into the Sea of Marmara right now.

For a moment he was unsure what to do. But then he recalled his father's words to him when he entered the empire's administration. "Play the game, Anthemius, but trust nothing and no-one except your own gut instinct. Keep your thoughts your own until you're sure they are true."

He would continue to play the game.

"Hunulf!"

"Sir?"

"Requisition a ship. We leave tonight for the capital."

Chapter 26

Constantinople, 6th May 396 AD

Caesarius was once again at his desk, overseeing his office in the golden palace. The news from Greece was not good. Further reports of attacks by Alaric were arriving weekly now. The prefect had sent out orders to all the Greek Cities' urban prefects to ensure their defences were repaired and the local units were stood to and prepared to mount defences of the cities. The Prefect of Illyricum was Eutychainus; the emperor, or rather the obnoxious Eutropius, had appointed him, despite pleas from himself and the senior generals, Abundantius, Timasius and Gainas. Eutychainus was firmly in the pocket of Eutropius and so did little more than nothing to help contain the situation. Thus Caesarius was reduced to trying to directly manage a war hundreds of miles away from his desk, an impossible and frustrating task.

He looked up and sighed. Aurelianus was approaching.

"Hello brother," he said, not looking up from his writing.

"Hello brother to you too, you look … busy." There was a trace of amusement in his voice.

Caesarius carefully dipped his quill back into its ivory ink pot and then continued to write. "More than you appear to be. What can I do for you, brother?"

Aurelianus sat down in the overly intricately carved chair across from where Caesarius sat.

"Flavius Anthemius …"

"That's your new and latest pet, if I recall?" sneered Caesarius.

Aurelianus ignored him and continued "Our highly competent procurator of the Constantinople Mint has been investigating a suspected ring of counterfeiters."

"Then tell the *Comes Sacrarum Largitionum*, don't bother me with such trivialities. Goodbye."

Aurelianus remained seated and carried on as if Caesarius had said nothing.

"He has recently returned from the Cyzicus mint with a very disturbing story."

"Don't tell me, the Phrygians are revolting." Caesarius' voice oozed derision as he continued to write, "and the empire is doomed. Tell me something I don't know."

"Brother, sarcasm does not become you. And I'm not here for an argument." Aurelianus picked up an ivory tusk that sat in a bronze holder and rolled it in his hand, admiring its colour and sheen.

"Then why are you here?" asked Caesarius, still not looking up from his work.

"To report an act of treason."

Caesarius stopped writing but didn't look up. He sat still and breathed in deeply. So, he thought, the games are already being played. So soon? He had wondered how long it would take before the wolves started circling the court, looking for their victim. Abundantius and Timasius had persuaded him to take up the mantle of Praetorian Prefect and he knew why. Eutropius had the emperor well and truly under his wing; he controlled access to the young Imperator, and he knew that his own appointment had been an effort by the army generals to try to gain some control back from the eunuch. Abundantius and Timasius wanted him to push back. He was proud of his own reputation for being fair and equitable, and someone who could be trusted by all parties. Diplomacy was a skill of his.

But that was no longer enough, he knew.

The "coup" that Eutropius had instigated via General Gainas was deeply entrenched now. Eutropius had manoeuvred his people into all branches of the administration. He knew that Eutychainus waited in the wings for his own job. Caesarius had no personal animosity towards Eutychainus; he seemed a capable man, and an *adequate* administrator, but he was completely under the thumb of Eutropius, who had gifted him lands and tax exemptions over the past year and now he did the eunuch's every bidding.

He also knew that his brother craved the post of Praetorian Prefect. He knew that his brother wanted to be rid of both the disgusting eunuch and the barbarians who plundered Greece. He wanted the Goth army defeated and ejected from the empire, and he wanted to curtail the opportunities for Goth citizens to gain power and influence.

He knew Aurelianus thought him too weak and too lenient with tribes and cities that tested the limits of what the empire accepted. He himself did not view it as weakness. The empire had to adapt, had to coerce those who otherwise sought to destroy it. Romanise them. Gainas was a decent man as far as he could see. Yes, he was a Goth, a barbarian, but he had fought for the empire against invaders, both Hun and his own tribes. He had served in the legions for nearly twenty years. He could not see how deliberately antagonising people such as him, who had sought refuge within the empire and then had been mistreated time and time again, could improve their current situation. Mistreatment was banal and vague term that hid the real act. Betrayal would have been more accurate.

Theodosius had not had many options when he had donned the purple and brought the empire back from the brink; but allowing the Goths to move around within the empire as self-governing units had been a disaster, as Alaric's ravages in Greece were now proving. Something had to be done to bring the barbarians under control, but confrontation was not the answer; of that, Caesarius was sure. He was equally sure that his younger, more flamboyant brother had a very different point of view; that the likes of Gainas should be barred from being a member of the senate or even a senior member of the military. But if a man was a good general, as plainly Gainas was, why make an enemy of him? It made no sense to Caesarius. Rome had been at its peak when it had absorbed and Romanised its enemies; it had to become that melting pot again or risk oblivion.

Shaking his head and coming back from his thoughts, he looked up and stared at his brother, whom he distrusted as much as any of the other senators or members of the emperor's consistorium.

"Treason?" he repeated without emotion. "That word, 'treason', is both overused and overworked, I think," he said. At least it was for him. It reeked of dark rooms and self-interest and was used to protect vested interests and drive personal agendas far more than it was used to protect the empire.

"I think you would agree that what Anthemius has uncovered meets the criteria of 'treason' more than most such charges brought against anyone recently," said Aurelianus, with that self-satisfied smile that irritated Caesarius so much.

His brother was clever, yes, smart, and ostentatious. He liked the good life, but not excessively so, like the eunuch was starting to do. But he was thorough, so if he had come to him with this information then he must at least have a degree of certainty about it.

"Very well," he said, placing his quill back into its holder. He leant back in his chair. "Tell me what you know."

"Anthemius is outside, best you hear it from him I think," said Aurelianus. Caesarius nodded and rang a small brass bell on his desk. Immediately a slave opened the door and bowed.

"Send in Procurator Anthemius."

Anthemius entered carrying a number of tablets and scrolls under his arms. He approached Caesarius desk and indicated with his eyes that he wanted some space on the desk to put down the items he was carrying. The Praetorian Prefect nodded, and he and his brother made room for Anthemius' collection of writings.

"Procurator Anthemius," said Caesarius, "we've not spoken for a while, please have a seat. Aurelianus here says you have a report of treason at the Cyzicus mint? That is a serious charge as you are aware, of course? But …" Caesarius waved a hand at the pile of tablets and scrolls before the procurator. "I see you have brought more than enough evidence with you."

"Prefect, thank you for seeing me. I appreciate you are very busy, but yes, this is a very serious situation." Anthemius sat opposite the prefect.

"Although it may be a little embarrassing for you," interrupted Aurelianus, smirking, "it is one that you need to act on, brother."

"Thank you, Senator," said Caesarius coldly and deliberately, turning to face Aurelianus. "That will be all. I will now speak with Procurator Anthemius in private. You may leave," and without waiting for a response, he rang his bell again and the same slave opened the door immediately. There was an uncomfortable silence. Aurelianus stared back at his older brother for several seconds, then he slowly got to his feet, settled his toga over his arm and walked from the room, giving Anthemius a small nod of the head as the door closed behind him.

The two men in the room looked at each other. The face of Anthemius was unreadable. Caesarius smiled and said lightly, "A wise man once said you can pick your enemies but not your family. More's the pity!"

The procurator said nothing.

"I know you consider Aurelianus your mentor."

"You are incorrect in that assumption, prefect," said Anthemius in a firm but friendly voice.

"Am I?" Caesarius raised his eyebrows in mock surprise.

"You are."

"You have had several meetings with him over the past months."

"Are you having me followed?" asked Anthemius; he asked as if he already knew the answer.

Caesarius laughed gently. "Not all the time Procurator, I just like to keep an eye on my family members. You see, I probably know them better that you do, and if I may, I would offer you a piece of what I consider sage advice."

Anthemius nodded.

"Aurelianus is my brother, but that doesn't mean I trust him. You should not either. He is ambitious beyond the norm and possesses the passion of a zealot, which in these times can be very dangerous. Our actions must be measured and balanced. At all times. Do you understand?"

"I do."

"With that in mind, do you still wish to inform me of an act of treason?"

"I do," repeated Anthemius.

Caesarius looked the younger man in the eyes, and they held each other's gaze. Then he nodded and said, "You may proceed then, but nothing of what you say to me now goes beyond this room without my say so. Is that understood?"

"It is."

"Go on then."

Anthemius spoke briefly and concisely of his dealings with the Persian moneychanger and his encounter with the Blues, the Jew at the docks, and his voyage to Cyzicus. He described the night-time vigils, the arrest of Balbus and Khaemet and their summary execution. He then showed the fake coins blanks and the die with Abundantius' face and name inscribed, though Anthemius had to read it to the prefect, who was not as adept at mirror reading.

Caesarius was stunned. His initial reaction was that this was a joke of some kind, for a party or birthday celebration, but the letter the procurator showed him left him feeling sick. Abundantius? Involved in a plot to overthrow the emperor?

He didn't believe it.

Truthfully, he didn't want to believe it. Abundantius was someone he had known for many years. He had always considered him a hangover from the old Roman Empire of Trajan and Hadrian, the old general fighting to keep the dream of the Roman Empire alive.

"What do *you* think?" he asked Anthemius. "Do you believe the general is going to attempt a coup?"

"I believe there is more to this than meets the eye," said the procurator without hesitation.

"Have you said as much to Aurelianus?" asked Caesarius.

"No."

"Why not?"

"He holds no official office, even though he holds much influence."

"I might tell him you said that."

Anthemius shrugged and seemed unworried. "That is unlikely, but if you do, it's merely the truth. As I mentioned before, and contrary to your belief, I am in no need of a 'mentor' and even less a 'patron'. I am, however, always willing to consider other opinions, solicited or not. But in the end, I keep my own council."

"If you were me, what would you do right now?" asked Caesarius, leaning forward.

"I would arrest General Abundantius and try him for treason. I have been shown convincing evidence that he is guilty, there is no reason not to act." Anthemius held the prefect's steady gaze.

"And yet…?"

"And yet, I believe there is more to this than meets the eye."

Caesarius blinked and looked away; he uttered a small blasphemy under his breath. It was difficult these days to know who to trust but looking at the calm and collected man across the table, he felt that this was one person he could at least begin to work with. Anthemius' reputation for thoroughness and honesty preceded him. His own brother spoke highly of him, so he had dismissed the procurator as another of his brother's sycophantic followers, or a desperate client who sought power or influence by association or proxy. This brief meeting had quickly dispelled those thoughts. The bronzed and immaculately dressed official he had in his office was no buffoon. He was sharp and clear-minded, independent, and not in thrall to anyone, it seemed. He mentally made a note to watch Anthemius closely and to consider making use of his talents. He needed allies and this was a talented man who would easily not fall foul of Eutropius' tricks and games, and neither plainly was he overly impressed by his own brother Aurelianus' reputation and influence.

"I agree, procurator. I will arrest the general and try him for treason as you recommend. However, you are to continue to investigate any avenue you see fit."

"Even if it is determined that one of the men who sponsored and supported your appointment as Praetorian Prefect is proved beyond doubt to be a traitor?" asked Anthemius.

"Yes," sighed Caesarius heavily. "Whatever that truth may be."

Anthemius stood up, looked at the older man for a second, then nodded and left.

Chapter 27

The Golden Palace, Constantinople, 10th May 396 AD

Saturninus, the co-judge for the trial of Abundantius, finished his speech announcing the guilt of the general and his punishment. "In view of your previous service to the empire, our gracious emperor has decreed that your punishment be exile in Sidon for the rest of your days, where you may dwell on your dishonour! God have mercy on you. Guards!"

The court guards grabbed the general's upper arms, but he shook them off, and glared at the dais on which the emperor Arcadius sat, but he didn't direct his ire at the emperor. He was solely focussed on Eutropius, with pure hatred in his eyes. He made to say something, then decided better and turned away. The eunuch's face was impassive and eventually, at the bidding of the court guards, the old soldier was escorted away.

Up on the dais, Arcadius rose, the rest of the court following suit and waited for the emperor to exit the courtroom. Surrounded by guards of the *Scholae*, the emperor and Eutropius strode down the corridor towards the court's main exit, where a further detachment of *Scholae* waited to escort the Imperator back to the golden palace.

Once on horseback, Eutropius and Arcadius were boxed in by the *Scholae*, forming a tight protective ring around the two men. "Lead on, Tribune," said Eutropius. The Tribune glanced at Arcadius, who gave the smallest of nods, and the party started off at a steady walk, out to the Mese and up the hill towards the palace.

"What now, Chamberlain?" asked Arcadius as they made slow travel up the hill.

"We will need to dispose of the traitor's lands and property." said Eutropius. "I will personally supervise the transfer to the imperial estates, of course."

"Thank you, Eutropius," said Arcadius. "I wouldn't know where to begin with that."

"That's why we have the administration, Imperator, so that you can concentrate on the important matters, and such mundane details like land transfers can be dealt with by my clerks." Eutropius' voice was light. "It seems unbelievable that such a veteran general could be guilty of plotting against you."

"I suppose so," said Arcadius absently, as if his interest in the subject was already waning.

"Yet, I suppose it's far from unprecedented; Vespasian, Severus – even your father – were all ex-army generals; it is only natural that those with armies at their command can pose a threat."

This seemed to stir a note of concern in Arcadius.

"You think others may be plotting too?"

"It's always a possibility, Imperator, we must always be vigilant. We were lucky this time that procurator Anthemius was so diligent and provided us with definitive evidence. The outcome was never in doubt. Even Abundantius' supporters had to concede his guilt in the end. But there may be others."

They rode on in silence for a minute, some onlookers had gathered along the side of the Mese to wave at the emperor's party as they plodded past.

"It is why I have taken the liberty of putting all armies under your direct control for now, until we have completed the redeployments and reassignments of senior officers and generals. It will allow us to prevent any such attempts at a coup and maybe, flush out any remaining traitors."

Arcadius nodded. The Chamberlain was not sure if he was confirming to the order transferring the command of the armies to him personally, or to the flushing out of traitors.

They concluded their ride, entering the Chalca gate, where they dismounted and parted company, the emperor heading back out to meet some friends at one of his hunting grounds just outside the city, whilst Eutropius made his excuses and headed for his rooms.

There he summoned his clerks and over the next three hours they set about the task of transferring the ownership of Abundantius' lands and properties to the Imperial Estates, under the direct administration of Eutropius' office. He ensured the parchment documents were all prepared and signed by his chief clerk responsible for Imperial land registry and made ready for the emperor's signature when he returned from his hunt. Eutropius then called for **Philoponus,** the person he considered his most loyal associate. He didn't consider anyone a friend.

"You have heard?" asked Eutropius.

"Our general is gone?"

"He is. The lands will be transferred to the Imperial Estates tomorrow."

"And the income from those lands?"

"Shall be used for the benefit of the empire," said Eutropius, smiling without mirth, "as usual."

"Good," said **Philoponus,** "I will wait for your summons on the matter. Will that be all?"

"For now, thank you."

For a while he sat there, absorbed in his own world. The days of being looked down on with scorn were at an end. Against all the odds, he, a eunuch, a mutilated boy, pitied, laughed at, abused and raped, now held real power.

Shaking himself from his reverie, the chamberlain took a tiny key out of his pocket and used it to unlock a shallow, almost invisible drawer under his desk. He pulled open the drawer and took out a sheet of papyrus. On it were a number of names. He took a quill, dipped it into his gold pot of deep blue ink, then carefully draw a line across the first name on the list: *'Abundantius'*. He gently replaced the quill pen, and blew on the papyrus to dry the ink, then he looked for some time at the second name on the list and smiled to himself.

Getting rid of Abundantius had been easier than he thought. He was grateful that the efficient Anthemius has been so diligent, it had made the whole job much easier. His finding the letter had sealed the general's fate, although the die alone would have been sufficient for a conviction.

During the trial the general had asked how he, a decorated soldier, was on trial while Eutropius, a mere eunuch, whom Abundantius had raised up to the role of chamberlain in good faith, could turn on him. Eutropius had calmly reminded the court that there was undeniable evidence that the general had plotted to overthrow the emperor, and that these proceedings gave him no pleasure. It was tragic to see his previous great benefactor fall so far from grace, and he begged the emperor to show leniency to the general for his past good deeds and service, which Arcadius gladly did, pleased that he could do a favour for his chamberlain.

But there were still others who could endanger him, those who held sway in the senate, and who could still influence the boy. They must be gotten rid of like Abundantius; only then would Eutropius' position be safe and unassailable. After that, who knew what possibilities lay ahead?

189

Chapter 28

Central Greece, 15th June 396 AD

At the head of a band of a hundred of Alaric's warriors Thiudimir rode confidently up to the gates of the village. The gates had been shut; he looked up and saw a number of men, their head and shoulders just showing about the stout wooden stakes that made up the village defensive wall. The fields surrounding the village had been tilled, but the crops were barely showing this early in the season. There were orange and lemon and date tree orchards surrounding the village amongst the patchwork of fields, but close to the village was only bare ground, to provide no cover for any approaching enemy. They had seen them coming, no-one was in the fields.

Beside Thiudimir rode a stocky man, who wore a Roman cavalry helmet, and the cloak that every Roman cavalry officer wore. He was clean shaven too; he looked every bit the Roman. Except he wasn't. His name was Demetrios, and he was a member of band of Greek mercenaries who Alaric employed as spies, scouts, and intermediaries.

"Greetings!" called Thiudimir in his best and only Greek, giving a friendly wave.

He got no friendly wave in return. "What do you want?" said a bald-headed man.

"Food and supplies." Demetrios called up. The man responded with a stream of Greek that Thiudimir patiently waited for the mercenary to translate.

"They've none to spare, the winter was hard, they're relying on next year's crops. The fields are still growing, there is nothing to give, blah, blah, blah …"

"Is he lying?" asked Thiudimir.

"Probably," replied Demetrios. "I was born and raised in a village like this; none of these people are wealthy, but they don't starve, there will be food and fodder stashed away."

Thiudimir shrugged. "Tell him they can give us what we want, and we'll be on our way, or we'll just take it and then some." The message was shouted up to the ramparts; the blad-headed man responded in an angry voice.

"He says the local Roman garrison has been alerted and are on their way. He advises us to leave now." Demetrios translated.

"Bullshit" laughed Thiudimir. "And in any event, I don't think they'll be anything we need to worry about. Let's go."

"We're leaving?" asked Demetrios, surprised.

"Of course not, you idiot, but we'll need a battering ram to get those gates open and those woods back over there look like they have some decent sized trees. But don't you tell him that!"

They turned their horses and headed off towards a coppice they had passed on their approach; jeers and shouts from the villagers following them. Thiudimir issued orders and the men dismounted, grabbed their axes, and began felling trees. A big one for the ram, and small ones to make the rig on which to carry it. It was mid-afternoon, and hot, but the men got on with the work without complaint; the opportunity for plunder had buoyed their spirits and there was banter aplenty as well as boasting of prowess on the battlefield and in bed. Using ropes they had brought with them, they lashed the trunks together to make a simple ram, with the large, pointed trunk sitting on top of four thinner but sturdy trunks which, when hauled up and resting in the elbows of the eight strongest warriors, would do the job. There wasn't time to fashion any protective cover, so Thiudimir instructed eight more men to stand between the ram carriers and hold shields above to make a protective barrier. When all was ready, the warriors walked the ram back towards the village.

The villagers were no longer jeering. They had been watching the Goths from the ramparts. They could see what was happening but could do nothing to thwart it.

Thiudimir was indifferent to the plight of the villagers at this point; they could have opened the gates at any time, they still could. But they didn't.

He ordered the ram forwards.

As they approached, a dozen arrows flew from the village's wooden ramparts and thumped into the ground ahead of them. Thiudimir yelled "Halt!". This should be easy, he knew, but he could not be over-confident or reckless. An arrow could still kill, even if fired by an utterly unskilled farmhand.

"Archers, keep those bastard's heads down!"

Twenty warriors surged forward with shields locked together. Behind them twenty archers scuttled forwards bent low, priming their bows. The captain of the archers, called out orders, and a volley of shafts flew towards the village. The villagers ducked smartly down behind the ramparts.

"Forwards lads," called out Thiudimir. The wall of bowmen made their way ahead. The squad carrying the ram following as fast as they were able, holding the ropes supporting the make-shift ram with one hand and their shields in the other.

But twenty archers were not enough it turned out. There were more than enough farmhands and artisans it seemed in the village who wanted to fight. Arrows were now coming thick and fast from the village. Suddenly, two of his archers were down, one dead, one wounded. They stopped. Thiudimir poked his head above the shields seeing the ramparts of the village full of bowmen. He thought he could even see women there. They must be desperate, he thought. Roman women fighting? This was a first.

"Back away! We'll try something different.". He called out. The warriors backed away in tight formation, and when at a safe distance, they circled together to assess the situation. Thiudimir was relieved there were no more casualties. The wounded man had an arrow in his right shoulder, he made no sound, but the sweat pouring from his brow and his gritted teeth betrayed the agony he was in. The dead warrior had been dragged back with them in the retreat, he was one of Demetrios' men. A lucky or unlucky shot depending on your point of view. An arrow straight through the eye socket.

Thiudimir looked around at the group, they looked sullen. Nobody liked being beaten, least of all by a bunch of farm workers.

"We'll get in there lads, don't worry."

"How?" asked several of the men.

Thiudimir looked around at the expectant faces, at Demetrios and then down at the dead man.

"Let's give Frideric a proper send-off."

The Goths encircled the funeral pyre of Frideric. They stood in solemn silence as the flames built and engulfed the fallen warrior. They had shared food that evening, two hogs that Demetrios and his mercenaries had tracked and killed. Barely enough between a hundred men, but it was better than nothing. Night had fallen an hour ago, and the fire was intense, lighting up the surrounds where the Goths stood. Demetrios said prayers for his comrade. The men chanted a prayer they had all learnt as children, a prayer for the dead and departed, those who had gone to that better place with God. They had made a big display of the funeral under the watchful eye of the villagers.

As the intensity of the pyre started to fade, the men started singing songs and started dancing, making a lot of noise. Then a flaming arrow, a cloth soaked in pigs lard wrapped around hit's head, was loosed into the air high above the pyre, the arrow arced high, reaching the zenith of its flight and then plummeted to earth burying itself in the ground, still aflame just a few feet away from the archer. Another arrow went up , then another. Cheers and laughs sounded out loud as the arrows landed closer and closer to the archers.

Thiudimir heard the cheers and shouts behind him and prayed for the villagers to keep enjoying the show. With faces blackened with the ash from the pyre and only wearing dark cloth out garments, his men had one by one secreted themselves away from the pyre. Thiudimir hoped the light from the fire was damaging the guard's night vision. He had them lie on the ground forming chains of men who passed from hand-to-hand wood and kindling scavenged from the orchard and coppices, the final man in the chain placing it carefully against the village wall.

Once he was satisfied, Thiudimir signalled for the men to withdraw. They returned to the singing and dancing men where Thiudimir sought out Demetrios and simply said "let's go!". Demetrios yelled out orders, the men quickly scattered, most to their horses, but one group remaining with the ram built earlier.

Thiudimir had his signaller blow out three blasts on the horn to signal the attack. The ram squad picked the ram and ran forwards towards the village. Simultaneously from behind them, burst sixty horse archers lead by Demetrios, each with four shafts ablaze with fire, they launched the first volley directly at the eastern village wall. Arrows hammered into the walls still burning, many went over the walls into the village. Thiudimir didn't really care, that was the first volley. The horse archers then veered south and fired another volley this times at the walls and the base of the walls. The rain of fire struck as desired. The kindling placed earlier burst into flame and within seconds, the whole south wall, tinder-dry from the summer sun, was ablaze, smoke billowing in clouds up into the star speckled sky above.

The ram squad were nearing the walls. Not wishing to repeat the mistake earlier Thiudimir had kept back twenty horse archers to circle the ram and to fire arrows at the village to keep the ramparts clear. The archers were good. They kept the ramparts clear.

Within two minutes they were ready for the final charge. Thiudimir behind the ram crew saw Demetrios returning from the north side of the village. He sent a runner to tell him to send half his men around again with as many fire arrows as they had left, the remaining half were to make running passes past the front of the gates. This done, he nodded to his signaller, and a horn sounded again three times.

The archers charged forward, loosing off a barrage of arrows. Simultaneously, the ram squad picked up their load and charged headlong at the village gates. The men carrying the ram were the largest and strongest men and they hit the gates with a bone-breaking and satisfying crash. There was the sound of splintering, then a hail of arrows hammered into the raised shields from above. A cry sounded from within the ram squad as an arrow found its mark in a leg. The man rolled away in agony, but another threw down his bow, grabbed the injured man's shield and stepped into his place. "Again," yelled Thiudimir. "Back five paces." The ram squad, as one paced back, then Thiudimir screamed, "Charge!" and the ram raced forwards again and struck the gates dead-centre, with yet another deafening crash. Thiudimir heard more wood splintering and yells of concern from the other side.

"I think they're shitting themselves now!" laughed one of the ram crew.

"Shut up," shouted back Thiudimir. "Ready again!"

The ram crew backed away, and at Thiudimir's command they raced forward and threw all of their strength into the third blow. There was a decisive crack as the bars on the inside either shattered or pulled loose of their restraints. The gates bowed inwards and then parted. "Let's go, lads!" yelled Thiudimir. The ram crew dropped the ram and surged their way through the gates. The first warriors immediately dropped to their knees and formed a shield wall, and the following men did likewise. Arrows peppered the wall of shields, some burying themselves in the wood and leather, others skipping off.

"Archers! Ready," yelled Thiudimir. He glanced behind him and saw that Demetrios had the archers on the ramparts pinned down. Now he could see into the village, he saw the arrows sent over earlier had set fire to houses and animal pits. The scene in front of him was a stark confusion of smoke, flame and of people and animals, running and screaming. No time to hesitate, they had to get to the grain before it catches fire too. A glance to the south showed the flames there starting to rise above the wall. Fire now encircled the village.

"Archers forward!" he yelled. The warriors in the shield wall crouched down to allow the archers to come right up to their shoulders. "Loose!" The shields were dropped, and the archers fired a volley of arrows at the line of villagers who were the last line of defence of their home. The arrows found their targets. Men dropped to the floor, blood gushing, or they hobbled or crawled away, and yet still, many stood fast and returned fire.

"Archers, reload! Wall, forward two paces!" Reforming the menacing wall, the men stepped forward two paces, keeping their discipline. The manoeuvre was repeated,` the archers unloading their deadly cargo into the desperate villagers. But the villagers held on, though Thiudimir could see they were on the point of breaking. He felt a pang of sympathy and admiration for a moment for the men he was fighting. But then thought of his wife and children back in the main baggage train of Alaric's army; they were skinny and hadn't eaten well for two weeks now. Food was scarce and this raid was risky, as the village was no pushover. To underline that thought, a well-aimed arrow found its mark in a man in front of him. He collapsed to the ground without a cry, blood gushing from his ruptured neck.

"And again, archers!" Thiudimir screamed. His blood was up now and pounding in his ears. "Loose!" Another lethal hail of arrows scythed down a dozen villagers, their screams piercing. Again, the shield wall reformed and again they paced forward.

"Watch the sides!" yelled Thiudimir. He glanced up to ensure that the flanks were dealing with the archers on the village ramparts, which were now slightly behind them as they edged their way forwards into the village. Thiudimir commanded to his signaller "Call the cavalry!", and the horn sounded a third time.

There was a rumble behind them, and the horse archers led by Demetrios, hurtled into the village around the ends of the shield wall. The cavalry had stowed their bows and now brandished their long swords. They smashed into the already dwindling line of defence the villagers had put up. Swords were raised and slashed down as the people turned and fled. It was all but over.

Thiudimir shouted above the din. "Secure the walls! Find the village elders, but don't butcher them… yet!". Two detachments of soldiers broke away from the shield wall and clambered up the ladders onto the walkway and set about clearing the walls of any last remaining defenders. The villagers knew they were done for, so most dropped their weapons and fell to their knees begging for mercy. Some got it, some didn't. Thiudimir let his men decide for themselves how generous they were feeling.

His retinue gathered around him, and he strode through the smoke from the burning houses. Around him he heard the crying of the children and the screaming of the women. They walked on through the centre of the village into what passed as the local forum, where he could see a small group of men and women, all aging. The village elders. With Demetrios beside him he strode towards the waiting group.

He didn't wait for introductions and said simply, "You should have given us what we asked for in the first place, then none of this would have happened." Demetrios translated his words without prompting.

A man stepped forward boldly, an old man. He leant on a wooden stick, and though he was blind, with milky eyes, he appeared to stare directly at Thiudimir.

"God will punish you for your evil work today," said the man hissed.

"Perhaps, but I've got women and children to feed, just like you," said Thiudimir through Demetrios.

"Jesus taught us that to kill is a sin and to steal is a sin; your soul will be damned for your work today, unless you repent!"

"You worry about your own soul, let me worry about mine!", Thiudimir was in no mood to debate with anyone now. "Shut up preaching to me, old man."

He looked over the man's shoulder to the other village elders, one or two of whom he assumed would be the decurions. "Show us the grain and fodder stores and bring out any food, drink, gold, silver, silk and spices." Demetrios translated.

"We need that grain" replied one of the elders.

"So do we." said Thiudimir.

The decurions muttered amongst themselves until Thiudimir's patience ran out.

"Show us the grain store or we will level the village, slaughter all the men and take all your women and children as slaves. Decide quick!"

They decided instantly.

It was two hours later amongst the ruins of their homes the villagers watched in silence as a train of wagons rolled by, laden with grain, food, cloth, spices, and fodder.

Houses smouldered and bodies lay in the open, feral dogs beginning to sniff around. Nobody seemed to care; they just stared after the departing wagons that rattled slowly away down the track in the growing light of the early morning and soon, though they were gone, still the villagers just stood and stared.

Chapter 29

Thessaly Thrace Border, 15th June 396 AD

Caius and Sextus paused their horses and dismounted. Sextus pointed to the way marker by the roadside. It read 'Milion CL'. Caius couldn't read. He had never been taught, but Sextus had taught him some rudiments of Greek as they had travelled. He could read numbers now. One hundred and fifty miles from New Rome.

"This is it," said Sextus calmly. "We're finally in Thrace. Another week or so and you'll be in the greatest city on Earth."

Caius crouched down and touched the marker with his hand. He still couldn't quite believe it. Here he was, further from home than ever he had imagined. One hundred and fifty more of these markers to pass and he would be at the home, the palace of the emperor. Just the thought of it scared him slightly. He stood up.

"So, what are you going to say to him when you see him?" asked Caius.

"Who?" Sextus looked confused.

"The emperor, of course."

Sextus spat on the ground. "You're the one who wanted to petition the emperor, you should be figuring out what it is you want to say or write rather."

"Write?"

"Of course. You don't just wander up to the palace and knock on the door and ask to see the emperor! Or was that your plan?" Sextus was looking at the young farmhand almost sadly.

"You never said anything about writing! I can't write!" exclaimed Caius. He felt a sense of panic start to well up. All this effort to make it to the capital to plead his case to the emperor, he had never actually considered how he would go about it. He had never thought that far ahead, if he was honest with himself. Just getting to New Rome was proving to be far more complicated and exhausting than he had imagined.

They had manged to avoid any real trouble on the way. They had been challenged by squads of militia and soldiers several times as they had ridden from town to town. They had met with some hostility as they attempted to gain entry to villages and towns, but then again others had been welcoming. The hostile towns were those that seemed to have suffered the most at the hands of Alaric, so Caius thought their anger towards strangers was understandable. He still felt fury in the pit of his stomach every time he thought about Tiberius. As he went to sleep at night, he still saw his brother's innocent face, yelling at the Goth riders as they plunged the spear into his body.

They had finally got onto the Via Egnacia, the road that ran from Dyrrachium to Constantinople, about four days ago, and had made good progress since then.

True to his word, Sextus had taught Caius the basics of handling a sword. It still felt heavy and unwieldy to him, and although the old solider had encouraged him and praised him, he knew in reality, if he was forced to fight, he stood little chance of defeating an enemy who was in any way competent. But he swore to keep practicing until he could use the sword to defend himself. So, every day he asked for Sextus to stop, and they would fence and spar for two hours. Sextus would also give him boxing and wrestling tips and tricks. Caius was strong from working the fields since his youth, and he had fought with his brother for fun, of course. But he had never been properly trained to fight or wrestle. Sextus said it was vital that a soldier knew how to defend himself, with or without a weapon. Caius grew fonder of his surly travelling companion each day; he found him to be a brave, careful, and thoughtful man with a kind heart. Not what he had expected of the Sextus he thought he knew back in the village.

"Well luckily for you I can write, so when we get to the capital, you're going to have to tell me what it is you want to say."

Caius breathed a sigh of relief. "What do you think I should say?"

"Aphrodite's tits Caius! Do I have to do everything for you?" snapped Sextus, but with a smile. "You tell me what to write, I'll write it. It's your petition."

Caius was silent. Then he said quietly, "I'll have to think about it."

Sextus snorted his laugh again. "We've got about a week, so start thinking. But don't expect the emperor to drop everything just to read your petition. He gets hundreds of requests for audiences and help every day, I'm sure."

"But he does see people, right?"

"No, he sees his ministers , the senators, the wealthy people, people who own land, people who own property. He'll never see the likes of us."

"Then how do we petition him?"

"We need to find a sponsor or a patron, someone who can get to see the emperor." Sextus got back onto his horse and signalled for Caius to do the same and they set off down the road at a gentle walk; the afternoon was hot, and they wanted to preserve the horses.

"But I don't know anybody in the capital," said Caius.

"I'm sure I can find someone to help us. I knew several men back in the army who came from families who served in the Blues and Greens guilds. I can start with them."

"Aren't they just the chariot teams in the games?"

"Caius, my poor innocent friend," responded the soldier, "The Urban Prefect thinks he runs the city, but the guilds know they run the city. The Urban Prefect can only do what he does at the pleasure of the city

202

guilds. And the Blues and Greens are two of the most powerful. Sure, they control the charioteers and train them and race them, but you don't drink, eat, serve food, whore, gamble, trade or work in most of the city without their say so. So, we need to get in with them and find someone who can help us. I'm sure they will. Last time I spoke to the men in the army they had no love for the Goths, and many, like me, had friends and family killed at Adrianople. So, any chance to help bring down Alaric, they'll jump at, never you mind about that."

"Do you hate the Goths?" asked Caius.

"Hate them? Sextus was silent for a second, "As a whole, I suppose I do hate them. I guess you do?"

"Well, I've never met one, except the ones that … that , you know, killed Tibby," Caius said. "Are they all that cruel?"

Sextus "Most of the ones I've met were either trying to kill me or I was trying to kill them. Either that or they'd been killing or raping or plundering some poor sod. But I've met a few Gothic traders and they were just people like you and me. Maybe their women are good too, I wouldn't know, I've never seen one. Though I've heard some fight alongside the men, if you can believe that."

Caius hadn't heard it but the thought of it scared him even more. He sighed and said, "Well, I hope we can find someone who can get us to see the emperor. Then perhaps he will send the army to get rid of all of the Goths."

Sextus looked sideways at his traveling companion and shook his head. The young man was an innocent. He still believed that the emperor would respond to his personal request for help. That took a special kind of naivety, or perhaps just a special kind of faith. He once had that belief in the power and wisdom of the emperor. That belief had died at Adrianople in the chaos of the slaughter, when the emperor had died like any other man, a sword run through his chest, facing the screaming hoard of Goths as they fell onto the legions in their thousands. He hoped the young man was right that the emperor would send and army to help.

But he knew in his heart that was never going to happen. There probably was no army to send, or else they would already have been in Greece.

Chapter 30

Delphi, Greece, 17th July 396 AD

The Gothic riders thundered up the pass and onto the small plateau. They reined in their horses and dismounted, dusting themselves off. Around them the mountains, their grey, jagged peaks shimmered in the summer heat. All was still. The only sounds were the chirping of crickets, the faint clang of a blacksmith's hammer way down in the valley below, and the occasional echoing bleat from a herd of goats as they wandered around the ruins, grazing on the wild shrubs and grass that had sprouted up between broken slabs and crumbling walls.

Only a handful of columns remained of the once great Temple of Delphi. Alaric gazed up at the columns.

"So, this is Delphi?" he said.

One of his officers laughed and said, "Looks like the oracle didn't see this coming!" Others joined in his laughter, and Alaric smiled. He was a Christian, yes. He had converted to the one God religion years ago, originally because he felt it would increase his chances of getting what he wanted. Roman lands for the Goths and a real military appointment.

Now he had his own priests in his army to baptise, to confess and to marry as his men required. He wanted a place for his people within the Roman lands because he had believed that God protected the Roman Empire. Certainly, the Romans believed that. But was God still on the Romans' side, he wondered? He looked up again at the columns of the temple. It had been dedicated to Apollo. The Roman Sun God, the God of Prophecy. For centuries the oracles had issued prophecies, some of which had come true, some which hadn't. But he supposed it was how you looked at things.

A small hut caught his eye on the far corner of the ruined temple. Smoke came from the chimney hole in its roof. A figure dressed in white stood outside the door of the hut. It was a woman.

Alaric turned around; his officers were still chatting and laughing, pointing to various sights down the hill.

"Wait here," he called out and turned and walked towards the hut. He heard the men starting to follow him, so he stopped and repeated the order. This time they stayed.

The woman was middle-aged, small but still beautiful, though lines were showing on her face marking the passage of time. Alaric looked down on her, waiting for her to speak. She said nothing but indicated that he should enter the hut. He ducked down through the doorway and found himself in a dimly lit single room. In the middle of the floor was a circular hole and, suspended over the hole was a metal tripod, holding an urn from which vapours emanated, infusing the air in the room. He found himself feeling slightly light-headed.

"Sit," the woman said gently her voice surprising low for such a small person. She pointed to an old semi-circular roman chair. Alaric sat.

"You came here looking for answers?" she asked.

"I came to see the temple," said Alaric.

"Disappointed?"

"A little."

"The Romans came and destroyed it all." She sounded sad.

"But you're still here. The oracle." It was a half-question, half-statement.

"That would be illegal."

"You have nothing to fear from me," said Alaric.

Neither said anything for a few minutes. The air was thick with the essence that smouldered in the urn.

"Do you believe the old Gods are still amongst us?" asked Alaric.

"Do you?"

"I don't know. Perhaps. Do you believe the old oracles really could see the future?"

"I don't know. Perhaps. I think you want to believe they did." The woman narrowed her eyes, looking intensely at him; he nodded.

"You're right. I would find any insight into what is to come useful."

"Is that why you came? Hoping to find some remnant of the oracle that could tell you your future? That's what the kings of old and the emperors all wanted." The woman knelt opposite Alaric, on the other side of the metal tripod. She started to add incense to the urn. A fresh smell struck Alaric's senses, relaxing him further.

"Maybe it's what the kings of today want too."

"Kings like you?" The woman smiled.

"You know who I am?"

She laughed. "Of course. King of the Tervingi ."

Silence again.

"What will become of me?" asked Alaric

"The emperor forbids it. It's un-Christian, it's heresy to predict the future." The woman held his gaze.

"I don't care about the emperor." Alaric returned her stare.

She stood up, walked around the urn and knelt in front of the king. She took his hands in hers and asked, "Are you sure? What if I told you that when you walk out that door, you will be killed?"

"I'll go out the window."

She laughed briefly, took a deep breath and squeezed Alaric's hands. She held them for a minute, then opened her eyes and gazed at his face. She seemed to study it closely, then she released his hands and sat back. She looked at the floor and said quietly. "You will be driven to destroy that which you seek."

"What do you mean?" asked Alaric.

"I don't know what it is you seek, only you know that."

"Why would I destroy what I'm looking for?"

"I think you are a man who will not rest until he finds what he is looking for."

"How do you know that?"

She replied simply. "Maybe I'm an oracle." She closed her eyes and knelt there motionless. After a few minutes Alaric got up and left. He blinked in the bright daylight and saw his officers surrounding the hut.

"Are you alright, sir?" asked one.

Alaric nodded and said they should leave and return to the army. As they left the plateau, he turned in his saddle and looked back at the hut, but there was no sign of the woman. He was quiet on the return journey and slept little that night.

Chapter 31

The Emperors' Court, Constantinople, 15th September 396 AD

Timasius sat in the accused's chair in the court and looked up at the child emperor sitting in the judge's seat. To him, Arcadius was still a child, even though he was now eighteen years old. The face was devoid of intelligence, the eyes drooping, the fat lips pursing. He fidgeted and looked for all the world as if he just wanted to get out the room. Never mind that the future, or life even, of one of his most senior generals now hung in the balance.

Timasius was under no illusions as to why he was here; he looked at the imposing figure of Eutropius at the left shoulder of Arcadius. *The puppet master of Constantinople*, he mused. He had eliminated the power of Abundantius a few months back by some preposterous nonsense of a plot to depose the emperor, a plot backed up by dubious evidence, to say the least. But Timasius knew that in these types of trial, a "treason trial", evidence was of secondary importance. Despite their pretence of legal standing, hearsay and rumour would take precedence.

His own arrest had happened two nights ago, palace guards knocking on his door, firmly but apologetically requesting that he accompany them to the palace, where he was to be detained by order of the emperor. Timasius read the warrant on the scroll; it was written in the name of the emperor but signed by Eutropius. There was little if any detail as to what the charges were, although the word "treason" was scattered amongst the wordy but vague paragraphs. He had been kept without any access to his legal counsel until right now, when he had met him in the court room. He had been treated well, and his room in the palace was comfortable enough, but a comfortable prison was still a prison.

There was a gallery of observers, some law students with their tutors, many senior and wealthy senators, some serving judges who were present to take over from the emperor if he so directed. That was a rare occurrence, but it was allowed by the law. There were several of the *illustrii* present as well as the praetorian prefect, Caesarius, who sat stony faced, but Timasius saw Aurelian there, seated at opposite end of the gallery from his older brother; he gave Timasius a small nod of recognition.

The court clerk had brought the session to order when Arcadius had arrived and sat in the judge's seat, with Eutropius standing beside him. All was now ready for the court to hear the formal charges. Timasius switched his gaze to the clerk, who had risen and was reciting from a marble tablet.

"… and the accused Timasius is charged with treason against our most exalted Emperor Arcadius, in that he has plotted to depose the rightful emperor and place himself as Emperor of the East."

Timasius' jaw tightened, he gritted his teeth and started to rise, words of indignation running through his head and about to burst forth into a tirade.

But his counsel placed a firm but steadying hand on his shaking shoulder and whispered sharply in his ear for him to stay calm and say nothing.

"How does the accused plead?" asked the clerk.

"Not guilty," responded Timasius' counsel, clearly and loudly, and with a subtle hint of derision.

"Very well," acknowledged the court clerk, "the court is now in session, the Majestic Emperor Arcadius is presiding."

There was a general murmuring from the gallery and court staff, then the counsel for the state stepped from his side of the court and said, "The state calls their witness, *Praepositus* Marcus Aurelius Flavius Bargus."

The blood drained from Timasius' face, and he watched the commander of his own bodyguard walk onto the floor of the chamber and stand before the court. He was dressed in a simple tunic and sandals.

The counsel for the state said, "The witness is now ready for your questions, Imperator." Arcadius shifted in his seat and spoke in his slightly effeminate voice. "Identify yourself."

Bargus drew himself up and said, "*Praepositus* Marcus Aurelius Flavius Bargus."

Timasius' counsel interjected. "Where is your uniform, *Praepositus*?"

"I have resigned from the employment of the accused, as I do not wish to be associated with a traitor."

Timasius sprang to his feet and roared, "What? You …" before his counsel grabbed him by his shoulders and implored him to be seated and to calm down.

The emperor glanced across at Timasius, looking slightly apprehensive. The old general stared back into the eyes of the emperor without fear. He was too angry to be afraid of the weakling. Arcadius asked his next standard question. "And what was or is your current association with the accused?"

Without hesitation, Bargus replied, "I was the commander of his personal bodyguard." The emperor seemed uncertain as to what to do next, so turned to Eutropius, who whispered in his ear. Arcadius nodded in understanding.

"What is it you wish to tell this court?"

"Only that I have on many occasions witnessed the accused declare his wish to be emperor, and that he has had meetings with many senior army members who share his view that he would be best placed to rule the Eastern Empire."

Arcadius pursed his thick lips and glanced at Timasius, who gritted his teeth and shook his head. The general's counsel stood and faced the emperor. "Imperator, may I ask a question?"

Arcadius looked at Eutropius, who shook his head. "No, not at this time." But he paused, not knowing what else to say.

The council took his chance. "Imperator, there is no legal precedent on which I may be refused. Your father was one who was always deemed fair and would give every man, no matter how lowly or exalted, the opportunity to prove his innocence. I stand humbly before you to defend the honour of this man, who has so loyally served your father and yourself. Surely if the case of the state is so solid, a mere question from me cannot change what is already pre-ordained?"

The emperor looked genuinely perplexed, and the counsel knew he had made his point. To refuse the allow the question would be to go against the precedents and the beliefs of his father, who the emperor and many in the court still revered. To allow the question and thereby allow the pre-eminence of Roman Law was the only honourable option.

Arcadius nodded and waved the counsel to proceed.

The counsel stepped forward and stood before Bargus. "*Praepositus* Bargus, what was your employment before being commander of General Timasius' bodyguard?"

"I don't see how that is relevant."

"Your occupation, please?" insisted the counsel. Bargus looked at the counsel then glanced at Eutropius, who stared back impassively at him.

"I was many things," muttered Bargus, dropping his gaze to the floor.

"Then you should be able to provide a lengthy answer to the question," said the counsel.

Eutropius learned over and whispered in the emperor's ear and Arcadius asked, "The point of this question is, counsel?"

212

"I wish to bring to your attention, Imperator, and to the attention of everybody in the court, who we have here as a witness. What type of man we have, who stands here accusing a faithful servant of the empire of many years?" The counsel turned to Bargus and said, "Again, I ask, what was your employment before being commander of General Timasius' bodyguard?"

Bargus remained silent. He glanced at Eutropius again, now with a little more desperation in his eyes. The eunuch remained unmoved, switching his attention to the gallery as if checking the reaction of the audience.

"Imperator, you have granted me permission to ask the question, please request that the witness answer." The counsel had just the right amount of firmness and reverence in his voice, thought Timasius.

Arcadius looked sullen and impatient, but for all his power, he had to abide by the rule of law, so he sighed and said, "*Praepositus* Bargus, you must answer the question."

"I was a merchant," said Bargus sullenly.

There was a small, dissatisfied murmur around the gallery and court.

The counsel pressed further. "A merchant of what?" Eutropius whispered in Arcadius' ear again, but the emperor said nothing. Bargus looked towards the dais; Timasius couldn't tell if he was looking to the weakling or the eunuch. Inside he felt a boiling rage that churned his gut. Somehow that damned eunuch had got to his man, turned him against him. What had he offered him, he wondered?

"A merchant of what?" pressed the counsel.

"Sausages," said Bargus quietly.

The counsel pretended he hadn't heard, cupped his ear, and asked, "I'm sorry; can you say that louder for everyone to hear?"

"I was a sausage seller," said Bargus, louder but not with any pride.

The murmurs from the gallery were more pronounced this time; there were a few badly suppressed laughs as well. Aurelian, however, stood and called out, "May I speak, Imperator?"

Arcadius looked confused. He had not spent much time in court rooms and emperors were only expected to preside in cases of high treason such as this, and such cases normally drew much emotion from supporters of both sides. Before Eutropius could stop him, the emperor nodded and said, "Of course, Senator Aurelian."

"My thanks, Gracious Imperator," replied Aurelian, bowing gracefully. "I am not an officer of this court, I understand, and if the accused is guilty, then he deserves the severest of punishments, but as Romans, the law is sacrosanct to us, it must be based on the truth, and truth comes from honourable men. Are we really entrusting any credence to this man? A trader in offal has been called to testify against one of our most distinguished and honoured generals." Aurelian turned to the gallery. "Fellow senators, are we really going to indulge this case, to have service and loyalty belittled by a meagre tradesman whom none of us has even met?"

There were shakes of the head and mutterings of agreement from many of the gallery observers. The teacher was whispering urgently to his students, some of whom looked amused. Caesarius stood too and said "Imperator, may I?" Again, the emperor nodded; he was losing control of the proceedings, he knew, but these intelligent and eloquently spoken men intimidated him and he did not know how to refuse their requests. Eutropius looked annoyed, which pleased Timasius, who nodded his appreciation to Aurelian.

Caesarius now was speaking. "Many of you know my brother and I agree on few things." There was a gentle laugh around the gallery. "But on this matter, I must concur. How can the word of this man be taken with greater weight than that of our long-serving and honourable friend, General Timasius? Imperator, why are we even here, if this is all the state has to offer?"

Arcadius looked around the room, appearing flustered. He turned to speak to Eutropius when Caesarius continued. "Imperator, if I might make a suggestion; for this case we should appoint two judges, one chosen by you and one by the senators, so that we may get a balanced perspective on the case. Let them preside; you may then attend to more important matters of state, as this matter hardly seems worthy of your time."

There was another round of murmurs, but with nods of the head. Arcadius looked relieved that he had been given a way out, but nevertheless turned his drooping eyes turned to Eutropius. The eunuch whispered a few words then stood back.

"Very well then," said the emperor. "I appoint Saturninus as our first co-judge."

Caesarius motioned for those senators present to converse with him, and after a few moments a thin, middle-aged man with a receding hairline stepped forwards and announced that he was to be the second co-judge.

"Procopius is it not?" asked the emperor.

"Yes, Imperator," said Procopius, bowing low. "It will be my honour to serve you and Rome."

"Very well, then, you may proceed." And with that, looking thoroughly relieved to be spared any further potential conflict with the senators, Arcadius gathered up his robe and walked from the court, accompanied by his bodyguard.

The clerks brought up a second chair and placed it next to the one the emperor had been sitting in, and the two judges took their seats. Eutropius spoke in Saturninus' ear for a minute and then stepped off the dais to take a seat in the gallery and observe the proceedings.

"We will continue with the statement from the witness Bargus."

Saturninus had seniority and spoke first. There was more muttering from the gallery. Timasius, however, was not surprised. Saturninus was old, experienced and had a notable history in dealing with the Goths. Theodosius had entrusted him with negotiating with the barbarians fourteen years ago and he had done well. But he was not a principled, forthright character; he bent whichever way the political wind was blowing, so it was no surprise that the emperor, at the urging of Eutropius, had nominated the veteran. Timasius did not dislike Saturninus. He judged him to be a weak and mainly irrelevant figure these days, so he spent little time considering him. Perhaps that had been a mistake, he mused, seeing that his future now lay very much in this man's hands. As for Procopius, Timasius always judged him to be a bit of an oaf. He often spoke before he thought, and even when backed into a verbal corner by good rhetoric or argument, he often as not stuck to his point of view whether there was merit in doing so or not. *Stubborn as a mule*, thought the general, *and about as intelligent, but nevertheless, he is a more honourable man than his co-judge.*

Bargus meanwhile, was speaking.

"I became aware that General Timasius had designs on the Imperial Diadem only in the few months since the death of the traitor Rufinus. In casual conversation he often said that ... that ..." but he paused and looked at Saturninus, as if worried about the consequences of his next words.

"Go on man, speak up!"

Bargus took a deep breath and said, "That the emperor was weak and listening too much to corrupt officials." There was a collective intake of breath from the observers, except from Eutropius, who sat expressionless, and Bargus was now a little more confident. "And that were he in power then the situation would be very different."

There were mutterings from the gallery and around the court. Timasius had started to rise in indignation, but the hand of his counsel held firm on his shoulder, and he sat straight back down. His counsel whispered, "Stay calm, General, that is most important. You will do yourself no good by letting your anger rule your words."

And indeed, it seemed his counsel was correct. Saturninus started another question. "And how would things be different?" when Procopius, the co-judge interrupted. The small thin man stood and spoke with a surprisingly powerful voice. "Enough of this!" He looked at Saturninus and then at Bargus with thinly disguised disgust.

"What is it that we do here?" he asked. "General Timasius is a veteran of the legions, he served with the great Theodosius, he has fought and won over the enemies of Rome and has shown loyalty again and again, committed no crimes and continues to serve Rome at the highest levels within the senate." Procopius looked around at the gallery, his eyes fixed on Eutropius. "It seems to me that this trial is nothing more than a ruse to politically discredit a great man, in order to further political ambitions. How can we take the words of a known criminal, a known trickster, a man who has returned to this city despite being ordered from it for petty crimes?"

Saturninus stood. He had been a big man in his prime, and was still imposing, though stooped with age, his greying hair wispy and somewhat unkempt.

"My enthusiastic co-judge speaks from the heart," he said. Procopius made to interject but Saturninus raised a hand and continued. "However, we are not here to listen to our hearts, but to listen to the facts, and whether you believe this witness or not, the assertions he makes are borne out by independent documents written by the accused himself, documents found in his properties by the witness."

Timasius looked at his counsel, frowning. The counsel stood and spoke to the judges. "We are not aware of any such documents. May we see them?"

Saturninus nodded to the court clerk who, after rifling through several scrolls and books, located a worn papyrus scroll. The counsel unrolled it and scanned the contents. He frowned and handed it to Timasius, who read it himself, his eyes widening as he read the words.

"Are these documents not written by yourself?" asked Saturninus.

"No!" snapped Timasius.

"And yet that is your handwriting, is it not?"

"No … well, yes it looks like it, but I never wrote those words, I swear!" insisted the general.

"It is your handwriting, yet you never wrote the words. Who could have possibly written them then? Bargus here?" Saturninus pointed at the silent witness.

"Him?" snorted Timasius ironically. "He doesn't know how!"

"Then who?" asked Saturninus, but before waiting for an answer he inquired, "What is the date on those documents?"

Timasius wasn't even looking at the letter now, he knew what was in it. He could see the trap opening for him now. "It is dated five years ago. 27th June."

"It's a long time ago, General. I understand, you can't possibly remember every single note you have written. I certainly can't," said Saturninus with a sly smile, expressing empathy with a man only slightly younger than himself.

"Insulting the accused is unworthy of you!" snapped Procopius, but he was less bullish now in defence of the general. Still, he attempted one last defence. "How can we believe what this man Bargus says? General

Timasius was kind to him in offering him a place in his guard, and this is how he repays him? By accusing him of treason, by stealing his personal papers?" There was a murmur of approval from some senators in the gallery.

Saturninus turned to Bargus and asked, "How did you come into the possession of these documents?"

"The general gave them to me to dispose of. 'Burn them,' he said to me."

"And why did you not obey your master in this?"

"My loyalty has always been first to the empire," said Bargus, but he was interrupted by a barking laugh from Procopius, who turned to the gallery and spread his arms.

"Fellow senators, can you in any way believe what this man says?"

"Let the witness speak," interjected Saturninus.

"Oh, I think he has spoken quite enough!" Procopius persisted. "He stands there before us, and you attempt to give his words credence over a decorated and loyal general."

"The man is a witness called by the state."

"The man is a known criminal and a liar."

"And on the authority of the emperor," Saturninus countered, talking over Procopius, who was still objecting "And my seniority by right of age in this court, the court *will* hear his testimony, or will I have to recall the emperor to remind you, sir, of your duties to the rule of law."

At that threat of action, Procopius ceased his attempts to talk over his co-judge. There was talking and a few shouts from the gallery, some in support of Procopius, others insisting that the witness be heard. Eutropius sat silent. Saturninus turned and looked for Caesarius and asked, "As praetorian prefect, what is your view?"

"The law is quite clear. Any witnesses called by the state or defendant must be given due opportunity to answer questions or make statements."

Saturninus turned back to Procopius and said, "Bargus merely handed us these documents, and whatever his motives, what is in them is damning. The witness was doing the empire a service by bringing them to us!" Without waiting for any further comment, he whirled and turned on the accused, who sat fuming in anger. "And where were you on the 27th of June of that year, General?"

"I was on campaign in Macedonia with the emperor," said Timasius quietly.

"And what had happened that day, General?" asked Saturninus.

Timasius looked across at Eutropius and then back to Bargus, then back to the judge. Cautiously and deliberately, he said, "We had won a victory against the barbarians. They were on the run."

"And what did the emperor want to do?" Saturninus asked confidently; he was in full flow and knew what he was doing. Timasius knew what he was doing as well but could not see any way of stopping it. "He wanted to continue to pursue them through the night."

"And why didn't he?"

The general sat silently, staring back at the old man in front of him. Saturninus has been a soldier too, not a very good one it was said, but no coward. But that was long in the past, Timasius knew. Now, he only seemed to care about a comfortable and ostentatious life in the capital. He threw lavish parties, which were attended by many senators. Eutropius too had been seen there many times. Maybe he thought he deserved a little luxury after all these years. Timasius was aware that Saturninus made sure he fell in line with whoever was calling the shots at court and was never afraid to trade comfort and convenience for principles, if he had ever had any in the first place.

Timasius gritted his teeth. He knew if he lied about that day, his lie would be immediately seen and countered. If he told the truth, he would damn himself. He sat staring at the scroll in front of him.

"I did not write these words!" Timasius growled angrily.

"Why didn't Theodosius pursue the barbarians, General?" insisted the judge.

Timasius breathed in deeply. Better to die with a clear conscience than betray one's own principals.

"Because I convinced him not to."

Saturninus stood back and turned to the gallery and echoed the words. "Because you convinced him not to!"

"I was concerned for my men."

"You were so concerned for your men that you filled their bellies with food and drink to the point they fell asleep, even the sentries and guards!"

Timasius was silent. Saturninus let the silence have its impact, then he continued in a low voice. "That night the barbarians crept back into your camp, past your snoring soldiers, and attacked our emperor as he slept. It was only the swift action of his bodyguard that prevented him from being captured or slain! Is that not the truth of the matter?"

Timasius glanced sideways and looked at his counsel, who shook his head. Timasius held his silence, though his gut was churning, and he was barely containing the outrage that boiled within him. It hadn't been like that; it had all been a horrible mistake. Saturninus pointed a gnarled and crooked finger at him. "Read the letter that lies before you!"

Timasius shook his head and said, "I did not write those words. I have been tricked! This is a deception. I will not be a party to this!"

Saturninus dramatically stepped forward and snatched up the scroll and unravelled it with a theatrical flourish; he was in his element now. He faced the gallery and read aloud.

"Perhaps one day, my chance to rule the empire as it should be ruled will come. Perhaps in a year, or perhaps today. Who knows what fortunes or pitfalls the battlefield offers? A lazy guard, a sleeping sentry could allow through a silent assassin, and in the blink of an eye, the empire will need a new ruler. I pray that I am there that day to step into that most sacred of duties and do what needs to be done to preserve this greatest of man's ventures: the Roman Empire."

The gallery was silent. Saturninus turned and looked at Timasius. Procopius too was silent; he looked shocked.

"Is this your handwriting?" asked Saturninus yet again.

"I swear I did not write those words," replied Timasius.

"Is this your handwriting?"

The general closed his eyes and breathed deeply. Opening them, he glanced across to where Eutropius sat. There was an evil glint in his eye and a nasty smirk on his lips.

"Yes, that is my handwriting."

Later that evening after Timasius had been escorted to the docks and put on a boat for his exile in North Africa, Eutropius was back in his private office. Having dismissed his aides, he once again took the small key out of his pocket and unlocked the shallow drawer. He took out the small sheet of papyrus and laid it carefully on his desk. Dipping a quill into his gold pot of deep blue ink, he gently drew a line through the second name on the list: *'Timasius'*. Placing the quill back into its gold holder, he blew on the papyrus and stared at the third name on the list with just a hint of a smile on his lips.

Chapter 32

Streets of Constantinople, 10th October 396 AD

Caius drank the remainder of his wine and looked across the tavern, to where Sextus was in deep conversation with three men, all wearing blue smocks. The tavern was poorly lit, it smelt of stale wine and sweat, but it was cheap; and for the last three months, upstairs in the small, musty smelling and creaking room, it had been home.

They had arrived at the gates of the city in late June. Caius had never seen anything like it before. The walls of the city were imposing from a distance; up close they towered over him. The walls of Emperor Constantine, said Sextus, the founder of the city, over half a century ago. The Mese, the main street, was enormous, paved in marble and fine stone; it carved through the heart of the city and there at the end of it, in the distance at the hilltop, the façade of the golden palace. There, in his mind's eye, sat the emperor, magnificent in his power, surveying and smiling kindly on his people below. He was convinced that the emperor would act once he knew the true suffering of his people in Greece. He had to. Caius had wanted to go straight to the palace, but Sextus had insisted they instead go towards the outer streets on the south side of the city. There they would meet people who could put them in touch with other people, who might be able to put them in touch with a patron who might be willing to petition on behalf of them. On their way, Caius had been dazzled by Constantinople, its buildings and its people.

He stared wide-eyed as a group of tall, slim women, dressed in fine silks, walked past them, laughing and giggling. Their dresses shimmered in the sunlight, and he caught a tantalising glimpse of what lay beneath the silk. He noticed priests on the steps of a small church, frowning as the women walked past. Caius blushed and turned to follow his friend, who was waiting at a corner of a building just off the side of the Mese.

"Put your tongue back in, lad," growled Sextus.

"Did you see them?" asked Caius.

"Pretty much all of them," agreed the older man, but he pointed at the priests and said, "But they'll be in trouble for sure; it doesn't look like the churchmen approve, even though they've probably all got a massive hard on just watching them go by. Come on, we have to go."

They passed shops and traders' stalls that lined the sides of the smaller street; heard the raucous laughter of businessmen, the yells of the traders, the squawks and clucks of cockerels and chickens, the grunts of pigs and the bellowing of oxen. A cacophony of noise that threatened to overwhelm Caius. He walked mesmerised, turning his head this way and that, nearly colliding with others and being cursed for his clumsiness. Sextus had had to grab his arm and steer him through the throng of people, weaving and barging all the time.

They passed by churches and shrines, taverns, orphanages, more churches, some impressive looking houses of two storeys, which Sextus dismissed as mere "traders' hovels", compared to the mansions occupied by the wealthy senators.

Caius was going to ask how much further they had had to go, but before he could open his mouth, Sextus pointed to a two-storey building set back off the street, with a small square in front of it. The building was quite small, and Caius could see it was a tavern; out in front were tables and chairs where men, sat drinking and making loud conversation.

"I know people here," Sextus had said, and he had told the truth. He introduced Caius to several of his old veteran friends, who slapped him hard on the back and plied him with drink for the remainder of the day. He hadn't remembered much else, but he had woken up the next morning in a rough wooden bed, to the sound of creaking floorboards. He had looked up bleary-eyed to see Sextus getting dressed. Then he had slid out of his narrow bed and stood there looking down. He had seen and heard through the cracks in the floorboards people milling around the tavern below; the smell of cooking wafted upwards making his mouth water.

That was how it had been for several weeks; him wandering the streets, gazing in wonder at the buildings and the people. And what buildings they were!

His little village had only single-storey buildings and a simple wooden barricade marking the limits. Larrissa had seemed massive with its walls and two-storey buildings. But here?

Here, there were three-storey buildings and higher still. There were squares and forums with columns that seemed to soar up and touch the sky. He had walked the length of the Mese many times, listening to the merchants and their servants shouting and yelling across the street, trying to catch the ears and eyes of the passing wealthy men and women who browsed the store fronts. City militia patrolled the upper Mese, moving on beggars and dragging away thieves and pickpockets. The smells of the lower Mese were those of cattle and pigs; these morphed into the sweet incenses and perfumes of the upper Mese, so that when you stood before the walls of the golden palace, the pleasant smells of flowers and trees that wafted from the palace gardens mixed with the fragrances of the street, filling the head, and calming the spirit.

He had marvelled at the Hippodrome. It seemed too large to have been built by mortal men, freemen, or slaves; surely giants or God himself must have raised it from the ground? The lower arches supported the middle columns and then the upper colonnades, towering above the roofs of three-storey buildings in the neighbouring streets. Caius wondered how men had made such a structure. Truly this city was the work of God.

The people, too, mesmerised him. In his small village a stranger was talked about, studied and if disliked or feared, ejected from the community. Here, half the people looked strange to him. There were

225

people with pale skins and long hair and slim noses, who Sextus said were called Verengians, who came from the far north, where in winter they never saw the sun. "Which is why they are so fucking pale!" laughed Sextus.

Then there were others whose skin was as rich and as dark as the night, their hair black, their lips full. Sextus called these people Moors or Numidians, and said they came from the scorching deserts in Africa, south of the lands commanded by the emperor, where they rode horses as fast as the wind. They dressed in white, held strangely shaped swords, wide at the tip and narrower at the hilt and were, according to Sextus, often slave traders, selling captives from raids on the coast of Hispania and Gaul.

Many of the traders on the streets were Jews. Jews had visited his village in the past, so Caius knew about them. He had seen people from Greece too. Thessaly, Sparta, Attica; places he knew of better than most. People had passed his way from those lands and cities; workers, artisans, entertainers, soldiers, so they were the ones that seemed "normal" to him. But there were others who looked positively outlandish to him. According to Sextus there were Gauls, Ionians, Hispanics, Slavs, Italians, Syracusans, Persians, Mesopotamians, Cretans, Macedonians, and a host of others he failed to remember the names of.

There were Goths too.

That shook Caius.

How could these people be allowed to live in the city of the emperor? How did the emperor allow it? These people had murdered his brother Tiberius in cold blood, without so much as a second thought. Yet here they were. He saw them everywhere. In the taverns, in the brothels, buying from traders; some were traders, and unbelievably, some were wearing the uniform of Roman soldiers.

"Why?" he asked Sextus. "Why are they allowed to live here? After what they have done?"

"It's a complicated world."

"No, it's not!" replied Caius sharply. "These animals murdered my brother and burnt our village, and yet the emperor doesn't punish them?"

They had been in a tavern, seated in a corner waiting for Sextus' blue-garbed friends to arrive.

"Keep your voice down!" hissed Sextus. "You're inviting trouble." He glanced around the room, but luckily no one appeared to have heard the outburst.

"There are Goths who live and work in the city, just like everyone else," said Sextus, a little more calmly, and with more consideration for what was plainly a sensitive subject. "They had nothing to do with what happened to us. To your brother."

"But their people did!" Now it was Caius' turn to hiss a reply.

"Well, you can't hold every Goth responsible for the actions of a few of Alaric's soldiers." Sextus made a short laugh. "But … well … I do hate the Goth bastards too, though I try to be a little more discerning about which particular Goth bastards I hate."

Caius drank a large mouthful of wine and burped. "So, when do we get to petition the emperor?"

"Soon, Caius, soon. We're here to meet some men who can help us, or rather you, to get in touch with a patron to whom we can appeal our cause."

Caius watched Sextus approach the three men who entered the tavern a few minutes later. They all looked like men who had endured hard lives, but they greeted Sextus warmly and proceeded to sit down and talk and joke loudly. Caius was desperate to rush across and demand they somehow get him an immediate audience with the emperor, but his friend had been quite firm.

"Let me do the talking, keep your mouth shut!"

So, Caius let Sextus do the talking and kept his mouth shut.

Chapter 33

Corinth, Greece, 10th October 396 AD

Thiudimir screamed as he and the charging line of Goths slammed headlong into the front rank of the city's garrison troops. Around him his comrades hurled themselves into the fray. They dodged the thrusts of the spears of the defenders, who had formed a less than exemplary shield wall. Some spears found their mark and screams, not of fury but of pain, erupted around him. He sidestepped a vicious thrust, sliced his heavy sword down onto the helmet of a defender. The helmet held but the blow stunned the man. He fell forwards, senseless, to the floor. Thiudimir stepped over him and slashed upwards at the man who had stepped forward to fill the hole. The man sidestepped the swing and jabbed his spear, but Thiudimir batted it away with his shield. Bringing his sword around in a ferocious arc he sliced the unbalanced man's left shoulder, almost severing the arm. The soldier fell to the floor screaming, blood gushing from the wound. But the defenders held fast. Next to him Demetrios was drawing his sword from the guts of a man who was still writhing and screaming on the ground, the mercenary stamped his heel into the man's face to silence him, then looked up for his next target.

Thiudimir looked to his left. He heard the rumble of the heavy cavalry and heard the crash and cries of soldiers being run down and trampled by the horses as they did their bloody work. Some of the defenders looked the same way and saw the carnage being wrought on their centre, but then Thiudimir heard a deep voice barking out words he didn't understand. Thiudimir saw the man yelling the orders. He was back two rows in the wall. He looked every inch the experienced veteran and unlike many of the defenders he looked like he knew what he was doing. "Who's that?" he yelled across to Demetrios.

"No idea! But he's telling them to keep eyes front and to hold their position". Thiudimir nodded. Running would be suicide, holding formation was the only way to survive.

Not so easy, then.

He stepped back and yelled at his own men to form up again. The message rippled through the ranks and Alaric's men quickly locked shields. A second line fell in behind them and a third. He saw archers forming behind the defenders' wall, and heard an order go up.

"Archers!" yelled Thiudimir, and the shields were raised just in time as a thousand or more lethal shafts thudded into the Goth shields, shocking arms and shoulders. Thiudimir took a deep breath and then thundered, "Forward!" As one the attackers hammered their shields from behind with the pommels of their swords and took a step forward, the sound like that of a giant stomping across the land. Thiudimir peered forward and saw some of the defenders wince at the sound. He smiled and yelled, "Again!" The deafening beat of war sounded again, and the attackers took another step forward.

Peering through a small gap between the shields, Thiudimir saw the enemy archers ready to launch again. He sounded the alarm. Again, the deadly rain of arrows was largely nullified, though several screams of agony told him that some had found their mark.

"Again!"

Another pace, another relentless thudding step, then another and then Thiudimir yelled out, "Engage!" The Goths took three long strides and crashed into the defenders' shield wall, throwing their combined weight forward. Thiudimir's shield, like his men's, had a rounded boss with a sharpened point which drove into the defenders' shields and locked the front rows together. Some of the enemy spears slid through the gaps. Some buried themselves in flesh. Most were deflected, many broke, as the sheer weight of men and shields were crushed together.

Now it was simply a deadly game of push and shove. Thiudimir thrust his sword forward, trying to find a target. He was jabbing half-blind, keeping behind his shield, and the enemy did the same. He was pinned into his own shield. He could barely move or breath; it was stifling hot. He smelt the stench of urine and faeces as men died and voided their bowls.

"Ready!" he yelled. He counted down from three and his men heaved forward, trying through brute strength to drive back the defenders. As the collective strength of his men surged forward, he stepped on some poor bastard's guts, slipped, and nearly went to the floor. He grabbed the leg of the man next to him and just stopped himself. To fall was to invite almost certain death. Stay on your feet, he told himself.

Again, he gave the order to press on. Again, the Goths surged forward. He could see the whites of his enemies' eyes now, and they showed fear, but still they held on. He could feel that his shield was locked hard into his opponent's; he couldn't move it sideways, and he couldn't draw back because of the pressure from behind him.

Another crushing surge: it was getting really hard to breathe now. There were shouts and screams all around. Anger, fear, hatred, excitement, all the emotions, all extreme. He was being crushed between the enemy and his own men, minute by minute.

He sucked in some precious air, peered through the small gap between shields, and saw the veteran directly in front of him, a row back. Nearly there, he thought. He forced some space for his body, filled his lungs and barked out the order for another surge. This time when they heaved forward, something gave way.

Maybe one of their men slipped, maybe they had weakened, whatever, it didn't matter, Thiudimir himself nearly toppled forward as the pressure of the defenders evaporated and they turned and fled. A dark shape thundered in front of him. The cavalry.

They had managed to break through at last and had outflanked the wall. Now it was just a glorious rout. Those defenders who could still run dropped their shields and swords and fled back to the city.

Thiudimir didn't pursue. He found himself face to face with the veteran soldier, who wasn't running. Without thinking, he charged at him, but was battered to one side by the man's shield. Demetrios thrust his sword at the man, but with lightening reactions he slashed away the sword and hammered his shield into his attacker, sending him crashing to the ground amongst the moaning bodies and the already dead. The veteran showed no fear and crouched, ready to take on others, even though he stood alone, his army running for their lives. By now he was surrounded by Thiudimir and his men. The man slowly circled looking each of his attackers in the eye, daring them to make a move. All around the circle the screams and cries of the rout continued, but none of them really heard them. The man uttered a stream of words. Demetrios who had picked himself up said, "he's telling us bastards, it's about fair now. Six against one. And apparently, we're fucking barbarian scum" he laughed.

Thiudimir couldn't help but admire the man. Not in the least bit scared. Challenging them, baiting them to come at him. One of his men took the bait and lunged at the veteran, who calmly stepped aside, ducking under the slicing sword, and then hammered his shield across the man's back, and using his sword pommel he stunned his attacker who dropped to the floor like a stone, then he spun around to deal with the next attack. It never came.

Thiudimir felt exhaustion start to roll over him. He lowered his sword, and yelled to his men, "Enough!" Immediately they all took a step back and lowered their weapons. The veteran narrowed his eyes and spat out some more words.

Demetrios said he's asking if the big bad Goths are scared of one little Greek boy?"

Any other day Thiudimir might have challenged this man to single combat. But not today. They had been fighting on and off for months. Today had been a long, hard-fought battle; skirmishers and then finally this last hour-long clash with the final line of city defenders. He was exhausted. The army around him too was slowing their chase of the city defenders. The bloodlust of battle was giving way to relief, exhaustion, delayed fear and above all prayers of thanks for their survival after another day of carnage.

"Tell him to go home," said Thiudimir to Demetrios. The man listened to the mercenary then barked out a short laugh and pointed to the city, where plumes of smoke were already starting to rise.

"Go home to what?" relayed Demetrios.

"Then walk away and start again. You're a brave man." Thiudimir sighed. "We don't want to see you dead."

"His family are in there," said Demetrios after another round of translation. Thiudimir looked towards the city and then back to his men.

"You all saw how this man fought," he said, and they nodded. "We all agree he lives?" They all nodded. "We all agree that life without family is no life at all?"

"Aye," said several men.

"Then let's reunite this man with his family." Thiudimir sheathed his sword, looked around and picked up two small daggers from two corpses at his feet. He took several steps towards the city. When they didn't follow him, he turned and yelled, "Well, come on then, you lazy bastards! And you, yes you, you stubborn Greek idiot, let's go find them, and get you and them out of the city."

Confused, but used to following the commands of their leader , the Goths formed a tight group around the Roman veteran, and he, equally bemused by this turn of events, placidly walked in their midst across the trampled and bloodstained soil and grass, towards the city gates.

All around them they saw the carnage of the battlefield, they heard the moaning, crying, weeping men, pleading for their lives, or pleading to be put out of their misery and pain. Around them were the dead, crushed, contorted, unrecognisable as human in some cases, a feast for the crows and vultures who even now had started to gather overhead.

Ahead they saw the rest of the city garrison running for their lives, the Goth cavalry amongst them, slashing and hacking as the runners tried to make it to the city they were supposed to be defending.

Now it lay open to Alaric's army.

On the far side of the battlefield, on a small barren hillock, surrounded by his bodyguard, Alaric watched with a small smile of satisfaction as his army chased down the fleeing defenders and slaughtered them. *That is the price of defeat*, he thought, *may I never taste it...* He saw the smoke rising from buildings on the outskirts of the city as his men began the sack. He had ordered that churches and shrines remain un-desecrated and that any who sheltered in them or around them be spared. Death would be dealt out to those of his own men who defied his orders. Alaric feared the wrath of God as much as anybody. Outside of those places, though, he knew he had to let his men have free rein. He just hoped that the city inhabitants had heeded the warnings he had sent in by messenger two days earlier, to stay in the protected buildings.

He would send in his commanders soon to restore some order, but he had to let his men reap some of the spoils of war; that was the order of things. He did not want his men to raze the city to the ground; that would break the bargain he had made with Eutropius. But he knew there was gold somewhere in the city and he needed gold urgently. He'd sent his most trusted officers to find the hoard and guard it against all-comers, especially his own men.

He turned away, mounted his horse, and signalled his entourage to follow him into the city. This place had not been attacked or threatened for over a century. It had no walls to speak of, and the people here had grown soft with wealth and comfort. There were plenty of trophies and spoils to be had, and there was the gold of course, but more than that, this city was the gateway to the home of the most famous of all Greeks: the Spartans.

Corinth had fallen.

Chapter 34

House of Eutropius, Constantinople, 12th December 396 AD

Eutropius sat alone on a chair, on a raised platform at the centre of a large circular room. He was hosting a party at his large city mansion. It lay just off the Mese, just ten minutes' journey by litter from the palace. The house had belonged to General Timasius. But now he, the castrated chamberlain, lived in it on holidays. On other days he rented it to senators and wealthy foreign visitors who liked a certain kind of entertainment. He had kept the original staff on, distributing bribes and handouts liberally, ensuring that not even the lowliest worker in the gardens was left out. A few unappreciative members of staff, who had shown misplaced loyalty to the old general, had refused the money. They had been dismissed. He had even freed all the slaves, giving them paid work. Some of those ex-slaves were young boys and rather comely women who he brought to these parties to help entertain his guests.

The house had spectacular views over the southern reaches of the city, out over the Sea of Marmara, but this room had no such view; its windows were tall and thin, but high on the walls, practically at ceiling height. Shafts of light illuminated the room during the day, but at night, the room was lit by powerful torches hung around the walls, and by three huge copper candelabras that hung from the vaulted ceiling, each hold a hundred candles.

All around Eutropius were men and women drinking, eating, and fornicating. Men with women's heads between their legs and women with men's heads between their legs. One adventurous woman lay on her back servicing an old senator with her mouth, whilst another, Eutropius had to admit a very attractive young woman, pleasured her. He hoped the senator's heart held out; he could do without the inconvenience of disposing of another body.

A naked servant walked close to him with a tray of drinks. Eutropius waved her over. Her lithe body and perfect breasts made eyes in the room follow her wherever she went. "Take two drinks to the two palace guards outside the front door. I don't want them to feel left out. But tell them from me that if they fall asleep, I will have them castrated!" He grinned a humourless grin. The servant bowed and headed for the main door, hips swaying.

Eutropius observed all of this dispassionately. His maiming at an early age meant no desire to take part entered his mind. He had been the target of older men's baser instincts for many years. He didn't feel shame, he was past all that. He realised now that all those nights of being fucked by soldiers and senators had been an almost spiritual experience. A sort of baptism of pain and humiliation that had hardened and tempered him for this time. It felt good to be the object of people's yearnings for recognition at court, for recognition of their importance by the emperor. And Eutropius was the gatekeeper to the emperor. Now they didn't queue up to bugger him, they queued up to flatter him and to pay him respect. It was sweet revenge on all of those powerful men who had used him as a sexual plaything without a second thought, and he intended to exact every last ounce of pleasure in that revenge. He enjoyed watching the sexual antics of others, not because it aroused him in any way, he wasn't capable of that. But it made him feel superior. He had no need to partake in such ridiculous acts to provide himself with pleasure.

Power was his pleasure. Power over people. And he had that now. He had power over the emperor. The poor, feeble boy who wore the purple lacked any real desire to rule. He only enjoyed fucking his wife and killing innocent animals. He had shown no interest in getting involved in matters of state.

"You always explain thing so well, Eutropius," the emperor had said, after one particularly long and boring session discussing the issue of Alaric.

Gainas had again pressed for action against Alaric, but Caesarius had recommended no engagement at present, for perfectly valid reasons, which Eutropius had not actively supported but had not dismissed either. The organisation of the new praesentalis armies was nearly complete; commanders were being assigned next month. Next year would be the time for action, if necessary, but even then, both Caesarius and Eutropius preferred diplomacy and, if necessary, bribery to keep the peace. War was dangerous and expensive.

"I know I can count on you, Eutropius, to get this dealt with." That, or something similar, was Arcadius' contribution to most meetings of the consistorium. And Eutropius loved hearing it. He loved hearing it because it handed the power of the emperor to him.

He loved hearing those words, because he could see how much the other members of the *illustrii* hated it. They all craved power, influence, and recognition from Arcadius. But it was only he, Eutropius, who really had it.

Eutychainus, that sycophantic fool, hated it, but he was now so in debt to Eutropius through his gambling addiction that he said nothing. The chamberlain could see that he despised the emperor's favour towards him, and that gave him pleasure.

Caesarius, praetorian prefect of the East, hated the emperor's trust in Eutropius too. Caesarius was meant to be the most senior individual at court, but Eutropius had managed to wrestle that power from him. All meetings with the emperor saw Eutropius sitting by his side or in his stead, steering the conversation. If he could not be there, which occasionally happened, he made sure his most trusted deputies were present, and that the emperor declare them proxies for Eutropius.

Caesarius was no fool, and not easily swayed by the chamberlain's games; he had succeeded in keeping a distance from the eunuch and had been instrumental in getting the reformation of the military up and running. Gainas had provided the necessary military expertise, but the administration had been all Caesarius'. He would soon be redundant; his independence needed to be curtailed, and with the new deployments complete, Eutychainus, who might be useless at gambling, was at least a competent, if unimaginative, administrator. Eutropius now needed to do something about Caesarius, and he of course he had a plan already in motion.

Gainas hated the influence Eutropius had. Now *that* was a source of particular pleasure. Eutropius didn't really know what it was about the Goth General that caused him to want to torment the man. He was capable militarily; after all, he had done him a huge favour in eliminating Rufinus. He just felt he needed to keep that particular beast on a leash; demeaning and undermining him seemed to be the best way at present to keep him neutered and powerless.

Then there was Aurelian. Now that man really did hate Eutropius' influence on Arcadius, with a passion. The younger brother of Caesarius was smart and had ambition to match the eunuch's own. He had been a potent Urban Prefect; his tenure was still admired and still caused senators to stop dozing in the senate building and sit up and listen when he spoke. Of all his opponents, Aurelian was the most dangerous. He had his own network of supporters and spies everywhere, inside and outside of the city. And Eutropius had heard rumblings of some kind of a plot against himself, which could have originated from Aurelian, though he doubted he could prove it. He must be on his guard. He had come too far now to be brought down by his aristocratic enemy.

Other members of the consistorium were of no concern to Eutropius: John the *Comes Sacrarum Largitionum* was in his pay. He had been handed lands and wealth confiscated from Abundantius and Timasius, though of course Eutropius had retained the most beautiful and the most profitable for himself, and he had kept records of transactions which could be easily brought out and used against them if they had a change of heart.

The Magistri Militum were all currently unassigned. Stilicho in the West arrogantly held onto the title of *magister utriusque militiae* but nobody in the East recognised that. Finally, there was Hosius, the *Magister Officiorum,* the Master of Offices, the man who controlled the palace guard, the weapons arsenals, and the state post. This was the man of most use to Eutropius; his network of informants brought information from all corners of the Empire, and for Eutropius that was the most valuable asset he had.

And he was putting those assets to use already. His man Dius had returned from Africa bringing good news. The next year looked like it was going to be even better than this last one. Next year would see him achieve even greater things.

A particularly loud moan from the woman on her back, as the cunnilingus from her female companion hit the mark, woke Eutropius from his reverie; he looked around smiled to himself. Who would have thought that he, Eutropius, that mutilated child, would rise to these heights, where he could hold these parties right in the centre of the Christian empire and nobody dared to challenge him? He checked himself. Don't get too pleased with your own success, he told himself. Pride before a fall. Always move forwards, always keep your enemies guessing.

He stood and walked from the room, leaving the writhing and moaning bodies to their night-time exploits.

Interlude

Gerung settled back on his bunk. "That was the worst ever guard duty!"

"What do you mean?" asked Gadaric. "How easy was that? Standing outside a house full of naked people, I mean come on."

"That's what I mean. We were outside, you twat! We should have been inside." Gerung snorted and rolled over onto his side. "Gods above, I had a stiffy on most of the night just listening to those women moaning and groaning."

Gadaric laughed. "Me too. So why don't you go see Octavia, get some of that frustration out of you?"

Gerung sighed. "Not my night with her. Besides, I'm a little short right now; not seen much gold lately."

"Why don't you go try your luck with the Empress?" taunted Gadaric.

"Fuck off."

Gadaric smiled and laughed quietly. He rolled over and closed his eyes.

Chapter 35

House of Gainas, Constantinople, 18th December 396 AD

Gainas sat in his favourite chair in his house. It was a good house, not far from the palace, three storeys, its own atrium, garden, and baths. Befitting a senior senator, that he knew, and he had been gifted it supposedly by the emperor himself. For services rendered. But Gainas knew the gift had come from Eutropius. He controlled everything the emperor did. The lazy shit probably had the ball-less chamberlain wipe his arse for him in the morning, simply because he had been told it was the right thing to do.

He had willingly come to Constantinople with the Eastern Army a year ago. His wife and children had moved to the capital on his insistence two years ago, as he knew it to be the safest place in the whole Empire. He had used up every influence and favour he had had at the time to get that to happen. Normally only Roman senators and military men were granted leave to live in the city, so close to the palace.

There had been rumblings and mumblings about letting Gainas move in to this area. A Goth living in one of the big houses in the city? But Eutropius has sailed into the debate in the senate and in his own inimitable way, combining oily persuasion with thinly veiled threats to life and limb; the vote went in Gainas' favour, and soon his wife and children had been recalled and were now firmly part of the set of families of senators and military men who hovered around the *illustrii*, hoping and happy to grab whatever slivers of power or influence came their way.

His wife had gone to bed, his children too. He sat in a swinging chair, on a balcony on the third floor of his house that had breath-taking views over the city and the golden horn. He sipped a particularly good wine, which came from his own cellars four levels below where he sat.

The grapes came from his own vineyard. His life as a soldier in the empire had been good to him.

To Alaric, he was a traitor, a deserter, someone who had abandoned the true faith of their people and thrown his lot in with the empire, the enemy.

He had never seen the empire as the enemy. It was packed full of selfish, arrogant, stuck-up bastards who would never accept him as a real senator. But even so. Would those same bastards ever accept him as an equal? But that didn't matter for now. He knew what was coming. He had seen the Huns ravage his town, destroy his family's crops and then his family. They were the true enemy. They were what forced his people to seek refuge within the empire. They were what drove his people across the rivers in the cold of winter, to knock on the gates of the empire and plead for from relief from their Hunic tormentors.

He recalled the winters in the Roman camps on the Southern side of the Danube. They had been cold, hungry days. He remembered his mother crying a lot. Somehow, he had survived that, and as a young angry man he had fought the Romans at the camps, escaped with his people and started to raid the local countryside. He had expected huge houses and fat Roman families wallowing in gold and silver. But all he had seen were people like himself, struggling to make a living day to day. His people had ended up fighting an impossible fight against the Roman army, and in the inevitable end, they had been cornered, rounded up and given an option. Join the Roman army or be sent back across the river to die. Gainas hadn't thought twice. He had joined the army.

He was glad to do so; he wanted no more part of the raids his people had made. He still felt, even today, the shame at his actions, for the family's livelihoods he had stolen, for the killing of innocent men, which he had failed to stop, which he himself had done.

He was a Christian, he had been baptised and hoped that in some way serving in the army of the Roman Empire, that empire blessed by the one God, might allow him to atone for the sins of those raids. He prayed every night for forgiveness. He prayed that he might gain enough power so he would be able to stop the senseless attacks that Alaric was still engaged in. Some senators still muttered about why he, a Goth, should be allowed in the senate building, when his fellow countrymen were out ravaging Greece. He felt no kinship towards Alaric; the man was a great general, but so was he. The man had ambition, but so did he. The only difference Gainas could see was that Alaric sought power and riches as the head of the Goth people in their own right. Gainas wanted the same power and riches, but as a leader of the Roman Empire. As part of true civilisation, of the one civilisation blessed by God. He wanted to be where Eutropius was now. He wanted the power to influence Arcadius to do right by the Roman people, to put right his own sins.

Eutropius had done nothing but wheedle and connive his way into power. He, Gainas, had fought bloody battle after bloody skirmish, seen his friends and family members die for the empire. He had been wounded many times, he had tasted the fear of the shield wall and the smelt the stench of dead and dying men in the mud of Illyricum, and in the hot sands of Syria. He had been the willing tool of Stilicho and Eutropius because he had believed it would serve both the empire and himself.

But now he sat here in New Rome, powerless and ignored.

Not for long.

He fingered the letter that had arrived that evening, delivered to him by a hooded figure who said nothing and who had managed to disappear without trace, despite Gainas ordering his men to follow him. The letter was from Stilicho. It wasn't signed by him, but Gainas recognised the script. The message read "Our mutual friend must go". Gainas understood the message perfectly. He smiled to himself, drank up his wine and went downstairs. He instructed a servant to go out and find Euthymius.

Chapter 36

The Senate, Constantinople, 20th December 396 AD

The senators cheered and clapped as the final vote of the year was announced. Caesarius smiled and nodded and waved a small wave of thanks to the gathered senate. The consulship was his for the next year. It was a powerless appointment. Long ago, in the days of the Roman Republic, it came with the power of a king, but those days were long gone. Now, the consulship was toothless, but somehow it still carried prestige and was a chance to gain some popularity with the city folk through the consular games. Caesarius was a big fan of the chariot races but not of much else. The animal baiting and hunting was popular with younger people, but the act of provoking and then killing a mindless beast did nothing for him. He was mindful of the need to avoid any lewd dramas to avoid antagonising the priests and bishops. So, the games would not be outstanding, but he would make sure the people had fun.

He had successfully navigated the year. Keeping Eutropius at bay had taken a large amount of time and effort, and he had managed to do some good, he felt. Several stupid, vindictive laws put in place by Rufinus due to his feud with Tatianus and Proculus, had been revoked. That had pleased the Lycians. More skilfully, he had allowed the Arians to make wills. The fact that they were heretics didn't seem any basis for stopping them passing on property. Their children could always be converted; what was the point of alienating future generations?

The one thing that irked him was Alaric. The barbarian seemed immune to any kind of action. Eutropius was right that the armies had been in no shape to attack the Goth horde this last year. But by all accounts, from Gainas' reports it looked as if this next campaign season, the reformed legions should be able to do something. And yet, there had been no enthusiasm by the emperor or Eutropius when anyone had suggested an attack.

There seemed to be a duality forming at court. Those who followed and supported Eutropius, and those who resisted his machinations.

He looked around the senate chamber and saw, on the senate floor, the chamberlain talking with Eutychainus and Saturninus, the latter glancing towards where Caesarius sat every now and again. Hosius joined them, as did two other senior and wealthy senators from Anatolia.

He shifted his gaze to the upper levels of the senate and was surprised to see Gainas, the Goth General Fravitta and his own brother Aurelian, deep in conversation. Looking at them you would not have thought a duet of barbarians was talking to his brother; all were dressed in their ceremonial togas, as befitted the occasion.

Yes, the opposing sides were forming their strategies; the outcome of the silent war was yet to be decided though.

"Eyeing up the teams, Prefect?"

Caesarius turned and saw that Anthemius had sat down beside him and that he was observing the same groups as himself.

"What do you mean?" he asked, knowing it was a dumb question. The procurator turned to him and looked him directly in the eye.

"You know exactly what I mean." He tilted his head at the room and continued. "Battle lines are being drawn right now. I can feel it, so can you. The battle for influence. Influence is power, as you know."

"And which side might you be favouring, procurator Anthemius?"

"My current position and reputation are nowhere near elevated enough, to concern myself with such matters, am I right?"

"You acquitted yourself this last year with dignity and professionalism," Caesarius said genuinely.

"I thank you for that, but you've answered my question anyhow, by avoiding a direct answer." Anthemius smiled. His dark eyes reflected the light from the upper windows of the senate building, where the late afternoon sun trickled in.

"As you yourself did to my question," said Caesarius.

"My simple answer is, I serve the empire, not the court, and I will continue to do all I can to ensure the survival and growth of the empire." Anthemius' words were without irony.

"Spoken like a true Roman."

"I hope so."

They sat in silence for several minutes. Caesarius had the feeling that the procurator wished to say something more. So, he waited whilst the senators around them slowly dispersed. Many came to offer their congratulations on his consulship, many sincerely, and a few, like Eutropius, utterly insincerely, but who knew appearances must be maintained. Eventually only he and Anthemius remained. At this, the procurator stood up and looked down at the Prefect. His dark eyes glinted in the light and held Caesarius' own gaze.

"The trials of the generals this year were rigged; no, don't feign surprise, you knew that as well as anybody. I am committed to exposing who was behind their downfall, so that others may not share their fate. But it may take time. I pray that you have that time. Congratulations on your consulship, and I wish you a Happy Saturnalia."

With that Anthemius turned and walked away, leaving Caesarius alone with his thoughts.

Part 3

397 AD

Chapter 37

House of Eutropius, Constantinople, 7th January 397

Eutropius was eating breakfast with his errand boy, Zafur, at his city house. They were waited on by another boy and a girl. Philoponus knocked and entered. He waved a skinny male servant ahead of him then told the boy and girl to leave the room.

"You need to hear this," said Philoponus without preamble.

"Good morning to you too," said Eutropius before sipping his freshly squeezed juice from a silver goblet.

Philoponus told the servant to repeat what they had just told him. The servant stammered, "I ... I ... have a friend your honour, well m... m ...more of an acquaintance really."

Eutropius held up his hand.

"Sit down, man." He pointed at the chair opposite him to the left of where Zafur sat; the boy was working his way through some smoked fish and dates. After a bit of encouragement, the terrified servant sat gingerly down in the chair. Eutropius did his best to smile, something he was not very good at.

"Have a drink; yes, have some fresh juice." Eutropius indicated the jug and glass. "Philoponus, pour the man a drink, looks like his hands are not steady enough." The man looked down at his hands; they were shaking uncontrollably.

"What's your name?" asked Eutropius.

"Th...Th...Theophanes Psellus, your honour," stammered the servant. Philoponus poured a drink and handed it to him.

"Well, Psellus, what is it that you have to tell me on this fine morning?" Eutropius tried to sound as interested as possible. He was in no mood for frittering away time on morons, but he trusted Philoponus as much as he could trust anyone, and if he thought this was important then it probably was.

The man held his drink with both hands and took a small sip. His eyes opened wide at the rich smooth taste, and he drank another draught, this time more deeply. Zafur sat at the table looking at Psellus with an expressionless face, idly putting dates into his mouth and chewing them deliberately, then letting the stones roll off of his tongue and drop into his bowl.

"A … a … as I said your honour, I have this acquaintance. A soldier."

"What type of soldier?"

"A legionary, an infantry man."

Eutropius didn't respond, so the man glanced at Philoponus nervously and continued. "We've got to know each other over the past few weeks since Saturnalia, and we have drinks together. We come from the same town in Dacia, you see?"

"Yes, I see," replied the chamberlain without enthusiasm.

"Well, I assumed it was just him being friendly on account of us both coming from Scupi, and he was just happy to chat about his home, us being so far from it."

"Get on with it, man!" snapped Philoponus.

Psellus started at the tone, then nodded quickly and continued. "Well, over the last week he has been asking about the household here. All stuff about you, your honour. He said he was just interested in how one of the *illustrii* lived, but then he asked about when you go out and when you come back and so on, who goes with you and was the house left empty and so on?" He took another drink of the juice, then set it down. "That was when I got suspicious, and I didn't know what to say or do. But I know asking those kinds of questions might be something a thief would do, to see if the house was empty before trying to rob the place."

"What did you do, Psellus?" asked Eutropius.

"I didn't say anything, I didn't do anything your honour, honest. I didn't tell him anything, I just tried to change the subject, but he kept trying to bring it back, so I left in the end; I made some excuse about being late for preparing evening meal. He said to keep our conversations between us and that he knew a way we could both gain some real gold. I said I wasn't interested."

"When are you seeing him again?" asked Eutropius.

"Well, I don't think I should, your honour, I think he is trying to steal stuff from this house. Probably him and his soldier friends. Everyone knows soldiers are always broke, spending their money on whores and wine all the time."

Eutropius rose from the table, signalled Philoponus to join him and told Psellus, who had immediately stood up too, to sit back down and have another drink of juice, and for Zafur to pour him one. The two eunuchs huddled together at the far end of the dining room. The chamberlain looked at the veteran and said, "Well?"

"I've never known an active serving soldier to plan a robbery of a house in the city; in the countryside yes, city no and certainly not from one of the mansion houses." said Philoponus. "There's something else going on."

Eutropius nodded. He was thinking hard.

"What should we do?" asked Philoponus.

"I think," said the chamberlain, "that our man Psellus should go for another drink with his soldier friend."

Chapter 38

Cyzicus Mint, 11th February 397 AD

She sat huddled in the dark. The room was cold in the winter, and she was allowed just the one tiny candle for light, which gave out on a the feeblest of heat. Her ankles were chafed and sore; the ring of metal rubbed her ankle. She had been chained to the post in the middle of the room for months now. She was allowed out only under the guard of two slaves, both mute, and then only for the purposes of doing her toilet; once a month she had been allowed to bathe after her time of the month had ended.

In her mind she still saw the headless bodies of her brother and husband lying on the grass outside the mint. Pertacus had ordered his guards to fetch her from her house and confine her to the locked room in the mint building itself. She had struggled to escape, hoping to run, and for a few seconds she had managed to, but the guards had been too fast and too strong; they caught her easily and brought her back.

"Don't worry, my beauty, nobody is going to dirty you." Pertacus had caressed her face with his podgy, slimy hand. She had shrunk back from the touch, but he had smiled with his fat lips and continued. "As long as you keep doing what you are told to do, nobody will harm you. But you must do *everything* you are told to do." The fat procurator leaned in and rubbed his fat jowl against her cheek and whispered, "Everything; you understand?"

She had said nothing. So, they put her in the room, the door locked, with just a small candle for light.

She often had no idea whether it was night or day, but every so often Pertacus would visit her and bring a table and chair and documents to write. All of the documents were lies of course. All written in the script of other men and women, all fakes.

255

But then that was what she was good at. It was the only thing she was good at. And before it hadn't mattered that it was a few invoices or receipts that she had forged, or a few lovers' letters, or even a few death notices. That had been for the Blues and had given her money and protection from harm. But now, she was a prisoner and she had been forced to forge the handwriting of soldiers and court officials. The demands were getting harder and harder, and the forgeries were getting more and more audacious. She felt sure that they would be discovered, and she was no fool. It was her work, her actions that were the crime. And she, a mere woman in the empire, who had no status, who would believe her word against the word of Pertacus?

In the dark, she sighed. She railed against her captives. She cried.

And she plotted.

Meals were brought to her by another slave, a fellow Egyptian; gradually they became acquainted. He at least acknowledged her and occasionally they talked for the few minutes he was allowed to be with her. When the guard ordered him out, she had pleaded with him to allow him to stay so she could just talk. She had flashed her smile at the young guard and used all of her remaining femininity to persuade him, and eventually he relented.

She had formed a plan. She had been working on it for a while now, but part of it revolted her, and she wasn't sure she could carry it through. But she saw no other way. She had to get out, had to flee this place. No matter what. The last forgery had been about week ago, she guessed, though it could have been longer. Another set of lies to discredit a local official and place another of Pertacus's men in his place, and documents to implicate an innocent soldier in an assassination attempt. The procurator would be back soon, she knew. So, she wiped away her tears, and breathed in deeply; slowly but surely Nephtys made her plans.

Chapter 39

Streets of Constantinople, 13th February 397 AD

Caius sat in a tavern off the Mese and nursed his goblet of warm wine; he also he nursed his bruised hands and arms. Sextus was off with two comrades from the Blues he had been cosying up to, doing something, he wasn't sure what, but it probably involved drinking and women or drinking and fighting.

Caius had been getting more and more agitated and frustrated as the days passed. They had been in the city for several months now. Sextus has been easily accepted into the ranks of the Blues as a veteran. Caius less so. He was not a natural at socialising. The people in the city always seemed to be in a rush, going somewhere where they weren't, always having some place to be. There was a continuous din of talking, shouting, cursing. On street corners there were beggars and priests and monks, all calling out to help them, give coin for food to them. Caius found them intimidating and avoided them as best he could.

The first month had been hard. He had been totally reliant on Sextus, but one day early in January things had changed.

It had been cold and he and Sextus and three other Blues men were on their way back from the south docks, where they had collected several crates of goods, which they carried between them back towards the city houses where Priscianus held his "court", as he liked to call it. It was just a meeting house where he and his lieutenants socialised and planned and where he received gifts and payments from his clients.

From seemingly nowhere, eight men in armless green tunics had jumped them and attempted to steal the crates. The street was crowded, and passers-by had screamed as the fighting broke out. The city ordinance banned non-soldiers from carrying weapons of any kind, so the Greens had been armed with simple wooden clubs. Before Caius fully understood what was happening, three of the Blues were already down on the ground, blood gushing from head wounds, leaving just Sextus and himself standing. They had ducked under the blows and stood back-to-back, facing their attackers. Caius had remembered the training that Sextus had given him on the journey, and he waited for the first move, which came from two men facing him. Both lunged at him with their bludgeons, but they were too close together now. Caius had ducked, though one of the clubs caught him a glancing blow on the shoulder and rammed his head into the midriff of the mugger on his left, forcing him back into another of the attackers, and all three of them crashed to the ground, smashing into a row of amphorae from a merchant. The merchant screamed and yelled, he and his servant tried to pull Caius off the men, cursing him loudly.

Caius disentangled himself quickly and shoved the merchant back, apologising as he did, but seeing that both the assailants were winded, he decided to take Sextus' advice and ensure they didn't get back up. He grabbed the club from the first man and smashed it against his head. The second man was trapped under the first, so Caius simply balled his fist and hit him across the jaw as hard as he could. The man's head snapped back, and he lay motionless.

"Look out!" called a small boy who was watching the chaos unfurl with wide eyes and a big smile. Caius instinctively dodged to one side and a club whistled by his head with an inch to spare. Again, he ducked down, spun, and grabbed his new attacker with both arms around the waist, then he forced himself upwards with a jerk. He felt the top of his skull impact on the man's chin. The man went limp and dropped like a stone to the floor. Caius now turned to a fourth assailant, who was unarmed but put up his arms in classic boxing pose. Caius didn't hesitate now; he'd boxed with Tiberius and Sextus. He stepped forward and threw a right-handed punch at the man's head; the man dodged it but ran into Caius left-handed swinging blow. He went down and on the way to the floor encountered Caius' knee coming up.

Get them on the floor and make sure they stay there. Sage advice from Sextus, he thought.

Looking around, he saw Sextus had downed two of his attackers and was attempting to spar with the final two. One had a club; the other was unarmed. Suddenly Sextus tripped over an unconscious Green on the floor as he stepped back to steady himself, and the two men took their opportunity and jumped on him. One raised his club to brain Sextus, but at the apex of his swing, Caius stepped in, grabbed the arm and wrenched it back, spinning the man off his feet. He wrestled the club from the attacker's grip, causing him to drop it. He kicked the man behind the knees to bring him to the floor, and then stomped down on the man's crotch. The scream was ear piercing. The final man was still struggling with Sextus on the ground. The veteran, however, had regained the advantage and slowly gained the upper hand, trapping the man in a neck hold. Sextus held it until the man passed out, then dropped him. They both stood and looked around, panting heavily. They were in a circle of bystanders who stood silently looking at the bodies in the street. Sextus and Caius suddenly smiled at each other and laughed.

In the aftermath, Priscianus had rewarded them generously with gold coin, and had encouraged Caius to go in for some boxing bouts between the Blues and Greens. Word on the street had gotten back to the Blues patriarch about how he had floored five of the Greens muggers with no weapon, and he knew a good way to make money when he saw it.

"My patron loves boxing; if you're good enough, he may even come and watch you!" Priscianus had joked.

The bouts were not strictly legal, the emperor Theodosius had disapproved of boxing and had banned the sport from his games, but that hadn't stopped the fights. They were frequented by many of the elite who still loved the sport and who bet large amounts of money on them, so nobody cared. In the two months that followed, Caius had fought four bouts and won them all. He was starting to make a name for himself. He found that he quite liked the attention, and he quite enjoyed the fighting. But he felt pangs of guilt too. He was not here to enjoy himself. He was here to help his people. So, after his third fight, he had demanded that he be allowed to fight a half-Goth, who was a member of the Greens.

He had won that fight eventually. It was brutal and bloody, and he had screamed at the end of it to the crowd that he'd won it for all the oppressed and terrorised people of Greece. There were cheers around the fighting pit. The people of the city had heard the news from Greece, and they, like him, wondered when the emperor would act. Any strike at the barbarians, even a purely symbolic one, was music to the people's ears. Priscianus had told him to tone it down, that there were a lot of Goths or half-Goths living and working in the city, that they were paying customers, and his anti-barbarian antics would turn them off, and that would affect his profits.

But now he sat in the tavern on his own, feeling guilty. Here he was, gaining coin, gaining a name, enjoying himself, whilst his village suffered, whilst Greece suffered. Sextus had told him to stop worrying.

"Relax, Caius, my friend. Alaric won't be travelling in the winter, he'll be holing up somewhere in Southern Greece, building up his strength for the spring. As long as we petition the emperor by the end of the month, there will be time to send an army to meet him in April." For some reason he wanted to keep Caius' spirits up and to keep him believing that he might influence the emperor. He didn't know why. There was little chance that the emperor would even hear the petition, and no chance he would change imperial military policy simply because Caius asked him.

"You make it sound so easy," Caius had muttered.

"It is. You just continue to box, I'll just do some jobs for Priscianus, do them well and he'll help us. I made a deal with him."

Priscianus scared Caius. The man seemed to have no scruples; he was coarse and rude, and ordered his men and women around without thought for their feelings. He had heard rumours that Priscianus had killed several men with his bare hands, though Sextus scoffed at that. "He's about my size; believe me, it takes a special skill to kill someone with only your hands. They're just stories to scare people shitless. Besides, the way you can fight now, he's hardly any threat to you."

"There's many ways to kill a man, and he still scares me," said Caius without humour.

"Relax, we've made a deal, we work these jobs for a month and provided he is happy with the work, he'll introduce us to his patron. After that we're free to go."

"Will he really?"

"Priscianus is a bastard, a cold heartless bastard," said Sextus casually, without anger. "He would sell his own grandmother into prostitution if he felt she could make any money. But his strength lies in his ability to control his men. Most of his men are like me, ex-soldiers, and we have a code. A deal is a deal. He breaks that trust, his own men will kill him, sure as you and I are standing here. I've got to know a lot of them. They don't like him, but they respect him, as long as he keeps his word."

"You're sure?"

"Absolutely, because if the others don't kill him, I will. A deal is a deal!"

"I'm not an ex-soldier."

"No, you're not, but you're under my protection, I made that plain when I came here. So, we do the work, and we'll get the contact. You make your pleas, we go home."

Caius wasn't so sure. Maybe he wasn't as streetwise as Sextus, maybe he wasn't as worldly wise, but when he looked at Priscianus he didn't see a man who kept his word, or his part of the bargain, unless it was in his own interests to do so. So, he had come up with his own plan. He was just getting enough courage from the wine to go and see the Blues patriarch. He took a deep breath, downed the remaining wine, stood up and strode out of the tavern and across the road to Priscianus' "court".

Chapter 40

Constantinople, 18th February 397 AD

Gainas handed the necessary papers of recommendation and assignment back to the man standing before him. "I see you've been granted the rank of tribune in the praesentalis legion, in charge of the 2nd cohort," he said.

"Thank you, sir," said Bargus, his eyes gleaming.

"Don't thank me. If I had my way you would be swinging from the gallows. These orders come direct from the emperor. You plainly have friends in very high places." Gainas made no effort to hide his disgust.

"I think I do sir," Bargus smiled.

"Get out!" snapped the general.

Another day, and another set of orders putting Eutropius' men in key positions in the legions. A snivelling sycophant called Leo had reported to him yesterday to inform him that Gainas was to hand command of the Southern Praecental legions to him on completion of the troop redeployments and housing. Today that gutter trash Bargus had turned up with signed orders to take up post as Tribune in the Northern Praecental legions. Gainas still held out faint hope that those legions would ultimately be his command. The appointment for Bargus was lucrative, as it involved controlling access across the Hellespont and bribes for queue jumping were accepted as part of the ongoing costs of travel. The bribes went to the military officer in charge of operations, in this case that was now Bargus.

Bargus, the snivelling bastard who betrayed Timasius. He hadn't really got to know the old soldier well in the end. He didn't believe for one minute the so-called conspiracy of Timasius against the emperor; it was all a concoction of lies by Eutropius. Of that, he was sure.

He was concerned now that Eutropius' attention was turning to him. And the presence of Bargus in one of his own legions worried him. A lot.

Chapter 41

The Peloponnese, Greece, 5th April 397 AD

The rider came hurtling into the camp on a sweating and exhausted horse. He leapt from the beast's back and ran to the pavilion at the centre of the camp, where Alaric held court. He was expected. The curtain of the tent was held open as he strode into the darkness within. He paused and blinked to adjust his eyes to the small amount of light coming through the vents in the high roof of the tent. Once he had some vision, he walked to where Alaric sat, not on any throne, but on an ordinary wooden chair at an ordinary wooden table with his generals and aides.

Alaric stood as the messenger approached and asked, "Well?"

The messenger was still breathing heavily. "I've ridden from Pheia in the West Peloponnese. Sir, Stilicho is there. He has landed and is unloading his army as we speak."

A murmur went around the table and around the aides and servants in the tent. Stilicho here already? It was too early in the season; this must be a mistake. Alaric raised his hand to silence the voices.

"How many?" he asked.

"I estimated two legions sir, with about three hundred cavalry each."

Alaric nodded.

"I saw him sir, he's here himself."

Again, the murmurings. Some of worry, some of disbelief.

"Thank you," said Alaric, and directed an aide to ensure that the rider's horse was properly tended to. Then he invited the messenger to be seated and told a servant to fetch him food and drink, as much as he wanted.

Alaric turned to his generals and said, "Time to pack, gentlemen." The generals left. Alaric sat back at the table and called for parchment and ink. He wrote a short note but did not sign it.

Our mutual enemy is back in the Peloponnese, two legions and cavalry at Pheia. He can be delayed, but only an imperial intervention will stop him. You can trust this messenger; send your reply with him.

Unlike the eunuch, he didn't consider his men expendable. He sealed the parchment, placed it in a leather holder and added the token he had received from the chamberlain. He waited patiently until the rider had eaten and drunk his fill, called an aide and then instructed the rider to get a fresh horse and ride with all haste to the capital and deliver the message to the palace. The token would mark him as a messenger of the imperial court and guarantee his safe passage, unlike his predecessor.

At least that is what he wished. He watched as the aide escorted the rider to his new horse. He hoped he would see the man again.

Chapter 42

Constantinople, 15th April 397 AD

Caius stood on the arena floor. The crowd was murmuring and chattering, waiting for the fight to start. The whole event was taking place in a private arena in the grounds of huge mansion owned, Priscianus had said, by a very senior member of the emperor's inner circle. They had just been treated to a particularly arousing display of dancing by a troupe of Persian dancers, who were greeted with smiles and claps and cheers from the crowd when they had finished. Caius had watched from Blues preparation area and Sextus had to get him to focus back on the upcoming fight.

Sextus had initially been against it. He could not believe that his farm-worker friend had walked up to the Blues Patriarch and demanded to fight the best of the Green's boxers, a Goth named Visimar. Sextus knew of the man. He was an ex-foederatus of the legions, bald except for a narrow ponytail at the back of his head. He was about two inches taller than Caius and had not lost a bout for twelve months.

"Are you mad?" he had asked his friend.

"I can beat him, and when I do, Priscianus has promised us an audience with his patron," said Caius with full confidence.

"This barbarian hasn't lost in a year," Sextus reminded him.

"Then he will be over-confident and will want to pummel this country boy into the ground. That will be his big mistake."

"You hope," growled the veteran.

So, now he stood on the arena floor. He stared at his opponent, who stood a few paces away. The Goth grinned nastily, showing a mouth full of pointed and blackened teeth. Caius' hands were wrapped and prepared but caestus, the small shards of metal embedded in the tough leather, were not allowed in this fight. Not out of any sense of care for the fighters; the crowd and in particular Priscianus' patron, just wanted the fight to last as long as possible. Visimar's hands were likewise bound. Both their torsos and legs were bare, as were their feet. Unlike the boxers of old, though, who fought naked, they both wore short tunics and g-straps to protect their genitals. Christian tolerance did not extend to two men rolling around in the nude grappling each other. In this case Caius was glad of that particular taboo; he bet his opponent was too.

The fight referee, his long switch in his hand, signalled they were ready to start and looked up at the owner's box for the signal. Caius didn't look around. He knew that somewhere up there was Priscianus' patron who, according to him, loved his boxing with a passion and had eagerly offered to stage this fight. Caius had promised them the fight of the year and asked only that, if he won, Priscianus' patron would grant him a five-minute audience. Somewhat to Caius' amazement, word had come back down that the patron had agreed and was looking forward to seeing the young farmhand deal out some punishment to the barbarian. But, if the fight was over too soon, no audience. If he lost, no audience. He had to please the patron. Provide some good entertainment.

The signal came and the crowd, full of enthusiasm, joined in the referee's countdown to the start.

"Five! Four! Three! Two! One! Go!"

With lightning speed, the barbarian rushed in and crashed into Caius, knocking him to the ground. He raised his fist to strike an early hit, but Caius palmed away his foe's arm and rolled out from under him, regaining his feet quickly. The crowd clapped in approval. Putting up his two-handed guard, he stepped around one way then the other, and then started to work his way into his opponent. He aimed some big blows at the Goth's head, which the bigger man easily dodged. Visimar attacked Caius' torso, which he managed to fend off, then aimed a left-handed jab at the farm-worker's head, which Caius avoided by a hair's breadth. This cat and mouse trading of blows and standing off continued for a while, then Caius saw a chance. Visimar had over-committed himself on another left-handed punch and for a moment was off-balance. Caius stepped in with his right leg behind Visimar and shouldered him to the floor and leapt on him to pin him in place. The Blues section of the crowd loved it, and screams of "Kill the bastard!" echoed out.

Sextus, watching from the side-lines, could not help but admire his friend's bravery. Fighting in a battle was scary, but at least you had your armour, your friends, and your weapons. Here you had only your hands and your wits to help you. He hoped his friend knew what he was doing. It was the Green's crowd turn now to roar as their man had grabbed Caius' arms and was attempting to knee the farmhand in the back to get him off him. There was a momentary stalemate, as neither contestant gave ground, then Visimar arched his back and rolled, taking Caius with him. Caius lashed out with his foot to stop his opponent from turning the tables on him. Pinning him to the ground he caught the Goth on the shoulder, which was enough. The two men sprang to their feet, ready and facing each other again.

Away from the fight, in the mansion house, a large, hooded figure crept slowly across the immaculate gardens, keeping to the shadows until he was up against the wall of the house. The figure slowly made its way around the house until it came to a small doorway, a sturdy wooden door with metal hinges. He carefully tested the latch, which lifted without any noise, and then entered the house, closing the door quietly behind him. Once inside the house he made his way through the house noiselessly, then up the marble staircase to the second floor. There were only a few servants around; he avoided them all effortlessly and came to the master bedchamber, where the owner of the house slept. He passed through the bedchamber and onto the balcony that looked out over the sea. Below and to the right was the arena; he heard the shouts and jeers and clapping. The fight was in full swing.

Caius hit the floor hard this time, on his back. His opponent had used the same tactic as earlier and unbalanced him after he had fully committed to a right-handed punch. With the wind momentarily knocked out of him he didn't fend off the punch but managed to just pull his head to the side, so his foe's hand punched only the sand of the arena. It must have hurt; he heard the Goth bark a curse. Now he swatted away another punch, and another. He heard the Green section of the crowd start to cheer. He hoped they kept cheering; he needed to silence them properly soon. He hoped the patron was enjoying the fight. Visimar kept throwing punches but somehow Caius managed avoid their full power. He decided he had given the crowd enough to cheer about for the moment, so he reached up and grabbed Visimar behind the neck and jerked him towards him and viciously head-butted the Goth. Unprepared and stunned, he rolled off Caius, who rolled in the opposite direction then stood up and side-stepped around his opponent who still was kneeling on the floor shaking his head. The Blues supporters went wild, jumping up and down, clapping and yelling.

"Get up!" screamed Caius at his opponent. Visimar turned and glanced at the farmhand and, just for a second, a look of worry crossed his face, then he gritted his pointed teeth, growled to himself and slowly stood up.

Caius continued to circle the stationary barbarian. The Greens booed, not liking the way they felt Caius was disrespecting his foe. The Blues, however, were loving every second of it.

Up on the balcony of the mansion house the figure looked around and found the place he was looking for, a dark corner behind yet another statue; he drew out a long knife. It glinted in the torchlight from the arena. He felt the keen edge and was satisfied; all that was left now was to wait.

Visimar had regained his composure again. He matched Caius' side steps and watched for an opportunity. The pause in action had given both men the chance to recover, so Caius decided it was time to move the fight on. He took two strides towards the Goth, who quickly shuffled one way then the other. Caius took another step forward and then threw a right hand at Visimar, then a left; both were short and the seemingly amateurish punches gave the barbarian confidence; he too stepped forward and aimed his own left-handed punch. Caius opened his hand and grabbed the balled fist as it came towards him, then he grabbed the Goth's other wrist as it came at him, but Caius had his full weight behind him, and he forced the blow back almost onto Visimar. There ensued a simple battle of pure strength, as both men tried to force the other into a position they could not maintain. As they grappled, Caius tried to trip his opponent, but the Goth was too nimble and kept his legs away. Suddenly Visimar leant forward and bit Caius' on his exposed forearm, the sharpened teeth piercing deep. The Blues supporters were incensed and roared in outrage. The shock of the illegal move caused Caius to let go, and Visimar pressed home his illicitly won advantage by delivering a hammer blow to Caius' right cheek that spun him away and caused him to stumble back, his head reeling.

The referee struck Visimar on the back with his switch several times, giving Caius a moment's respite, as the barbarian turned on the man, snarling. The spectators now were jeering at each other as much as at the combatants. Food and goblets were being hurled between the two factions and some of the crowd who were close to the divide started their own brawl. Then soldiers appeared amongst the stands and the threat of cold steel soon dampened the supporters' urge to spar amongst themselves.

Caius regained his composure and turned to face his foe again. He looked Visimar straight in the eyes and cocked his head back, challenging the barbarian to attack.

"Come on, you Goth bastard!" he yelled. He had no idea if his opponent understood him, so he made some rude gestures which he felt sure he would understand and continued to goad him. It worked. The barbarian decided he had had enough and rushed at Caius. He raised his hands in classic defensive posture and weathered a flurry of blows, then when Visimar paused to catch breath, he aimed a low punch at the torso, which connected well. He heard the breath go out of the Goth, who doubled over, so he quickly followed through with a right-hand punch, arcing downwards, which also connected, this time with the Goth's head. His opponent tried to fend off the attack, but Caius gave him no time to recover, and he struck again, and again and again. Visimar collapsed to the floor. The Blues section of the crowd leapt to their feet and cheered and yelled. The Greens too were in uproar and screaming at their man to get up.

Caius stepped away. The barbarian tried to get up onto one knee. Caius let him; Visimar stood on both legs but was still bent over. Caius walked up to him, and as the barbarian looked up and tried to raise a defending arm, he hammered home the final punch, sending the barbarian to the area floor, where he stayed motionless.

Caius stood there for a second, bent over, gasping for air, then he straightened up and raised both hands in victory. The crowd erupted. "Caius! Caius! Caius!" they chanted. He looked up at the owner's box, blinking as the sweat stung his eyes. He saw a number of lavishly dressed men on their feet applauding. He had no idea who the patron was, but since they were all smiling and nodding and clapping, he reckoned that he had done enough to earn his audience. A feeling of relief and euphoria came over him. He walked to the front of the Blues supporters and fell into the crowd, who lifted him on their shoulders and proceeded to parade him around the arena like a conquering hero.

It was about an hour later, when the crowd had quietened down and the arena was now deserted, that Caius finally got his wish. Above, the stars twinkled in the deep blue night sky, and around him the torches flickered dimly as Priscianus led him and Sextus up the steps and into the area where the noblemen sat around drinking wine, except one. He sat on a chair placed on a small dais within the box observing the entrance of the little party into the box. The Blues patrician led the two men in and walked directly up to the man sitting in the chair.

"Most honourable Eutropius," said Priscianus, as that is how the man liked to be addressed by common people. "May I present the winner of the main bout tonight, Caius Plautius Paulinus, and his fighting coach Sextus Cassius Velus."

The man, who Caius noticed was bald and overweight, but quite tall, leaned forward and said in a surprisingly high-pitched voice, "So this is the farm boy who beat the unbeatable Goth?"

"It is indeed him," confirmed Priscianus. Caius noticed he avoided the use of the word "honourable" now.

"Well, boy," continued Eutropius without humour, "you apparently wanted to speak to me?"

"I do, most honourable sir," stuttered Caius. He kept his head bowed, not meeting the eyes of this powerful man. He had heard the name but had never dreamt that this is who Priscianus' patron was. He had

273

learnt during his time in the city that this man was really a eunuch, but that unlike other eunuchs, who were mere domestic servants, this one held real power and influence in the empire. That alone was enough to make him unpopular, it seemed. But he also he knew that this man had the confidence and ear of the emperor.

So, he carried on with a confidence that surprised himself. "I wish to plead to you to … to send the army to save our people from the barbarians."

Eutropius raised his eyebrows.

"Are there not soldiers in Greece to defend you?"

"There are soldiers sir, but they do not fight, they cannot battle so many. The barbarian numbers are so vast. They are like a plague!" Caius said forcefully.

"Indeed?" The eunuch raised his eyebrows and turned to another man standing next to him. Caius hadn't noticed him before, but as he looked at him, he was shocked to see the man sported a Goth style long hair, though he wore Roman clothes. "What do you think of that, General Gainas? This man says the Goths in Greece are like a plague!"

Gainas looked at Caius and then at Sextus. Then he spoke to Eutropius. "I agree, the farm boy has sense. We should be attacking Alaric and driving him off. I'm glad to see even the humblest of our citizens can see what some of our most elevated cannot." Turning back to Caius he said, "Well fought tonight lad, you take the hits well, and thank you for putting on a show." Gainas winked at Caius, a small act of familiarity that caught him off guard. "We both know you could have ended that bout inside of thirty seconds. Visimar is quick and strong, but he's an idiot, and an arrogant idiot at that."

With that, Gainas took up the folds of his robe and strode out of the gallery. Eutropius snorted and said, "You'll have to forgive the general; he has much on his mind at the moment. You have my word, Caius …

Caius?" Caius nodded. "The situation in Greece is being worked on and will be settled and dealt with before the end of the year."

"You will be sending the legions to Greece then, sir?" asked Caius eagerly.

"By this time next year there will be many of Rome's legions in Greece and the Goth threat will be no more. That I can guarantee."

"Thank you, sir, thank you. The people are starving out there. The Goths have taken the food, killed the men, the livestock ..."

"Yes, yes, I've heard it is a terrible time for the people of Greece," interrupted the chamberlain curtly. "You will have to excuse me; I am needed at the palace shortly. I must return to my quarters to ready myself. Thank you, Priscianus, for introducing me to your latest find; he's quite the fighter. Now I must go. Zafur! Where is the little runt? Zafur?" Eutropius strode away.

Caius and Sextus stood there with Priscianus awkwardly for a few seconds, uncertain what to do, until the Blues patrician said, "Let's go. He's a busy man, and you had your five minutes with him as promised. Let's get you cleaned up; we've a party to go to, to celebrate your victory! Tomorrow, we need to talk about your next fight."

Caius wasn't listening. He was watching Eutropius as he exited the arena gallery. Was he lying? Were the soldiers going to be sent to Greece. Would Alaric be thrown out of the Empire? He wasn't sure. And furthermore, he wasn't convinced that Eutropius had taken any notice of him. He felt deflated and suddenly depressed. Was that it? Was that all he was going to be able to do? All the travelling, the miles, the hiding, the fighting? He bit his lip and looked askance at Sextus, who shrugged his shoulders and said, "He's a fucking politician, what did you expect? We've done what we can, let's go home."

"Home?" asked Caius.

"Home?" echoed Priscianus suspiciously.

"Yes, home. Greece. Let's go back to the village. We've done what you wanted to do. We've spoken to the emperor; well, as good as spoken to him. It's not up to us what happens next. It's in the hands of our betters."

"We can't go," said Caius.

"No, you can't go," agreed Priscianus. "He has more fights to win!"

"Fuck your fights!" snapped Sextus.

Priscianus bristled. "Mind your tongue soldier, you forget yourself."

"We came to the city to help his village, not to make you money," Sextus retorted.

"If we hadn't taken you in, you'd have starved to death by now, you ungrateful bastard." Priscianus' voice was low and dangerous. He clicked his fingers and two of the Blues men stepped alongside the Blues leader; bodyguards, veterans like Sextus, albeit slightly younger. Tertius and Septimus. Sextus knew them both and had gotten drunk with them both several times. Tertius was from Thessaly, like Sextus and Caius, whilst Septimus came from Illyricum. Septimus had lost his eye in a skirmish with desert nomads on the Eastern borders, but he was strong and fast despite that. The eye patch he wore only added to his menacing looks. Tertius had lost his left hand in Gaul and wore a brass hand shaped like a balled fist. Sextus had seen him use it and had no wish to be on the receiving end of that punch.

Caius turned to his friend, grabbing his arm and said, "We can't go home yet Sextus." Looking at the group of retreating dignitaries following Eutropius out of the hall, in a lower voice he continued, "We need to see if the patron will keep his word and will send the legions to Greece." Sextus considered his words and nodded. Caius turned back to Priscianus. "I'll fight for you, but not if you harm my friend here." The Blues Patrician motioned for Tertius and Septimus to hold their positions.

"You don't set the rules, I do," he snapped.

Sextus stepped in front of Caius and put his face close to the Blues leader. "Not for me you don't," he said. "The deal was we work for you, …"

"You don't get to decide …" retorted Priscianus

"…you get Caius here a meeting with your patron …" Sextus persisted.

"… how things are done…"

"… we kept our side …"

".. you …"

" A deal is a deal!" Sextus screamed in Priscianus' face.

" … won't walk away from this!"

Priscianus' spittle struck Sextus in the face as he yelled, nearly apoplectic with rage at the insolence.

Nobody had ever challenged him like this before. He whirled and pointed at Sextus "I'm changing the deal! You're just another useless , self-interested vet, I can buy two of your kind for a Nummus, like these two." Priscianus thumbed Tertius and Septimus next to him, and growled, lowering his voice dangerously. "Why do I need to keep you around, or even alive?"

Caius elbowed past Sextus and broke in. "Let's calm down. Look," he met Priscianus' angry gaze. "I'll fight for you. Alright?"

"Caius …" began Sextus.

"Shut up!"

Sextus stared at his friend. Caius had changed, matured he saw. He wasn't the naïve farmhand he had set out with across the empire. So Sextus shut up. Caius continued, sounding conciliatory. "We're grateful for your help, of course we are. But we can't stay forever; and we had a deal."

"I'm changing the deal. You'll do as I say!" scowled Priscianus. "Bring him" he ordered his bodyguards, pointing at Caius, "and kill him" he pointed at Sextus. "No fucking grunt disrespects me." He muttered as he turned to walk away back down the steps to the arena floor.

But nobody else moved.

Caius and Sextus stood together and readied themselves against Tertius and Septimus, but the two Blues men stayed where they were. Then Septimus spoke deliberately and with a dangerous edge to it.

"A deal is a deal."

Priscianus stopped and turned around.

"What?"

Septimus turned and looked the Blues Patrician. "You made a deal. You should keep your word."

"And who the fuck turned you into a quaestor?" spat Priscianus. "Do as I say, kill the old man and bring the boy."

But instead, Septimus nodded at Tertius, and both lunged forward and grabbed the arms of Priscianus. They dragged him down the steps. He yelled out a stream of expletives and demanded that the other Blues men kill these traitors. A crowd started to gather on the arena floor. Most of the spectators had gone, but the loyal Blues men were still there, waiting to escort their leader and their champion back across the city. A small contingent of Greens was there too, tending to their defeated fighter. Everyone stopped what they were doing and looked at the growing commotion.

Tertius and Septimus dragged Priscianus into the arena and threw him onto the sandy floor. The remaining Blues men formed a circle around him.

Septimus said, "He broke his word to that man," pointing up at Sextus, who still stood in the gallery alongside Caius.

"A deal is a deal," said Tertius.

"Who the hell do you think you are?" snarled Priscianus, attempting to stand up, but several hands forced him back down.

"You make a deal; you stick to it," said another Blues man.

"Rules are made to be broken," snapped Priscianus.

"Maybe rules are, but deals are not," said another. There were murmurs of agreement.

"Vote?" said Septimus.

"No!" cried the Blues leader.

But the men all raised their arms. One by one they raised their thumbs, and then turned their wrists to point their thumbs downwards.

"No!" hissed Priscianus.

Septimus drew out a sharp knife. The Blues leader tried to stand and again was held down by other men. He continued to struggle. Strong arms grabbed him, and Septimus stepped behind him, placed the razor-edged blade against Priscianus' throat, leaned in and whispered, "A deal is a deal, you arrogant fuck!" The blade sliced across Priscianus' neck. Blood spurted and gushed out and the Blues leader fell to the floor, vainly attempting to stem the flow of his lifeblood. Within a few seconds he lay still.

Whilst Septimus cleaned his dagger, Tertius turned the body over and put his hand in a pocket of the bloodied tunic. He pulled out an object and walked back up the steps, to where Sextus and Caius stood. He held out his hand to Sextus, who held up his hands and said, "No way. Not me."

"What?" asked Caius, looking at Tertius's bloodied hand. In his palm lay a disk about two inches across; in the flickering torchlight it looked black.

"Take it," said the bodyguard. "We'll follow you."

Caius reached out and picked up the disk and looked at it.

"For God's sake, Caius!" cursed Sextus.

"What?" asked Caius.

"You've just agreed to be the new city leader for the Blues."

Caius stared at Sextus. Then he smiled. Then he gave a small laugh. "Who would have thought, eh?" he said.

"Do you have any idea what you've just agreed to?" asked Sextus.

"No," said Caius.

"Just as fucking well," laughed Sextus. "Otherwise you'd be shitting yourself. Come on," he slapped his friend hard on the back. "Let's go and get drunk!"

Chapter 43

House of Eutropius, Constantinople, 15th April 397 AD

It was nearly midnight by the time Eutropius got back to his private bedroom. The evening had gone well. His little, slightly illegal fight night had gone well; the betting had made a decent profit and his conversations with several influential senators had yielded new potential opportunities for expanding his own influence and power.

He had had his personal bodyguards escort him back to the house from the arena. They were all paid mercenaries of course, loyal only to the constant stream of gold that emanated from him. He trusted only a few of the eunuchs in the palace and the mercenaries. One of them apparently came from the far north, where he said it was dark for half the year. Eutropius couldn't imagine a more miserable place to live; no wonder he'd come south for a better life.

He had two guards just outside his bedroom door. No one was allowed in during the hours of darkness. At his bedroom door, his secretary Philoponus, briefed Eutropius that all was in order, that the house was secure, and asked if there was anything else he could do to be of service.

Eutropius said no and closed the door, locking it. He turned, lit a candle, and went out onto the balcony, took a long deep breath and surveyed the view. It was a beautiful night. Overhead the stars twinkled in a sky of deep velvet blue, whilst out at sea the lanterns of the night fishermen flickered as their boats bobbed on the sea in the gentle night breeze. There was still faint laughter and chatter from the arena at the edge of the property, which he knew would die down soon, as he had told the guards to remove everyone by midnight. He took his candle and, turning to his right, he held it high so that it illuminated the floor of the balcony. Quite clearly, he saw boot prints in the sand that he had deliberately left there earlier.

281

"You can come out now," said Eutropius.

Nothing happened.

"You cannot stay there forever. You're trapped here. Best give yourself up."

Suddenly there was a movement, and a hooded figure sprung up from behind a statue and rushed at the chamberlain. Before he could reach his target, another figure cannoned into the attacker. Together they crashed to the floor in front of Eutropius. There was a moment of confusion, as the two figures wrestled for control of what appeared to be a short dagger, which caught the twinkling starlight on its shiny blade. Then the weapon fell to the floor, and Philoponus, who had stayed in the room with the chamberlain, stood up and dragged the hooded figure to his knees with a short sword at this throat.

Eutropius walked to the door, unlocked it and called for his guards. Six of his personal guard came into the room. Candles were lit, and a chair was brought for the chamberlain, who sat directly in front of the kneeling figure.

"Strip him!" ordered the chamberlain.

Several strong hands ripped the tunic from him, hood, and all. Within a few seconds the man was kneeling naked, shaking, his head down looking at the floor. The eunuch thought he heard the man whisper a prayer.

"Swords," said Eutropius, and his bodyguard drew their swords.

"I've been reading some archives in the palace library," said Eutropius casually. "I found Dio's *Roman History* to be particularly good, especially his descriptions of the Mad Emperor Gaius, or Caligula, as he has become known."

He nodded to Philoponus, who pulled back the head of the kneeling man. The candlelight revealed a thin, scarred face. The man had been cursed with illness at one time in the past; little pockmarks littered his face. His beard was thin and wispy, and his eyes were sunken.

"Caligula liked to torture his victims slowly. Death by a thousand cuts, I believe it was called. Very nasty, very painful and very slow."

Eutropius could see the man was shaking. He leant forward and lifted his chin, looking straight into his eyes.

"You're not getting out of this room alive. This is where it ends for you. No escape, no trading of your life for information. You are either a few minutes from death or a few hours. If you choose the latter, you will have wished you chose the former, I assure you."

He signalled to the bodyguard and one by one, each of the bodyguards stabbed at the man. None of the wounds went deep, but all pieced his skin; blood ran from the wounds. At first the man made no sound, but at each subsequent cut he grimaced and cried out, begging to for them to stop. Eutropius held up his hand. The guards drew back their swords.

"I need the name of the man or men who sent you to kill me."

"I don't know his name," said the man. Eutropius nodded, and again the swords plunged into the would-be assassin, and more blood ran onto the floor.

"I don't know his name!" screamed the man, "I beg you! I don't know it!

"A description then, perhaps?" suggested the chamberlain.

Between sobs the man said, in a quivering voice, "A foreigner. He wore animal skins; a leather belt; long hair."

"A Goth?" prompted Eutropius.

The man grimaced as a wave of pain came over him, and said in a barely audible voice, "Maybe, I don't know, possibly."

283

Eutropius nodded, and the swords dug in again and again. At a sign from the eunuch, one of the bodyguards sliced the man's face from cheek to temple. He moaned, tried to reach up and stop the blood from rushing into his mouth, but Philoponus held him tight, his sword nicking his throat; more blood trickled down. His body was now almost completely covered in blood. Writhing and weeping, the man spat blood out and said, "Yes, yes! He was a Goth, but he carried a Roman sword! I remember a Roman sword!"

"Where did you meet him?"

"At the Artemis tavern, southern corner of the forum of Constantine," gasped the man in agony.

"And what were you to do when you had killed me?"

The man hesitated, and the swords stabbed and sliced again. Some of the cuts went deeper this time, at Eutropius' urging; more blood spilled, and the man whimpered through the agony. "I was to meet … back at the Artemis tomorrow morning, to get … my final payment." He coughed and blood spurted out. Flecks of it hit Eutropius in the face and spattered onto his robe.

"What time tomorrow?"

"An hour after sunrise."

Eutropius' eyes gleamed. "One last time, can you remember a name?" he asked.

The man sobbed and shook his head. Another nod, and the swords dug into flesh, deeper this time. One dug into his left eye; white liquid gushed out and the man screamed aloud now, all sense of defiance gone. "I don't know, he never said! I don't know," he sobbed, trying to reach his ruined eye, but the fierce grip of Philoponus held his arms in place as he struggled in his pain. "I don't know!" he yelled and continued to repeat over and over. "I don't know! I don't know!" He was weakening now; he'd lost a lot of blood, which was running across

284

Eutropius' bedroom floor. The assassin started to recite a prayer, a Christian prayer.

Eutropius sucked in a deep breath. He looked at Philoponus, who shook his head and said, "He doesn't know." The chamberlain considered his options, then acquiesced. Philoponus viciously drew his sword across the man's throat, then drove the dagger he had taken from the assassin through the man's back, into his heart.

"It's not enough is it?" asked Philoponus, as he looked at the mutilated body lying at his feet.

"No, not enough to convict anyone now, but it may be enough to catch our conspirators, and at worst send out a warning to stop anyone trying anything else. Here's what we're going to do..."

Chapter 44

Streets of Constantinople, 16th April 397 AD

Philoponus nursed a warm wine drink at the taberna Artemis. He was sitting at the end of a long bench outside on the street. His drink steamed in the cool morning air. He had got there early and stationed a number of his men, disguised as day traders and street beggars, so that they had every angle and approach to the tavern covered. He wore the tunic that the assassin had worn, with the hood up. Eutropius' house staff had done a swift repair on the garment, but a good repair; to the casual eye, you didn't notice the extra seams.

There was a buzz of conversation around the tavern; the word on the street was that the emperor's chamberlain had been attacked last night and that he had been badly injured and was on his death bed. A procession had been seen going from the Chalca Gate of the palace to the house of Eutropius, and it was taken as fact that the emperor was visiting his chief advisor, possibly one last time before he departed this earth. Philoponus heard their words. One old man was saying he thought it would be no bad thing for the eunuch to die. "It isn't natural for one of his kind to have so much power!" he growled before taking a long draw on his wine. "Next he'll be wanting to lead an army, who ever heard of such a thing?" He was interrupted by his companions, who pointed out that the eunuch was simply helping to guide the emperor, and the latter was just the public face of the Imperator. "You believe what you like," said the old man. "Mark my words, he'll be wanting more and more, and that young emperor had better keep an eye out, or that eunuch will be stabbing him in the back and wanting to be emperor himself! I've seen it before." The groups all broke out talking over one another, some defending the eunuch, others condemning him.

Philoponus pondered on his own view. He disliked Eutropius. He thought him arrogant, cruel, and self-indulgent, but right now, the empire needed someone who could keep a clear head and steer a sure course, and the chamberlain appeared to be able to do that. Philoponus knew that the work done with the army and provincial reorganisation was good and long overdue; he had worked with Eutropius, Caesarius and Gainas on the deployments, which should, assuming no major upsets, all be in place this spring. The emperor was evidently incapable of ruling by himself, but he was a necessary figurehead. The Theodosians were still seen by everyone as the legitimate rulers of Rome, so powerful and legendary was the legacy of Theodosius. Why go through the turmoil of establishing a whole new dynasty when you can just keep control of an existing one? So, he was prepared to work for this eunuch and to do the tasks set for him, until he found gainful work elsewhere, or until the eunuch overstepped himself. There was only so far that he would go.

He looked up, keeping his face hidden under the brow of the hood, and saw a figure approach across the forum, weaving between the increasing number of people who criss-crossed the vast open area surrounding Constantine's stunning victory column. It was a Goth soldier, precisely as the assassin had described. The man walked right up the table where Philoponus was and sat down. Philoponus kept his head down and took a sip of his wine; it was cheap, acidic, and steamed gently in the cool morning air. He put down the cup and said in a loud whisper, "You're late."

The soldier simply said, "I heard the news about the chamberlain. He's not dead. You said he would be dead."

"Not my problem," said Philoponus and lifted his head and threw back the hood. "But it will be yours."

The soldier gasped, sprang back off the bench and made to run. But two of Philoponus' men, who had been also sitting on tavern benches, tackled him and threw him to the ground. Philoponus stood over the struggling soldier for a moment, then looked around at the crowd that was gathering; his eye landed on another figure, not Goth this time. He could have been from anywhere, but his eyes were darting between their captive and directly at Philoponus. When he saw the veteran's eyes on him, he dropped his head, and dodged behind some onlookers.

"Stop that man!" yelled Philoponus to three men who were close to the fleeing man. A brief scuffle ensued, but within a minute both men were on their knees, surrounded by Philoponus and his men, all with swords drawn.

"Bring them!" snapped Philoponus, and the two captives were bundled roughly to their feet and dragged away into a back street, where a cart stood, pulled by two mules. The men were loaded onto the cart, and to the driver, Philoponus said, "Take them, Publius," and the cart with the two captives and an escort of guards set off. Half an hour later they came to a large mansion. The guards dragged the prisoners from the cart and through the doors of the mansion, kicking and punching them to keep them in order when they started to struggle. They were taken downstairs to a cellar. It was dark and cold, the only light coming from a small high window, which only illuminated the area where they were forced onto the floor on their knees.

"Strip them," said a high pitched and cold voice. The clothes were ripped and cut roughly off their bodies.

"Swords!" said the voice out of the darkness again. There was a rasping sound as the guards drew their weapons. Both men, shaking now, peered into the gloom in front of them.

Suddenly there was the flash of a flint, and a candle was lit. It lay on the floor in front of the two men. The candle threw up a yellowy light and revealed the form of a big man, seated. The man was fat, with drooping shoulders. The light from below partially illuminated his head, but shadows mixing with the light made his face take on a hideous look of a demon.

"I've been reading some archives in the palace library," began Eutropius.

A few minutes later the screaming began again.

Chapter 45

Cyzicus Mint, 25th April 397 AD

Nephtys was patient. For the plan to work, she had to be. She also had to swallow what little pride she had left.

For the last ten days she had subtly courted the young guard who escorted the slave who brought her food. She had smiled at him coyly with her best smile and tried to behave like the submissive women she knew would be expected by any Roman man, dropping her eyes, being demure. She showed him her chafed wrists and asked for some salve. The next day he had slipped her a small jar of ox-grease.

Over the following days, they had started to talk; at first just one-word exchanges of "Hello," and "Thank you," and stilted phrases. But these had blossomed into sentences and then into conversations.

She asked him about his family, his hopes, his dreams. She found out he was the youngest of four brothers. His name was Gallus Rabirius Petrus.

The oldest brother was a *praepositus* in one of the Eastern Legions in Syria, the second was a teacher to a wealthy family in Constantinople, the third had died in his late teenage years of fever, leaving Gallus to remain here in Cyzicus to tend for his aging father, his mother having died when he was very young. He loved the art of fighting, as he called it. He had grown up fighting with his brothers. They had bullied him at first, but he had decided to stand up to them one day and, despite receiving an almighty beating from them, they had ceased the bullying that day and the four of them had practiced together, the oldest teaching them everything he had learnt in the legions when he was home.

Gallus wanted to join the legions too. But his brothers insisted he must stay at home and care for his father, whose health and strength were failing. So, he did some local boxing and wrestling when he could to keep his hand in. Someday soon his father would die, and then he would sign up and join the legions. But until then he was trapped here, a slave to his family, as much as she was a slave to Pertacus.

When he asked about her, she said she had been enslaved in Egypt and brought here when she was young, with her brother. They had managed to escape their owner but had not managed to get back to Egypt; instead, they had survived on the streets until they were spotted by Pertacus' staff and brought in to work in the mint. Of course, she was employed to forge those documents for Pertacus as well. Her marriage to Balbus had seemed initially like a way to get out from under Pertacus, but it had proved fruitless, as her late husband had been a weak man, unable to stand up to the gross procurator.

One day, during a conversation with Gallus when she was being brought her food, he said he was sorry about her brother, and lowering his voice he said he thought the procurator was wrong to kill them without a trial. In fact, he suspected that they were only killed to cover up another crime. But he had no idea what that might be.

Another day, whilst he guarded her when she was taking air down on the private dock, he said that he wished things were different between them, and that she wasn't his prisoner, and he wasn't her guard. Later that day Nephtys, when she had the opportunity, whispered to the Egyptian slave who brought the food for her to speak to Gallus and say that it didn't have to be that way.

So, slowly but surely, Nephtys and Gallus grew closer. Still, she told herself, be patient, you will only get one chance at this. Be patient.

Chapter 46

The Consistory, Constantinople, 25th April 397 AD

The consistorium was in session, with the emperor seated on the imperial throne, on a raised dais. In a large circle gathered the *illustrii*, the most noble of the nobles, the elite of the city. To the left of the emperor, on a lower step stood the chamberlain and to the right at the same level stood Caesarius. Each of the officials had their own specific place in the consistorium, all at subtly different heights, to make it plain who was superior in rank to whom. The Urban Prefect, who stood on a step below Caesarius and Eutropius, finished off his normal introductory announcements and, at the chamberlain's bidding, the ever-apathetic emperor suggested that they get down to the business of the day, which was, yet again, Alaric.

"What is the latest from Greece on his whereabouts?" asked the emperor to the room at large, though he didn't seem to care whether an answer was forthcoming or not.

"He was last reported as holding up in the Peloponnese, waiting for the spring, Imperator," said Caesarius.

Eutropius coughed and spoke. "I don't believe that Alaric is the one we should be concerned about, my honourable friends. We have a much bigger problem."

All eyes turned onto the eunuch. He savoured the moment for a few seconds, meeting their stares one by one around the room.

"Well, Chamberlain?" prompted Arcadius with a short sigh, "Don't keep us on tenterhooks!"

Eutropius felt mildly annoyed that the emperor had interrupted the focus of the room, but nodded obediently and said, "Stilicho."

"My brother's regent?" Arcadius looked genuinely surprised; the heavy-lidded eyes for once were wide open.

Murmurs and mutterings of consternation swept around the room. Caesarius, amongst others, frowned and turned to the eunuch.

"Please enlighten us, Chamberlain, on what you know and why you believe Stilicho is any kind of a threat to us?" inquired Caesarius.

"Very simple, Prefect. Stilicho has landed in the Peloponnese with two legions and cavalry." Eutropius held Caesarius' gaze. "I'm surprised, prefect, that you didn't have knowledge of this yourself already."

The slight hit home and Eutropius could see that Caesarius was annoyed, but he had nothing to strike back with. Oh, how he loved these political games, and this was just his opening gambit. Aurelian however was not so stymied. With a calculated amount of indignation, he said, "And I'm surprised, chamberlain, that you didn't share this knowledge with us sooner."

"I have only just come into this knowledge myself, just before this meeting," replied the eunuch smoothly, "through our good and honourable friend Eutychainus." That was a lie of course; the prefect of Illyricum had not seen the message that the chamberlain had been handed from Alaric that very morning. But Eutychainus had been primed already by Eutropius for some surprises; he was not unintelligent. He kept a straight face, merely nodding as the eyes of the room turned on him, as if acknowledging the act.

"Then why, pray did you not bring that message directly to me?" snapped Caesarius angrily. Eutychainus didn't flinch. "I only received the news minutes before this gathering and after discussions with the chamberlain, we agreed that the emperor should be the first to know, and since this meeting was about to go into session, it seemed the logical thing to bring it to all your attentions as soon as possible."

The room nodded and murmured in agreement; the argument was sound. Eutropius felt satisfaction as Caesarius seethed silently, unable to say anything without making himself appear selfish and pre-occupied with his own appearance of competency.

"And how did you come by this information?" asked Aurelian casually.

"The normal post riders report to me weekly from Illyricum," replied Eutychainus. "But this one came directly to me overland and by sea. The provincial commander is no fool and knew this was critical information for the emperor and us to know."

"And have you been informed of his intentions?" Caesarius asked, determined to get back some control over the conversation and wrest it from the eunuch.

"No," replied Eutychainus.

Arcadius looked at Eutropius and spoke. "Surely he is here to help us get rid of Alaric. My brother would not send him otherwise."

"I doubt your brother sent him knowingly, Imperator," replied Eutropius softly and respectfully. "We cannot trust this half-Vandal, who touts himself as regent and claims some kind of authority over you. Stilicho's vanity, arrogance and duplicity know no bounds."

"And you of course are the picture of piety, modesty and temperance, are you not, Chamberlain?" Caesarius was uncharacteristically caustic.

Eutropius turned to Caesarius to make a retort but thought better of it. He needed to maintain the high ground here, not get into verbal mudslinging with the Praetorian Prefect.

Caesarius continued. "What does he want?" he asked. "You seem to be knowledgeable, Chamberlain, on his comings and goings? What exactly is he after?" The prefect made no attempt to keep the sarcasm from his words.

There was an uncomfortable silence in the consistorium. The officials and generals were watching the two most powerful men in the empire slug it out verbally, standing either side of the emperor. Arcadius, for his part didn't seem to know what to do. His two chief advisors were sparring right in front of him, but he did nothing, he just sat there. Aurelian watched the scene with derision. Arcadius was pathetic. Eutropius was a scheming bastard, and his brother, who was no fool but was acting like one, was letting himself be baited by the eunuch.

"Might I suggest we all calm down?" Eutychainus spoke eventually. His low but melodic voice had exactly that effect. "Prefect," he turned to Caesarius, "what should we do?"

Eutropius glanced at Eutychainus, not sure what he was doing. He stayed silent and waited.

"I will send an envoy to meet with the general, and request that he assist us to expel Alaric from Greece," said Caesarius. Aurelian mentally applauded his brother's stance, but knew it was completely impractical. He too wanted the barbarian army out of Greece, but meeting it headlong in some kind of fixed-piece battle was never going to work. Alaric was too canny an enemy and had too many warriors compared to the legions that were available.

"And what happens if or when Alaric is beaten?" asked Eutychainus.

"Then Greece has its salvation, and both East and West can celebrate a triumph," replied Caesarius.

Eutychainus shook his head. "Followed by Stilicho marching on New Rome with an army, bolstered no doubt by the remains of Alaric's men, to claim regency over our emperor!"

There was a chorus of voices clamouring to speak. From the angry voices and urgent whisperings, the chamberlain could sense that the room was against this ever happening. He joined the fray.

"General Stilicho is practically a usurper; he dictates policy in the West. To all intents and purposes, he holds the most magnificent Honorius hostage in this own palace! This army of his that he has landed, we had no notice of it, nothing from our glorious emperor's kin in the west to say that it is an officially sanctioned venture, so we must treat it as it seems to us, to be that of an invading army!" The chamberlain finished with what he hoped was enough anger and passion to get those fence-sitters in the room to jump across to his way of thinking. But Caesarius wasn't finished. He turned and looked into the face of the emperor

"Imperator, these are legions of Rome! Not some marauding barbarian hoard," snapped the Prefect. "We cannot send our own troops against them. Your father fought too hard and long for a united empire to have us all throw it away in civil war!"

Arcadius nodded. "I agree, prefect, but what can we do?"

Caesarius paused. He had no immediate answer.

It was a political trap, pure and simple, and he had walked right into it like a junior quaestor barely come of age. He cursed to himself silently.

If he sided with Eutropius and tried to get rid of Stilicho, they risked civil war, and that was unthinkable. The empire was recovering after Adrianople and after the wars of Theodosius the coffers were still low. The armies were still not in a state of readiness, and although they were getting close to being combat ready, throwing them into a battle too early could be catastrophic. Another civil war could fracture the empire forever and perhaps spell the end of it. There were plenty of enemies on its borders just waiting for a chance to strike; everyone knew that.

But if they let Stilicho loose in Greece and sided with him, yes, he might defeat Alaric, but Stilicho was a charismatic and popular general. What was to stop him, out in the field, being proclaimed Imperator and then marching on Constantinople to claim regency over both Eastern and Western emperors, something he continually claimed Theodosius had granted him the right of when he died? What was to stop him claiming the throne for himself as saviour of the empire? A half-barbarian emperor didn't bear thinking about.

He shook his head. He realised that the room was silent, waiting for him to speak.

Into that silence, Eutropius cleared his throat and said, "We declare General Stilicho an enemy of the people."

"What?" exclaimed Caesarius.

"We declare General Stilicho an enemy of the people," repeated the eunuch.

"And how will that help exactly?" asked Caesarius acidly.

"It will force him to withdraw, Prefect." Eutychainus spoke in his silky voice.

"Why?"

"Because he knows that he will never get the support of the east that way. It removes all legitimacy," the Prefect of Illyricum said smoothly.

"It makes no difference at all." Caesarius was dismissive of Eutychainus. "He can still engage with Alaric, perhaps even negotiate with him, and they can all still march on this city, perhaps even with our own legions. He'll remake his own legitimacy through the sword!"

"It's lucky then, that we have a way to get him to leave," Eutropius announced. He was smiling that nasty smirk. Caesarius braced himself; he was starting to get the feeling that this whole situation had been engineered by the eunuch and had been leading up to this moment.

Eutropius turned to Arcadius, drew out a scroll and read it out loud.

To our most Magnificent Arcadius, Son of the Great Theodosius, we the people of the province of Africa hereby duly declare our eternal allegiance to you as your loyal subjects, and will serve and obey your edits, laws and any other you see fit to send us from time to time.

297

Your loyal servant

Gildo

"There is much more legal wording and other minutiae, but in essence, Imperator, we have managed to obtain the pledge of Gildo, who has broken his ties with old Rome and pledged Africa's allegiance to New Rome and to you."

There was stunned silence around the consistorium. Eutropius smiled as he looked at each of the officials and generals who encircled the throne. "I needn't remind you all of the vast resources of Africa, and not just the annual grain supply that is now ours to control." He turned to Arcadius and said, "And this is why Stilicho will choose to leave, Imperator. He cannot allow this to happen. He will have to sail for Africa and try to reclaim the province for Ravenna."

"What if he succeeds?" asked the emperor.

"Then we will be no worse off than we are now, majesty, and it buys us the time to deal with Alaric and to bring our legions up to full strength. If he fails, then we have acquired vast resources that will assure our wealth and security for centuries to come."

Arcadius stood up and began clapping, slowly at first then faster; everybody else gradually joined in, except Caesarius, who stood ignored and humiliated. He was the Prefect of the East, nominally the most powerful man in Constantinople beside the emperor, but he had been made to look like a lowly procurator. The applause continued and Eutropius wallowed in his victory, but he eventually raised his hand in mock modesty, bowed low to the emperor and said, "I thank you for your applause and appreciation, but I have to tell you all that this marvellous diplomatic coup has been achieved by our honourable friend the Prefect of Illyricum, Eutychainus!"

Arcadius turned and led the room in another extended round of applause for Eutychainus. Eutropius looked at Caesarius. The latter returned the look without expression. Across the room, on a lower step, Aurelian was clapping with the rest of the room, but was watching his older brother, standing isolated and dejected. He knew he was finished. He felt no sympathy for him. He had been outplayed. He knew the price of failure in this game. It was now just a question of whether to resign or whether to wait until the emperor replaced him.

But without doubt, within a day or so, they would have a new Praetorian Prefect of the East, and it would be Eutychainus. Eutropius had out-manoeuvred them all. There was no doubt in Aurelian's mind that the eunuch had been behind it all. Eutychainus was a very able administrator, but utterly devoid of the cunning and imagination needed to pull-off such an impressive diplomatic coup. No, it was Eutropius who had masterminded the removal of a potential threat to the throne and, in the process, gained an immensely rich territory for the East, which would ensure a reliable supply of food and resources for Constantinople. And as a reward, he would have his man as Praetorian Prefect of the East. But more than that, for all intents and purposes, Aurelian knew that Eutropius, a eunuch, now totally controlled the Eastern Empire. He would have to do something about that. It was an unacceptable situation, and he knew who might be willing to help rectify it. Not right now, but someone who he believed was just as eager to control Arcadius and into the bargain had an actual legitimate claim to do so.

Later that evening, in his private office, Eutropius drew a line across the third name on his list: *'Caesarius'*. He carefully replaced the quill back into its gold holder, and blew on the papyrus to dry the ink, then he looked for some time at the next name on the list but this time he did not smile.

Chapter 47

Praetorian Prefect of the East, Constantinople, 1st May 397 AD

Eutychainus, the new Praetorian Prefect of the East, surveyed the hustle and bustle below him. His clerks and officers busied themselves transcribing orders, edicts, organising supply trains for the legions, ensuring the soldiers were fed, clothed, and armed, not just in camp but those on the march across the empire. He smiled. He was content. He was rich. Very rich. Thanks mainly to Eutropius, who had seen fit to lease him lands confiscated from Abundantius and Timasius. Of course, the chamberlain still wanted his rent, which amounted to a considerable sum, but the remainder of the income from those lands was more than all but the wealthiest Romans would ever see in their lifetimes. Things could not have gone better for him over the last twelve months.

And now it looked like things were going to get even better. Peace was coming at last to the empire. Alaric was going to be nullified. Stilicho was going to be ejected from the East, and the East had acquired an extremely wealthy province with an inexhaustible food supply. He had no idea how Eutropius had managed to persuade Gildo to switch his allegiance to Arcadius, but in truth he didn't care. Eutropius had seen fit to hand the glory of that political masterstroke to him. That was sufficient for him.

Now they controlled the East, he and Eutropius would benefit immensely in the coming months, and the empire would of course benefit too, with the peace that they were bringing with their work. If things went as planned, he was confident that he would get that consulship next year.

He finished reading the final set of orders for the day. They had been signed by the emperor and he countersigned, satisfied that they were clear and comprehensive, and had the necessary seals imprinted on them to confirm their authenticity.

He sat back and mused. Peace was coming at last to the empire. The legions had been re-organised and re-deployed, the barbarians to the north seemed to have calmed down. The Persians were keeping to the terms of the most recent treaty between Rome and Ctesiphon and, most importantly of all, Alaric would soon no longer be a threat; Eutropius' and his own plans would see to that. Peace was good for business and for building wealth. War was not. And Eutychainus liked building wealth, especially his own.

Calling for a clerk, he handed the orders to him and said that they were to be delivered to the recipient with all haste. The post riders were to ride through the night to ensure the instructions reached their destination within three days. The clerk bowed and strode swiftly down the corridors of the palace and to the offices of the Imperial Post. He passed on the message from the Prefect and within ten minutes a rider had set off through the Chalca Gate, down the Mese, through the Golden Gate in the Walls of Constantine, and disappeared down the Via Ignacia, towards Greece.

Chapter 48

Western Peloponnese, Greece, 7th May 397 AD

Thiudimir looked ahead. The mountain path wound ahead around boulders, down invisible dips, and led towards to the head of the pass that lay a mile ahead. The path was wide, and the valley was green, studded with trees and boulders as far as he could see in the distance, but he had to know if they could get the baggage train over the mountain pass. They had been sent ahead by Alaric to find safe passage, as scouts had spotted Stilicho's forces a few miles away. They were driving Alaric's forces up against the hills, making him choose certain paths to keep the baggage train together and protect it. For an army, the baggage train was the centre, the heart of the unit, where weapons, food, drink, shelter and pay were based. An army nation such as theirs that lost its baggage train was beaten, defeated; the regular imperial soldiers could still run back to their homes, to their cities.

Alaric's people had nowhere to run. They had no home. The baggage train was their home. Hundreds of wagons, oxen and heavy horses transporting women, children, slaves, servants, weapons, food, coins, books, tents, hearths, cooking pots and utensils, family heirlooms, items of sentimental value and all the other things that go to make up lives of people. It was the tribe. It was their life. And the cunning Stilicho had timed his expeditionary force's arrival and deployment perfectly. They had landed at the port of Pheia, cutting off the easy path, north, round the edge of the Peloponnese. They had to take the rising land to the north. Alaric had been quick to get the Gothic army moving; Stilicho had been slow to get out of Pheia. He had beaten Stilicho to the first obstacle, two valleys with a narrow ridge between them, which the locals said had an easy exit to the north and onto the route to the port of Patrae, which seemed to be where Alaric was taking them. Both armies had spies and scouts out keeping an eye on each other. He had no doubt there were eyes on him now, either a hidden scout or one of the natives in the pay of Stilicho.

The main body of men remained behind, forming a defensive line, whilst the baggage train had moved slowly towards the entrance of these two parallel valleys. But Alaric was unsure whether the exit route was suitable for the baggage train, so he had told Thiudimir to scout ahead with his men.

Thiudimir was not a natural rider; many of his people were, but he was never comfortable on a herd-obsessed four-legged eating machine with a mind of its own. He preferred to trust his own legs, but time was pressing; a horse was way faster than he was and that outweighed his misgivings. The horses were actually sure-footed ponies and used to the rough hilly terrain. They had been taken from local farms a month back and were proving their worth. He looked back but saw nothing. If the Romans were out there, he could not see them. He wondered if they were bothering to follow them at all. Their usual horses were not used to this terrain; they had sailed across the Adriatic and were trained for fixed battles on the open plains. But he didn't want to take any chances, and it was no good finding a way through the mountains if they never lived to tell the tale to Alaric. So, he wasn't just looking for the way through, he was looking for a place where he could stand and fight and kill any Romans who happened to follow him. It was them or him. He glanced up at the sky. The sun was past its zenith and getting lower in the sky; he had to get to the head of the valley before sundown. He asked the local guide they had paid to show them the way how long to the head of the valley down to the north. Another two hours, came the reply. Thiudimir urged his men forward along the valley.

Chapter 49

Cyzicus Mint, Anatolia, 7th May 397 AD

Gallus had taken Nephtys to the dockside for her evening air. There were no boats in the dock, though a supply ship was due in that next morning, he said. He was quiet this evening; she asked him what was wrong, but he said nothing at first.

"My father died yesterday," he said quietly.

Nephtys instinctively reached for the guard's hand and held it between hers, gently pressing. Inside, her thoughts were racing. What did this mean? Was he now going off to join the legions, would he abandon her?

"I'm sorry for your loss, Gallus. I truly am," she said as calmly and as sincerely as she could. She realised that she really was sorry.

They stood there silently for a few minutes, then he turned to her, still with her hands wrapped around his and said, "Why are you doing this?"

Nephtys looked confused and asked, "Doing what?"

"This between you and me?"

Nephtys tried to smile her most endearing smile. "I like you; you've been nice to me."

"The others say you're only being nice so you can bewitch me and escape. They say that you've mystical powers from the East."

"Who are these 'others'?"

"The other guards."

Nephtys looked at the young man and realised that she really did like him. It had been all just a ruse to start with, to escape. She still needed to escape, but she really had gotten to care for this young man, who seemed so polite, yet sometimes so intense.

"I'll tell you the truth if you answer me truthfully one question right now." She looked up into his eyes, and he nodded.

"Now that your father is dead, are you going to leave this place?" She tried to keep her voice steady and neutral, though inside she felt her heart throbbing in her chest, hoping for the right answer for her.

"Yes," came his simple reply.

She gripped his hand tightly and spoke deliberately but with the intensity of the truth. "At first my only thought was of escape, it's true. But after all these weeks, I have come to look forward to our time together more and more. And whilst I want to get out of this place and break free of Pertacus, I fear losing you more; you have protected me from the worst. With you gone, I don't think I will survive."

Gallus looked down at her face. That beautiful face. "I won't let them harm you," he said. "I promise, so help me God."

They stood on the dockside for a while, then together walked back up the corridor, where Gallus re-attached her chains for the night, and lit two candles, placing them within reach of Nephtys; then he closed and locked the door behind him. She heard his footsteps fade away into the distance.

Chapter 50

Western Peloponnese, Greece, 7th May 397 AD

Thiudimir stood on a boulder, looked north and smiled to himself. The job was half done. They had reached the top of the valley late afternoon. The sun was settling behind the Western Hills and in the evening light he could see that ahead the slopes descended smoothly, and where he stood now was not that rocky; wagons could get up the path they had ridden, and from what he could see they would easily get down the other side. In the far distance, in the failing evening light, he saw a few small lights that were moving steadily east: fishing boats on the isthmus between the Peloponnese and Illyricum, some heading to Patrae, he guessed.

They would need to get boats themselves or build rafts, but they would manage it. Better than getting trapped back at Corinth by incoming armies from the east. Alaric did not want to get caught between two armies. This way they made their own choices and had more options. So that was the good news.

The bad news was that they had spotted Roman scouts behind them, blocking the way back to Alaric. He hoped that Alaric would send reinforcements to help them; he reckoned there were as many Romans as his men, maybe more. He had told his men to not stop and look behind; he didn't want the Romans to know that they had seen them.

Thiudimir considered his options. They could try a straight charge at the Romans, but in the poor light they wouldn't be able to go at any speed, the ponies could break a leg or throw their riders. They didn't know how many of the enemy there were. Hurrying back to his men, who were waiting nervously with their ponies, he said urgently, "I've got an idea, but we need to go now. You two," he pointed at the local guide and an older warrior, whom he trusted implicitly. "Start down the valley and lead the other horses, slowly now, make sure you're seen; the rest of you, come with me. Keep low!"

Two minutes later they were scrambling amongst the steep ridge among the rocks and boulders, climbing higher and higher off the valley floor, keeping as low as possible and off the skyline, on the side opposite to where the Romans were approaching . Two of Thiudimir's men, young Braga and Getica, led the way. They were agile and had been brought up in the central highlands of Germanica, so were used to rocky and mountainous terrain. All of the men, including Thiudimir carried a bow and a dozen arrows. Not his favourite weapon, but useful for foraging and hunting, so the scouts always carried them.

Thiudimir brought up the rear. He wanted to keep a close eye on the pursuing enemy. The sun had disappeared behind the hills now; the moon was in its last quarter and not due to rise for a few hours. Thiudimir hid behind a large rock, peered through a gap and saw the Roman riders slowly pass below. They did not look wary or show any sign of concern that they might be being watched. Good, he thought. The dark figures below had reached the summit of the pass and had gathered in a large mass. Thiudimir hissed in a low whisper for his men to stop moving and to stay low. In the sudden silence of the clear windless night, he could just hear some voices from the officers, but he couldn't make out the words.

Suddenly there was a shout and several of the figures pointed down the pass towards the north. Thiudimir smiled. They had seen the two men. The Romans came together as a group, presumably to discuss what to do; whether to follow or whether to go back to Stilicho, he guessed. He counted a dozen men. This was doable. They had to get them all. He could not risk one of them getting back to Stilicho.

Thiudimir hissed a command to his men. All six men stood up sharply, braced themselves and launched their arrows at the group. The distance was not great, the bows powerful and the Romans were totally caught by surprise. Four of the arrows found their mark. Two of the enemy fell from their horses; the other two men managed to stay on their horses, with the shafts showing from their shoulders. The final two arrows hit horses, one in the rump, the other in the neck. The beasts panicked and threw their riders, and alarm spread through the whole group. Those that could control their animals whirled around to try to see their attackers.

"Again!" Thiudimir shouted; no point in being quiet now. Another volley slammed into the group; this time three more men fell from their rides.

"Braga! Getica! Go!" The two mountain men threw down their bows, leapt off the rocks and rushed towards the frantic Romans.

"Again!" shouted Thiudimir. A third volley struck the group and two more fell from their horses.

"Keep firing!" he shouted. He studied the scene. There had been twelve men; only two remained on their horses. They had seen Braga and Getica rushing towards them. Instinctively they turned and rode hard at the two men on foot, easy targets. But they were rushing directly into the line of fire of the archers.

"Make sure you hit the Romans, not our men!" yelled Thiudimir. The archers did not miss. One man was struck in the chest by two arrows and must have died instantly; he collapsed from his mount in a second. The other rider took an arrow through the shoulder and the shock of it made him drop his reins. He tried to stay on, but within a few seconds he too was on the ground, the arrow's shaft snapping as he fell. He rolled to his feet and stood, only to be hacked down by Braga's sword.

"Let's go!" said Thiudimir, and he and the remaining three archers jumped off the rocks and ran to join the others, closed in on the remaining Romans. Three were already dead when they got up close; the remainder were all wounded. Three stood as the Goths approached, swords drawn, but they were in no state to fight. Two had broken arms and the third had blood streaming from a gash in the head. Thiudimir didn't hesitate. This was no time to be squeamish or merciful. He stepped forward and delivered a deadly blow to the first of the Romans, his sword slicing into the man's neck. Braga easily parried one of the men with a broken arm then buried his sword in the man's chest; Getica did the same with his opponent. The other men then dispatched the other wounded Romans. It had taken less than five minutes; all twelve Romans lay dead.

Breathing heavily from the run and short fight, Thiudimir said, "Braga, get our horses and guide back. The rest of you, start heading back." When the men looked at him with questioning stares, he said, "No we're not staying. We don't have time. These bastards will be missed soon enough, and we need to get the baggage train through here as quick as possible, so we go back tonight!" There were a few mutters, but Thiudimir was used to that. "Get going now! We'll catch you up with the horses. You won't have to walk all the way if that's what you're worried about, ladies!"

Chapter 51

Cyzicus Mint, Anatolia, 8th May 397 AD

She thought it was early evening but in her windowless room, she had no real idea. On the other side of the door, she heard nothing. Normal work had ceased, as the teams in the striking room had either departed for home, or in the case of the slaves been locked in their cells.

She sat on the rough straw mattress that Gallus had got for her and waited for either the next meal with the young guard as company, or for the next visit from Pertacus with his documents to forge. The number of times the procurator had visited lately had lessened. That didn't bother her; the less she was around the flabby, sweaty, lecherous man so much the better. But there had been no forgery work put before her; that worried her. That work had been her insurance, it made her important enough to keep alive at least. For over four weeks now she had worked on Gallus, to build that relationship with him. She wondered if it had been enough time. She didn't want to rush this, but she had to decide soon.

Then she heard faint footsteps, multiple footsteps; they grew louder and then paused. The door lock rattled, the bolts were being drawn back. Nephtys stood up. Her face lit up briefly as Gallus stepped into the room, but his face looked grim. A second later another guard, an older man, stepped through the door; he could not have been more of a contrast to Gallus. Where Gallus was big, tall, and well-muscled, he was small, thin, and bony. Whereas Gallus had bright white teeth, the few teeth this man had were yellow or black. Gallus had a full head of hair and was handsome, this man was nearly balding, his face was pockmarked with the scars of disease, and his left eye did not look in the same direction as his right. Gallus abjectly looked at Nephtys and she saw him gently shake his head. The new guard grinned nastily and eyed her up and down. She felt like he was undressing her in his head. She shivered.

The procurator came in.

"Ah, good evening my dear," said Pertacus. "Meet your new guardian; his name is Metilius. I am assigning you to his tender care from now on. Unlike Gallus here, who has been relieved of this particular duty, as I think he has become a little too attached to you."

Pausing briefly to catch his breath, the procurator continued, "Now … Metilius can't speak. Show her, man." Metilius opened his mouth. He had no tongue.

"Yes, silenced forever by some eastern desert barbarian, so no little lovers' conversations between you two in the future." The procurator was leering at her, little beads of sweat on his brow; his eyes held no humour.

Then he said what Nephtys had been dreading. "I'm afraid that my use for you as a forger is over." The procurator nodded at her widening eyes.

"Yes, my dear, there has been an improvement in my circumstances with my masters in high places, and your services in that area are no longer needed." Nephtys watched in horror as he started to undo his buckle, which held his cloak on his shoulders. "But something as beautiful as you should not go to waste." The procurator began to unbutton his tunic. "I was told to kill you by my betters, but somehow, I just can't bring myself to do so. Well, not unless you fail to please me and, after me, Metilius. After that I'll maybe let Gallus have his turn. I think he's in love with you, and perhaps you might even care for him too, though I suspect your little game of courting our young man here was just part of a plot to escape." Nephtys looked at Gallus with wide eyes and shook her head.

"Metilius! Undress her!" snapped Pertacus.

311

The older guard stepped forward and Nephtys shrank back.

Gallus didn't move. He stared at the floor.

Metilius, however, reached forward and grabbed her forearm; she tried to slap him away but, though his hand was as skinny as the rest of him, the grip was like a vice, and he simply caught the raised hand and spun her around. He used one of her arms to trap the other and, gripping her dress at the shoulder, ripped it from her. She wore loose undergarments covering her torso and waist, but Metilius tore those from her too.

Pertacus' lips glistened, his eyes roaming over Nephtys' perfect body, the curves and lines made more alluring to the procurator by the flickering candlelight .

Gallus shook his head and turned away. Nephtys thought he was mouthing some prayer or incantation. She wasn't sure; she couldn't hear, couldn't feel, couldn't keep track of what was happening. She felt sick in her stomach; fear washed over her like a wave. This couldn't be happening. Not now.

"Gallus, please," pleaded Nephtys in a pained whisper. "Please."

"Gallus, please!" mimicked Pertacus, laughing. "He will obey orders as he always does, as all my men do, my dear." The procurator undid his belt, which supported a pair of ceremonial knives in scabbards encrusted with jewels. He dropped the belt and knives dramatically to the floor to one side. It was the only thing that held his flabby belly in place. He removed his breeches, and stood there expectantly, his erect penis almost hidden by the folds of fat.

"Yes, please, now Metilius," said the procurator, his eyes wide with anticipation, and the scrawny but powerful guard forced the now struggling Nephtys to her knees within a foot of Pertacus. Desperately she forced her head back, trying to delay the first contact, but Metilius held her arms in a vice-like grip and started to force her head forwards onto Pertacus.

"Yes, my dear, that's right, that's right," hissed the procurator. Suddenly he coughed, then choked, then coughed again; his face was suddenly aghast as blood erupted from his mouth, spattering the hair, shoulders, and breasts of Nephtys and the face of Metilius. Shocked and surprised, Metilius let go of Nephtys; although she was still shackled to the wall, she was suddenly free of her captor and rolled away to one side, to avoid being crushed by the bulk of the procurator as he toppled forward, clutching his stomach.

Nephtys looked up and saw Gallus holding his sword, dripping with blood. Pertacus' blood.

The procurator was not dead but was writhing on the floor in agony, blood streaming out of the wound in his back and gushing from his mouth. He was making gurgling and choking sounds but unable to speak.

Now Metilius darted forward to get to the door, but Gallus slammed it shut and rammed the bolts home. The older guard looked this way and that but found nothing else he could use as a weapon, so he drew out a long thin knife, about half the length of Gallus' blade. But he didn't threaten Gallus. Instead, he stepped lightly over the still squirming procurator and grabbed Nephtys, pulled her up by her long black hair and held the knife to her throat, daring Gallus to approach.

But Metilius suddenly made a sound like a barking dog and stared down in horror at the knife protruding from his thigh. Finding herself free, as the guard grasped his leg to staunch the blood, Nephtys whipped around and stabbed at him with the second of Pertacus's knives. This time the knife hammered straight into his left eye. Making horrible noises, Metilius buckled to the floor and thrashed around in agony. Gallus calmly stepped over him, slammed his heel into the wounded guard's neck to hold him still, then drove his sword into his chest.

Gallus waited until the life had drained from Metilius and wrenched the blade free. He turned to the procurator, who lay twitching on the floor, his eyes still moving, still trying to mouth some words, but no sound could be heard other than a rasping noise. Gallus kicked the obese official onto his back with his boot, then very deliberately placed his sword point over the middle of Pertacus' chest. He looked him in the eye, saw the fear in the face of the procurator, thrust the sword downwards and left it there, protruding like a crucifix over a grave.

He spent no time looking at the dead Pertacus or Metilius. He crossed the floor and gently lifted Nephtys to her feet. He pressed her close to him for a second then sat her down on her rough bed. Studiously avoiding looking at her nakedness, he fetched an old blanket and wrapped it around her shoulders. He unshackled her from her chains then he offered his hand to her; shaking, tears running down her cheeks, she took it. Without speaking he led her to the door; as they passed the body of Pertacus, Gallus pulled his sword free. Letting go of Nephtys, he slowly and quietly pulled back the door bolts, opened the door quickly and stepped out.

The striking room was empty.

Gallus reached back and to grab Nephtys' hand, but she drew back. "No!" she hissed. Tears were running from her eyes, but somehow, the haze and the horror of the last few minutes cleared slightly, and she remembered her plan. Wiping away the tears, she darted back inside the room, the blanket dropping from her shoulders. She located Pertacus' belt; on it was a metal ring with keys. Her hands shaking, she unhooked the ring of keys and grabbed one of the torches that burned still inside her prison room, then she stepped out of the room, and whispered to Gallus. "Follow me!"

Naked apart from some shreds of the clothing that Metilius had missed, she ran through the striking room, down the corridor leading to the mint officials' offices. She paused behind the archway into the office area. She nervously peered around the corner into the large columned area which normally teemed with clerks and administrators. But it was dark, and no sound came from the room. There was no one around now, the working day had long ended, and the officials and clerks had left hours ago before evening set in. No sane worker would be walking the streets of Constantinople in the dark. But there would still be guards patrolling the building.

She heard Gallus step behind her. Before he could speak, she said in a shaky whisper, "We need to get into Pertacus' office!" Gallus had no idea what she was up to, but he had just killed two men for her, to set her free. "Why?" he hissed. "We need to go now, before the night guards find us. And you need to get some clothes on!"

She turned to Gallus, who tried to look away, but she turned his face towards her. "Gallus, you saved me. I'm in your debt, but you and I are now criminals. They will hunt us down. We need to find protection. Someone who will protect us."

"How will breaking into the procurator's office help?" he asked.

She drew in a breath, sniffed, and wiped her eyes again, smearing dust across her face. "Do you trust me?" she asked. He nodded. Checking again for the night guards but seeing none, they ran across the room; within a few seconds Nephtys had the doors unlocked. They entered, then she locked the doors behind them. In the torchlight, shadows flickered across the walls. There were chairs and couches and desks scattered through the huge office. But Nephtys didn't hesitate; she headed straight for the largest desk and ducked behind it. Pertacus' secure box.

"What's in this?" asked Gallus.

"Hope," replied Nephtys. She looked at the young guard. "Can you find me something to wear? Pertacus had lots of clothes." When Gallus paused, she smiled weakly and said, "Or perhaps you want me to go outside like this?" Gallus started looking for clothing.

Nephtys opened the strong box and, sure enough, inside was exactly what she hoped for. She smiled more fully; now they had a chance of survival.

Chapter 52

Northern Peloponnese, Greece, 8th May 397 AD

The first wagons of the main baggage train had begun to roll away by late-afternoon. Night was falling now as Alaric watched them labour their way along the track towards the mountain pass. Lit torches gave away their position. The Romans rarely, if ever, fought at night, and he hoped they continued with that tradition. He turned to Thiudimir, who stood waiting for his king. The soldier had found a new shield and had acquired a new knife as well as a short-handled axe.

"You did well," said Alaric.

"They'll send more scouts."

"Of course, but they'll not be against half a dozen men this time. I doubt they'll give us much trouble. Unlike Stilicho's army."

"We're going to fight them?" asked Thiudimir, raising his eyebrows.

Alaric laughed. "What do you think? Honestly?"

"I think it would be a close fight."

"I agree, but that aside, I've no intention of giving the good Vandal General what he wants." Alaric put his arm around Thiudimir's shoulders and walked him back towards the waiting group of senior commanders. "He wants a pitched battle, of course. A moment of glory, to sell to his enemies that he alone can rid the empire of the accursed Alaric. Have his triumph in Rome on a white steed, with me being dragged behind him in chains. Oh, how he would love that." The Goth general laughed. Then his face changed as he looked at the lines of Roman soldiers on the plain below.

"I never wanted this, you know," he said quietly. "I just wanted a place for our people to settle, somewhere where we could farm in peace. That's all."

Thiudimir suspected Alaric was going to ask him to do something dangerous. He had noticed this habit of talking around the subject when he had unpleasant things to say.

"King Alaric," said Thiudimir. "Just tell me what it is you want me to do."

"You're not going to like it," said Alaric with a sad smile on his face.

"But I'll do it anyway, you know that, so just say it."

Alaric grasped Thiudimir's shoulders, looked him in the eye and spoke. "You're a good man, you know that? If every man in this army were like you, we'd be invincible …Invincible."

"The task?" insisted Thiudimir.

Alaric looked at the thickset blond soldier again, sighed and told him what his task was.

Chapter 53

Near Cyzicus, Anatolia, 9th May 397 AD

Nephtys awoke with a start and looked around, then fell back on the mattress, her heart thumping. For a second, she was disoriented and thought she was back in her cell and all of last night had been a dream. But looking around again, it was not. This was not her cell. It was a small room, but light with the morning sun shining through a small, high window. The room was well-furnished and clean.

Then she recalled she was in a holy house, run by Christian women, where the sick and poor were tended. She remembered Gallus taking her there late last night and telling her to stay there until he came back for her. Then she remembered the letters and momentarily panicked until she saw the leather satchel at the foot of the bed. She grabbed it and, opening the clasp, she checked inside and sighed with relief; the letters were all there. Securing the clasp, she rose from the bed and went to the door. It was unlocked, so she got dressed and placing the satchel over her shoulder, opened the door and walked out into the corridor. It was narrow but short and led into an open courtyard, where a central fountain spilled out of a statue, a statue of no one she recognised. One of the women of the holy house, dressed in a pale-yellow dress, directed her to where food was available. She was offered dried fruit and bread and a cup of milk, which she took to a stone bench next to the fountain. The sun was still low, and the courtyard was still half in shadow, but the sunlight just touched the tip of the fountain streams, and Nephtys sat there gazing as the light of the sun danced and twinkled in the water. She thought about the night before and her hand trembled at the memory as she ate her bread.

Having escaped the mint via the private dock, they had clambered along the seashore and doubled back into the city. They had talked last night on the way to the holy house. She had told him what she had to do. She had to find her son, the boy taken from her to force her to do the things she had done for Pertacus and his masters back in Constantinople. She knew who had him. But they were powerful, so powerful she had seen no way to get near them. But now she had the letters.

The letters were a mixture. Some of them were hers, written in her hand, but in the style of others: politicians, bureaucrats, soldiers, traders, administrators – she had lost count. But others were letters from the men in the capital with instructions on what to do. Why Pertacus had not burned them she could not work out. Maybe he felt so invincible and untouchable in his role that he thought they would never be found. There again, maybe he had kept them for insurance so that should he be found out, he could perhaps trade his life for those who had given the orders to commit treason.

It didn't matter, because now she had the letters. A treasure trove of deceit, illegal orders, and instructions to commit outright criminal acts, all written by the men in Constantinople. The men who held her son. Now she had a chance to get him back. She would trade the letters for her son. It was risky, but she had to try. First, she had to get into the city undetected, because she was sure that once Pertacus' body was discovered. and she and the letters were missing, messages would be sent to the capital; they would be hunted from that moment on. Her son was in danger now too; without her under their control, he was of no use to them. But he was only a young boy; they couldn't kill him, surely. She had to hope that. She just had to hope.

So now she waited for Gallus to return.

Chapter 54

Northern Peloponnese, Greece, 9th May 397 AD

It had taken a whole day to get every wagon, cart, horse, mule, woman, child, and slave ready and sent up the mountain pass. The valley floor was wide, no barrier to the Roman cavalry or infantry. Alaric had managed to deploy his soldiers and cavalry across the mouth of the valley until now, but at some point, he had to pull back. He hoped the line looked too thin to withstand any concerted attack. He had deliberately made himself look vulnerable to having his line broken, because he wanted to lure Stilicho into the valley.

But his old adversary was nowhere to be seen. He was savvy enough to know that, at some point, Alaric would have to break his own line and reform his army into marching order to protect the baggage train as it wound its way up the valley and down the other side. Alaric had sent out scouts to the mountain tops and ridges to observe what was happening, but none had yet returned with any news. He was blind as to what Stilicho was doing. Was he only following them? He doubted it. Was he sending a portion of his force around the mountains, to intercept Alaric as he emerged on the northern shore of the Peloponnese, towards Patrae? More than likely, but there was nothing he could do about that. He could only hope that he could get across the hills and valleys first. They had the lead. He sat on his horse with his commanders and bodyguards around him and watched the last light of the day die on the horizon in the southwest.

"Clear night, King Alaric," said one of his senior commanders, Edica. "And a late moon. It will be dark, harder for the Romans to find us."

"Oh, they know where we are, for sure," said Alaric. Then addressing the whole group in a louder voice, "My friends, there are going to be some long nights and longer days ahead. You have your assignments, but I will stress one more time. Protect the baggage train at all costs, with your lives if you must! Now go, rally your men, and we'll meet on the other side of the mountains. God bless you all!"

"God bless you, King Alaric," the commanders replied one by one as they turned their horses and rode away, all moving slowly in the half-light, not wishing to endanger their mounts.

The king turned to his bodyguards and his remaining commander, Theodahad, and said, "I will remind you of our plan. Athaulf is leading the front and knows his orders; that is to get to the north coast as soon as possible. Our task," he paused and looked at the men in the dark, wrapped in furs and heavy tunics in the dark they were like night wraiths, big and imposing. "Our task is to defend the rear of the baggage train, to prevent the Romans from gaining a foothold in our lines. Theodahad has command of his infantry and cavalry units and will provide the main defence. We," he indicated his bodyguard "will act as shock troops to bolster Theodahad when he needs support. You will act on my command alone. No-one so much as fires an arrow at the Romans without my say -so, and if I say fall back, we fall back. No heroics. No challenging Romans to single combat. Our aim is simple. To survive the next days. Do you understand?"

In the faint light he saw the heads nod and heard a few muted "ayes". The soldiers would not be happy; they lusted after battle and booty, but this was not the time for that. They were vulnerable and they had to make sure Stilicho could not exploit that. They were running, pure and simple, but as God was his witness, he was going to make damn sure that this was an orderly retreat to establish a new base in Illyricum, and not a panicked rout, scrabbling for survival.

Chapter 55

Forum of Constantine, Constantinople, 10th May 397 AD

In the forum of Constantine, Anthemius sat beneath a cooling willow tree, many of which grew on the edge of the forum providing shade for the thousands of people who came there to relax in the afternoon, when the working day was done.

Anthemius had had a full life over the last months, since getting back from Cyzicus.

He had got married. Lucia was from an influential family; the daughter of a senator, and she came with a large dowry. It was a good match. Her family were comfortable *spectabiles*, the second ranks in the senate. They had kept their lands despite the efforts of Rufinus, and now Eutropius, to acquire it off of them. His wife's father knew the emperor personally through a long history of service with his father, and by all accounts they got on well. She was not unattractive, and they got on with each other well enough, there was no love there but that didn't matter. They were very comfortable, happy in their own polite way, and they had started the process of producing children, as was expected of all good Roman marriages.

Then there was work. He had been active in ensuring the constant supply of coins into the economy, local and remote. There had been transportation problems with raw materials, raids by barbarians on the mines and on the wagons. In truth, they had gotten away with very little, comparatively speaking, but with Alaric still rampaging in the Peloponnese, any signs of insurgents from other Germanic tribes got the emperor and consistorium very nervous. So additional protection had to be arranged; that meant more organisation for the guards and associated logistics. There seemed to be no end to the paperwork.

Ever since the trials of the two generals last year, he had set aside some time each week to work on the puzzle of the counterfeit coins. But time and time again, he had come up short. He could not see how to pursue his investigation. So, lacking ideas of any use from his subordinates and getting no active enthusiasm from his peers to pursue what appeared to be an already concluded affair, he had decided to go outside of the imperial administration and seek help from more unorthodox circles.

So now he found himself sitting at a small table for two, drinking a cup of cool wine with Quaderi, the Persian money changer.

He had come to see his companion for his advice. He hesitated to call him a friend, because he regarded him as both trustworthy and unscrupulous. The former in the sense that he trusted his discretion when dealing in sensitive matters; the latter in the sense that the rule of law was seen as an option in life, not a guiding principle or obsession as it was for the citizens of New Rome.

"So let us go over it again," said Quaderi. "From the beginning."

"Very well," said Anthemius. "You were passed a number of fake coins over a period of time from several sources We tracked the other sources to be sure, but none gave us any further leads, except a small blue bag full of coins."

"Priscianus, the Blues leader," said Quaderi, "who came to an untimely end about a month ago."

"I heard."

"He will not be missed!" laughed the Persian and raised his cup in a toast. They both drank.

"Priscianus said he had been given a bag of the coins as a gift from a wealthy lady for one of the Blues charioteers whom she admired, but we thought that unlikely, so we followed him to the Jew on the docks, who told us that he had been ordering coins from Cyzicus and they all came in blue bags, and we suspect they always were fakes."

"Almost certainly."

"The bag from Priscianus was the only bag of coins that we know of. All the others were individual coins."

"Yes," agreed Quaderi.

"When I put the bag in front of Priscianus he seemed … annoyed, surprised … I'm not sure what. But he definitely was not happy about seeing it again."

The Persian nodded. "Which maybe indicates he was not aware that the blue bag had been given to me."

"That's possibly it. It might explain his reaction."

Quaderi tugged at his short beard absently as he thought. "Having a whole bag of newly minted fakes is a far riskier undertaking than putting around a coin here and coin there. In fact, the gambling shops at the Hippodrome and arenas are far safer places to mix those coins, which is where I would imagine most of them go."

"I agree. So why risk the whole bag?"

They were silent for a minute, the chatter of people around them as the people of the city bustled by carrying pots of grain, loaves of bread and amphoras of wine. The moneychanger said, "Didn't you say Priscianus said he was ill the day the money was due to me?"

"Yes, I didn't believe him."

"Perhaps you should," pondered the Persian. "I think a mistake was made by one of his subordinates. A message to pay me on the day he was ill; but they didn't get the instructions about not mixing fakes with real coins. They must simply have taken the money from the strong box and handed it to Maurinus, the charioteer, to bring to me. Yes … a mistake."

Anthemius considered the suggestion. And the more he thought about it, the more he felt his companion was correct. It was careless to bunch so much counterfeit money together. The subordinate must not have known the coins were fake; why should he? No reason for Priscianus to say; the fewer who knew about it the better.

The act itself was reckless, or perhaps done with no knowledge of the reality of the coins. Maurinus certainly seemed genuinely surprised. Why not others?

"So Priscianus was genuinely ill," said Anthemius.

Quaderi nodded.

"The subordinate, on his instructions, simply took the first available amount of money from their strong box to pay you off."

Quaderi nodded again.

"Because they decided to switch to the Jew, now that the supply of counterfeit coins from Cyzicus was becoming more reliable."

The Persian nodded again and added, "And always in those little blue bags. How quaint."

Anthemius continued. "When we arrived at Cyzicus we were expected and given the tour. Pertacus denied all knowledge of any forgery or fraud."

"As you would expect him to."

"But as soon as the culprits were discovered, they were executed, indicating that Pertacus did not know of the treason."

"Or was just covering his tracks and eliminating anybody that might implicate him?"

Anthemius took a small sip of his wine and placed the cup gently on the table. "It does all seem far too convenient, in hindsight," he said. "Pertacus suggesting my men help with the guarding. Why do that? At

326

the time I saw no reason not to and I guess I was keen to solve this problem, and I trusted Hunulf and his men far more than I trusted Pertacus, so it seemed like the right thing to do at the time."

"And now?" prompted Quaderi.

"And now, I think he was putting on a show for me, or for Hunulf and his men. Showing us what we wanted to see. He was willing to forego a bit of glory in order to throw me off, by giving me the perpetrators and a raft of evidence to support the guilt of Balbus and Khaemet."

"And what evidence?" asked the Persian

"Papers, letters from Abundantius; the writing matched the general's; I checked."

"But letters and writings can be forged, can they not?"

Anthemius nodded. "Yes, of course they can. But since Balbus probably did the forging, we can't prove it."

"Why do you think Balbus forged the papers?"

"His wife apparently forged some documents when she was younger and working with the Blues in Cyzicus; she most likely taught him how to do it."

Quaderi nearly choked on his wine when he laughed out loud. Some spatters hit the table, and a couple landed on Anthemius' arm, staining the white cloth. The Persian was unabashed and continued to chuckle.

"What's so funny?" he asked, somewhat annoyed as he tried to remove the stain with his own spit and a finger.

"Oh," laughed Quaderi. "You Romans are quite funny, are you not?"

Anthemius furrowed his brow. "What do you mean?" he asked, a slight testiness in his voice.

"You really think Balbus' wife taught him how to forge?" The Persian took another drink of his wine.

"Why not?"

"Why not?" echoed the moneychanger. "My dear procurator, you've told to me how beautiful this woman was, how enchanting."

"I have? I barely recall mentioning her."

"Precisely. I think your words to me earlier were, a 'comely' woman, though some might say attractive." Quaderi smiled. "I've never known you skirt around a subject with such vagueness; your eyes and face lit up when you mentioned her. My conclusion is that she was in fact a woman of rare and enticing beauty?" He stared at Anthemius intently and lifted his bushy eyebrows. "Tell me I am wrong."

"She was … stunning," admitted Anthemius.

"Hah!" barked the Persian, loudly so that several people on other tables turned and looked at him, but he waved at them to mind their own business. Then he leaned forward and lowered his voice. "I can see why you have had difficulty getting to your next step. It's in your Roman nature, is it not, to demand that a woman be seen and not heard?"

"No, not at all."

"Then why are woman not permitted to serve as senators or administrators?"

"That's not work fitting for a woman."

"What is then, tell me?"

"She has great responsibility for the next generation of Romans."

"Oh please. You Roman men, you philander, you cheat on your wives, openly have mistresses and everyone dismisses it as nothing of consequence. Indeed, I've heard that if you Roman men actually love your wives, you're made fun of ..."

The Persian was enjoying himself, Anthemius could see that; he tried to interject, but Quaderi continued on, " ...yet if your wife is unfaithful to you, or fails to bear you children? Why, they're denounced, cast out, scorned as being an actress or prostitute, and then thrown out onto the street, to be just that in order to survive. The hypocrisy is laughable."

"It's not like that at all!" insisted Anthemius.

"No?" laughed Quaderi. "Then, tell me this, most noble procurator of the city mint." Sarcasm oozed from the money-changer. "How is it that you, possibly the most intelligent of all the people I know, cannot see the most obvious next step in your investigation, when it is right in front of your nose?"

Anthemius placed his cup down and said, "Go on then, Persian; enlighten me."

"Balbus' wife did not teach him how to forge the letters," said Quaderi. He looked Anthemius in the eyes, and raised his eyebrows again, encouraging the procurator to think.

Then it hit Anthemius. He closed his eyes and nodded.

"The wife."

The Persian smiled and nodded. "The wife."

Chapter 56

The Northern Peloponnese, 10th May 397 AD

E Berwolf, the commander in charge of guarding the rear section of the baggage train, screamed, "Shields!"

The men raised their shields over their heads as a murderous rain of arrows slammed into them. Curses and screams went up as some arrows found their target.

Eberwolf saw the attacking cavalry wheeling away, then he saw Theodahad, leading his detachment of riders, race across the ground to their right, towards the retreating Romans. The Romans stopped and turned back, Theodahad did the same; now he was being pursued by the Romans, back to the baggage train. Theodahad headed back towards where Eberwolf and his men stood behind a thin, two-man-deep shield wall, which they had created to protect themselves.

The rear section of baggage train was in trouble. One of the wagons had broken its axle. It was old and had travelled hundreds of miles; it was a miracle it had made it this far. But now it blocked the main route, spilling its contents of valuable food and supplies across the track. The wagon itself was of no consequence, it needed to be abandoned, but the supplies were critical, and other wagons and carts were trapped behind it and vulnerable to the Roman attack. The Romans hadn't missed that. A unit of cavalry, who looked like Hunnic mercenaries to Eberwolf, had seized on the confusion and were harassing them mercilessly, trying to find a way through the line of warriors lining the side of the track.

Theodahad's men headed straight towards the shield wall, then split and broke left and right; the Hunic horsemen were taken by surprise and found themselves in front of the wall of shields. Eberwolf yelled, "Loose!" and a storm of spears and arrows was launched by warriors in and behind the shield wall, which scythed into the attackers. Horses and riders screamed and fell. The ground was rocky and hard. Many horses broke their legs falling. The earth was littered with battered and broken men and beasts. Before the fallen could rise to try to stagger away, Theodahad's men had circled back, crashed into the injured and dying and driven away the few survivors. The men making up the shield wall cheered and beat their sword hafts on the wooden backs of the shields. The attack was over for now.

Eberwolf surveyed the landscape and saw no more immediate threat but ordered the front line of the shield wall to stand fast, and for the rear line to get their arses back and help shift the broken wagon, reload the spilled goods onto other carts and to get the wagons and carts moving again. They had been at this for nearly two days now. It had been relentless, and progress had been dismally slow. The men were tired, and the Romans had been harassing continually. It was now midday again; the sun was high in the sky, dipping behind puffy white clouds from time to time, but the heat was really starting to tell on them. Water was to hand in the river which wound down the valley, but that was away from the baggage train defences and a previous squad of men sent to refill had been attacked and killed to a man by a Roman cohort that had hidden themselves in amongst the rocks and tussocks. Nowhere was safe away from the track. Stilicho was no fool; he knew how to unsettle his enemies. Eberwolf stared towards the head of the valley, which seemed an awfully long way away. It was going to be a long day.

High up on the hilly ridge, directly above where Eberwolf was cajoling his men to get the baggage train moving, Berimund fought for his life. A Roman spear was lodged in his shield making it awkward and difficult to hold. A legionary hacked at his shield, the impact sending a painful shock through Berimund's arm and shoulder. "Fuck you!" he swore at his enemy, and he thrust forward with his shield and barrelled into the man, sending him sprawling backward. He slid off his shield and wrenched the spear from it. Out of the corner of his eye he saw movement and whirled around with the spear, stabbing it forward into the chest of another legionary, who screamed in agony. Berimund dropped the spear and whirled around again to block another attack from the first Roman with his sword. There was a loud metallic clang as metal hit metal, and the two men found themselves almost face to face as they braced one against the other in a deadly contest of strength. Berimund screamed in the face of his opponent, who flinched. It was all he needed. He kneed the man in the crotch, then slashed down on the back of his head with his sword.

He retrieved his shield and turned and surveyed the scene. The Romans were backing off. But it would only be a temporary respite.

Alaric surveyed the valley from a vantage point about half a mile behind the rear of the baggage train. Below him, the baggage train was slowly, oh so very slowly, crawling down the track. He could see Theodahad's cavalry patrolling the rear of the train. There appeared to be a broken wagon near the rear, which men were now pushing to one side. Above him, to the left, the units of soldiers he had posted on the high ground to the West looked like they were holding onto the ridge top. He could see them fighting from where he sat, but they were holding the Romans back. But further down the valley, to the West, he could see some troop movement and cavalry forming up. Stilicho was not messing around this time. But this couldn't be his whole force; it was still too few. The main force had to be lagging behind them, on the other side of the mountains by the northwest shore. Patience, he told himself. It's still all going to plan at the moment. But it all relied on Thiudimir. If he failed, they would all be doomed.

At the bottom of the valley Athaulf, Alaric's brother-in-law, directed the mass of people: men, women, children, warriors, slaves, and whores as they reached the flatter ground. The wind blew from the west down the valley, though the sun was hot. They had two wagons loaded with wine and water to give to the thirsty people before they continued across the plain towards another group of small hills, which hid the northern coast. Another senior commander, Sarus, scowled as the people passed. "What the fuck are we doing here?" he muttered loudly. Some of the people glanced at him and frowned. Athaulf pulled Sarus aside and snapped, "Shut up! These people need encouragement, not you whining!"

Sarus wrestled his arm free and hissed, "Your brother-in-law is leading us to our deaths! We should meet with Stilicho and discuss terms." Athaulf straightened and then punched the man in the face, so quickly he had no time to brace himself. Sarus sprawled on the floor, shook his head, then picked himself up and drew his sword. He found himself facing half a dozen men, surrounding Athaulf with weapons ready and pointed at Sarus. He snarled. "Hah! The brave Athaulf hiding like a woman behind his guards? Let's settle this now."

Athaulf barged his way in front of his bodyguard and strode forward menacingly, sword drawn, forcing Sarus to retreat. Sarus raised his sword, but Athaulf easily batted it aside, then he blocked a counter thrust from his opponent and stepped in close, holding the other's sword arm in a vice-like gripe, immobilising him. "Listen, you piece of shit. Your job is to scout ahead, find out what defences the towns ahead have and help identify how we can start to prepare the defences that will be needed. Now get your sorry arse across the plain around that headland, or so help me I'll kill you now, to put us all out of our misery!"

The two men locked eyes for a few seconds, then Sarus shook himself free and, cursing and muttering to himself, took himself to his horse, mounted it and then rode off hard across the plain, a small group of his men following him.

"He's going to be a problem, that one," said one of Athaulf's bodyguards.

Athaulf silently agreed. Sarus was nothing but an ever-present pain in the backside and had been ever since Alaric had one of his family executed for extortion and stealing.

Athaulf turned looked around and saw the people had stopped and were staring at him. He angrily waved at them to keep moving and yelled, "Keep moving you lot, don't you know the fucking Romans are right behind us? Now move! You and you, help that old bastard with his cart, and you two, make sure the children get a drink when they get here. Keep it moving!"

Berimund yelled to his men to fall back again. The ridge was narrowing as they went lower, and it would be ever more difficult for the Romans to pass them by. The drop on either side was becoming steeper and steeper. It was impossible for cavalry, so only the infantry were pressing the Goths back. The wind was strengthening. Below he could see the baggage train winding its way down along the path. Across the other side of the ridge, towards the sea, he could see the Roman army building in strength as more and more infantry units amassed. But their own job was to ensure that no units of Romans managed to sneak around the secondary valley below them, to cut them off. So far, they had seen nothing, except the Romans who had had the same idea as Alaric and were trying to take the high ground to the northwest, above the baggage train.

He heard a yell and ducked instinctively. A volley of spears had been launched. Most were caught by the wind and clattered harmlessly amongst the rocks. One skidded off of Berimund's shield and another struck a glancing blow to another warrior, but his helmet saved him, though he staggered and nearly fell from the ridge, until willing hands grabbed and steadied him. "Return fire!" shouted Berimund, and his men quickly gathered the spears. On his count, they launched them back at the Romans just below them. The spears had a following wind, and judging by the scream, at least one found its mark.

Suddenly a dozen Romans leapt out from amongst the rocks and threw themselves at Berimund's men. He found himself facing two legionaries, one young, one older. The older one didn't hesitate and surged forward, dodging Berimund's sword thrust and slicing his own sword at the Goth's leg. Berimund stepped quickly back, avoiding the attack. The young legionnaire hadn't moved. He was unsure what to do and dangerously near the edge of the ridge, with little room to manoeuvre. The older roman pressed his attack. He was good, but not as used to hand to hand combat in the open as Berimund. He fended off a vicious down stroke with his shield and rammed it into the Roman. The point on the boss was not long, but it was razor sharp and pierced the legionary's leather body armour, drawing blood and a string of curses. The Roman attempted to steady himself and pushed his own shield forward to block Berimund, but the Goth sidestepped, hopped onto a rock and allowed the Roman to topple forwards past him. He hacked at his opponent's exposed back, drawing a howl of agony. Berimund whirled and drove his sword into the Roman's upper back and down into his heart. Wrenching his sword free, he spun around and saw the young legionary still standing there, frozen in terror.

"Go home, son," growled Berimund, pointing his sword at the roman youth. "No need to die today." He glanced to his side; his men had driven off the skirmishers again.

"Fall back!" he yelled to his men. One by one they clambered over the jagged and twisted rocks of the ridge. Berimund was the last to retreat, holding his sword out. He called to the youth, "Don't follow us, son! You'll only find death here."

But next moment, there were more yells and another dozen soldiers came leaping over the rocks. This time, they had bows. Hun bows. Berimund realised these were not Roman conscripts, they were steppe warrior mercenaries; he knew they were in trouble. He just had time to yell "shields!" when a volley of arrows hammered into them. He heard a cry of pain and then of terror as one of his men with an arrow in his thigh and another in his arm stumbled and fell from the ridge. He heard the warrior's cry fade as he fell and rolled down the near vertical drop to their side.

Another rain of arrows created havoc and more casualties. All they could do was cower behind their shields.

Eberwolf had got the rearmost wagons moving again; his men had heaved the broken wagon off the track. Theodahad's cavalry was crossing the rear of the baggage train, giving the Romans no opening to attack. At one point Theodahad came up to Eberwolf and yelled for him to move faster, to which Eberwolf yelled back that if he thought he could make a pack mule with a hundred pounds on his back run like a fucking horse, he was welcome to come and try for himself.

Eberwolf had got every able-bodied man, and some of the women, to form up behind the last wagons to provide a small mobile fighting force capable of forming a final wall of defence if needed, if the Romans broke through Theodahad's lines.

"Come on people, move!" shouted Eberwolf again and again, but the pace was painfully slow.

The Tervingi defences were stretched thin now. Alaric could see that plainly from his vantage point. He had a view down the valley and could see that Theodahad was holding the rear-guard well. Above him on the ridge line, though, he could see arrows flying at his men, not a good sign. The Romans had called in archers, to which his men up there had no response. To the northwest on the plain, he could see small units of Roman infantry and cavalry, keeping pace with the baggage train. Every now and again, if a wagon found itself isolated, these units would start to head for the lone wagon, like a pack of wolves trying to isolate a sheep. Then the soldiers guarding the wagons had to form up to provide a defensive shield, or a detachment of the Tervingi cavalry had to rush down from the upper valley to drive off the intruders. The bugles and horns sounded every few seconds as orders were yelled out and passed down the line. But so far, the Goths had held fast, and the Romans had had no real impact on the retreat. Almost as if they were herding the baggage train to a destination. *Let them think they're doing just that*, thought Alaric.

But then, towards the northwest, he saw a dark mass moving, hundreds of horsemen. Alaric swore. This was the one thing he had prayed not to happen. Stilicho had sent his shock troops ahead to intercept them. The Huns were coming.

Eberwolf heard them before he saw them, a sound like the rumbling of distant thunder and a vibration in the earth, vaguely felt. No sooner had he registered the sound than he saw their own cavalry heading back towards them, Theodahad waving madly at their head. Instead of stopping, the majority of the cavalry raced past them, heading up the valley, but Theodahad and his bodyguards galloped to where Eberwolf stood.

"Form up defence! Upend the carts and wagons, the Huns are here!" screamed Theodahad.

Instantly Eberwolf was barking out orders; there had to be immediate action, or they all were going to die.

"Off the wagons now!" he yelled. "Turn them on their sides!" The men leapt off their carts and wagons, the women too; they bundled the children into a group and, using a steep bank of the valley side to their

337

backs, they rolled and overturned the carts to form a barricade. Pots, clothes, food, bedding, furs, and valuables spilled over the path, their livelihoods and homes upended in a desperate bid to survive. Eberwolf glanced down the plain to the northwest and saw, about a quarter of a mile away, a wall of black horsemen heading straight for them. He yelled to his troops to get the old men, women, and children behind the barricades, to arm as many as they could and to use anything they could for shields, then with the Huns only a minute out, he screamed and yelled and cajoled the able-bodied men into a solid shield wall surrounding the upended baggage train. He only had a dozen or so archers at his disposal, and he kept them safe behind the barricades. The rest of his men were armed with long spears that they dug the end of into the ground and pointed forwards to make a lethal wall of metal onto which the horses and riders would charge at their peril. That was the plan, of course. The Huns were outstanding archers but only average foot soldiers, so the defenders just had to survive the initial onslaughts and bombardments of arrows and wait for the re-enforcements to arrive.

"My men will be back to drive them off, with Alaric's help!" called out Theodahad, who had joined the defensive line.

"They better fucking well had!" cursed Eberwolf. "I've no intention of dying in this God forsaken place." He glanced between the shields and screamed out, "Brace yourselves!"

High above, Berimund endured another battering of arrows. His men had sheathed their swords; they clung onto the steep and jagged rocks with one hand, holding their shields in their other. Bit by bit they edged back along the ridge, moving in groups of twos and threes, shielding each other as best they could. There was no opportunity to create a solid defence; this was just the desperation of trying to survive the next onslaught. Every so often they managed to launch a spear down the ridge, but it was immediately answered by another barrage of shafts, which clattered amongst the rocks or buried themselves in the wood of their shields. Berimund muttered a short prayer, "Lord, if you can hear me, do something to help!" He didn't know what else to do. They could not attack; they would be cut down instantly. They could not keep retreating, that would lead the attackers right into the heart of the Tervingi army at the head of the valley.

And then it happened.

The temperature seemed to plummet and suddenly they were enveloped in fog, and the world around them shrank to nothing but a featureless white and grey.

Alaric saw Theodahad's cavalry heading up the pass towards him. He urged his horse and his bodyguards forward to meet them. The officer in the lead rode up to Alaric; gasping, he requested that the king go to the assistance of Theodahad, to relieve the rear of the baggage train. Alaric nodded and said he had already ordered his messengers to quickly head up the valley and bring down another unit of cavalry. They were already on their way down.

"We will form up when the reserves arrive and drive off the Huns. No quarter!" he announced. He ordered his third in command to remain and ensure that the other Roman units did not exploit the absence of the cavalry units, which he knew they would try to do, as that was exactly what he would do himself in the same situation.

Whilst he waited for the reinforcements, he looked up to the ridge above him. He could see nothing of the skirmishing up there now; clouds were swirling around the ridgetop. Who knew what was happening up there now? Berimund was a good man. If anyone could prevail up there, it was him.

Berimund banged on his shield with his sword haft, and out of the gloom he saw his men appear around him like wraiths. They were only two dozen now and they only had swords, plus a few spears and arrows retrieved from the ground. They had no bows. There was no time to lose; the cloud might vanish at any moment. "We attack!" he growled. "Any of you fuckers disagree?" None of them did. "Let's go, then!" They rose up, and together they screamed a Tervingi war cry and rushed back down along the ridge, leaping from rock to rock. Arrows flew at them, but the Huns were now firing blind, and they aimed high and wide. Within seconds Berimund saw a dark shadow in front of him and he launched himself at it, battering it to the ground with his shield and hacking at it with his sword, blood streaming from the blade as he slashed again and again. He stepped over the body and saw another shadow, in profile, raise its arm, holding a ghostly bow. He barrelled into the figure, heard a yell, and hacked down. He saw the bow clatter to the floor, and a quiver of arrows spilled its content onto the ground. All around him he heard his men screaming their war cry. Another figure rose up beside him; instinctively he whirled and slashed at it. He heard a cry and the figure fell to the floor, a sword making a metallic clang as it struck a rock. Berimund saw the blood gushing out across the ground. Then the cloud thinned for a moment, and he saw his enemy. It was the young Roman soldier he had spoken to earlier. He lay there, his life blood running from his neck, unable to speak, looking up at his killer.

Berimund knelt beside the boy and gripped his hand. "I told you to go home, boy. I'm truly sorry. May you find peace with our Lord…"

The young lay trying to stem the flow, but it was useless. Berimund watched as his life slowly left him.

A few minutes later, his men found him kneeling next to the young Roman soldier, in prayer, and informed him that the enemy was fleeing back down the ridge and that the position was secure. Berimund nodded and stood, tears flowing down his cheeks. Around them, the cloud lifted, and the late afternoon sun appeared, bathing the rocks in golden sunlight. Below they saw the dark hoard of Huns heading directly for the rear of the baggage train.

The shock of the arrows hammering into his shield nearly bowled Eberwolf backwards. Others in the wall suffered likewise; one or two shields splintered under the murderous assault , but as far as he could see, miraculously nobody was hit this time. The Huns peeled away, and Eberwolf yelled out to his archers to hold fire and not to waste arrows. He glanced up the hill to his left. No sign of their own cavalry yet. He looked back at the Huns who were already wheeling around and coming back for another attack. One of his archers behind him called out, "there's another group of them gathering further out, with fire!"

"Hold fast! Keep your positions!" growled Eberwolf, but he himself stood up and looked to where his man was pointing. Sure enough, about a quarter of a mile away he saw another wave of the Hunic mercenaries circling a column of smoke. They were lighting arrows wrapped with cloth dipped in grease, and he could see them starting to head towards them. He cursed and yelled to his archers to fire at the returning Huns. The archers did their best to keep up a rate of fire, but there were too few of them, and their bows were inferior to the Huns. The enemy thundered close to Eberwolf's shield wall and launched another volley of arrows, this time taking out two of the defenders, but the holes in the shield wall were instantly filled. Willing hands from inside the ring of wagons hauled the injured soldiers back to temporary safety.

But now the third wave of Huns was heading towards them, a pall of smoke trailing behind from the lit arrowheads. This time the Huns did not get so close; they simply galloped towards the rear of the baggage train, loosed their arrows high and then wheeled away. The Goths could do nothing but watch as a rain of fire slammed into the wagons, ground, and animals all around them. Chaos ensured.

Mules and horses squealed in pain and panic as the arrows hit. Several beasts bolted, fire exploding across their backs. In their terror and anguish, they ploughed into people and carts, breaking bones and heads and sending wheels, wooden planks and splinters, pots and clothes and food, flying across the ground. The defenders had been hit too. Some had manged to staunch the flames, but others were screaming in agony, their compatriots trying to help them by rolling them on the ground. Eberwolf could only watch in horror as petrified creatures panicked, people burned, and their defences collapsed around them. The shield wall was pointless against the attack. Eberwolf whirled around and yelled to his men. "Get these people out of here now." They scrambled across the ground, back up onto the path and pushed and shoved and hauled the women, children, and men, who were crying, yelling, and cursing, from behind the wagons and onto the open path. Some were complaining that they were leaving their homes behind, but Eberwolf's men yelled at them to run. They ran.

They were now exposed as a group. The main baggage train had moved on; they were isolated. Looking down the hill he could see more Huns were heading back to them, again with more fire arrows. But now, too, a small section of Roman cavalry across the valley was taking an interest; seeing the separated group, they were heading towards them. They were a lot closer. Seeing the group on foot, they sensed blood and Eberwolf saw them urge their mounts forward. He turned to Theodahad, who was still with them, and shouted at him and to all his men around him. "Come on, get these people up the hill as fast as you can! Carry them if you have to!" He glanced over his shoulder and saw the Romans and the Huns bearing down on them and his heart sank.

But then he heard cheers and yells of joy and the sound of more thunder, not an ominous sound now, but glorious. Alaric and his cavalry had finally arrived. Five hundred men, charging at full speed, cannoned into the Roman unit, swatting it aside like insects, swords ringing out as they clashed on armour. Eberwolf saw the Roman cavalrymen thrown from their horses amongst the carnage and chaos. Alaric and his men raced on and headed for the Huns who had been focussed on the baggage train and now, too late noticed the Goths heading for their right flank. Some managed to lose off arrows at their attackers, but most didn't notice until the swords and spears of Alaric's men cut them down as a scythe cuts hay. The Huns broke and ran, Alaric's men chasing them, harassing them. Eberwolf looked after them and sighed. He would live to fight again, it seemed. He offered a short prayer, then he turned said to his men around him, "Come on, you loafers, let's get going. They'll be back soon enough no doubt; let's get up this fucking hill as quick as we can. Come on!"

It was early afternoon. Sarus had reached the hills on the far side of the plain and had circled around the north side of the low hills of the valley on the north side of the mountain, onto the narrow path, close to the sea, and some miles ahead he could see a walled town. Patrae. It was further than they had thought; it would take them the rest of the day to get there. The baggage train would take much longer. It was hotter down here than up the mountain side. He had a small group of men with him, and they rode cautiously down the narrow track, picking their way carefully, alert for any signs of the enemy, any sign of Stilicho's army. None were apparent. They could hear nothing but the wind and the occasional chirping of crickets and birds. In the distance they saw deer, so at least there was game here to hunt. They might yet not starve to death, thought Sarus, despite that idiot Alaric's best attempts. They rode on, keeping their eyes behind them on the west. If Stilicho was watching them, that's where he would be.

The afternoon wore on. Eberwolf urged his people on. Theodahad had remounted his horse and re-joined his men, but the cavalry unit now remained closer to the baggage train. The Romans, for their part, seemed content to keep their distance, with only the occasional foray towards the Goths. Their attacks were mainly limited to rude gestures and yelled curses and insults. Eberwolf's men and women gave back as good as they got. He assumed that they had not figured on losing quite so many men unnecessarily and were simply trying to keep them moving across the plain. He had no doubt Stilicho's main force lay behind them and was making its way around. Eberwolf trusted Alaric implicitly, but even he could not see how they were going to be able to fight their way through this time. Stilicho must know, with the help of local guides, exactly where they were going to come out of the mountains. They were heading for Patrae in the hope of finding ships to get them across the sea to northern Illyricum

Stilicho had all the time in the world to prepare, whilst they had yet to get their baggage train across the plain, around the low hills to the south of Patrae, and then somehow take the walled town. And judging from their current pace, it was going to take much, much longer than they thought to get over to the north shore. Not one day, more like two or three, and they were going to get more and more strung out as time wore on. Nobody spoke now, the only sound was that of sandals and boots on the ground, the creaking of the carts and wagons and a few muffled cries from the babes. He looked around him. The men were tired from the fighting. The women were tired from the stress and the work of helping to haul the wagons and carts and to keep the children under control; the younger children were tired and hot, hungry and thirsty. Their homes, possessions and food and drink lay scattered and burning behind them. Theodahad and his men were delivering food and water from further down the baggage train, but there were many mouths to feed and many thirsty people. Eberwolf shook his head as if to wave away the worries. *No use dwelling*, he thought, *take each day as it comes*. He looked up ahead, he still could not see around the low hills ahead across the plain. He cursed and trudged on.

Chapter 57

Near Corinth, Greece, 11th May 397 AD

The rider had been on the road for ten days. He had lost count of the number of changed horses, or how many hours he had been in the saddle. He was sore, tired, and badly wanted to just lie down and sleep. But he knew he could not. He rode with a dozen soldiers and had been with them since Athens. He had delivered his message to the *Magister Militum*, who was still in Athens. The city had held out against Alaric and survived.

The rider had delivered the letters from Eutychainus to the general. The old soldier looked shocked as the read the contents and the rider heard him mutter some profanities. He saw him straighten up, then he turned to him and said, "Go to the commissary and get fed and get some rest. I will send a slave to get you in a few hours."

The rider looked blankly at the general; he was so tired he hadn't really taken in anything the old soldier had said.

"Go!" yelled the general. He went, found some food, then found a comfortable spot in the corner of the commissary room and fell asleep as soon as he lay down.

He was shaken awake sometime later from his camp bed by a Numidian slave. It took him a moment to remember where he was; his sleep had been so deep he was momentarily confused. It was still dark, but he rose, rubbed his gritty eyes and followed the slave through the camp. When he reached the stables, there was a bustle of activity, through which he was escorted to the general.

"Right, there you are," said the general. "This is Tiberius Julius Marullus, one of my senior officers; he will accompany you on your journey onwards to ensure you arrive safely and deliver both of your letters."

"Both?" the rider was surprised.

"Yes, both messages, and it's likely that you will be riding into the middle of a battle, so I have my orders to provide you with an escort."

"Two letters?" the rider repeated.

"Yes, man, two; are you an imbecile?" snapped the general. "You have one for King Alaric and one for General Stilicho. Both signed by the emperor himself, may God protect him!"

So, they had ridden out, and within two days they found themselves at Corinth. Corinth had not escaped the ravages of Alaric's army, though the damage was not catastrophic. Stonemasons and carpenters were busy at work, repairing the city walls and gates. They sought out merchants who traded with the Goths, providing food and drink and clothing, and who had just returned to the city. They had been with Alaric not ten days ago and they had seen the whole army moving to the north.

That didn't make any sense to the senior officer. There was only sea to the north; Stilicho could trap Alaric easily there. The rider was worried. He now needed to get one message to Alaric and another to Stilicho, and he wanted to deliver them before they came to blows. The soldiers with him laughed and joked about battles and fighting, but he just wanted a quiet life. He loved riding through the countryside on horseback. Riding into a battle was not what he thought he would have to do. The recruiter never mentioned this when he had convinced him to take the job.

So, they left Corinth behind them, nursing its wounds, and trying to return to life after Alaric. It was now early morning, the air was cool; but soon the sun, already climbing up in the east, would quickly heat things up and they could not afford to slow too much. They pushed their horses onwards.

Chapter 58

Southern Docks, Constantinople, 11th May 397 AD

Hunulf fumed. "Do I have to go in this fucking boat again?" He walked up the gangplank onto the same vessel that they had travelled in previously, with the same swarthy, taciturn Persian Captain, who eyed Hunulf with disdain.

Anthemius smiled and replied, "It's a short trip, Hunulf, stop complaining. I don't hear Sigeric and Videric whining like a little girl, do I?"

"They don't spend all day and night chucking their guts up, do they?"

"Stay on deck; you will be fine. And seriously," Anthemius lowered his voice and leaned into the Goth guard. "You must find this woman and bring her to me safely; it is a matter of the greatest importance."

"If she's dead?"

"Find out who killed her and bring them back to me."

"Why can't you come along?"

"Remind me. Exactly why I am paying you?"

"Good point," conceded Hunulf. "We'll see you in a few days, I hope."

Anthemius nodded and walked to the bridge to find the captain, who turned to him with a frown on his face.

"Procurator, I see I have the glorious company of your barbarian friends again?"

"Captain, please make all haste to Cyzicus, it is a matter of great urgency."

"How urgent?" asked the captain.

347

"Thirty gold solidarii urgent."

The captain mulled over the huge sum he had just been offered, Anthemius smiled inwardly; he knew the captain was trying to seem unfazed, pretending to not be impressed by the sum. But the procurator knew exactly how much this captain made in a year of sailing and it was only a tiny fraction of the amount he had just been offered. Anthemius needed this trip to go smoothly and quickly; there was no time to waste, and he needed to ensure the loyalty of this man for the duration.

The captain stuck his hand out, and they shook.

"I will give you five solidarii now for expenses. The remainder will be paid to you on your return, provided my men are returned safely, along with the woman that they will have in their custody. " Anthemius handed over the coins.

"And if they don't?" inquired the captain casually.

Anthemius drew close to the man and looked down on him. In a calm and measured voice, he said, "Captain, if I hear so much as a whisper of mistreatment of my men or the woman, you will never sail the sea again. I will lock you in a windowless cell for the rest of your days. You sell them to slavers, and I will personally hunt you down and disembowel you. Are we clear?" He held the captains' stare until the latter blinked, coughed briefly and looked away, adjusting his turban.

"Very clear, procurator, very clear," he said. "Have no worries, I will look after your men and treat them like kings ... even though they are barbarians." he finished petulantly.

"You will do more than that for the small fortune I have paid you, captain" retorted Anthemius. "The big stocky one you don't like, but who is likely to spend most of the voyage throwing up over the side is called Hunulf. *He* is in charge of this trip. You will follow his orders to the letter, do you understand me?"

Anthemius could see the captain bristle at this demand, but he had little choice if he wanted the windfall. The procurator saw him mentally weigh up the pros and cons and then nod his head. Anthemius insisted they shook again; it wasn't a guarantee, but he felt that, despite the captain's harsh looks, he was a man of his word. He just hoped that he had not misinterpreted him.

"Very well, have a good trip," he said.

Returning to his men, he told them that he expected no trouble from the captain, and that Hunulf had overall command of the mission, but please could they not antagonise the captain? He said he would see them on their return, hopefully with the woman.

They all shook hands and Anthemius left the ship down the gangway, deftly avoiding the sailors loading the ship's supplies, and waited on the dock. Another small contingent of palace guards waited for him. He loitered for a short time watching the ship prepare to leave, then mentally deciding that there was nothing more for him to do here, he waved briefly to Hunulf, turned, and walked back towards the city.

He had done all he could now. It was up to Hunulf, Sigeric and Videric to complete their mission.

Chapter 59

The Golden Palace, Constantinople, 11th May 397 AD

In the emperor's private rooms, Eutropius sat with Eudoxia and Arcadius. Eudoxia was starting to show her pregnancy; she was keen to talk to the eunuch and to ask how investigations on his attempted murder were proceeding.

"It's been over two months now, how have your investigations gone?" she asked.

"Very well, Empress, we have spent much time in tracking down several conspirators," said the chamberlain with feigned modesty. "I trusted my man Philoponus to do a thorough job."

"Have you apprehended the plotters?" asked Arcadius.

"We had the man, of course and two of his immediate accomplices, and we know of another who was involved."

"Who were they?" asked Eudoxia eagerly.

"The men we apprehended at the tavern have been questioned, tortured and executed, of course. Both were soldiers. Both served in the returning legions from the West last year. Both served in the Northern Praecental legions. We suspect that they were not alone, and indeed we've identified two of their officers who enlisted their help in the conspiracy and arrested them. We found some incriminating letters in the first officer's quarters. His wife, whom he has been estranged from for some time, also provided us with some letters. I have them here."

The chamberlain snapped his fingers and Zafur stepped forward and handed him several papyrus scrolls. He handed them to the emperor and empress. They read the letters and shook their heads. The emperor frowned as if trying to recall something.

"This is the officer's handwriting?" asked Arcadius.

"Indeed," asserted the chamberlain.

"And he organised the attempt on your life?" Eudoxia inquired.

"I believe so."

"But he was the witness at Timasius' trial!" exclaimed Arcadius. "Am I not correct?"

"Indeed, Imperator, you are quite correct. It is the same man. Bargus."

"Does that mean Timasius is innocent?" asked Eudoxia.

"No empress, not at all, that was a different matter."

"He has been arrested, this Bargus?"

"Unfortunately, no. When our men went to arrest him, he made a run for it. My spies saw him entering the city and I am told he is trying to escape to Anatolia. My men are tracking him down as we speak."

"And what about the second officer?" asked the emperor.

"Ah yes, Imperator," Eutropius said with some satisfaction. "We still have him in the cells. He may prove to be extremely useful to us in revealing who was behind the plot to kill me. I will be interrogating him with General Gainas when he gets back in a couple of days."

"Why Gainas?" asked the empress.

"It's one of his men."

"Do you think Gainas was involved?" pressed the empress.

The chamberlain with a hint of terseness. "Right now, I don't know what to think. The next few days will bring me answers, I'm sure."

Eudoxia stayed silent. She had not liked the condescending tone of Eutropius' voice. But Arcadius just nodded and smiled. "Good. Now, you had a suggestion about deterring this type of thing in the future, I believe?"

"Yes indeed. I think that to stop this type of treasonous behaviour, we need to make it legally treasonous, because right now it is not."

"No?" the emperor raised his eyebrows, surprised.

Eutropius snapped his fingers and Zafur handed the emperor a tablet.

"This is a proposal for a new law, it is not a full inscription, merely a first draft" Eutropius explained. "Under current laws what happened to me was attempted murder of course, which is a very serious crime of course."

"Of course." said Arcadius. Eudoxia kept silent, she was watching the eunuch closely.

Eutropius continued "But how much more is the loss and cost to the empire if our most valuable citizens are attacked and killed? The people who serve the empire at the highest levels need more protection than the average citizen. They contribute more, and therefore *their* murder should be a higher crime."

Arcadius nodded enthusiastically and said, "I agree, Chamberlain, it makes sense. We will direct Eutychainus to issue the law." He made a show of reading the draft law, then handed the tablet back to the chamberlain, who shook his head. "There is work to do yet on the wording, as you no doubt have noticed, but it will be ready within a few months."

"Why did he do it, do you think?" asked Eudoxia interjected suddenly.

Eutropius was momentarily taken aback. "Who are we talking about now?" he spoke without deference.

The empress frowned at the eunuch's impoliteness. "Bargus. Why did he do it, do you think?"

Eutropius relaxed and said smoothly, "I have no idea; perhaps he regrets his testimony against his old employer and in some way blames me for his guilt."

Eudoxia rubbed her belly and shifted in her seat. "It seems to me he should be grateful to you. You recommended him to his current command, yet he turns on you?"

"Who knows what goes on in some of these provincial minds?" said Eutropius absently.

Suddenly Arcadius got up and called for his horse to be readied and declared he was going to go hunting, as it was such a good day for a ride. Both Eudoxia and Eutropius rose as he spoke, and with that he was gone. After looking at one another for an awkward few seconds, Eutropius made his excuses to the empress and departed, with the little Zafur in tow.

After he had gone, Eudoxia sat alone and pondered. She had felt uncomfortable with the eunuch for the first time. Something had changed. Up until now she had always felt Eutropius was very much her supporter and champion. But he appeared to be getting a little above himself, a little too self-indulgent. She had overheard several of her handmaidens whispering about the chamberlain, how he had taken to speaking to senior officials in a dismissive fashion. He had just been dismissive to her.

She would have to keep a close eye on the eunuch.

Yes, a very close eye.

Chapter 60

The Northern Peloponnese Shore, 12th May 397 AD

Sarus and his small troop of riders were resting on the beach. The waves lapped the shore; the men had bathed in the waters in the early morning, after arriving late in the afternoon, close to the town. It was the first real wash they had had in months, and it had felt good. They had hung their clothes up to dry in the morning sun and the light sea breeze, draped over the tall grass that lined the dunes.

"Shouldn't we be getting back, tell them about the walls around the town?" asked one of the men, a keen young man called Leovigild. He was new among Sarus' riders.

"No need," replied one of the older hands. Sarus nodded. They had not been spotted by Stilicho's army, although the townspeople undoubtedly could see them. Sarus looked back and saw, coming around the headland, the start of the baggage train. At its head were Athaulf's warriors, thousands of armed Goths. *The people in the town must be pissing themselves about now*, thought Sarus. Athaulf himself was riding at the head of his men. Sarus cursed. He mounted his horse and rode out to meet the Goth general.

"What are you doing here?" snapped Athaulf.

Sarus was sullen. "You said to scout the town. We have. It has walls."

"I said towns. This is Patrae; there is another further up the coast; Rhium. Which the locals tell us does not have walls and is nearer to the north shore of the isthmus. Get your men and go do your job!" Sarus bristled, but he could do nothing. Athaulf sat at the head of an army. He turned his horse around and headed back to his men. Sarus could not see why Alaric had chosen this place to retreat to. There was nowhere to go. Yes, there was port here, but they had no ships big enough to take them across the sea. The only two ways out of here

354

were the way Alaric was coming, or a narrow pass which butted up to the sea, along the coast from the east. But Stilicho was behind them. The Goths had beaten the Romans to Patrae. It was a simple race. But now they were trapped. All Sarus could see around him were hills and the walled town ahead. Sarus cursed Alaric for his stupidity. He should have done a deal with Stilicho, joined with him, and marched on the capital. But no. He had to lead his people to freedom, whatever that meant. Perhaps he fancied himself as some modern-day Moses. He spat on the ground.

"What are we going to do now?" asked one of the men when he got back to them.

"Apparently there is another town further ahead without walls," said Sarus irritably. "We check it out and report back."

Athaulf had ridden ahead to make sure Sarus was doing what he was meant to do. But he wasn't. He had had to bawl the man out and tell him to go do his job properly. Patrae was not the aim, according to Alaric. It was too well defended and could be resupplied by sea; if they put up a fight, they could get bogged down in either a siege or being besieged by Stilicho if they did manage to get into the town. But Rhium was a different matter. It had a good harbour by all accounts, but few defences. That's where Alaric had told him to lead his men. But he wanted to be sure.

"Sir!" cried a scout. "Stilicho is coming!" He pointed behind them to the West. The hills sloping to the sea hid the view. All he could see were his men and the baggage train winding its way around the headland and following him

"How long?" asked Athaulf.

"I don't know sir; we could only see the glints off of their spears." The man was young and inexperienced and didn't know how to quickly judge numbers and distance.

"Take me to where you saw Stilicho," snapped Athaulf.

Chapter 61

Eastern Peloponnese, Greece, 12th May 397 AD

The riders drank from the stream and found a spot where the horses could do so as well. The water was cool and clear. The leader of the riders glanced at the sky. It was well past noon now. He took out some dried figs they had purchased at the last small village he had passed. The men there confirmed that the road, as it was, was clear of rock falls and snaked alongside the sea at the foot of the hills, all the way to the north shore of the Peloponnese. The villagers had not seen any sign of Alaric. They had heard he was about, but their local contacts had corroborated the reports he had heard; that Alaric was indeed moving north, but still no one knew why.

The men checked their horses over and it was agreed that they would gain nothing by over-working them now. Once they were closer, they might need to urge them on. But they were at least half a day away, maybe more, from their destination. They took their mounts' reins and led them in a slow walk for an hour, trying to find shade where they could, and let them graze on some good ground they came across. After an hour the officer checked the sun again, then mounted up, ordering his men to do likewise, and coaxed his horse into a steady trot towards the north: towards Alaric.

Chapter 62

The Golden Palace, Constantinople, 12th May 397 AD

Gainas followed the chamberlain through low, narrow, dimly lit corridors, deep under the Golden Palace. Here was where all the most dangerous prisoners were kept: traitors, usurpers, anyone who threatened the emperor or his immediate family, either physically or politically. Sometimes they were kept for less than a day before they were executed, sometimes they were kept for years, just in case.

Their boots echoed along the narrow tunnels as they strode along at pace. Gainas was not familiar with the layout and was thoroughly lost.

"Where are we going, Chamberlain?" he asked tersely.

The eunuch paused and turned, peered around one of his personal bodyguards and said quietly, "You will see shortly, General."

And soon enough they came to a thick wooden door with huge iron hinges and bolts, and a small iron grille at head height. Two large palace guards stood outside silently, and also waiting at the door with a set of keys was a hunched and disfigured man, one side of his face drooping. Gainas was disgusted to see saliva dribbling out of his mouth, and dripping onto the floor, yet the wretch seemed unaware of it.

"Open it up, Bardanes," instructed the chamberlain. The cripple dutifully pulled a large set of iron keys from his belt and, with a shaky hand, unlocked the cell door. The door swung open and Eutropius and Gainas, accompanied by two of their bodyguards, entered the cell. The ceiling was high, so they did not have to stoop, and the room had six torchers burning in it. The air was stifling and hot and there was a stench of urine.

At the centre of the room was a wooden bench and tied to the bench was the splayed figure of a man. The man was naked, and his body was bruised, battered and bloodied. There were long open wounds across his chest, his breath came erratically, through clenched teeth. The man turned his head to look at him and Gainas started as he recognised the figure. Euthymius. The man who had struck the head of Rufinus from the hated Prefect's body. The commander of his bodyguard. His most trusted man, his friend of many years.

He whirled on the eunuch. "What is he doing here?" he snarled, "like this?"

"I would think that is obvious, General," Eutropius purred in his almost falsetto voice. "He has committed a crime and I am attempting to elicit his accomplices."

"What is his crime then?" asked Gainas stiffly. He already knew the answer.

"He conspired to have me killed," said Eutropius calmly. "The question is, did he arrange it himself, or was he ordered to do it?" The eunuch nodded to Bardanes. He hobbled over to the bench, took out a curved knife and stood there, looking askance at the chamberlain. "Just a slice, Bardanes."

Gainas winced as the cripple took his knife and sliced a portion of Euthymius' thigh, like he was carving a slice of ox or game. The officer attempted to stifle his pain and convulsed as the blade cut through him. Blood poured from the open wound. Bardanes shuffled to a bucket, reached in and took out a handful of white powder.

"I think we need to continue our talk, don't we, *praepositus*?" Eutropius leaned over the twitching figure. "Answer me this," he looked at Gainas as he spoke. "Who ordered you to have me assassinated?"

Euthymius made a rasping sound as he gasped for air between his clenched teeth. Sweat poured from his brow, mixing with the blood on his face His eyes were clenched tight shut as he fought against all instinct to scream aloud. Gainas found he was holding his own breath.

Euthymius hissed two words "Fuck you!" and he spat in the eunuch's face, blood and spittle staining face and robe. The chamberlain closed his eyes, then signalled with a small wave of his hand to Bardanes. The cripple sprinkled some of the white powder onto the open wound. Salt.

Euthymius screamed, letting out his agony without restraint. He hurled a tirade of profanities at the eunuch. Gainas turned away, his stomach churning at his friend's suffering.

"I ordered it!" screamed the officer, "I planned it! You disrespected my general!"

"He ordered you to kill me?" Eutropius interjected strongly.

Euthymius laughed. "No , you idiot; arrgh!" he shrieked as Bardanes threw more salt at the exposed, bleeding flesh on his leg at the eunuch's bidding. But the officer broke into a choking laugh through the pain. "He would never … do … that!"

"Then why?" insisted the chamberlain, sounding vexed.

"Because I could do … what he could not!"

"Why?"

"He is my … General … and … my friend." Euthymius was weakening, his breath rattling as he tried to speak.

Gainas swung around looked helplessly at his old comrade. He gritted his teeth and drew in breath through his nose as he tried to calm his own temper. He looked at his two bodyguards and placed his hand on his hilt. This was madness, but he felt that he had no choice; this had to end. The eunuch had to die and now. He tensed his arm, ready. The chamberlain's bodyguards were no novices; they felt the tension in the room. They too tensed. The chamberlain glanced between the men in the room and smirked in triumph.

"And what, pray, is going on here?" said a smooth musical voice.

Both Eutropius and Gainas turned and saw Aurelian standing in the doorway. The pounding of blood in Gainas' ears subsided, as Aurelian's words broke the tension in the room.

"How long have you been there, senator?" asked Eutropius, standing back, looking and sounding a little annoyed at the interruption.

"Long enough."

"And what have you learned?"

"That you are unnecessarily cruel and also wasting your time. That he is plainly telling the truth. You should just kill him now and put the man out of his misery."

Eutropius turned and took two steps towards Aurelian. "This is none of your business, senator," he snapped.

"But it is certainly business of mine," said a female voice that Eutropius knew well.

Eudoxia, wife of Arcadius and Empress of the Eastern Roman Empire, stepped into the room and immediately Aurelian, Eutropius and Gainas and their bodyguards drew back and bowed low.

"Empress, what are you doing here? This is no place for …" started the chamberlain, but Eudoxia waved him to silence.

"A woman, you are going to say. This place, as you call it, is my home. I live here, Chamberlain, lest you forget; the palace is my home, and I will go where I please in my own dwelling." She turned to Aurelian and said, "You were right to bring me here, thank you, senator."

Then she turned and walked up to the table where Euthymius lay. She looked at the man as he lay shaking in agony, sweating and bleeding, his breath rasping through gritted teeth. She seemed unmoved.

"This is the man who plotted to kill you, Chamberlain?"

"Yes, Empress, one of them."

"The ringleader?"

"So he claims."

"You're not convinced?"

"No."

"Why do you think he is lying?"

Eutropius looked at Gainas with cold eyes and said, "I think he is protecting the man who really ordered the attempt."

The Empress turned to look at Gainas.

"This is one of your men, General?"

"He was, Empress. Though he no longer serves me directly," Gainas said truthfully. Euthymius had been transferred and promoted to one of the new legions in Phrygia, whilst Gainas had recently set up camp in Thrace, in the hope of command of one of the new praesentalis legions.

"You knew nothing of this plot?" Eudoxia looked at Gainas directly, with hard eyes. He felt her stare go through his skull and right into his brain, as if she was reading his mind.

"I had no prior knowledge of this attempt." He hoped he sounded cool and deliberate. It took all of his self-control to speak evenly and sound sincere, even though there was some truth in his words. He had no details of what was planned, he did not know the means or the date of the attempt, or who would be sent to do the deed.

"You did not order this attempt?" pressed the Empress.

"I did not, majesty." Gainas bowed as he said it. Again, there was truth there, it made it easier to say.

"So, if there was someone who ordered this man to make the attempt, who would it be if not you?" Eudoxia kept up her unnerving stare and her tone was cold and determined.

Gainas stood straight and, looking back at Eutropius, said, "That I do not know, majesty. I only know that our chamberlain is not short of enemies, and he should not be surprised that there are people who want him dead."

Eudoxia looked amused. She glanced at the chamberlain then back to the general; Gainas saw her muse over something in her mind then she seemed to come to a decision. She pointed to one of the chamberlain's guards and said sharply, "You! Kill this man and hand his body over to General Gainas." The guard didn't hesitate, he drew his sword and with two brutal strokes he severed Euthymius' head, which hit the floor with a loud thud. Eutropius stepped back as the blood gushed from the gaping neck.

Eudoxia turned to him. "Chamberlain, you've found your man; justice has been served. General Gainas is a long serving and respected member of the army. This man was his friend. In the interest of good relations between all of you, he will be given the body of this man to bury as he sees fit."

"He committed treason!" snapped Eutropius. "The body should be cast from …"

"He did not commit treason, Chamberlain," interrupted the Empress. "He did attempt to kill you, but you are not the embodiment of the empire, so no treason was committed."

"There is a law …"

"Which is not yet in effect and not yet approved by the emperor!" snapped Eudoxia.

The silence lasted several long seconds. Then the chamberlain relaxed, smiled and bowed and said quietly, "Your majesty is right, of course. I have let my personal feeling overrule my better judgement. I unreservedly apologise."

Eudoxia too relaxed at this. Her faced softened and she smiled. "I understand, my good Chamberlain. You are a good advisor and friend to both the emperor and me. This whole episode has been upsetting for all of us."

She turned to Gainas and spoke. "I am sorry about your friend, General; you are free to give him the funeral you wish."

"I am grateful for your words, Empress."

"Now gentlemen, if you will excuse me." Eudoxia left the cell. As her footsteps and those of her personal guard receded, Aurelian sighed a big sigh and said to the room, "That, I believe, settles things for now?"

Eutropius stared at Gainas across the ruined body of Euthymius, then he stepped around the table, not caring that he splashed through the puddle of blood on the floor. As he approached, Gainas' guards tensed again, but he relaxed them with a wave of his hand. Eutropius leaned over Gainas and hissed, "Don't think for one moment that I don't know this was you. You are now mine, General. You might have a new friend in the Empress, but one little word to the emperor and your head will go the same way as your friend here, make sure you remember that!"

Gainas held the stare of the eunuch, who turned away and stormed from the room with his two guards. The sound of the chamberlain berating his guards for following the Empress' order echoed back down the corridor. Gainas guessed the guard would not be a palace guard for long. He might not live to see the day out.

"Thank you, senator." Aurelian's voice broke through Gainas' thoughts.

"What?"

"You might at least say 'thank you senator'," repeated Aurelian.

"Why would I need to thank you?" asked Gainas.

"You were about to draw your sword and run it through the eunuch."

"Was I?"

"Oh, come, General. You've nothing to fear from me."

Gainas strode up to the senator and pushed him back into the wall. He heard the sound of steel on steel as his own guards and Aurelian's guards drew their swords. "Hold!" ordered Aurelian.

"I've nothing to fear from you?" echoed the general sarcastically. "The man who betrayed us to Eutropius?" He saw the accusation hit home. Fear momentarily flashed in Aurelian's eyes, then he regained his composure.

"Well spotted, General. Of course, I told Eutropius. It was a ridiculous plan!" Aurelian said dismissively. "An assassin in the dark on the balcony? Really? Was that the best you could come up with? I lent you good men for this and you squandered the opportunity. Now they're dead, your friend is dead, and *it* knows you were behind it."

"You were behind it too."

"But he doesn't suspect me, he only suspects you." Aurelian smiled.

"I could tell him."

"Hah! And of course, our Chamberlain is in a mood to believe everything you say. There is such trust there." Aurelian laughed. A mocking laugh.

"No, I'm afraid, General, you've got yourself in a tight spot. On the battlefield you might excel, but in this world, you're blundering about like an adolescent idiot. I suggest you stick to what you are good at, good old-fashioned soldiering, and let me handle Eutropius."

"And how do you intend to do that?" asked Gainas, stepping back and releasing Aurelian.

"Our Empress doesn't seem quite so enamoured with her eunuch benefactor as she once was, didn't you notice?" Aurelian smoothed down his toga.

Gainas nodded.

"Now *that* is worth knowing."

Aurelian straightened himself up and ushered his guards out. As he left the room, he turned and looked back at Gainas and said, "I'm genuinely sorry about your friend, but both you and I know, his blood is actually on your hands. Good day, General."

Interlude

Palace Guard Barracks, 12th May 397 AD

Gadaric and Gerung were both quiet as they undressed and packed away their uniforms for the day. Their guard duty down in the cells that day had not been pleasant.

They settled into their bunks and rolled over to sleep. There was only the sound of insects chirping through the window in the roof of their room.

"Poor bastard," muttered Gerung.

"Yeah. Poor bastard. May he rest in peace."

"Did you hear what the general and that senator said?"

"I did"

"I don't think I should tell Octavia that bit of gossip."

"Not if you value your head."

Chapter 63

The Northern Peloponnese Shore, 12th May 397 AD

E vening was closing in; the wind was rising and coming from the west. Clouds were gathering. The sun settled into a bank of grey cloud, and the gloom of dusk came swiftly. All day the baggage train had rolled around the headland and gathered near the town of Patrae. A delegation under a white flag came out to meet with Athaulf and asked what the Goths wanted. Athaulf told them just supplies. This seemed to surprise the men. The town's administrators had been expecting demands for surrender, but Athaulf reiterated that they just wanted fresh supplies of milk, meat, fruit, and grain. They agreed that the food would be brought out to them. Then he asked them about the port of Rhium.

"It's in bad disrepair," said the town decurion. "Our docks are in constant use, but they only deal with small fishermen normally; the Romans removed all the walls, so it's open. Here it's well protected. Why do you ask?"

"We need docks for ships," said Athaulf.

"What ships?" asked the decurion, looking perplexed.

"They're not here yet."

"When are they coming?"

"Soon." Athaulf did not want to give away too much.

"What sort of ships?"

"Big ones, I hope."

The decurion turned to his officials and Athaulf heard whispers amongst them but could not make out the words. Then the group seemed to come to a decision. Nervously, the decurion returned to

Athaulf and said, "Rhium will be no good to you. We're prepared to let you use our docks, but we ask that you pay the normal levy."

"You do realise who you're talking to?" smiled Athaulf, "Why should we pay you?"

"B-Because we know that Stilicho is behind you, and that you need to get to your ships, wherever they are, to get away, or you'll have to turn and fight him. You m-might lose." The decurion was shaking as he spoke. A bead of sweat ran down his temple.

"We could just take your town by force."

"You could, but it would take time, and you don't have time, from what I understand. You could be trapped between the walls and Stilicho's army."

"But if we pay you, you'll let us into your town to use the docks?" Athaulf smiled; in a way he admired the decurion's blatant cheek.

"On one condition."

"Which is?"

"You control your people; they pass directly to the docks and board your ships when they arrive. No looting or stealing."

"What is your price to use the docks?" asked Athaulf

"Ten pounds of gold."

Athaulf blinked at the price; it was not outrageous. They did have a lot of people to move through. But the town were asking for more than half of their entire remaining gold reserves. He could just go ahead and pay it, and he might do so if things got bad. But things were not yet that bad. There was still no sign of Stilicho, and they had settled into a cool but not antagonistic relationship with the town.

"I'll have to speak with King Alaric."

"I thought you were King Alaric." The decurion looked surprised.

"You never asked. No, I'm his brother-in-law. Alaric will be here shortly. In the meantime, we'll gather our troops and baggage train outside your walls. You don't attack us; we'll not attack you. I assume you have a garrison in town?" Athaulf indicated the two militia men who stood with the group of town officials. They each held a spear and wore a sword, but neither looked like they knew what to do with them.

"We do, and likewise you don't attack the town and we will send out some traders to sell you food and goods."

"Sell us?" snorted Athaulf. "You press your luck decurion"

"If you try to steal from us, we'll close the gates, and you will have to fight it out with Stilicho. W-we have livelihoods too." The decurion's voice quavered, but he held the Goth's stare.

"And what happens when Stilicho arrives and finds out that you've helped us escape?"

"We'll offer him the same deal. We're just trying to ensure that our townspeople don't starve. We need money for that. We'll help him cross and chase after you. This is not our fight." The decurion continued to hold the Goth's stare, though he was visibly shaking.

Athaulf stared back then burst out laughing; he looked around at his men and they laughed too.

"You have some balls, decurion, I will give you that. Very well, I will send my men to tell you what we need; send out your traders, and we will pay you for your goods. When Alaric arrives, we will negotiate terms of use of your docks. Agreed?" Athaulf thrust his gloved hand out, the town decurion took it and they shook.

The decurions rode back to the town with two of Athaulf's quartermasters, who would tell the town what they needed in supplies. In the meantime, Athaulf barked out orders for the warriors to direct the baggage train to gather outside of the town's main gates and to begin building fortifications to defend it.

Shortly after Sarus returned, reporting that Rhium was indeed without walls, and the docks were small and looked in poor condition. Athaulf told him about the deal he was brokering with the town decurions.

"You sent me on a fool's errand?" Sarus retorted.

Athaulf did feel a little bit awkward. He didn't like Sarus, but in his shoes he would probably have been equally annoyed.

"I did not expect the town to be so accommodating. We thought they would bar the gates, but it appears they are a bit more business minded," said Athaulf. "I apologise for wasting your time, but time is now of the essence. I know you don't like me, but we need to make our position defensible. Alaric is coming; he needs to agree to pay the town to let us in. Only he can make that decision." Athaulf looked behind him to the west, hoping he might spot Alaric's banner.

"He'll be a fool if he doesn't," snapped Sarus.

Athaulf leaned across and grabbed Sarus' forearm in a vice-like grip. "Because we're desperate here and need every man, I'll forget you said that, this one time. Start helping the men build the defences. We don't have much time."

Sarus pulled his arm free, wheeled his horse around and rode off with his men.

Athaulf looked back as the baggage train and warriors continued to round the headland and head towards the town. Light was fading. A month earlier they would have stopped for the night; the terrain was rough. It was difficult to see, and the chance of losing a wheel or breaking a leg, human or horse, was high. It just wasn't worth it. Athaulf was in no mood for normality. Stilicho knew exactly where they were heading and if he was close enough behind them, in the morning, he would surely launch his forces at them. Athaulf wanted the baggage train secured behind the defences. Here they would stand. Here they would defend until salvation came. They just had to hold out long enough.

Athaulf was relentless in his work. He cajoled the men who were lazy, swore at them in jest when they worked hard, encouraged the younger men, and asked the advice of the older men. Throughout the evening he rode up and down the line of wagons, encouraging them to keep moving and telling them that warm food and wine was waiting for them after they had finished. Around four in the morning, Eberwolf finally brought up the rear of the baggage train, and they rumbled slowly through the line of defences that had been constructed throughout the night. Stilicho's men had not attacked. Athaulf looked back towards the headland. Alaric, Theodahad and their men were still not back. He assumed that they were staying back to ensure that the Romans either did not make it down the valley or were engaged in fighting them off. He had expected them back by now, but there was no sign of them, although the early morning gloom made it hard to see. He stared hard, but his mind or his eyes were playing tricks; every time he thought he saw movement, he didn't see it again.

The last wagon made it through the still incomplete but formidable defensive line. As expected, he heard a barrage of expletives followed by, "Thought we would never fucking get here." said Eberwolf.

Athaulf dismounted and walked over to him and asked how his journey had been.

"Fucking great," Eberwolf snapped. "Had my arse roasted by some Hun arrows, lost my supply of wine, my fucking wagon and nearly lost my wife."

"Never thought you cared!" laughed a woman close by.

"Shut up, woman or I'll toss you over the barricade when Stilicho and his bastards come calling!" Eberwolf roared back.

"At least they might treat me better than you do, you miserable old sod." There were more laughs from the men and women around them; this was normal in the Eberwolf household, everyone knew.

Athaulf too was smiling. "Well, I will leave you in your marital bliss to get yourself settled and fed. Get some rest if you can. Though I don't believe you'll get much. Our friend Stilicho will be visiting us soon, I think!" He glanced east and saw, above the line of steep hills, the dark of the night giving way to the deep blue of early dawn. He remembered something and called out to Eberwolf. "Any sign of King Alaric?"

"He said he would hold back, make sure we weren't followed."

"Did he say his intentions?"

"No. He'll be down soon though, I'm sure."

Athaulf, looked again towards the headland. The increasing light still revealed no sign of their leader. Had he made it, he wondered? He put that thought out of his mind. Stilicho did not want Alaric dead. He wanted him to surrender, to fight with him for Rome, like they had done before. A force of twenty thousand warriors was an army the like of which the West or East could only barely match themselves; adding in the Tervingi numbers would bolster Rome in the coming fight against the Huns. And that fight was coming. It might be next year, it could be in five years, but Athaulf knew soon, the Tervingi and the Romans together would have to face the Hun menace. But that was today. Today was all about survival and not losing.

It was about an hour later when the shout went up from the lookouts on the defensive line. All eyes turned west and there, forming up on the plain in the early morning light, was Stilicho's army. Athaulf roared out his orders; camp orderlies sounded the horns and the men rushed to gather their shields, helmets, spears, and swords. Cursing and cajoling, the men were formed up into lines, behind the defensive wall. The cavalry he held back, protecting the left flank away from the town the walls, which formed a solid barrier on their right flank. If the Romans broke through, he would send in the cavalry, but right now they would stay put. He didn't expect the Hunic mounted archers to go after his cavalry; both were as good as each other at manoeuvring, and they could easily run circles around each other all day to no great effect. No, Alaric expected Stilicho to use the Huns to harass the infantry, his warriors, to go for the static lines. Athaulf went over his orders from Alaric in his head. They were simple. Get to a defensible area by the sea. That was critical, it must be by the sea, and then hold out. Don't attack, don't force the battle, don't risk casualties unnecessarily. Above all else, protect the baggage train and the families. Well, he was doing that, he hoped.

He turned and looked behind him. In front of the city walls was the centre of their world. A mass of wagon and carts, handcarts, horses, mules, and goats. The huge baggage train with the women, the children, the men too old to fight, the cripples too broken to fight, although a few still wielded a sword in case they failed to halt the Romans. Athaulf knew it would never come to that. Stilicho was not looking to destroy them. He wanted to add their strength to his. Smoke drifted up from the campfires and he saw small figures running around. The children, playing, oblivious to what was happening less than five minutes' walk away. He turned back to face the Romans. He remained mounted at one end of the defensive wall. Here he could see the ground stretching out and dropping gently away to the sea. The defences were basic but should prove effective, he thought. Trees had been felled and then buried in the ground as stakes at an angle, with the exposed end sharpened to a point. The men had slaved all night so that these ran in an almost unbroken line from the rocky outcrop on which Athaulf sat on his horse all the way down to the sea. Boulders, branches and rocks had been rolled into the ground between and behind the stakes to break up the surface and make the terrain as difficult as possible. Athaulf did not think for one moment that it would permanently hold off the Romans, but it would certainly slow them down.

"Why won't those bastards let us in the gates?" asked one of his officers.

"They want to see who is going to turn out victorious here. No point in picking sides at the moment, is there?" replied another.

Athaulf grimaced; the man was right. The town could just do nothing. They had bolted the gates. If Alaric's army proved victorious, they had already made a deal and they could pay for their passage. If Stilicho was victorious then the town could not be proved complicit in any anti-Roman activity. The town decurions were not stupid, that was for sure.

"Hold your positions!" he roared. His orders repeated down the lines by the officers. The shouts and calls died away in the wind. For a minute there was silence, only the sound of the wind in the grass and the occasional cry of a gull could be heard. Then it came. The sound of the *cornus* and *lituus* signalling the Roman infantry and cavalry to start their attack.

Eberwolf stood in line with his old friend Berimund. The two of them had fought many battles together, so this was nothing new to them. They heard the sound of the Roman horns and readied themselves. It wouldn't be long now. Eberwolf was nervous, but not afraid. He wanted to feel nervous, it kept him sharp.

"Ready?" he asked, looking forwards at the approaching Romans.

"Ready," replied Berimund calmly.

"I'll bet you a week's ration of wine I'll get more of the buggers than you." Eberwolf issued his normal challenge to his friend.

"You cheat."

"How?"

"You count them even if they're not dead."

"I only count them if they're not able to continue fighting."

"Whatever. Here they come, now!" Berimund steeled himself.

The first wave of Romans ran towards the defensive line, stopped and hurled their pilums hard and fast, as one unit, and the lethal rain of iron arced and plunged into the defensive line. Many struck the ground, some bounced off of the stakes and boulders, but a few struck the shields of the defenders. The heavy shafts disturbed those warriors, and they dropped their shields and attempted to remove the now bent pilums buried in the wood.

"Shields!" yelled out the officers and the second rain of spears hurtled towards them. There were some cries of pain as a handful of men caught without their shields were struck down. No sooner had this deadly downpour stopped than the sound of horses reached the ears of the warriors. Peering between the shields they saw a mass of cavalry archers bearing towards them, racing in from the direction of the sea. They galloped along the line of defences peppering the defenders with arrows. Most of the arrows were stopped by the shields, but a few found their targets. Now a new line of infantry had formed up. Once the archers had gone another wave of pilums were launched at the defences, this one causing the defenders to edge back. Athaulf saw this and ordered his officers to instruct the men to hold their ground. But it was no use. The Romans continued to pound the front ranks of the Goths with arrows and pilums. Bit by bit they were forced back from the defensive line. Not uniformly; some sturdier, more experienced groups were holding fast, whilst others, younger and more inexperienced, were giving into their fears and trying to get out of the range of the constant bombardment. The Romans had seen the movement and now they concentrated their efforts on a few places where the wall of defenders had edged back. The mounted archers concentrated their fire on these areas; the foot soldiers targeted these areas with their pilum. Alaric had guessed right; Stilicho was ignoring the Tervingi cavalry.

"Stand fast!" screamed out Athaulf again, his order echoing down the lines, but it was no use. The Roman infantry had got to the defensive line in three places. Under the cover of the mounted archers, they worked their way through the defensive works. The defenders attempted to throw back the pilums that now littered the ground and they let off a few arrows, but the solid, imposing line of defence was just not there, and the Romans smelled a speedy victory. The first Roman infantry struck at the Goth shield wall, thrusting their pilums and spathas to attack the thin and irregular line.

Almost isolated now from the retreating defensive line, Eberwolf and Berimund and their men held steady against the initial onslaught. They were used to this. They simply had to weather the storm; the Romans were bound to run out of spears and arrows soon. Then the rain of metal lessened and Eberwolf saw what had happened. The line was badly disrupted.

"Back off, but slowly!" he ordered. Together the men kept their shields locked and slowly stepped back. But they were too far in front of the rest of the wall and an easy target for the attackers. Suddenly they found themselves beset on three sides. Eberwolf dodged aside as a spear was thrust between his and Berimund's shields. He returned the thrust but hit nothing. Berimund did likewise and felt his sword strike home.

"One to me!" he roared above the cacophony of shouting, screaming, yelling and the ringing of metal on wood and metal. There was a scream and a curse. Glancing behind him, Eberwolf saw that the three men nearest the main defensive line had been cut down.

"Close up!" he yelled. The group closed up and now they were isolated. Two dozen men surrounded by an army. With shields locked together in a circle, the men thrust and sliced, holding back the waves of Romans. Eberwolf and Berimund held their ground, shoulder to shoulder, hunched behind their shields. The Romans beat on the shields, hacked at the circular wall, but could find no way through. Eberwolf felt a red-hot pain as a pilum sliced his arm. He felt a pressure on his shield arm; a huge Roman legionary tried to force his way into the circle. Eberwolf braced his foot and shoved forward. A small gap opened between him and Berimund. He saw the sword thrust come at him from the other side but managed to parry it somehow with his shield. That opened the other side. "Fuck this!" he screamed, and he shoved his shield forward and upwards. It found a target; somebody yelled in pain. He hacked forwards with his sword and hit something, blood spattering up his arm, so he hacked again and again found something. Suddenly the pressure on his shield gave way and he almost stumbled forwards. Looking up, he stared directly into the faces of two young Roman legionaries, both with swords raised, so he screamed at them and lunged forward, slicing his sword down. He hacked at them again, whirled around as he sensed another threat behind him and swerved aside to avoid a spear thrust. He dropped his sword and grabbed the spear, pulling it towards him, along with its owner who foolishly had not let go. He punched the man in the throat. He let go. Eberwolf stuck the weapon into the guts of one of the two young legionaries. He reached down, grabbed his sword and thrust it towards the other, but Berimund downed him a second later with a sword strike to the neck. The man's armour protected his neck, but the force of the blow knocked him over. Eberwolf thrust his sword into his neck under the armour and wrenched it clear, the man choking on his own blood.

"Behind you!" shouted Berimund. Instinctively Eberwolf ducked down, spun around and launched himself at his unknown attacker. They fell to the ground. Eberwolf found himself grappling for the assailant's short sword. He could hear the man's breath, smell his sweat and for a moment he was face to face with him, their helmets touching as they struggled for the weapon. They both had a grip on the sword. Eberwolf, grasping hard, lifted and smashed down the hand of his opponent onto a rock. The man yelled out in pain, as Eberwolf felt a bone break in the man's hand. The sword fell away. He grabbed it by the hilt and rammed the pommel into the Roman's face. Blood spurted. He hammered it again into the man's face, and again, and again, and again. There was a rushing sound in his ears, and he heard himself screaming and screaming.

"I think he's dead now," said someone close by.

He looked up, the rage flowing from him. He glanced around; the attackers were turning around and running away.

"What?" he asked, looking around.

Berimund stood beside him, looking down at him. "I think he's dead," he said again.

Eberwolf stood up. He looked at his hands; they were completely red with blood. Roman blood.

"The cavalry is here," said Berimund casually.

"What? Where?" Eberwolf was confused; it often happened in battle.

"The king." His friend pointed and Eberwolf saw horsemen, lots of horsemen, Tervingi horsemen speeding across the plain, streaming after the Romans, who were running back across the plain towards the west. Back towards Stilicho.

"So, Alaric and Theodahad got here in the end, then?" sighed Eberwolf.

"About two minutes ago" said Berimund. "But you were too busy smashing that man's face in to notice."

Eberwolf looked down at the man, or what was left of him, and shook his head. "That was madness."

"You mean leaving the shield wall and going on a one-man rampage against a whole Roman army?" asked Berimund sarcastically. "Perfectly normal for you, you crazy bastard!" He clapped his friend on the back.

"What now?" asked one of Eberwolf's men, covered in blood and grime. Bodies lay all around them, some of them moaning and crying. Most were still, though. The stench of faeces and urine filled the air. The smell of the aftermath of a battle. Not mentioned by the poets of old when recalling the daring feats of warriors on the field of war.

"Put the mortally wounded out of their misery; everyone else, get them on their feet, and send them back to Stilicho. They'll have a better chance to live with the Roman doctors. We're not animals, even if we are barbarians," said Berimund with a wry smile.

"No, I meant, what now for us?" repeated the warrior.

Eberwolf and Berimund looked at each other, shrugged and said together, "We wait for the next attack."

Alaric met up with Athaulf on the rocky outcrop overseeing the battlefield.

"Well met!" said Athaulf.

"It won't keep them off for long, but hopefully that will be it," said Alaric.

"How do you know. You can't be sure."

Alaric was staring out to sea. Suddenly he laughed and said "Actually, I can be sure. See that?" and he pointed to a sail that had appeared over the low headland to the west, behind Stilicho's army.

"What's that?" asked Athaulf.

"That, brother-in-law, is our saviour today."

They looked on as another sail appeared, then another. Then from behind the headland itself appeared a Roman trireme, and another, and another. Then a number of *Navix Acturias* also appeared, their thirty oars beating a steady rhythm. Athaulf saw the men pointing towards the ships. Some looked in askance back up at Alaric. Over in the distant Roman camp, Athaulf saw the Romans waving at the ships and he turned to Alaric, but the king held up his and said, "Wait".

The triremes headed towards Stilicho's camp, towards the enthusiastic army, waiting to receive their resupply and re-armaments, no doubt, thought Athaulf. But then he saw the men on the shore stop waving, then he saw them running away.

"Are those arrows being fired at the Romans?" he asked Alaric.

"Yes, they are," smiled the king.

"Who is on those ships?"

Alaric smiled again.

"Our good friend Thiudimir."

"How?" asked Athaulf.

"I sent him around to find the ships four days ago."

"But how could he sail all those ships? He only took a few men with him."

"Not just a few men. He took a whole lot of that gold from Corinth. And he bought us a navy. A navy that will take us across the sea to Illyricum."

Athaulf stared from Alaric to the boats and then back to Alaric. "He bribed the men who brought Stilicho to Greece to come and save us from Stilicho?"

"Yes," said Alaric. "Yes, that he did."

Athaulf burst out laughing, the officer's around him who had heard the conversation did likewise. They slapped each other on the backs and gripped wrists in the warrior's handshake, congratulating each other. They had survived . Again.

Athaulf pointed at the town and said to his king, "If we pay them, the town will let us use their docks."

Alaric nodded and smiled. "Good, we'd best get going then, hadn't we?"

Chapter 64

The Forum of Constantine, Constantinople, 12th May 397 AD

Awell-dressed man, wearing an in-fashion toga, walked away from under a large portico in the Forum of Constantine through a loud, chaotic crowd of people. He was smiling. Behind him, seated between marble columns, was Caius, surrounded by Blues hard men, including Sextus, Tertius and Septimus.

In front of them milled a crowd of clients, traders and citizens, all hoping to meet Caius and gain some favour; protection or a loan or having some grievance settled with without having to go to the expense or time of hiring a lawyer.

"That was a mistake," said Sextus, who sat back down next to his friend. More people clamoured for attention, but Caius held up his hand to signal the Blues men to hold back the throng.

"What do you mean?" he asked.

"The man owes us money; he's plainly lying about not being able to pay you back."

"He seemed genuine to me; aren't we meant to be standing up for the everyday Roman?" said Caius, though he knew it sounded naïve.

"You didn't stand up for that potter last week. He had his entire stock smashed by the Greens, who were still pissed that you beat their man," Sextus said pointedly.

"That was different."

"Oh, different," said Sextus, his voice dripping with sarcasm.

"Yes, different, I didn't like him and … well, I didn't trust him." Caius had been feeling more down these last few weeks. Not because of his

383

new-found responsibilities, which were far more onerous and complex than he ever imagined. No, there were other reasons.

"Why?" prompted Sextus.

Caius looked at him squarely "You know why."

"Because he was a Goth."

"Yes"

Sextus shook his head. "You need to get this fixation that all Goths are blood-thirsty maniacs out of your head …"

"I know that."

Sextus leaned close into Caius's face and hissed, "Do you? Really? Do you? Because all I have seen happen so far, since you inexplicably took this job, is you systematically purging any barbarian out of the Blues, Goth or any other."

"You know what they did to us! What they did to your friend too, or have you forgotten?"

Sextus settled back and sighed "Of course not, but you can't lump every single Goth we meet into the same bag as those who attacked our village. That potter was just a man trying to make a living."

"Then he should go back to where he came from."

"That's your answer, is it?"

"Yes, that's my answer. And it's why I took this … this … whatever this is. When Septimus held out that token, all I could think was, this could give me a chance to rid Constantinople of the bastards who killed Tiberius."

"These people didn't kill your brother."

"You're wrong Sextus, you're wrong. That's exactly what they did. Their kind have infiltrated the empire at every level, it's got to stop. They pillage and rape and burn and destroy our villages."

"Not these people…" Sextus tried to interrupt, but Caius talked over him.

"And I wondered why? Why did the emperor allow it? Why did he not stop it? Well, I see it now. That general at the fight; what was his name?"

"Gainas."

"Yes, him, Gainas. He was one of them; one of them, Sextus! A barbarian right in the heart of the empire." Caius realised his voice had gotten louder. His men were looking at him, frowning. He lowered his voice and tried to speak only to his friend. "No wonder nothing has been done, we've been taken over by the stealth and cunning of these savages."

"General Gainas is not a savage!" Sextus hissed. "He's served in the legions for years, he's well respected and well-liked by the men who served under him." He paused and then said, pointedly, "Men like me."

Caius reddened slightly and realised he had perhaps gone too far with his friend, but he wasn't willing to deny what he now believed. He thought about responding but decided against it. Anyway, the crowd around them were getting restless. His men apparently agreed. "Who's next?" asked Tertius tersely. Caius pointed to a young woman with a classic Roman five-braid hairstyle, holding a small and sickly-looking child; the Blues men let her through.

Chapter 65

Southern Docks, Constantinople, 12th May 397 AD

The sun had set about half an hour earlier. A figure emerged from the shadows of the docks warehouses and scuttled along one of the wharves, to where a lantern had been lit. He had been told by his contact that would be the sign. A small boat was there, bobbing gently in the water as expected; three men, as expected, waited at the end of the walkway, ready to take him to safety.

They ushered the figure into the boat; he sat down, facing aft. Then two of the men seated themselves forward of him, also facing aft. They took up oars and began to row. The third took the tiller and steered the small skiff out of the shelter of the docks into the sea; immediately they felt the current tug at the boat.

The man at the tiller gave a short whistle and the two men shipped their oars. Their passenger looked up at the steersman and said, "What's happening?" but the words had barely left his lips when he gasped. The blade of a sword appeared out of his chest. It was drawn back, and the man toppled forwards onto the bottom of the boat desperately trying to stem the flow of blood with grasping hands. One of the oarsman brought a lantern up and held it over him.

"You missed his heart, he's still alive."

The oarsman with the sword was powerfully built. He reached down and roughly pulled up the moaning figure, who was still clutching his belly, and leaned him over the bulwark. The boat rocked, but the other two men steadied the craft by moving to the opposite side. With a single vicious slice down, the swordsman decapitated the passenger, the head dropping into the water with a distinct plop. The blood, black in the dim light, poured into the sea from the severed neck. Together the men tied two large rocks they had brought with them onto the corpse's feet then heaved it over the side.

Philoponus stared at the obsidian sea for a while. The light from the stars in the deep blue night sky above caught the ripples every so often, twinkling and glimmering in the waves. The water slapped on the gunwales of the boat as the tide took a hold of the small craft and drove it northeast, toward the Golden Horn.

"Goodbye, Bargus," said Philoponus quietly, and returned to the tiller, whilst his two men sat back down and started to row.

Chapter 66

The Golden Palace, Constantinople, 13th May 397 AD

Eudoxia lay naked in the steaming bath, surrounded by her slaves and her servants. The water was a perfect temperature, slightly milky thanks to the minerals and salts thrown into the water before she arrived. Nobody spoke. She had instructed them to be quiet. She needed to think. She had a lot on her mind, mainly about who wielded the power at court.

When she was been betrothed to the emperor she had been delighted. The eunuch Eutropius had done her and her family a huge favour by tying them into the Theodicean family. It had been the most wonderful day of her life. True, the emperor himself was a halfwit and a bore as well as being only passable to look at, but who cared? He was the rightful emperor and that was all that mattered. Anyone associated with him was, by virtue of knowing him personally, also legitimate. Being married to him made that relationship unbreakable. She bathed, and she revelled in that legitimacy. Except …

She was acutely aware from the beginning that she herself seemed to wield little or no power. Rufinus had hated her, because she had replaced his own daughter, who he was trying to marry to the emperor. It was a good job Gainas had done away with him; she had been getting worried for her own safety. But now Eutropius had stepped in and appeared to be the person who had most sway over Arcadius. She blamed herself, as she had encouraged him to listen to the eunuch, rather than Rufinus, and she had been right. Rufinus had been a real threat; at that point the chamberlain had merely been the chamberlain. But now? Now things were very different.

She had heard how he had manipulated Caesarius and deposed him in a spectacular political coup. She could not help but admire the smoothness of his operation, making it seemingly impossible to disagree that Eutychainus was a far better candidate for Praetorian Prefect than Caesarius. With the eunuch whispering in his ear day and night, Arcadius had certainly been convinced. But dullard that he was, the emperor could not see what everyone else could; that Eutychainus was Eutropius' man through and through, whereas Caesarius at least was his own man, albeit often blinded by his antipathy towards his younger brother, Aurelian.

Aurelian. The man was cold and calculating and ruthless. He was also unafraid of Eutropius. Caesarius and Aurelian were the youngest members of a hugely influential and rich family owning vast tracts of land across Thrace, Moesia, and Anatolia. Despite the huge amounts of property that Eutropius had acquired during the last two to three years, he still held less than Aurelian and, in addition to that, when Aurelian spoke the Senate listened. When Eutropius spoke, the Senate turned their collective noses up in disgust. Although the Senate in reality was nothing more than an old men's debating club with no imperial power at all and only some Urban power in the city, collectively they owned just about all the land in the empire outside of the imperial estates, and that meant that if they wanted to be awkward and make things difficult for the imperial family, they could.

Eudoxia splashed the warm water gently up her arms and across her breasts and nodded to one of the handmaidens, who gently tipped some more salts into the pool and stirred the water. The empress breathed in deeply and slipped her head beneath the water briefly, enjoying the sensation and letting the water swirl around her head. She sat back up and ran her fingers through her hair, squeezing out the excess water. She ran her hands over her swelling belly; two more months and the first of a new generation of Theodosians would arrive. She wanted it to be a boy, but something told her that it would be a girl. Her old midwife had been non-committal about it being a boy, and despite visiting the shrines in the Hagia Sofia and praying hard and often, she could not shake the feeling that this would not be the heir that Arcadius was hoping for.

For that reason alone, she needed to secure her position at court. She considered herself empress, but in reality, she was merely consort to the emperor, and consorts were far easier to dispose of than Augustae. Her mind turned back to Aurelian.

He had come to her over the incident with Gainas' man. Why? She had jumped at the chance to impose some kind of influence over the situation, and it had felt good to make the decision and to take control. Or at least, at the time she had thought she was in control, but now, thinking about it, she was not so sure. Was Aurelian manipulating her? If so, to what end? Or was he trying to court her favour? If so, to what end?

She sighed. She suddenly felt restless and in need of company. Arcadius was fairly competent in the bedroom, if unimaginative. He was out hunting though; as always, it seemed. She dismissed all the slaves and servants except for Siduri.

She was a dark-skinned, dark-haired beauty. A Sumerian servant who had come to her as a slave when she still lived in the house of Promotus, before she was married. She trusted Siduri with her life and her deepest secrets. They had known each other since they were young; they had had their first bleed the same month, both had lost their virtue the same month and had since shared all their secrets. On her marriage, Eudoxia had freed Siduri and insisted she accompany her to the palace and had placed her at her side instead of the established handmaidens and servants who might have expected the position.

Siduri had been threatened by the other girls more than once because of that. But she was tough; when one of the chambermaids had attacked her out of jealously for a lost position, Siduri had not hesitated, and had killed her attacker. Too late, the chambermaid had realised you don't mess with Sumerian men or women; the desert is not an easy place to survive. The incident was used by many of the palace staff to demand Siduri be dismissed, exiled or hanged even. Eudoxia had not dismissed, exiled or hanged Siduri. She had thanked her, rewarded her, and instead dismissed anyone who had accused her.

Siduri could be trusted. And she trusted her now.

"Can you bring him?" Eudoxia whispered to Siduri. She smiled gently, nodded and slipped away quietly, closing and locking the door behind her.

Eudoxia closed her eyes and lay in the steaming water thinking about Aurelian. Was he trying to undermine Eutropius? Was he hoping that she might turn on her benefactor? The one who had placed her in this place? She felt slightly annoyed that he might think that.

She was grateful to the eunuch, but she had to admit, his attitude latterly had become tiresome and on occasion bordering on rude; he lacked the deference he once used to show her. She didn't mind that he was lining his own pockets, everyone did that. She didn't even mind that he had plainly removed the two generals, Abundantius and Timasius, on less than convincing accusations of treason, but there was a line of decency over which you did not cross when you were a eunuch, and the chamberlain was awfully close to crossing that line. Perhaps he needed to be taken down a notch or two; she certainly wanted to have him around Arcadius less. Perhaps Aurelian might be one person who she could work with to face off against the chamberlain. Another would be Gainas. He certainly hated the eunuch; he made no attempt to hide his feelings. And she was certain that he had been behind the failed attempt on Eutropius. He had already murdered one Praetorian Prefect; murdering a chamberlain would hardly cause him any sleepless nights. The fact that his men had not given him up spoke volumes about how highly they regarded him.

Yes. Aurelian and Gainas. Strange bedfellows. The first an aristocrat from a long line of aristocrats from the administrative school, with a heavy disdain of the military and an even heavier disdain of the Goths. The second a long-serving Roman general of Goth extract, a military man through and through, with a heavy disdain of administrators and aristocrats. Yes. Strange bedfellows. She laughed a gentle laugh to herself. This should be fun, she thought.

She heard the door open and Siduri came in. Behind her came a man of medium height with long, blond hair. But he was no Goth. He just wore it in the fashion of the barbarians. He was handsome, muscular, an excellent swordsman, deferential yet witty and cheeky, and an excellent lover. He was the *Comes Sacrarum Largitionum*, the man with the money; she smiled to herself. He walked in and stood looking down at her, his face neutral.

"Good afternoon, John," said Eudoxia, standing up.

"Good afternoon, majesty," said John, showing no embarrassment at her nakedness.

She looked towards the door and said, "Thank you Siduri. Please lock the door and post two guards outside. We are not to be disturbed."

Siduri backed away, closing the door behind her. Eudoxia heard the locks click. She held her hand out to the man standing in front of her. John dropped his cloak, removed his sandals, tunic, breeches, and underclothes, and already showing his arousal, stepped into the bath, taking Eudoxia's hand then embracing her, kissing her. They knelt down together. John rubbed his hand over her belly. "Are you sure?" he asked.

"I command it!" she giggled and reached down between his legs. She breathed in sharply and closed her eyes involuntarily as in response he immediately reached between her legs and started massaging her. He was good. She lay back slowly in the water and let the pleasure wash over her. A battle for power within the court was under way. She was late to the battle, but before she engaged in the fighting, she just wanted to enjoy this moment.

Chapter 67

The Northern Peloponnese Shore, 13st May 397 AD

It had taken the whole of the previous day to load up the ships and sail them to Illyricum to the north, and then return overnight to collect the remainder of Alaric's people. The crews of the ships had all been paid handsomely to ensure they stayed loyal, and they had been efficient in their work.

Stilicho's army had withdrawn and made no further attempt to engage or harass. Alaric wondered what was going through his old adversary's mind right now. Was he raging? Was he philosophic? Was he depressed? If he knew anything about his nemesis, he judged that he would be annoyed but not rabid. The attack yesterday had not been much more than a skirmish, but it had cost him men. Probably more than he had bargained for, he judged; and if the Romans were short of one thing that was fighting men. Sure, they had the foederati of Huns and Gepids and other Goths, but they did not have an endless supply of men. Stilicho wanted to deal with Alaric, not destroy him. But letting him get away again would not do the Vandal general any favours back in the West, in Ravenna. The old senators over there would be gossiping that the Vandal general had let the Goth general go. Again. They had met many times in battle and every time he, Alaric had gotten away. Yes, tongues would be wagging in the corridors of power in the West.

It was early evening, as he was about to step onto the last ship preparing to leave the Peloponnese, when Alaric saw riders approaching the docks from the town. A dozen men, riding hard and fast. They headed directly for them, causing one of Alaric's bodyguards to draw his sword, but the king waved at him to sheath it.

The horsemen pulled up twenty feet away, just short of the boardwalk that ran along the length of the dock front, and the lead rider, a senior cavalry officer by the looks of him, dismounted along with what looked like a rider from the *cursus publicus*, the Roman postal service. Both men looked tired and worn out, as did the horses they rode. Alaric and his guards stepped off the gangplank and walked towards the newcomers, along the dock.

"Where is King Alaric?" the cavalry officer asked.

"Who is asking?" replied one of the bodyguards, stepping towards the Roman soldier. He placed his hand on the hilt of his sword.

"This rider has a personal letter for Alaric, King of the Tervingi ," said the soldier, holding up his hands to signal his peaceful intent and pointing to the messenger.

Alaric looked at the Roman sizing him up. He didn't think the man meant him harm, so he nodded to his bodyguard, who stepped forward and held out his gloved hand and said sternly, "Give it to me, and I will ensure the king receives it."

The soldier looked uncertain and replied, "I must give it to the king personally; those are my orders."

"Then give it to me," said Alaric, "I am he."

Something in the way the king spoke must have convinced the soldier, because he looked for a second at the Gothic king, then bowed in deference and waved the rider forward. The latter handed a letter to Alaric and stepped back. The soldier told the rider to get on his horse, then he ordered his men to back away, out of earshot. Once he was sure they were far enough away, he turned back to the Gothic king and his bodyguards and said, "Permission to approach you, King Alaric, there is information I must share with you privately."

"Your name?" asked Alaric

"Marullus."

The king nodded, although he sensed his bodyguards stiffening, readying themselves for the slightest sign of treachery. But Alaric looked at the Marullus's face as he approached and was satisfied that this was a man of honour.

"Please open and read the letter, sir," said the soldier.

Alaric opened up the latter and read it.

It pleases his majesty the Emperor Arcadius to appoint King Alaric of the Goths, to be Magister Militum per Illyricum and he is granted access to all the Imperial Armouries, Supply Depots and Barracks as he sees fit to accommodate the housing and deployment of his infantry and cavalry. An annual allowance of grain and gold will be made available to you for the victualing and reward of your army to the amount of ...

There was more, but Alaric had seen enough; he closed his eyes and smiled. He had it.

At last.

He had been granted everything he had been pressuring, cajoling and praying for over the last three years. He smiled at Marullus and thanked him for bringing the message. The soldier cleared his throat.

"There is more?" prompted Alaric.

Marullus nodded and said, "I have also been authorised by the Praetorian Prefect of the East to inform you that General Stilicho, who I believe is commanding the army that who has been pursuing you ..."

"And who is now camped over there," noted the king with a wry smile, pointing west.

Marullus glanced over the king's shoulder and nodded, not having noticed the encampment until now. "Um, the general has been declared an enemy of the people of the Eastern Empire, and I will be riding to him to deliver orders to him to immediately leave Greece and to return to Ravenna. Any failure to do so will be considered an act of war, and the Prefect would then command you to engage and destroy the general's army." He finished his message in a stilted tone.

"You are not pleased about that last bit, soldier?"

"Not my place to say sir," said Marullus stiffly.

"Say it anyway." Alaric's tone was soft but conveyed an order that was to be obeyed. The old soldier nodded, and said, "Without meaning any disrespect, to order a Roman army to be attacked by a … a …"

"A barbarian horde?" prompted Alaric with that wry smile of his.

"Yes, well, that does not sit right with me. I'm sorry, sir."

Alaric looked at the man. He saw a man of the Empire; loyal, dedicated. He bore scars of his battles. He could see them on his face and arms. But he saw a disillusioned man too.

"It's a new world, Marullus; things are changing for everyone."

The soldier nodded, and said, "If you will excuse me, I have another letter to deliver, but I don't think he will be as pleased to receive his as you were yours." With that Marullus bowed, turned, and strode back to his men.

"God be with you!" Alaric called after the man. Marullus paused for a moment, but then carried on walking.

Alaric read the letter again, and then again. It seemed almost surreal.

Everything he wanted.

He watched as the riders set off in a steady trot back into the town. In the west, the last rays of the sun lit up the high clouds with reds and oranges in the early evening light. He turned around and walked up the gangplank and onto the trireme. Somehow, he knew that he would not be traveling this way again.

Chapter 68

Cyzicus, 13th May 397 AD

Hunulf, Videric and Sigeric sat in a tavern on the outskirts of Cyzicus, finishing off a meal of roasted fowl and root vegetables. They had had a rough trip across the sea, poor weather had forced the captain to take shelter in a cove for one day then two days later they had spent heaved to on an anchor riding out a second bout of stormy weather. Hunulf had spent five days not eating and barely drinking, so he was making up for it now.

When they had arrived, they used the seal that Anthemius had given them to gain entry to the mint. They had expected to be met by Pertacus only to find out he had been murdered by a guard, who had also stolen private papers of the procurator and taken the widow of the previous deputy with him as hostage, or so they had been told. When they spoke to the commander of the guards, they were told he had been attempting to organise a search party, but their duties meant they could not leave the mint, so the local garrison had been contacted and a small squad of local militia had been sent out to track down the runaway guard and hopefully retrieve the woman as well.

Hunulf was relieved that the woman was alive. He had thought that she would probably have been kicked out on to the streets once her husband had been executed. The streets were a hard place to live as a man, let alone a woman, especially one as beautiful as she was. The local pimps would have seized her as soon as they saw her and put her to work. But apparently that had not happened. According to the mint guard commander, the woman had been kept within the mint and only the procurator and this guard had had access to her.

Strange to say the least, thought Hunulf. But he guessed all would be revealed when they found her. Anthemius had said they must find her, so find her they would. It was just going to take them a little longer.

They had purchased horses, again courtesy of the token Hunulf carried from Anthemius, and they had also obtained provisions. After asking around all the local stables and wagon hauliers, Hunulf had found a man who had loaned a horse to a "young couple", one very beautiful foreign looking woman and a local lad. They had headed out the eastern gate of the city in a hurry and travelling light. Hunulf knew it had to be them. That was five days ago. The Goth cursed the weather at sea. They could be anywhere by now. But best follow the trail they had and see where it led.

So Hunulf and the two brothers finished up their wine, downed the last of their hot food, then left a generous tip for the tavern owner. Anthemius was paying. They walked to their horses and leading them through the eastern gate, they mounted and rode off east to wherever the trail may take them, in search of a woman carrying a secret.

Chapter 69

The Consistorium, Constantinople 20th May 397 AD

The Consistorium was in evening session, messengers had returned from Greece. Eutropius had just finished briefing the assembled *illustrii* outlining the terms under which Alaric had been appointed *Magister Militum per Illyricum* replacing Eutychainus who was now confirmed as the Praetorian Prefect of the East. There was also news that Stilicho had indeed left the Peloponnese to head back to Italy and then to North Africa to try to bring Gildo back under the Western Court. Eutropius' move had worked perfectly, the Vandal General had no choice but to abandon any attempt to try to move on Constantinople.

The emperor as normal sat on his throne on the dais. Two large *Candidati* guards stood behind the throne and two were positioned three steps below the dais. Eutropius stood to the left of the throne. He had barely been able to contain his excitement as he read the news. With Hosius as *Magister Officiorum* and Saturninus controlling the judiciary, Eutropius held the reins of power across the Empire. The army, the administration, the infrastructure and the courts. All were at his bidding. It seemed that there was nothing he could not achieve.

A despised eunuch now had the power of life and death over all of the men in the room except the emperor, and he was barely worth a second thought. He was only needed as a figurehead , a puppet who only had to respond to whichever string Eutropius decided to pull. The mood amongst the other members of Consistorium was in sharp contrast to the eunuch's palpable joy.

Caesarius stood stunned at the news. He could not believe it. This was nothing short of a base betrayal of the people of Greece. Alaric had plundered his way across the country behaving like nothing more than a band of marauding bandits. He should have been brought to

Constantinople in chains, and the remaining Goths broken up into manageable groups and resettled across the Empire. He shook his head. How low had they sunk, all in the name of maintaining power. And who had the power? That creature that stood by the emperor's left hand. That thing that even now the pathetic excuse of an emperor was praising in glowing terms for preserving the peace and securing the borders of the Eastern Empire.

Aurelian was ambivalent about the news. He inwardly applauded Eutropius' clever moves, but it was unacceptable that the eunuch be given such a wide mandate of action. It was also unacceptable that he undermined the post of Praetorian Prefect. He could not understand why Eutychainus stood for it, but he guessed that Eutropius had something over him, same for Hosius and Saturninus. The actions were right, but the person executing those moves could not be allowed to continue in the role unchecked. Only two other people seemed to be either a concerned as he, or at least had voiced any kind of concern.

Aurelian glanced at Gainas. The general was not a full member of the Consistorium, but he managed to get himself into the meetings, normally at the behest of Eutropius, who he guessed wanted to keep a tight leash on the general after recent events. Aurelian studied the man. He was not good at hiding his feelings and there was one word that could be used described Gainas now. Apoplectic. The soldier stood swaying, shaking his head and grinding his teeth. He saw Aurelian watching him and glared back, fury in his face. Aurelian nodded slightly in return. He could use that fury to his advantage. And he would. The other person he would make efforts to use was the empress Eudoxia, who he knew was getting more and more disenchanted with her one-time supporter.

After another fifteen minutes of bland sycophantic praise towards the chamberlain the meeting broke up, the emperor retired to his private chambers, and groups of the *illustrii* gravitated together to discuss the proceedings.

400

Gainas normally left quickly as he had no wish to play the political games of the others, but today he strode deliberately to Aurelian, took his arm, non-too gently and hissed in the senator's ear. "Alaric? *Magister Militum*, what in God's name is going on? How can you people allow this?"

Aurelian whispered equally urgently "Control yourself General! Eutropius plays a long game, you need to learn to do that too. Alaric is a player's piece, the people of Greece are players pieces, it's all a game. You should know that. The game never ends and although Eutropius may have won this round, it doesn't mean he will win the next."

Gainas stared at Aurelian, his teeth gritted. "This is not a game! These are people's lives you're playing with."

"And what do you do on the battlefield General? You willingly sacrifice men to achieve an aim without barely a second thought."

"That's different" snapped Gainas.

Aurelian shook his head, "No, it's not general, it's exactly the same. It's just now the fighting isn't always with swords and spears, it's also with houses and farms and people's livelihoods."

Caesarius had wandered into the conversation and interrupted "And what will the people of Greece think, when they find out that the man who has terrorised them for the past two years is now running the army, and that army are the same men who raped their women, enslaved their children and burned their farms?". He looked in askance at his younger brother.

Aurelian merely shrugged, then looked at Gainas and said, "No-one said that life was fair. And you know that General. Personally, I think you're less concerned about the plight of the Greeks and more upset that you have been passed over again for *Magister Militum* and that it's gone now to one of your ex-subordinates."

The Goth snarled, uttered a curse and strode from the room. When the door had shut behind him, Aurelian gave a small laugh and said to Caesarius. "I think I hit a nerve there, don't you?".

Interlude

John's Tavern, Constantinople, 20ᵗʰ May 397 AD

Gadaric and Gerung downed another cup of wine and banged the goblets on the serving bench.

"Another two!" roared Gerung.

The tavern was crowded, and people were pushing and shoving to get to and from the serving area. The two Goths doggedly held their position against the surge of people. It wasn't hard. Both were over six feet three inches tall, most people in the tavern knew who they were and avoided them if they could. It wasn't wise to upset a palace guard, especially not one of the *Candidati*.

"Can you believe that about Alaric?" asked Gadaric.

"I always knew he was a lucky bastard!" replied Gerung, looking across the packed room, "I bet he doesn't have to pay for it."

"For what?"

"Sex."

"I wasn't talking about sex." said Gadaric.

"Oh."

"He's now a fucking Roman General in Greece, you realise that don't you?" Gadaric grabbed a fresh cup of wine and took a gulp of it.

"Who?"

"Alaric, you idiot. Who else do you think we're talking about?"

"Oh yes, Alaric. Lucky bastard." Gerung said absently.

"Why do you keep looking around?" asked Gadaric.

Gerung smiled and looked at his friend and said, "I'm waiting on Octavia. It's my night tonight."

Behind the serving bench, the tavern worker signalled to a small man wearing a blue sash sitting at the end of the bench. The two leaned into each other and the tavern worker whispered, "Those two palace guards just said that Alaric has been made a General in the Roman army!". The small man nodded, slipped the server a silver coin, then slid off his stool and went out the side door.

Outside he broke into a run. He knew Caius would want to hear this news as soon as possible. But then he slowed his dash, and then slowed still further to a steady walk as it dawned on him that the leader of the Blues was not going to like hearing what he had to say.

No, he was not going to like it one bit.

Chapter 70

Eutropius sat in his private office and re-read the parchment that Zafur had just brought him. It was from Eutychainus, who in turn had received it from Count John, the finance minister. The procurator of the Cyzicus mint had been murdered along with one of his guards. The suspect was another guard who had also taken with him one of the mint's slaves, a woman.

He sat and pondered the news. He was unsure what this meant. Perhaps nothing. He glanced at the boy who stood there waiting to be told his next orders. Then he grabbed another piece of parchment and wrote a short note to Eutychainus, recommending a replacement for the procurator. The son of a senator whose wife recently had been caught in a compromising situation with an actor. The wife was the one with the money inherited from her family who were wealthy shipping merchants. He could not afford a scandal which would seriously impede his penchant for gambling, so Eutropius was happy to help out the senator on occasions and call on favours when it suited him, especially when he needed a ship for special services. Putting the son in the position of responsibility would further endear him to the senator.

He finished off the note and held it out to Zafur, who went to take it, but the eunuch pulled it back. The boy looked at the chamberlain without emotion.

"Take this to the prefect Eutychainus." said Eutropius. "Then come back and I'll take you to the forum in my litter, where I'll get you a treat. Would you like that?"

The boy nodded. Eutropius gave him the parchment and Zafur rushed away out of the door, his bare feet slapping on the stones and echoing down the corridor.

Chapter 71

Constantine Walls, Constantinople, 21st May 397 AD

Flavius Anthemius and Quaderi stood atop the walls of New Rome, looking westwards at the setting sun.

"The Greeks used to call this place Byzantium. Did you know that?" Quaderi said casually.

"Yes, I did actually. But I think Constantinople is a better name."

"You would, of course."

They stood in silence for a few minutes more. A light breeze blew to their backs, cool but not chill, refreshing, with a hint of the sea.

"Beautiful evening," said the Persian.

"It is," said Anthemius.

"But that is not why you brought me up here, is it?"

"No, I brought you to see the walls up close," said Anthemius.

"Why? You can see this anytime."

"Not this close. You need to be an Imperial Official to get up here."

"You just keep thinking that."

Anthemius looked across at his companion. He decided to ignore the comment.

"Look around at the stonework," he said, gesturing with his arm.

"I have, it's not the finest piece of Roman engineering," Quaderi put his hand into a large crack. "Looks like it's seen better days."

"And there are buildings outside the wall now."

"And there are buildings outside the wall," agreed the Persian. The two men walked along the battlements of the walls for a while, noting where stones had dropped away, cracks had appeared and where people had constructed dwelling which were butting right up to the walls on both sides.

"You know of the Huns, of course?" asked Anthemius.

"We've all heard of them. Fearsome warriors. Good archers," Quaderi replied. "My people have fought them off in the north. They argue too much between themselves to be too much of a threat."

"A bit like the Romans, then?" Anthemius smiled and his companion laughed.

"Why, procurator Anthemius, I do believe you are mocking your beloved Empire."

"Maybe."

"However," continued the Persian. "From what I have heard, if ever the Huns get together … well, that would be a very different story."

"Why? The barbarians know little of siege craft." Anthemius was dismissive. "Alaric could not penetrate these walls, and he only managed to get into cities in Greece through bribery."

"Ah, my friend, that was Alaric, a Goth." Quaderi turned and looked him directly in the eyes. "We're talking about the Huns here. City walls such as you see here would not stop an organised band of Huns. Not for one moment."

Anthemius nodded. He knew the Persian spoke the truth. He too had heard the rumours of cities in the north and east taken with ease by Hunic raiders. He turned again to the west and watched silently as the sun's rays lit up the high clouds, turning them red and orange.

"You're thinking about the future then, procurator?" prompted Quaderi.

Anthemius nodded, looking at the clouds darkening the horizon. "I am concerned that a storm is coming, and that we may not weather it. Not unless we start to ready ourselves now."

The two men, one born of Rome, the other of Persia, stood together on the walls of Constantinople, watched together as the sky darkened from blue to indigo. The stars appeared, one by one, in the dark velvet sky above. Eventually they wrapped their cloaks around themselves and, descending the stairs, returned to the city street below. There waiting for them were the two tall palace guards who had been assigned to Anthemius to guard him as he walked the city streets.

The four of them walked back to the forum of Constantine, where they parted company. The Persian bid his farewell and entered his shop. He slept in the room above. Anthemius walked back through the dark street, to his family quarters within the palace complex. One slave removed his cloak, a second led him to a bowl of water where he washed his hands and face. He dismissed them both and made his way upstairs to the bedchamber. His wife was already asleep when he climbed into his soft bed. He doused the night light candle and lay back.

Staring at the ceiling, he thought of the Huns, he thought of Constantinople, and he thought of Rome. And as sleep took him, he wondered about the future of them all.

To be continued ...

What Comes Next ...

The Guardians of Byzantium : Book 2

The following is a sample of the first chapter of
"The Guardians of Byzantium : Book 2"

Chapter 1

Paphlagonia, Northern Anatolia, 22nd May 397 AD

The black flag snapped and fluttered atop a spear shaft in the biting, cold wind that blew down from the snow-capped mountains. The man called Uptar was holding the shaft of the spear and looking down with satisfaction. The point was buried in the ground, through the guts of a young Roman, choking on his last breath, mouth filling with blood, face contorted with agony, staring up at his killer in terror. Uptar stood and calmly watched the spirit of life flee from the brown eyes.

Every raid he brought along a spear like this. It was a Roman spear, which he thought was amusing and ironic. He used it to stake out where he had been. At first that had involved planting it in the ground at the centre of a village, but then he'd had this idea of using it to kill a Roman and leave it in the body with his flag. It served two purposes; it was a lot more satisfying to send another pathetic Roman farmer to meet his almighty God; it also made for a terrifying warning to others who might think about resisting him.

He wanted to ensure that the Romans knew who he was. He wanted to ensure that they feared him more than they feared retribution from Constantinople for failing to defend their homes.

So, the whole tribe had agreed that when they attacked the towns, they would take the beautiful women, the strong and vigorous men and the healthy-looking children as slaves. The rest they would slaughter except for one old man. He, they would blind in one eye, cut off three fingers of his left hand, then send him on ahead to the next settlement. A grim warning that the *Huni* were coming …

Book 2 of "The Guardians of Byzantium" now Available on Amazon.

Visit *https://www.amazon.co.uk/dp/B0B723BZ52* today to get your copy or scan the QR code below.

Historical Notes

The Roman Empire is a hugely popular subject for historical fiction. The lives of Julius Caesar and Mark Anthony have been immortalised in Shakespearean plays. The TV adaption of Robert Graves' *I, Claudius* is set in the middle years of the Julio-Claudian dynasty and was a massive hit in the 1970's. Another hugely popular Roman film was the 1990's film *Gladiator*, depicting the emperor Commodus as a maniacal, bloodthirsty narcissist. It was a massive Hollywood hit. *Titus Andronicus*, by Shakespeare, although a work of fiction, was supposedly set in and around the reign of Theodosius, but that is only hinted at. Then there was Charlton Heston as Ben Hur, and Kirk Douglas as Spartacus. All of these works of popular literature and films have focussed on the *Western* Roman Empire, the empire centred around Rome itself; the empire which fell in 476 AD.

Much less well known, except perhaps in academic circles, is the Eastern Roman Empire, the half of the empire centred on Constantinople, the half of the Roman Empire which existed well past 476 AD and indeed survived all the way to 1453 AD when, finally, the Ottoman Empire breached the walls of Constantinople and occupied the city.

Many people, I included, assumed that the Eastern Roman Empire was what morphed into the "Holy Roman Empire", but that is wrong. The Holy Roman Empire was a complex union of western European states and principalities within Western Europe. The Holy Roman Empire, which was dissolved in 1806 by Napoleon, was not the same as the Eastern Roman Empire.

No, the Eastern Roman Empire morphed into what is now termed the Byzantine Empire or just Byzantium. This was the named given to it by eighteenth-century scholars to distinguish it from the previous centuries of the Roman Empire. Byzantium is the original name of the town on the Bosphorus chosen by the Emperor Constantine I to become his New Rome. And this is the city that for centuries bore his name: Constantinople.

By 400 AD, the Eastern Roman Empire was a very different empire to that of Caesar, Claudius, and Commodus, and historians refer to the Eastern Empire after around 600 AD as the Byzantine Empire. But throughout its history, the men and women of the Byzantine Empire considered themselves Roman. They just happened to live in Constantinople and the surrounding lands and although they universally spoke Greek, not Latin, that didn't stop them being Roman.

Having discovered this incredible empire through the medium of Robin Pierson's *History of Byzantium* podcast, I became entranced with the complexity, the scope, and the resilience of the Byzantines. I wanted to try to bring some of this amazing history to life and to bring it into the modern genre of historical fiction.

I wanted to write this book, set right at the very start of the Eastern Roman Empire, during the immensely turbulent and influential last five years of the fourth century. This was a period of history which, before listening to *The History of Rome* and *The History of Byzantium* podcasts, I knew absolutely nothing about. I originally planned this book to start in 400 AD and to cover the 410s AD, ending with the sack of Rome, but after much reading and also listening to the *Byzantium Stories* episodes on John Chrysostom, particularly Part 2 : the Snake Pit, I decided to start in the year 395 AD, the year the Roman Empire is generally recognised as finally splitting into two distinct halves, with two separate diverging agendas, policies, and cultures.

Through the medium of the podcasts, I learnt of the court of Arcadius and the revolving door of courtiers who vied for power, prestige and influence in the presence of an immature and ineffective emperor. The battle of political wills in that court led to the threat of Alaric being ignored for nearly two years, whilst he went on the rampage through the central Roman Empire in an effort to force Constantinople to grant him a military rank of suitable standing, as well as a settled home for his people. The misery of the people of Macedonia (modern day Greece) must have been complete, their livelihoods wrecked, people enslaved or killed, as the Goths scoured their way through the ancient lands of Greece which, until that time, had known only peace for generations.

Most of the key figures in the book were real people. The emperor Arcadius is a well-documented figure, portrayed as dull-witted and easily influenced by the older and more experienced men and women around him. His consort Eudoxia is well known too for her flamboyance and love of the finer things in life. Court gossip also puts her and the Count John as not-so-secret lovers, though we don't have any concrete proof of that.

The opening scene of this book recounts the infamous incident when General Gainas, acting on orders from Stilicho, assassinated Rufinus, the Praetorian Prefect of the East, in front of thousands of witnesses. The complete absence of any consequences to Gainas or his men gives credence to the theory that the Eastern court were complicit in the murder. Nobody seemed to mourn Rufinus.

I found Gainas to be a somewhat tragic figure. A Goth who chose to throw his lot in with the Romans, as many of his race did, rather than to stay with his own people. A twenty-year veteran of many campaigns, he was a Roman General commanding Roman Legions, he apparently dressed as a Roman, had a house in Constantinople and his family lived in the city for many years. But in the times he lived in, his Gothic ethnicity played against him, both at court and amongst the populace of the city.

General Stilicho is referred to only in the third person in the book, a deliberate move on my part, as I wanted the complete focus on the book to be on the Eastern Empire. Stilicho was appointed by the late Emperor Theodosius as regent over the Western Emperor, Honorius, Arcadius's younger brother. He was viewed with suspicion and loathing by many of the Eastern Court. His claim that Theodosius had appointed him regent over Arcadius as well as Honorius, and therefore the whole Roman Empire, was the cause of many a political tug of war.

The Gothic King Alaric is a mighty figure in late Roman history, but we see him only in his early days here, leading his whole army nation through Greece plundering and generally making a nuisance of himself, trying to stir the Roman authorities to come to the negotiating table. But the Eastern Court were embroiled in their own internal battles and happy to have Alaric as a pawn on the chessboard. The Battle of Adrianople several years earlier had decimated the ranks of the Roman Armies as had recent civil wars. The armies of the Empire were just not in a state to take on the Gothic hoard. So, the court used Alaric's rampage as a political weapon to their own ends, and we leave this part of the tale as Eutropius finally gives Alaric what he wants. But spoiler alert … it won't last.

Athaulf was Alaric's brother-in-law and went on to lead the Goths in Italy for several years after Alaric's death. He eventually did kill Sarus who had decided to throw his lot in with an Imperial usurper named Jovinus. Unfortunately, one of Sarus' followers tricked Athaulf into sparing his life only to murder Athaulf shortly after as revenge for the death of Sarus. Late antiquity was oftentimes a brutal place to live.

The generals Abundantius and Timasius were distinguished and experienced Roman Generals and would have known Gainas. Yes, Timasius really did nearly get the emperor Theodosius killed through poor judgement. And yes, there was a sausage seller named Bargus who wormed his way into the good books of Timasius and then betrayed him to Eutropius.

And of course, Eutropius lived, an incredible character; a eunuch who rose to become as powerful as the emperor. He was despised by the senators and the elite of Constantinople and many sought ways to get rid of him. None more diligently than Gainas it is suspected.

There is no firm record of an assassination attempt on Eutropius, but a law passed later that year of 397 AD, ascribed to Eutychainus, and which appears in the Theodosian Codex, reads:

"If any person should enter into a criminal conspiracy with soldiers or civilians, or even with barbarians, or should take or give the oaths of a conspiracy, and should plan for the death of men of Illustrious rank who participate in Our counsels and Our Consistory, or for the death of Senators, who are also part of Our body, or, finally, for the death of anyone who is in Our imperial service, he shall be struck down with the sword as one guilty of high treason, and all his goods shall be assigned to Our fisc. For the laws have willed that the intent to commit crime shall be punished with the same severity as the actual commission of crime."

Up until then it was only treason if you plotted against the imperial family, so something must have happened to prompt this law, and some historians have suggested that it could have been an attempt on Eutropius' life; the most likely candidate as ringleader is Gainas. It certainly offered up a juicy subplot too good to ignore …

The brothers Caesarius and Aurelianus (Aurelian) are also well documented, in an indirect way, by Synisius and Zozimus, ancient historians. The cautionary tale by Synisius called *De Providentia* depicts the two brothers as Egyptians, in an apocryphal story mirroring the intrigues of the court. All historians have the protagonist of the tale down as Aurelian, but historians have had some disagreement on who the antagonist represents, whether it was Caesarius or actually Eutychainus. In any event Synisius the author certainly has his own political agenda, , and despite portraying (probably) Caesarius in De Providentia as scheming and evil, other historical records seem to indicate that it was Caesarius who was the more enlightened administrator, less belligerent and self-interested than Aurelian. The shutting out of Aurelian and his family from political life in the early 5th century by the then Praetorian Prefect indicates that the then incumbent did not trust Aurelian with any kind of power.

And who was that particular Praetorian Prefect? That was Flavius Anthemius, who we see in this book as a junior procurator, working his way up the administrative ladder of success. Little is known of Anthemius as a person or his history prior to 400 AD, apart from a reference to him being on a mission with Stilicho and Aurelian to the Persians in the 380s AD. As a result, I have taken several liberties with his character.

What is known is that he was a highly effective and highly capable Praetorian Prefect of the East who seemed to have no other agenda than to serve the Roman Empire. He came to prominence and power when the Eastern Roman Empire desperately needed a man of integrity and good judgement, and it seems Anthemius was endowed with these attributes in spades. We shall see and hear much more from him.

Hosius, another Eutropius sycophant, is noted as the *Magister Officiorum* a very powerful official, and Eutychainus was Prefect of Illyricum (modern day Macedonia, Albania, and Croatia) prior to being elevated by Eutropius to Praetorian Prefect of the East. This position was almost as powerful as being a co-emperor at the time, although during the age of Eutropius that post appears to have been subservient to Eutropius himself. Eutychainus is noted in the histories as being a very capable administrator, possibly the finest of the age, but there also seems no doubt that he was very much Eutropius' man, and so history perhaps has been a little unkind to him. Maybe Eutropius simply wanted the best man for the job? Who knows?

Saturninus was a real general who later served as a judge and did preside over the "show-trials" of the two generals Abundantius and Timasius, and therefore had to have been under the sway of Eutropius to a greater or lesser degree.

The Blues and Greens guilds very much existed and whilst originally, they were fan clubs of the various chariot teams at the regular Roman games in Rome, offshoots of the Blues and Greens spread throughout the empire, particularly where there were games. Their influence in popular and street politics is well documented, and nowhere more so than in several serious incidents in Constantinople over the years. There are suggestions that the guilds morphed into antiquity's version of organised crime gangs, and I loved that idea, so although I've probably overplayed that hand, I don't regret it, and it will continue as a backdrop as the story goes forwards.

All the other characters are fictitious but hopefully they are representative of people who lived at the time. I've tried to paint the picture of the fundamental nature of existence in late Roman times. How there was this incredible belief within the empire that the Romans were the only real civilised people. Everyone else was a barbarian, except perhaps the Persians. And yet in the years in which this story is set, there was an underlying fear that the empire itself was more and more becoming subservient to those barbarians. Those from outside the empire kept demanding tribute to not attack. And there seemed to be more and more influential barbarians inside the empire itself. People such as Gainas. The fact that these barbarians considered themselves Roman but were never really accepted as "real" Romans, became a huge source of tension. That tension will soon reach a breaking point, with tragic consequences for the citizens of Constantinople.

I hope you enjoyed the book. Our cast of characters will return soon, as we find out whether Gainas will finally get the respect and rewards he craves, whether Caius and Sextus mange to remain in charge of the Blues Guild, whether Nephtys gets to see her son again and whether Anthemius tracks down the people behind the counterfeiting ring within the Roman mints.

We will also find out how Alaric's elevation to *Magister Militum per Illyricum* is received, now that he is responsible for protecting the people he has just spent two years terrorising.

It will come as no surprise if I tell you that the answer to the last question is … not well.

Justin Isaacs, UK, 2022

Historical Dramatis Personae

The Eastern Romans

Abundantius. A General in the Eastern Roman Empire.

Aelia Eudoxia. Wife of Flavius Arcadius.

Aurelian. A Senator in Constantinople, and Ex-Urban Prefect (head of Roman Senate).

Bargus. Commander of the personal bodyguard to General Timasius.

Caesarius. A Senator in Constantinople, brother of Aurelian.

Comes John. A Senator in Constantinople, the finance minister, *Comes Sacrarum Largitionum*

Eutropius. The Chamberlain or *praepositus sacri cubiculi* (Provost of the sacred bedchamber)

Eutychainus. A Senator in Constantinople.

Flavius Arcadius. Emperor of the Eastern Roman Empire (eldest son of Theodosius)

Flavius Anthemius. Procurator of the City Mint and a Senator in Constantinople.

Gainas. A General in the Eastern Roman Empire of Gothic ethnicity.

Hosius. A Senator in Constantinople, the *Magister Officiorum*, the Master of Offices providing administrative oversight and intelligence.

Promotus. A General in the Eastern Roman Army, killed by Rufinus in 394 AD.

Rufinus. A General and Senator of Gaulish ethnicity in the Eastern Roman Empire, Praetorian Prefect of the East (Second in power to the emperor).

Theodosius. Last sole ruler of the Roman Empire (died January 397 AD)

Flavius Timasius. A General in the Eastern Roman Empire.

Saturninus. A General and Senator of the Eastern Roman Empire.

The Western Romans

Gildo. Ruler of the Province of Africa

Honorius. Emperor of the Western Roman Empire (youngest son of Theodosius).

Stilicho. A half-Vandal General in the Western Roman Empire and Regent of *Honorius*

The Goths

Alaric. Leader of the Gothic Army in the Eastern Roman Empire

Athaulf. Brother -in-law of *Alaric* and a General in the Gothic Army

Sarus. Chieftain in the Gothic Army

Acknowledgements

I would like to thank Robin Pierson creator of "The History of Byzantium" podcast for his fantastic support in the writing of this book. At no prompting from myself, he provided me with a wealth of research material and information about the Byzantine Empire in addition to his normal podcast material.

I would also like to thank Mike Duncan for firing up my interest in history through his epic and award-winning podcast series "The History of Rome". If you think like I used to think, that history is boring, I urge you to listen to both Mike's and Robin's podcasts, they will change your perspective on the past and also on the present.

I would also like to thank Becca Louise Hayes for the wonderful artwork used on the cover and on the section title pages.

Printed in Great Britain
by Amazon

26902994R00245